MW00934122

INSANE CIRCUMSTANCES

9/20/14

La cuiria,

Thanks for your support.

Be blessed!
Brenda

INSANE CIRCUMSTANCES

Brenda Smith

Copyright © 2012 by Brenda Smith.

Library of Congress Control Number:		2012903778
ISBN:	Hardcover	978-1-4691-7621-5
	Softcover	978-1-4691-7620-8
	Ebook	978-1-4691-7622-2

All rights reserved. No part of this book may be reproduced or transmitted in any form or by any means, electronic or mechanical, including photocopying, recording, or by any information storage and retrieval system, without permission in writing from the copyright owner.

This is a work of fiction. Names, characters, places and incidents either are the product of the author's imagination or are used fictitiously, and any resemblance to any actual persons, living or dead, events, or locales is entirely coincidental.

This book was printed in the United States of America.

To order additional copies of this book, contact:
Xlibris Corporation
1-888-795-4274
www.Xlibris.com
Orders@Xlibris.com
111341

CONTENTS

This book is dedicated to my parents, the late Samuel and Ona Belle Lane, A special thanks is given to my husband, Jerry V. Smith, my number one fan, the one who has kept my feet to the fire, who insisted that I do that scholarly work before I delved into fiction. And to my sons, Brian and Justin, who keep encouraging me!

I also appreciate my friend Jacquie Harper who provided editorial assistance. And a special thank you is given to my nephew, Rodney Elliott for designing the cover for Insane Circumstances.

PROLOGUE

It's funny how memories can lay dormant until jogged awake by some event, at some other time, in yet another location. Sheets of rain matched only by those of tears falling on her face blanketed the young woman's car windows in much the same way they had on the day Brandi had returned home from Claxville University. The only difference was this time, salty tears did not stain her face; they had been replaced with torrents of rage—rage enacted by the announcement on WJIV-TV about a black girl who had returned to her dormitory room and found "Nigger go home" scrawled in a childlike manner in thick blood-exterior lacquer on the floor.

When the morning news anchorman mentioned the school's name, Brandi Leigh Brown-Pennington, PhD in broadcast journalism, had looked upward at the monitor and outward into the recording studio to see her white male counterpart speak with his lips what she heard from the tube. He was saying that the girl had also indicated that other bitter atrocities had been committed against her while at the school, that she had been hazed throughout her entire matriculation at the school.

"However," the man said, "an in-house investigation has shown that she committed these acts herself," his unctuous regrets on the air insincere enough to make the viewer gag. "Furthermore," he added, "Elnora Jenkins, one of the first black students to enroll at the university, has been interviewed. And according to her, this was 'ludicrous.' She could not recall such incidents ever happening before."

While the anchorman spoke, the cameraman focused in on the visage of the victimized girl with grieving, heartbroken parents helping her pack for the return home; and the observer shuddered, for she had previously seen that look—the one which bordered on stark terror—before they cut away to capture the older woman, the one that Brandi herself had known years ago. The news commentator removed her glasses, blinked, and put them on again, disbelieving what and whom she had seen.

Brandi grew sick with disbelief. She threw her pen at the monitor. "The nerve of that bitch!" she said to herself, as she was sure that the young coed had told the truth; she'd seen that same look another time, in another place, in another city and state. In her own looking glass, she'd seen it. And she had not wanted to remember those times . . . that was over thirty . . . almost forty years ago; and she'd left Julie, Laura, Mary Margaret, Kirk and Chuck, Mr. Henri, Dr. McIntyre, Kris, Carmen, Dubblerville, Flo, Lou, and Elnora too—left them all buried in the recesses of her mind—that is, until today.

The woman left the office as soon as she could clear her desk and retrieve her overcoat, purse, and briefcase. Suddenly, she felt chilled, and her head ached, pounded; the facial veins in her temple pulsated, and the pain jagged to match a nonrhythmic tempo alien to the woman. Her eyes were flickering in an odd way, images of things past welling up inside of her; and she grew increasingly more nauseous, was getting sick to her stomach, didn't want to "puke" all over the station's floors. Housekeeping wouldn't appreciate that!

Brandi needed to get home to her desk to write—writing about noisome events always seemed to help. "Maybe," she thought, "if I send my notes to her, maybe they'll help her—help her to know she is not crazy, insane, a pure nut, a basket case, totally out to lunch . . . Maybe it'll help her to know that it happened to me too."

Bobbing, weaving drunkenly, blubbering, the woman made it out the building, into the parking lot, and in the car before the somber skies opened up. And when she was finally in the safety of her home, the woman collapsed on the bed and sobbed violently, bawling like the rains released from the sky's leaky clouds, until relief came. Then she began a letter of consolation.

And under the watchful eye of her beloved one, she laid aside the letter she intended to write and instead penned her story, his story—their story in the third person.

CHAPTER ONE

The Bus Ride

Morning came soon on the cool, damp early fall day that Brandi was to leave for the university. She hopped out of bed and took her usual morning trek down the worn path of red clay to the leaning fixture of graying, weather-beaten board with leaky roof and cracked cement floor that was the toilet, where she sat and reflected on the times past in the Wester community, thinking of the shiny future that today's happenings suggested.

When she got back to the house, her parents, Sara and Carruthers, alias Catkiller Brown, were already in the kitchen. "Rats!" she muttered as her father invited her to sit and talk with them. Brandi did not want to talk anymore because she and Catkiller had spent the last four months arguing about her decision to attend Claxville University.

Receipt of a fellowship for Negro students under the auspices of one of the nation's major manufacturers was reason enough for her to go off to the school. Cat, as he was lovingly called by Sara and those closest to him, thought that the girl should stay at home and work a while and attend a school for coloreds in closer proximity to their hometown—a school that other neighboring children had selected.

"Brandi," he began, "your mother and I love you and are just as supportive of your endeavors as we've always been. However . . ." "However," the oldest of their children chimed in with disgust, "we feel that it is not in your best interest to go up to that school. It's 'bout time you started to earn your keep. And besides that, you need to rest your head. It just ain't natural for a person to just keep learning all the time." She repeated the father's entreaties verbatim, albeit, in her head, as they were repetitious; she'd only heard them a zillion times—at least now it seemed that way.

The man's obsession with concerns about the probable diminishing of his daughter's morality, integrity, and dignity while up at the school was making life in the Brown household pure hell.

"Now, Brandi," the frustrated father argued, "you know that is not the main reason we don't want you going up there. There ain't but a handful of colored children up there—and I know you don' heard about the bad times they keep falling on."

"Daddy, that's them. That ain't me," the girl pleaded. "Give me a break! Don't compare me with anyone else—I know how to take care of myself."

"Baby, let me show you this newspaper clipping I got from Mrs. Barnes over at the high school," Cat continued, reaching for the paper which lay at hand, passing it diagonally to the place where his daughter now sat, nudging her tight-fisted hands with its corner. "Here, read it for yourself," the man persisted.

Brandi had already seen it, had hoped that Cat—though not a college graduate, yet an avid reader—had not read the feature story in the August edition of the now-defunct *Negro Collegiate Post*, which said that Negro students all across the country attending traditionally white colleges were under so much pressure that they generally felt depressed, lonely, and alienated; that they felt that the preponderance of their universities were "hostile" places where relationships with white students and professors were often quite demoralizing.

Yet she quietly scanned the article again to please her father, noting that under faculty-student relationships, the writer said, "Many students complained about an apparent belief of white faculty and students that all or most Negroes were 'special admits' or 'beneficiaries of quotas,' and therefore had no legitimate place on campus." "Hogwash!" she thought.

Her father, watching closely, anticipated the point at which she would look at some graphs on the magazine's page. The man leaned over, pointed to a huge star penciled in on the page's margin. "Look at that," he insisted, showing her that the school she'd chosen—Claxville University—ranked in the top ten in every area addressed and was the highest in many areas.

"Ah, come on, Daddy, you know I always make good grades. I study hard, and I made over a thousand on the college entrance exam," Brandi said soothingly to the man. "I ain't worried about none of that junk," she said, getting to her feet, desiring to finish packing.

"Baby, we—your mama and me—we can't hardly stand to see you go up there. Those folks aren't going to treat you right—why can't you just be like everybody else?" Cat wrung his hands in despair and winced, realizing that the "trump card" he'd sought from the high school counselor had failed to change his "headstrong" baby's mind. No hint of alarm had shown on her face; her demeanor remained the same. Her resolve showed in her countenance . . . she was going!

Cat took in a breath of air, and his pause for breath allowed Brandi to escape the conversation, to commence the retreat to the comforts of the tiny bedroom with two beds she shared with five younger siblings—the "lap" baby was still in Sara and Cat's room as Sara had separated them so the ones who still "peed in the bed" slept apart from the ones that were potty-trained. "Two to four," mused the escapee, "and minus me makes three."

The usually complacent father, losing it, jumped up from the table and retorted angrily to the girl, who quickened her departure, more forcefully than he'd ever been with his independent daughter. "When they find your ass dead, that damn company can bury it too."

Sara, seeing how vexed Cat had come, shushed him with a finger to her lips and pursued the girl into the bedroom. "Child, you better be careful up there. It would kill your daddy if anything happened to you!" she said when they were out of the man's earshot.

The duo, mother and daughter, scurried to get Brandi ready for the trip to the bus station, picking up the odds and ends that lay all over the room (on the dresser, nightstand, in the corners) and stuffed these small items, makeup, perfumes, toiletries, curlers, straightening comb, rollers, bedroom shoes, housecoat, dental supplies—rather, attempted to stuff it—in the suitcases already packed, repacked, and packed the container's corners again, revisiting a summerlong process that had been redone each time something new was bought. Mother and daughter worked tenaciously at it until the task was completed, leaving little to do except close the lids, fastening all Brandi's worldly goods therein.

Sara watched while her daughter opened the chiffarobe and pulled out the outfit she had set aside to wear that day. The mother picked up slivers of paper, price tags, string, and bits of wrapping paper from high school graduation gifts and made her way through the maze of luggage, trash cans, shoe boxes, toys, and the children's junk until she stood behind the girl, gazing in the mirror, noting how much alike they were. They looked alike; the girl had even inherited her own dogged determination to do what she wanted in life, to relentlessly pursue whatever tasks she was given; and now the sight of her made the older woman's face serene, her thoughts pensive. The whole room was spinning now, seeming to rock her from side to side; the floor seemed to tilt and sway beneath her. Sara's knees trembled, weakened, and her body began to sag.

"What's the matter, Ma?" Brandi questioned her mother as she turned around to catch the collapsing woman. The younger woman became concerned—her mother, her Rock of Gibraltar, appeared to be falling, to be crumbling before her very eyes.

Sara, simply overwhelmed by the day's events, wiped the solitary tear that was a part of her bout of despair, pulled herself together, removed herself from the girl's arms, led her back through the clutter, seated herself bedside, and drew her oldest child down to her.

Her daughter followed her lead; and when Brandi was kneeling directly in front of her, Sara stroked her hair, looked at her face, and rubbed it. The girl took the woman's hands and kissed her mother's knuckles. The woman sniffed briefly and cleared her throat so she could speak freely. "I was just thinking about how sorry I am that your daddy and I won't be taking you up yonder," she said. "I was rather looking forward to it." The girl's mother paused, sighed, shook her head at her own behavior, reconciling herself to the daughter's bus trip, and continued to study her daughter's youthful features.

"You know I want you to go to that college as much as you want to go yourself. Want the best for you." Sara spoke these words evenly, mentally dissuading her voice from cracking, quavering with emotion, breaking up, shattering. "You know that ain't so with your daddy. So for God's sake, be careful!" she exclaimed. "You hear me, Brandi Leigh Brown?" Sara strengthened her motherly admonition when she had her daughter's chin in her hand and had established full eye contact. "Be careful!"

The mother loosed her child, and Brandi vaulted to her feet. Then they renewed their efforts to finish the packing.

Getting the suitcases fastened proved to be more of a challenge than either had anticipated, but neither was willing to call Cat, to elicit the man's assistance; they had to complete this task by themselves. Sara wiped at her brow, the top of her sweating lip, erasing a beady mustache formed by the stuffiness in the tiny room and overexertion. "Open the window, child," she said, sitting down on the bed beside the bag before getting at it again. Brandi crawled across the bed, struggled to let the window up, and crawled back, seating herself beside her mama. An overwhelming urge to touch and to be touched by the small woman, one that everybody said looked like her sister, overcame Brandi. She leaned over and kissed the woman, who gleefully asked, "What's that for?"

"Nothing," her daughter said, smiling with love and gratitude, having realized in the last few minutes that things had been rougher for her mom than it had been for her in the last few months—the woman had had to sleep with the father who seemed pretty unreasonable to the girl who had not turned eighteen, wasn't even legal yet, wouldn't be until the first of the year.

"Let's get busy," Sara suggested as she got up from her bedside perch. "You sit on the suitcase, and I'll fasten one side, then the other," she said before she had a second thought. "Nope, uh-uh." Sara shook her head vigorously, saying to Brandi, who had turned around, preparing to leap up and sit on the lid real fast, holding tight to the edge of the bed while the woman snapped the closure, "That just ain't going to work. You'll be done pinched your butt. I wish you would wear something else besides that little bobtail dress you got on. I just don't like them miniskirts."

Brandi elected not to go into the dress issue again, had already fought that battle, so she quietly and quickly exchanged places. The taller of the two—her mother, a head taller than she—sat on the piece of luggage; and they succeeded in closing the baggage this time.

"Where you put your money?" her mother asked when they were finished. "Did you put it in your suitcase? What you do with the key? We need to lock this thing. Do we need to go back in, get your money out?"

"It's in my pocketbook," was the first response to Sara's chain of queries.

"All of it! You got all of it in your pocketbook?" the woman spoke with disbelief. "Gal, you get that money out of there! Somebody be done took that thing from you, and you won't have a dime when you get up yonder."

Sara left the room, swiftly returning with a flour sack that had been freed of its contents during weekday washing. She snipped at its threads with her teeth and tore a strip of material, which she strung around the girl's thin waist in spite of her protest, "Naw, Ma, no, I ain't going to do that, that don't make no sense."

She tried to back away from the woman, who snatched her back with a verbal warning. "Don't naw me, gal," the elder woman told her rebelling daughter. "We gonna tie all your money up in this belt, then pen it 'round you waist with some safety pins."

Brandi relented and lifted her arms in disgust while Sara set about her maternal task, nudging with her shoulders at the hem of the red miniskirted dress with white bodice and black patent leather belt bought especially for the trip. "You are gonna wish you had something on your legs, and your arms too. It gets mighty cold on them Greyhounds. Hold this skirt up, out of the way!" the mother argued.

And realizing that she had not gotten the safety pins, Sara ordered loudly, "One of you other young'uns, bring me a couple of safety pins out of my sewing box." With the pins secured from an obedient little one, the woman fashioned a money belt, secured it around her oldest daughter's waist, making sure that her treasure lay hidden beneath the black patent leather belt.

When mother and daughter had packed and all were dressed, the Brown family left for the bus station. Silence permeated the molecules of space left vacant by the occupants of the heavily laden Ford Country Squire station wagon that sputtered its way toward town. Not Cat, Sara, Brandi, nor any of the girls' siblings spoke. Neighbors lined in yards on both sides of the rural route waved, called salutations, bade adieu to Brandi, or tipped hats at Carruthers and his family as they passed by, their greetings barely acknowledged by the aggrieved family. One would have thought they were headed to a funeral instead of the bus station.

They arrived in plenty of time—Cat just believed "a person ought to be in place before any event. That way you don't have to be crawling all over folks to get where you going."

The man unloaded his daughter's luggage—such that the couple of pieces of baggage were; the girl nor her parents could afford a whole set. They had settled for two pieces of luggage. Sara, with Brandi's assistance, unloaded the rest of the children, placing them in strategic locations so they wouldn't get run over by other people coming to the Greyhound bus station; but they began to run around, so Cat ordered Sara to "sit them on the tailgate of the wagon," adding "all of y'all better stay put!" Each young'un was plopped into place and warned with a wagging motherly finger. "Stay right there, don't move!" She smacked each, briskly and sharply, on the thigh with her open palm to emphasize that she meant business. "Wasn't taking any mess today,"—couldn't!

Brandi's aunt Sylvia, Sara's oldest sister, had already gotten there, was sitting in the truck with her spouse. The woman, a small gray-haired replica of what Sara was to look like when she becomes "ancient," got out of the vehicle's cab limping as her leg had gone to sleep while she waited and called out to her favorite niece, "Gal, everybody sure is proud of you. You just keep on keeping on! Brought a little something for you to carry with you," she added, draping a heavy patchwork quilt of no particular design on the girl's outstretched arm. "Made it from scraps . . . it ain't much, but it'll keep you warm. I ain't never been up yonder where you going off to college, but I hear tell it gets mighty cold up there."

"And here's some tea cakes for you," the woman added before Brandi could extend gratitude for the prize. "I ain't had no tinfoil to put these cakes in, so I put them in this here light bread sack." The woman spoke almost apologetically as she handed the Wonder Bread sack to her niece.

Brandi took the light-bread sack, put it to her nose, and sniffed at it, trying to catch the aroma—she loved nothing better than these little sweet, flat vanilla-flavored biscuits for which there was no written recipe. The woman renewed her farewell monologue, "I hear tell it gets mighty cold up there . . . I ain't never been there, don't know which way to get there if I had to come find you . . . don't know where no Claxville is, but that's what I heard. I was hoping I had a piece of change to give you too."

At the mention of money, Sara broke the exchange between the two. "Sister, you already done enough. Brandi's got a plenty," she said while she nudged the eldest of her offspring to express gratitude for the old woman's generosity.

At the poke in her ribs, Brandi spoke. "Aunt Sylvia, I appreciate everything you've done. I'm going to make you proud. Just wait and see, I'm going to make all of you proud," she repeated, her voice swelling with assurance and volume as she glanced in the direction of the father who seemingly had become more pensive as time passed. Sylvia, always the surrogate mother for her many nieces and nephews when they need a little extra loving, took Brandi and baggage in her slender arms. She'd never been able to produce any of her own. This was one of her babies . . . she held the niece close to her breast.

By now the uncle had made his way over to the crowd. "Gal, don't you bring back no white boy for a husband," Uncle Jack, who stood nearby, emitted, and Brandi gasped audibly, not believing that he'd made the statement. Her mother held the back of her own head, looked downward studying the earth, toeing the ground as if to write a message in the dirt. Then mother and daughter looked to the father; and both caught Cat's eye, each silently pleading that the uncle's witty, wry, yet loaded remark would not renew a dispute laid aside for the moment.

"Get away from here with your foolishness!" Aunt Sylvia fussed at the man who was incognizant of the issue best left alone for the moment. The father paid little attention to them.

Sara and Brandi still watched Carruthers. Neither the girl nor her mother knew that the man had not heard the comment, and he quizzed them with his eyes . . . Cat stood remembering his own brief hiatus as a college athlete who'd reappeared prematurely at his parents' home with a simple "That place just wasn't like home." Mother and daughter shrugged and looked at each other, emitted sighs of relief, and wiped at their brows with the backs of their hands.

Sara had never asked her husband why he had not stayed in school—the teen had been so glad that her high school sweetheart had returned home and that he had married her.

Sara took the quilt and bag of cookies from Brandi. The girl went to her father. "Daddy," she said, "I promise I won't do nothing that will embarrass you and Ma. I'm going to make you proud. Just wait and see, I'm going to make you proud," the oldest of the Brown children spoke with confidence. Simultaneously, she elevated herself on tiptoe, reached for her father's neck, and nuzzled him at his collar like she used to when she was a little girl.

The big man melted. "Baby, I know you will. I know you will," he murmured, more to assuage his own fears—to exhibit the same unwavering faith the girl now possessed.

Tears welled up in Sara's eyes, and she stirred at the earth with her right foot.

Carruthers held his eldest a moment more and prayed that his little girl would indeed be successful, would return, and that she'd return unblemished. Then he kissed her and let her go.

"Where your money, child?" asked sister.

Brandi chuckled. "Ma done already made me pin it around my waist with a piece of flour sack," she told the woman, who nodded in approval.

"Good," she said. "That's steady, and you ain't got to worry 'bout nobody taking it off of you before you get where you going," inserted the uncle.

Brandi touched the bulge made by the strip of flour sack secured with safety pins that Sara had fashioned into a money belt before they'd left the house. The girl wondered how she would get the uncomfortable device, which was becoming saturated with perspiration from the folds of flesh increasingly encircling it as time passed, from her waist.

The Greyhound bus pulled up, and all too soon the driver was asking for her suitcase to place it in the compartment in the belly of the bus. "I want to keep this with me," the girl said of her belongings.

"Ain't got room for that big suitcase up front," he insisted as he placed the bag inside. Then the driver closed the door to the compartment and stepped to the bus's passageway for the obvious first timer's ascent.

"After you, ma'am," he said.

Brandi gave her daddy one more peck on the cheek and mounted the three short steps briskly, exuding much confidence. She bent at the final step's apex as if to curtsy and waved once more to Sara, her siblings, and the others before turning for her seat.

The sea of occupants engulfed the wayfarer—Brandi pivoted for a hasty retreat to the comforts of Wester. She was suffocating, suddenly drowning in a wave of uncertainty. It had never occurred to her that other passengers would be on the bus, that she'd be the only colored person on the whole bus. Brandi wanted to get off! "Find yourself a seat, missy. We got to get on the move," the driver insisted.

Brandi stepped to her immediate left and plopped down in the vacant seat. "I'm going to put your stuff here," the man said, reaching for the remainder of her goods.

The novice moaned a pitiful "that's okay" before the driver returned to his own seat and prepared for their departure.

All too soon the bus was en route; the first leg of Brandi's two-hundred-plus-mile journey began.

The young traveler sat motionless, except for the balls of her eyes which gravitated from one position to another as she tried to catch a final glimpse of Cat, Sara, and her brothers and sisters who waved frantic good-byes matched only by those of Aunt Sylvia and Uncle Jack who had come to bid her farewell.

Although she could not see through the dirty shaded windows or pass the visages of the other passengers, her peers persisted long after the bus left the station heading northward.

The bus lurched forward, speeding from the familiar to the unknown. As the miles passed, the terrain was altered, flats became mountainous, and where pines stood, oaks and other less coniferous vegetation appeared. Tall cotton became short, sparse, dried, brownish stalks, and soon there was no cotton at all. And the bus grew dim. Droplets of rain pelted the vehicle's windows before it made sheets of fluid precipitation.

As the sheets of rain swept their way from the windshield to their window midway the bus, the yet unknown seatmate's loosened lips released a sparkle that drew the girl's attention from the fogging windows to his rustic face. Whistling snores from the passenger to Brandi's left became snorts—deep, loud, and long.

The boy was about her age. His shoulder-length hair, thick mustache, and full summer beard hid his what was ordinarily clean-shaven apparition.

Where skin was apparent was a summer bronze that nearly matched her own pecan tan complexion. She laid her hand close to his, comparing. The man grunted, turning in his seat, and she withdrew her hand before his own plopped into the place hers had relinquished. She gasped.

Then Brandi's stomach rumbled—she had ignored Sara's admonition to "hurry up and eat breakfast" before she left home. She covered the member with her hand, trying to make it hush. "Child, you do not know when you are going to get your next mouthful," the sage had spoken to her daughter.

"Ma, I'll be all right. You know I don't ever eat breakfast when I'm going somewhere," she had persisted.

Sara ended the discourse with "All right, missy."

The contents of the Wonder Bread sack grew increasingly enticing as time passed, as the stomach growled. Brandi gave in, readjusted all that she bore—the purse and the overnight case she held in her lap were placed on the floor between her feet and the cumbersome quilt was unfurled on her lap and tucked around her bottom. She laid the sack of goodies atop her blanketed lap.

When she tried to open the sack of goodies, the aroma of its freshly baked contents escaped and the sleeping boy stirred in his seat. Brandi froze anew. He reached for the covers, loosening the end from under her tiny hips, and he covered his body with the loosened ends and rolled over to face the window. With his back to her, the man continued in restful repose. It was becoming cooler. The miniskirted, ineffably skinny teen now appreciated the warmth generated by the gift, yet she was reluctant to pull it back as she didn't want to disturb the young man.

Brandi took a tea cake from the sack and nibbled at it, savoring every morsel of the Watkins' vanilla-flavored delight. The man's snores subsiding, she munched as quietly as she could.

Soon, all the other passengers were stirring. Something smelled good. They started to walk to the lavatory at the rear of the bus, and conversations ensued everywhere. The passenger to Brandi's left woke up too. He didn't say anything, nor did he release his hold on the covers.

"Want one?" Brandi asked, widening the opening of the light-bread sack for the hand that responded by stretching itself out as its owner pronounced a sleepy "Thanks." The man consumed first one, then another couple of the delicacies before renewing his slumber.

The bus sped along. Brandi wanted to go to the bathroom so bad, was frozen to her seat by the unknown. She couldn't wait to get to the university.

Soon, the bus completed its first leg of the journey. Everyone got off the bus except Brandi . . . and him. The boy didn't move either.

The driver returned to the bus.

"Check your ticket, ma'am."

"Huh?"

"Your ticket, ma'am, I need to check it."

She reached for her purse and secured the ticket for the driver, who took it and punched it with a hole puncher.

"Aren't you going to get off and rest yourself, ma'am?" he inquired, returning the paper to her.

"No, I am going to wait until I get to the university."

"Suit yourself, ma'am," he said before he added, "it's going to be a couple of hours before we leave here. We have to wait for the next bus to come in, pick up some connections." The driver left.

The seatmate stirred in his seat.

Several passengers got on and off the bus again before Brandi would relinquish her seat.

The girl headed straight to the ladies' room when she got inside the bus station. A ten-cent sign at each of the facilities' stalls greeted her. Brandi was in a pickle—she had to pee and every dime she owned was tied around her waist. "Damn!" she uttered

She wanted to cry.

"Do you want to use this one?" A girl about her own age that freed the stall by which she stood was holding the enclosure wide open. Brandi thanked her and rushed in. She couldn't pull her drawers down fast enough—she frantically tore at the strip around her waist, stripping pins open, puncturing her flesh, ripping skin, making cat's claws. When she relieved herself, she remarked aloud about how much better she felt. From the aperture at the base of the stalls, the lady in the next stall passed the toilet tissue. Brandi thanked her and smiled.

In that tiny stall, Brandi set about reorganizing herself for the remainder of the trip to Claxville, for the rest of her life. She took the money belt from her waist, raised her dress high to inspect it, noting bloody, puffy, swelling trails made by the large safety pins, by her own fingernails when she tried to loosen the fixture as she tried to figure out how Sara had made it so secure. Then she took all of the money from the homemade contraption and placed it in her purse before depositing the shredded material and pins in the trash. Brandi just wanted to relax—the college-bound young lady wanted to be free of concerns about using the bathroom and of being afraid to go.

Thoughts of her family broke the boredom of the remaining leg of the trip. Her mind was constantly drawn to her father's warnings. She drew solace from her self-assurance that things weren't going to be easy, that though by all measures she was no bigger than a flea, couldn't fight gnats out of her own face, she did have some sense, knew how to take precautions, would be all right for she had become a younger version of Sara, had embodied and embraced the mother's teachings. Thus she would follow the rules, keep to herself, refrain from letting every Tom, Dick, and Harry know everything about her, keep her hands off other people's stuff, not touch anything that didn't belong to her—and when in the stores, wouldn't touch anything unless she had the money to pay for it.

Sara's commandments made her daughter's fingers curl at the knuckles in memory of the raps Sara had freely given the probing phalanges, anywhere, anytime, in the presence of anybody—at home, at church, uptown during their infrequent trips to the stores in Wester, at the rolling stores' tailgates.

Brandi would also be watchful, prayerful, would try to figure out other people's plans, reasons, inclinations before they did it; be welcoming and defensive at the same time; would pay attention to everything—the weather, numbers, her dreams. Sara's superstitions had been transmitted to the girl as well.

She shifted in her seat, and yawns escaped her parting lips. Eleven to twelve hours was an awful long time to just sit and do nothing. She shut her eyes and had drifted into peaceful revelry when the images of Sara, Cat, Aunt Sylvia, and her brothers and sisters visited her anew. Sara and her brother-in-law chattered cheerfully, while Caroline, Maureen, Pearline, Lil' Carruthers, and Benjamin bobbed up and down on the Country Squire station wagon's worn tailgate.

Her father spoke to her in a fog, continuing his relentless verbal tirade. He was no longer talking to her but at her. The man was angry—his anger humiliated her; his obvious lack of confidence in her ability to succeed in another world humiliated her. His words of warning cut her like raw green switches. The voiceless words spewed from his lips and hovered above her sleeping head, then dropped from the sky, cascading its cold drops on her warm, happy spirit.

Brandi stirred in her seat, shook her head from side to side. "No," she spoke in the air—did not, could not understand why her father was doing this to her.

The bus seemed to falter, sputter—the driver shifted its gears to accommodate the mechanism's needs for the now hilly terrain. Brandi awoke with a start, initially confused about where she was.

Momentarily, the bus was pulling up to the station. Brandi craned her neck to get a good look at her final destination.

CHAPTER TWO

The Arrival

When the bus arrived at the Claxville Bus Terminal, Brandi's inklings of apprehension resurfaced—now that she was in the college town, she was not sure of how she would find the campus and get to the dormitory. She struggled for a moment with the belongings in the rack above her head. "Step back, I'll get it down for you." The sleeping boy spoke up, got the goods down, and placed them on the seat as the young woman directed before he got off the bus.

Taking a moment to bid a nervous "Thank you" to the driver who sat updating his log, she proceeded with the dismount.

The driver, summoned from his task by these departing words, bounded from his seat and assisted the tattered traveler with her meager possessions before leaping back in the seat and speeding ahead to the next leg of his route.

Everyone else, having been met by some relation or friend, jauntily sauntered away, leaving the girl to her thoughts of what she needed to do next. She noted the sign atop the terminal that did indeed indicate she was at her destination—Brandi Brown was in Claxville.

A cursory glance to the right showed a lengthy, hilly knoll flanked by many eateries, service stations, and lodging places. The Varsity sign enacted a deprived digestive system with eleven hours of tea cakes and pop. A hamburger "all the way" seemed to be the balm needed to douse a rushing wave of sugary sweet hunger-induced nausea. "If I had somewhere to put this stuff, I could get a bite to eat, and then figure out where the devil I'm going," she thought.

A "Can I help you?" brought Brandi out of a pensive mood.

"Oh, I just need directions to Claxville University!" rushed from her anxious lips. "But before I go there, I want to get something to eat from that restaurant over there."

The previously unnoticed taxi driver immediately reached for her luggage, tossing it lightly into the back of his battered mustard-colored cab, sliding, amateurish lettering on its sides and banged bumpers with chipped paint abounding. A quick "At your service, ma'am," and a brisk bow with cap tipped toward the remainder of the seat set Brandi in motion anew.

She never got a glance to her immediate left, for had she made a small swivel in her seat or turned her head leftward, she would have seen that the bus station was right across the road from the entranceway to the university. Brandi would also have seen the back of her traveling companion as he disappeared through the black wrought iron archway with "Claxville University, 1887" slightly obscured by oaks' bowing branches and ivy's entwining vines. If she had been more attentive, the boy on the bus could have pointed the way.

Nevertheless, the hasty trip to the Varsity allowed no time for glancing over one's shoulders—for looking backward to what could have been. After placing an order for "a cheeseburger all the way, some onion rings, and a driver-recommended Varsity orange drink," the response to his inquiry about the passenger's destination was a garbled "Davis Hall."

With meter already engaged and running at its customary frantic, seemingly tampered pace, the driver turned right, hoping that his passenger, like many previous passengers, would not immediately advise him that he was going away from the university—away from its living quarters, toward the world of academe. He thought that with lady luck on his side he would be able to break even, to make his "gas money" and a "bit more" if he'd found one more passenger that day.

Thirty minutes later, with campus evaded, sufficiently crisscrossed several times, good, cheap cafes and Fraternity Row explored, the weary passenger, but full passenger—she had enjoyed the fast food from the Varsity—asked how much farther she had to go before she got to the dormitory. A "just around the corner" was followed momentarily by a view of a magnificent antebellum structure—Davis Hall. Brandi's mouth fell open—she was struck by such opulence, the likes of which she'd never seen; the black-and-white pictures on the university's brochures had not done the campus or its buildings justice.

Paid and overtipped for services rendered, the cabdriver left an almost listless Brandi, suitcase, purse, patchwork quilt, and remnants of the double-strength Watkins-flavored cinnamon and nutmeg tea cakes at a side door, one where other students, their families, and friends unloaded.

Before she could get a foot in the door, a gaggle of white girls dressed in light pink and baby blue shirts, with oversized towels in tow and bottles of oils and tanning lotion in hand, bounded from the exit, disengaging the young woman from her belongings. She dropped everything—everything except her purse whose shoulder strap proved to be a firm, gripping anchor. A renewed effort involved propping the massive door open with a gnawed, twisted piece of green oak limb which seemed to have served the same purpose many times and testing the door several times to ensure the stability of the prop before she regathered her fallen belongings.

When Brandi stepped inside, a long, semidark hallway broke in the middle by brilliance greeted her. The brilliance and aura of the setting nearly took her breath. For a moment or two, the young woman stood transfixed, glaring upward at a magnificent chandelier which she thought must have held hundreds of tiny candlelike bulbs. She looked to her left and to her right to the beautiful ornamental staircase that appeared to stop abruptly at the next floor. A glance around showed the lobby, which resembled a grand ballroom—full of overstuffed sofas and chairs, plants, magazine racks—whose floors were blanketed in piles of luggage, loose bed linens, bags and containers of foodstuffs, room-sized refrigerators, ironing boards, hair dryers, vacuum cleaners, brooms, mops, radios, record players . . . all signs of fall, of school's opening, of new beginnings.

A rumbling, nervous stomach made the bungling figure with all her belongings rush for the light. An overwhelming urge to use the bathroom activated the girl's sweat glands; beads of sweat peppered her "pecan tan" brow and upper lip.

Then the newcomer almost slipped on hardwood floors waxed to perfection. The lobby, dressed in reddish brocade of antebellum times, was in the middle of many labeled doors. A "come in" was given to Brandi's light tap on the door with a bronze plate labeled "Resident Assistant."

When Brandi glanced forward, a partially clad RA seated in a rumpled bed in an unkempt room reeking of a sweet, sickening, almost repulsive odor of cigarettes said, "I'm not ready for my room to be cleaned yet. Come back when you finish Ms. Winthrop's suite." Brandi slithered snakelike out of the doorway with caution learned upon her initial entry into Davis Hall. She faced others trickling in to check into the dormitory and instinctively fell in the line with them, managing to get her room assignment and to the bathroom with little more ado.

Bobby Dylan's deep throaty growl from somebody's radio ushered her to the third floor. He was singing something about blowing in the wind, at least that's what the disc jockey said concerning the song unfamiliar to the newcomer. Propelled by the unfamiliar yet driving, compelling rhythm from his guitar, the university student first found her room and stood momentarily at the room's entrance before placing the key in the keyhole.

Two bunk beds in a cool room, with decor incongruent with that of the exterior of Davis Hall and the lobby, greeted Brandi. Everything was coal grayish black metal—desk, lockers, chest of drawers, student's desk, venetian blinds—all reminiscent of a prison's cold furnishings. Although the room seemed quite drab after the opulence from downstairs and was not as magnificent as the exterior had suggested, the young woman noted that it was squeaky clean in spite of the cracking, busting tile and metal lockers blotched with rust—she determined that all was fixable. She toed the tile with a foot pulled from the shoes she had worn for the last twelve or more hours, deciding a little tar could cure that and that she could buy a little paint to touch up the rust spots peppered in the furnishings' metal exteriors.

Having become satisfied with the living conditions, the young woman wondered for just a moment about the room's other occupant before fragmented light from the venetian-blinded window beckoned her. She peeked through a slit in the blinds and watched the traffic flow; then she widened the slit to get a better view. The parted metal blades showed that the room was in the front of the building, facing a sandwich shop in a small shopping mall directly across the street. A downward glance revealed an imposing lawn blanketed by a browning sea of male and female students' oiled bodies. She couldn't understand how they could take all of that heat. It was hot enough to fry an egg on the sidewalk, a hundred degrees in the shade! An elevated dew point made it hotter than the thermometer actually showed. At least that was what she had heard on the radio while still in the taxi.

Farther on the horizon, Brandi could see what appeared to be ant-sized people walking around on buildings' flat roofs. "It's probably workers," the exhausted student voiced sleepily to the listening room. She lay on the bed for just a moment, was going to unpack in a minute. And she fell asleep. Neither the dull humdrum from other students checking in, sobbing mothers leaving their "babies" for the first time since bonding, nor the constant flushing of the commode from the bathroom diagonal to her room was distracting enough to keep the young woman awake. She was exhausted, had barely slept any the last week, was much too excited! Brandi was asleep before her head hit the pillow; sleep refused to allow her to dress it in the new linen she's bought for this occasion.

Brandi dreamed the door opened, illumination flooded the room, and her roommate stood at her bedside, peering at her as she slept. It appeared that others were with her, but they did not stay. They left as quickly as they came.

CHAPTER THREE

Games People Play

What actually transpired during Brandi's sound slumber was that Julie Blanchard, from over near Forest Hills, had checked in alone this year, for she was a second-year freshman, entered the room and found the sleeping "colored" girl on the bed in the room that she and another repeater, Laura Mackey, had agreed to share this particular fall. The room itself was in a strategic location. It was near the staircase and could be used at the discretion of the unruly ruffians at Claxville simply to escape, break curfew, and "party."

Julie, Laura, and their friends—all "ladies of distinction," many of whom had not been able to interest any sorority in allowing them membership—had pledged to "rule Davis Hall" upon their return to Claxville University that year.

Needless to say, Julie went from dorm room to dorm room touting her discovery. Soon, several of her "pseudo-sorors" joined her in the return to the room for a glance at the fully clad colored girl sprawled face down on the naked mattress Julie had claimed before summer vacation.

A slight stir from Brandi caused the snickering, gaping comrades to retreat more hastily than they had come. Yet the laughter, jeers, and pounding footsteps in descent did nothing to the weary resident in room 306. When the college students gathered in a room down the hall, they initially decided to catch up on the summer "happenings" and to have the resident assistant take care of the rooming situation the following day. Nevertheless, with a couple of six packs of "brew" consumed and a wrinkled "joint" wrested from a hole in the lining of the bottom of a purse, the conversation soon returned to Julie's discovery.

Suddenly, Laura Mackey, the Blanchard girl's chosen roommate, recounted a tale her mother had told her about "getting a maid fired for stealing" in retaliation for the woman's report of sexual trysts she and her friends engaged in with a stable boy when she was a teenager. As best as Laura could remember the tale, the precocious teens had removed valuables—family heirlooms, that is, pieces of silverware, combs with pearly spines, etc.—and buried them in dung behind the stables, leaving the impression with her parents that "coloreds would steal anything that was not nailed down."

"We could do the same thing to the colored girl in our room," was her proposition.

Initially Julie rejected the preposterous proposal to engage in that kind of horseplay with, "How dumb can you get, Laura! That girl can't steal shit because there ain't nothing in the damn room yet. All my shit's still in the car."

"But," Laura, lips curled up with glee, devilish twinkle in eye, insisted, "we can slip in there and put something in there while she's sleep."

"Suppose she wakes up? What are we going to do then?" asked Julie quite seriously. She shook her head because this was absurd.

"Stupid!" chimed in yet another friend. "If she didn't wake up while all of us was in there, she won't wake up while you put something in there."

"And if she did," another added, "all you got to do is introduce yourself and tell her you are her roommate. It's just that simple, dummy. No need to make a mountain out of a molehill."

While the girls bantered back and forth about the feasibility of recreating an old story, one of the current room's occupants reached for her desk and tossed a pack of pastel-colored writing paper with matching envelopes between the two. Her note of assurance "That'll do it!" was the catalyst needed to set the game in motion.

Dawn, accompanied by first the sputtering and then rushes of water from the lead pipes and shower heads that lay dormant during the summer months, the bustle and busy of a major thoroughfare through Claxville's main campus, and rays of light peeking through venetian blinds left cracked by the sleeping young woman, brought life back to the inert figure on the bare mattress.

Brandi swiped at the dried spittle that had accumulated on her face during the night, moaned aloud, and mumbled, "Damn!" as she felt her black square-framed glasses collapse under her body's weight. "Can't afford to break you, guys—you're the only pair I got," she spoke soothingly to the glasses needed for myopia. She was blind as a bat without them, could barely see what was directly in front of her.

An extended bladder, one accustomed to several trips during the night to the white porcelain pot with chipping edges, shoved her from the bed. Unusually stiff joints cracked; one after another they made themselves

BRENDA SMITH

audible. "Boy, I'm sore . . . and still sleepy too. I wish I could crawl back in the bed," she muttered.

Nearing the door, Brandi decided to gather all toiletries needed to prepare herself for the day. "I don't know who else is up—better do it now. Need to get this bed made up before my roommate comes," the occupant mumbled to the room.

She reached for her wallet, but common sense from the last day or two argued, "It's ludicrous to go through all that stuff you went through yesterday. Leave it in the room—it'll be safe here!" The lone occupant of room 306 replied, "I can't believe I let Ma talk me into wearing that rag around my waist like that—I'm glad nobody that I knew saw me! They would have thought I had lost all my marbles." She rubbed her hand across the scratches from the pins and her own nails on her midriff.

Bladder pushing harder, she hurried along to the community bathroom, as did others on the third floor.

Julie, Laura, and the remainder of their buddies patrolled the hallways, waiting for the right time to make their "hit." A hush fell on the floor of Davis Hall when Brandi appeared in the hallway. Following the night's strategic plan, each young woman took her place—one in the bathroom, preparing for showering. Another assumed her post at the door, shifting nervously from in and out to out and in.

When the signal was given that Brandi was in the shower, a trio hurried to the empty room. Julie, with stationery tucked under a borrowed nightshirt, was prodded by Laura and another to "put the damn paper down" and "let's get the hell out of here before that thing comes back in here."

When the pastel writing paper found a resting place in the middle of the bed, Julie was "out of there!" The remaining warriors, including the sentry who feigned preparation for showering, abandoned their posts for a retreat to the safety of "headquarters."

The lookout was interrogated by the others.

"Did she speak to you?"

"No."

"What'd she look like?"

"I don't know."

"Was her hair long or short?"

"How tall was she?"

"I don't know."

"I don't know!" was the response to the chain of queries from the comrades.

"What do you mean you don't know? She damn near stepped on your toes and you don't know what she looked like!" Julie shrieked in frustration amid the barrage of inquiries.

"I was just looking out, that was all I was supposed to do," argued the lookout. "Y'all didn't say I had to look at her!"

"Stupid bitch!" Julie exclaimed before she flung herself to the bed in frustration. All fell silent, waiting for more from her.

The sobering, rest-broken Julie added, "All I know is if that colored girl would have been a black snake, she would have bit all y'all's asses—and to think I listened to y'all. My daddy just did let me bring my scrawny ass back up here. He said one lick of shit out of me and I'd be back home before midnight."

Tears welling in her eyes, Julie pounded the flesh of the bed as the others set about reassuring their friend that everything was "cool."

"Shucks, Julie, ain't no sense in taking this thing so personal. Everybody is supposed to have fun while they're in college." One of the instigators piped, "You ought to hear some of the things my daddy said they did when he was up here."

"Your daddy . . . your daddy, I don't want to hear a damn thing about your daddy!" a distressed Julie shrieked at her companions.

"And your damn mama neither." She pointed at Laura, who nodded affirmatively at each comment.

CHAPTER FOUR

So Much for Advice

Brandi returned to the room as quietly and quickly as she left. Less than twenty minutes had passed since she had gone for her shower. Instinctively, the girl checked her purse for its contents, musing silently again to herself about having tied her money around her waist with a rag when she'd left the tiny, quaint, comfortable Wester Community.

She retrieved the letter regarding registration from the pocketbook, laying it on the cold steel nightstand separating one side of the room from the other. Then she continued with the dressing, first of herself and secondly the bed. Noting for the first time that the bed was already covered with a mattress pad, Brandi added the floral muslin sheets with matching pillowcases she'd bought with the "tobacco" money she'd earned just before coming to Claxville.

Once more, thoughts of her roommate surfaced—Sara had suggested that she wait to buy a bedspread because they, she and her roommate, would want to have matching ones. "Can't I just buy two? Then we can swap."

"Better wait, child," the mother suggested forcibly. "Ain't no used to wasting money."

Brandi finished unpacking, reread the letter, and left the room to begin the day. Drawn downward to the door she had entered just twelve hours before, she stepped from the blinding morning lights into shadows of humongous oaks surrounding the building. A somewhat disconcerted Brandi's feet slipped into a blanket of grass with dew still glistening on each blade. "No wonder those girls almost knocked me down yesterday," she emitted as her vision cleared and her feet steadied.

Looking around, she saw the traffic light—red, green, and yellow—neon lights in the sandwich shop that had beckoned her to the window just the day before. Brandi crossed the street and entered the sandwich shop.

"Good morning, ma'am. Can I help you?" called a young man behind the counter to the day's first customer.

"I'll have a bologna sandwich please," responded the individual who did not recognize pastrami, knockwurst, or many other foods on the menu. "Baloney meat," a chunk of cheese, and a large RC Cola were generally the choices afforded by the rolling stores, small crossroads groceries, and meat markets in the neck of the woods from which the young woman had come.

"The works—mayonnaise, mustard, lettuce . . . ?" he probed further. "Onion?"

"Yes, all of those," she stammered, mouth watering with anticipation. It had been quite a while since she had eaten. As a matter of fact, a whole day had passed. She preferred breakfast, but this would do . . . would have to.

"For here or to go, ma'am? Do you want to eat here, or would you like to take it with you?" the man asked, pointing toward the round tables with white heart-shaped wrought iron backs. Glancing at her watch, the young woman said, "I'll take it with me." It was nine o'clock, and her letter had indicated she was to meet with her advisor at ten. Cat's and Sara's warnings for her to "leave early, so you'll get there on time" and not to ask too many questions so people wouldn't know she was new came to her.

"Huh?" she responded to the server, who had already asked twice, "Something to drink, ma'am?"

"Oh yes, a soda . . . I'll have a Coke."

The man cut the sandwich in half, deftly encased it in waxed paper, and began to insert a bag of chips into the paper bag but was interrupted by Brandi's "I didn't order chips."

"Comes with it," he said, handing it and the poured Coke to her.

"That'll be fifty cents, ma'am."

The young woman with bag in tow marveled silently at its contents, especially the number of thin slices of meat the man had put between two slices of white bread. A person just couldn't get that much bologna for fifty cents in Wester. In fact, nobody Brandi knew would put that much meat on a sandwich. Sara used that much to make sandwiches for herself, Carruthers, the girl, and the remainder of the Brown clan.

Giving thanks, Brandi ate half of the sandwich while waiting for a bus to arrive. "I'll have the rest for lunch," she said to herself.

Brandi took the map to Reade Hall out of her purse to look for her destination and appointment time again. She was supposed to meet with a woman named Dr. McIntyre.

She decided to walk to the building instead of waiting for the bus. It did not appear to be too far from where she currently stood. And it wasn't. Once inside Reade Hall, Brandi found Dr. McIntyre's office with little trouble. A secretary smiled at her and opened another door to a larger office where the professor was standing behind her desk talking on the telephone. "Just have a seat," the woman said as she pointed to the seat directly in front of her desk.

When she was finished, the fiftyish woman with frosted hair, dressed impeccably in a pale blue business suit, greeted the student cordially and began her academic advisement. "So you want to be an interpreter—how interesting!" Dr. McIntyre told Brandi.

"All I know is I want to live in other countries and get to know other people, to speak their languages." Brandi was sure of that, so she spoke with authority.

"What was the catalyst for such thoughts—what made you so interested in studying languages?" the advisor continued.

After a moment, Brandi offered, "I don't know—guess it was because of Mr. A."

"Mr. A.? Who's Mr. A? Was he one of your high school teachers? One who taught languages?"

"No." The girl told her advisor of the clothier back in Wester and about his tales of faraway lands.

"That's very interesting, Brandi," she said delightfully when the girl had told of the man. "Of course, you know you will have to work very hard to achieve such a grandiose goal. You must already be a hard worker. You've gotten this far," the woman told her charge.

"Not many of you people get this far," the professor continued.

Now discomfort replaced comfort and the young woman's mind strayed from the present—Brandi grew tense. Dr. McIntyre was talking about "you people." Brandi didn't know about this "you people" thing. Carruthers had always talked about it. "Better watch out for them folks always talking about 'you people.' Don't trust them no farther than you can throw them," he'd said time and time again.

"Brandi," the professor brought the young woman to the present, "I'm going to sign you up for three classes, twelve hours. That's the minimum you can take and still be classified as a full-time student. If you take less than that during any given quarter, you will not be able to benefit from your scholarship. Do you understand?"

"Yes, ma'am."

"You stop by and talk to me sometimes," the woman said to her charge when they had selected classes, a meal plan and the like, and placed such on the appropriate forms, giving one to Brandi and maintaining a duplicate for her files. "I want to know how things are coming. If you have any difficulty, please feel free to call me. That's why I am here. If I am not in, you can leave a message with my secretary—her name is Kay—and I'll return your calls."

Dr. McIntyre made a mental note to talk about this student in the next department meeting. She was quite an interesting character, and the woman felt that she was worth salvaging. Besides that, they had never had a colored girl or boy graduate from the department. None could get past the "animal." By legend, Bob Henri was a monster—he was the meanest, nastiest, and without a doubt one of the worst bigots on the campus . . . the student senate received and passed along to the administration more complaints about him than any other instructor in the whole university system. The man was notorious for picking fights with students to gauge their mettle under pressure. Maybe, just maybe, if she ran interference this one time, this ambitious little waft could get by him.

Professor Virginia McIntyre realized immediately how difficult, challenging, and rewarding the task would be. She concealed her excitement and resisted the temptation to get up and pace about. "Kay!" she called to her secretary as soon as the girl had gone. "Ask Carmen to come by. We need her to tutor someone this quarter. We might as well put her on the payroll now."

Brandi left Reade Hall, humming a nervous tune while getting ready for the next step, advisement having gone well and Dr. McIntyre proving to be different from what she had anticipated, from what was presupposed, suggested, from that which she had refused to internalize—that which she proposed to refute. This kind, warm, caring lady was nothing like those in some of the articles she had read or heard spoken about, and the young woman was glad.

CHAPTER FIVE

Sweet Conversation

Brandi whistled gaily, as much as possible, hummed, sang at some tune until she got to the bus stop. Several students were already there—none paid any attention to the young woman as she scanned the posted routes, trying to discern what the various colors on the map's legend meant. Momentarily, a bus pulled up, and the passengers began to mount its steps. Brandi mounted it too.

A student in front of Brandi asked the driver, "Will this bus take me to the admissions office?" His "I'll let you know when we get there" gave the novice a bit of relief because that was also her destination.

Spotting a bronze face like hers, she proceeded to the rear of the bus and sat beside a dark mahogany-colored man wearing a green, brown, orange, and yellow kaleidoscopic dashiki. Brandi was exhilarated—she'd found someone she could talk to . . . or so she thought.

Brandi had hardly talked with anyone since she had arrived at the university—the cabdriver had talked to her, and Dr. McIntyre had done most of the talking. Brandi enjoyed talking too. In fact, the young woman loved to talk. Carruthers had always said that his eldest daughter talked when she "ought to been listening."

On the other hand, Sara defended her child's loquaciousness. The mother enjoyed talking to her, and she generally allowed Brandi to express herself freely as long as she wasn't "sassy."

When Sara spoke of her eldest child, she'd often begin, "Now Brandi, that child's something else. She loves to talk—she'll talk to a fencepost if it will stand still long enough!"

"Matter of fact, she came here squawking," Sara would continue. Brandi was born one of the few nights that the woman could ever remember snow falling so far down south. The night the baby came, Cat had started over to his mama's house to pay a visit. So Brandi's grandmother, Ma Grover, sent her uncle Baby Boy to catch him when Sara started "paining, 'cause she knowed Sara was gonna act the fool." "Don't tarry none," she said to the lanky teen, "you know how your sister is, and Cat need to be here too!"

"Stop by and fetch that midwife on your way," the elderly woman called out. "And tell her to bring some sassafras root or something to make that gal rest some, if she can. She might better bring enough for all of us," she added. "Ain't no sense in everybody's staying up all night, watching Sara act the fool. Never could take no pain, that one, never could."

Cat had turned around when the snow started, so he was already back at the house by the time Baby Boy had gotten the midwife to the house. It didn't take Brandi long to come into the world. When the girl, with "head clean as the top of Cat's receding hairline," made her entrance, the midwife prematurely announced, "I believe y'alls got yo'selfs a fine baby boy." The man, set to yapping by this pronouncement, stopped short when exposed genitalia showed that the squawking, hairless ball of fire was indeed female. "So you see," Sara would complete the story, "she came here with her mouth wide open."

Another favorite story Sara enjoyed telling about the talkative tot was about a day when she'd finally taken the three-year-old into town instead of leaving her at home with Ma Grover. "That child," she said, "spoke to everybody she saw—merchants and everybody . . . colored and white, didn't make no difference. She was just a talking. Every one of them storekeepers would be talking about what good manners she had and how good she could express herself."

One of the Rubenstein twins, clothiers who catered to mostly colored people in Wester and other small towns around there, noted that the child appeared to be reading names on the shoe boxes as she wandered aimlessly through the cluttered aisles while Sara was paying on her bill. "Come here, honey," Mr. A called gently to the toddler, kneeling down in front of her as she approached. "Read this for me, honey," he said, crawling down the crowded rows alongside the tot pointing at each word on the shoe-laden containers.

"Wrangler, Converse, Jones, Stebbins, Admiral, Stacy-Adams," she read with confidence; and when they had finished reading labels on all the shoe boxes on the aisle, he stood up and turned to the awaiting mother, inquiring, "How you teaching her to read at such an early age?"

"Mr. A, I just tell you the truth. I get so tired of her talking sometimes and answering all her questions 'til I thought I'd just teach her how to read. Then she can entertain herself while I do my chores," Sara spoke almost apologetically.

"That's all right," the man said approvingly, nodding for her, the customer, to continue.

"I started with her letters, and she learned them so fast. Before I knew it she was just calling out letters and saying, 'Mama, what that say?' That's all I know about her reading. Brandi, that child just don't never forget nothing." Sara threw her hands up and let them plop by her side.

And then, depending on the company, Sara would tell of another encounter she and Brandi had that first day in town and about the conversation that ensued. "Brandi made me so proud . . . she was still saying them French words Mr. Z done come over and start saying to her when he left the cash register."

"Well, anyhow, soon as we stepped out the door, Ole Tillie Mae Johnson —what Cat went with before me and him started going together—anyway, she come stepping her fat ass down the street by the time we hit the pavement good. Well, anyway, you know she hasn't said a word to me since me and him got married. She stopped her nosey tail and said to Brandi, 'You sho' is a pretty li'l girl.'

"I couldn't believe what happened next," Sara would continue, in embarrassment or delight, depending upon the company. "Brandi looked at her for a moment and then responded, 'You shore is got a fat butt.'" Either way the mother would break out in fits of laughter when she recounted this part of the story about Brandi's love for conversation—and inevitably the listener could not help but to laugh too.

Almost fifteen years after Mr. A and his twin, Mr. Z, had taught her a few French words while Sara did her business in town, Brandi seated herself beside the somewhat handsome stranger on the university's transport and prepared for some polite conversation. By the time she had placed her belongings in strategic positions, to facilitate a quick and easy dismount when the bus got to the admissions hall, the man was moving. The young woman thought the bus was nearing a stop. However, that was not the case—the mahogany man had disengaged himself from the seat with the colored girl and had moved to a vacant seat beside a white girl.

The cranky old overstuffed bus grudgingly climbed hills and fell in valleys of green, peppered with the yellows, browns, oranges, and reds of late fall and impending winter, stopping to take on more students at each stop, leaving behind those who had reached their destinations, giving those who waited vacated seats. Soon, the bus was stuffed beyond capacity; students at the university for registration for fall semester, standing, held fast to each other and the backs of seats to avoid falling over as the aging vehicle lurched toward its final destination. Every seat was filled—that is, every seat except the one beside Sara's daughter, who thirsted for sweet conversation.

Brandi was relieved when the bus stopped and the driver announced for passengers unable to see in the thickness, "Admissions Hall, straight ahead, up the walk a piece, and to the left. You can't miss it. There'll be a line," the man announced grumpily in a loud voice. The young woman made her way through the crowd—she wanted to get off of the vehicle . . . to be freed of the confounding dilemma, and was glad that she had not had to ask for help.

The student got in line, determined to forget about the mahogany man, to attend to the day's tasks. She just got in line, standing for hours while it crept mercilessly forward and stopped again and again before resuming its snail's pace. But the mahogany man wouldn't go away—he became a skeleton in her mind's closet . . . Brandi would never forget their brief encounter.

When lunchtime came, the admissions office closed and a few students opted to leave and return later; others stayed. Brandi found herself at high noon on the top step, mimicking the actions of others who had either publicly or privately resolved to stay until the staff returned, until she was registered. She sat and finished the remains of the "warm" bologna sandwich with wilting lettuce and already overripe tomato slithering freely from its wrapping. Then she sipped the warm, flat, caramel-colored remnants from the morning's Coke and lost herself in the magnificence of nature that embraced her.

As much as Brandi had always enjoyed talking, she began to relish the voice of beauty manifested through chattering, chirping birds, and hasty footsteps of squirrels skittering hither and yonder depositing winter's food in alcoves of the antiquated oaks decorating North Campus. Gray moss hanging from the left side of each grand oak moved with the wind, whispering a soft, sweet song.

"I think I'm going to like it here," she mused, wrapping her arms tightly around herself. When the doors had reopened and she'd taken care of her business, the young woman had more money in her purse that she'd brought to Claxville with her. The grant from the manufacturer had more than paid for her expenses—tuition, room and board, meals, books, all that she could possibly incur in one quarter was paid for. She had not had to use any of the money she's brought with her. Things were looking up for Brandi Leigh Brown!

CHAPTER SIX

For Better or Worse

When Brandi returned to the dormitory, she noticed a box of pastel-colored writing paper on the bed opposite the one which she had taken, walked toward it with outstretched hand, and withdrew the member before it touched the box's clear plastic lid, exposing its inviting, almost summoning contents. Sara's forewarning, "Child, while you up there, don't you put your hands on nothing that don't belong to you—you hear me—nothing!" rang loud and clear.

Stepping back a few steps, she almost fell on the other bed when the telephone on the desk blasted. It rang incessantly, several times before Brandi removed it from its cradle. "Hello," she spoke tentatively into the mouthpiece.

"Is Julie there?" a deep Southern bass drawled.

Brandi's "No, sir" yielded a loud, irritable, "You tell her her daddy called, you here!" Then the man was gone—he hung up without the customary good-bye; the line grew dead.

"Julie, that's her name—Julie," Brandi muttered, securing a piece of her own paper to scribble a note to the yet unseen roommate, which she laid neatly beside the box of stationery.

Then she decided to take a nap. It had been a relatively warm, as well as taxing day; the humidity almost sucked one's breath away. The young woman was glad the old oaks had shaded the environs while she waited for registration. She lay on the bed, had hardly made herself comfortable; her head had barely touched the pillow when the telephone rang anew. This time, when she said hello, all she heard were giggles; once again the phone was hung up.

Returning to her resting place, she repositioned herself on the tiny bunk for the early afternoon nap, but she was summoned a third time by the instrument's disturbing blast. "Brandi," the caller spoke with authority, "this is your RA. Miz Winthrop needs to see you in her office."

"Right now?" she questioned sleepily.

"Yes, right now. It won't take long," was the caller's response before she too had given proper protocol—again there was no good-bye, just the click of the telephone being placed back on the resident assistant's cradle.

Brandi looked at the instrument and shook her head in wonderment before she reluctantly picked herself up off the bunk to respond to the summons from the housemother.

Ms. Winthrop greeted the puzzled girl with "Brandi, I've received a complaint from several parents, including those of your roommate, regarding . . ."

"I ain't done nothing. I didn't touch anything in that room that wasn't mine. I ain't even seen no roommate," Brandi prematurely defended herself. "When I got back to the room from registration, her writing paper was on the bed, but I ain't touched it!" she exclaimed. "The only reason that I answered that phone was 'cause it just kept on ringing, and I thought it might be something important."

"Hold your horses, Brandi. We know you ain't done nothing," Ms. Winthrop spoke almost soothingly to the panicking student. "The situation is quite simple. Two girls who were here last school term had agreed to room together this year. It seems that they had already bought matching bed linens, towels, curtains, and bedspreads. And they had a rug cut to fit the room. So we decided to find you another room if that's all right with you.

"I had the resident assistant to start looking today," the woman went on, not giving Brandi a chance to say a word. "We got another colored girl on the fourth floor, and there's a girl from China down the hall from there. Both girls are a bit older than you, but we know you'll enjoy them, and they'll help you to get along while you're here." Pointing at the direction in which the RA had retreated, the woman said, "She's going to take you to meet both of them, then we'll decide where to put you. You understand?" she quizzed Brandi.

Brandi had not understood—did not want to understand; yet moments later, the stoic-looking woman was directing the resident assistant to take the "girl" to meet the other "girls." "Take her to May Lin's room first, then to the other 'girl's' room," the woman said to the resident assistant who had witnessed their entire conversation from afar.

"Girl!" How old does a colored woman have to be before she can be a woman? Brandi resented being called a "girl." Girls under ten were called

BRENDA SMITH

"girls," and she had long passed that. By the age of twelve, at the onset of puberty, they were usually alluded to as young lady. She had asked Sara how she felt about being called a "gal" all the time. Sara had dismissed her daughter's query with a warning, "All I know is you better respect your elders, missy."

Sara's daughter was having a difficult time with respect for elders up at Claxville.

The resident assistant, who was no more than a year or two older than Brandi, commanded her to "follow me!"

She took her to the Oriental girl's room first. The air in the room was thick—the odor of oils and sauces greeted the two visitors, yet neither remarked about the university's policy against cooking in one's room. They both had a task to attend to—the resident assistant to find a room for Brandi, and for Brandi, it was to remain in the room which she had originally been assigned; she was not sure when she had purposed to stay in the room, to make the relationship with the current roommate work, but she had, and the young woman was stubborn as a mule—if she put in for something, she was likely not to let up.

Once the resident assistant had introduced the two occupants of Davis Hall, she left them to their own devices.

Soon, it was obvious that Brandi had come at a very bad time. May Lin, a much older woman than even she anticipated, had just received a letter from her parents in the Orient. When she had offered the guest, "the girl with no room," a chair, she had taken the letter from the desk, displaying its contents to her. "This letter, it has upset me so my day is ruined—forgive me, it is hard to think of much else," she expressed sorrowfully before letting Brandi in on the nature of her disturbance.

May Lin's older sister Sue Lin, a student at a prestigious university in New Jersey, had met a young man from their homeland and had become engaged, but they were unable to marry because custom did not permit a younger sister to take a spouse until the older sister had found her own husband. May Lin wept openly as she spoke of the family's dilemma. Wails erupted periodically as she ran her finger downward on the pages, tracing the passageways of symbols and characters, interpreting the letter verbatim for the "girl with no room."

Odors from the pot boiling on a hot plate resting on the desk penetrating the air and May Lin's squeaky sobs caused Brandi to disengage herself from the setting. She had problems of her own—she just couldn't handle someone else's that day. The visitor thanked the hostess and excused herself. "I have another appointment. Perhaps we can talk another time," she said as she relinquished her seat and offered the departing handshake.

Next she went to room 406, which was directly above her own, to visit its occupant, a fortyish colored woman who lived about an hour's drive from Wester. Both acknowledged the coincidence and exchanged a few pleasantries before they talked about the real reason for her visit. Brandi's inquiry from the doctoral student about placement of two colored women and a Chinese woman in a dormitory for freshmen was met with a cool "I have been here two years, and I have been busy taking care of my own business. I'm here just to get my degree, and then I'm gone. If you want to succeed, you do what you're told." Brandi thanked the woman for her time and returned to her own room to sort out her own dilemma.

When she was back in her own room, the young woman renewed her efforts to take a nap, but sleep evaded her—she thrashed around, tossing and turning, never able to get comfortable, so she decided to write a letter to Sara. There was so much to tell. It seemed like a month or more had passed since she had left home, but it had actually been a couple of days . . . nevertheless, she wanted to tell her how she almost peed in her pants trying to get money out of the homemade money belt . . .

Moreover, she wanted her family, especially Aunt Sylvia, to know how the aroma of the tea cakes had permeated the air on the bus ride, causing dozing passengers to come alive. She wanted to tell of Julie's antics, about the girl from China, and the woman from the neighboring town. There was so much to tell.

Instead, she wrote:

Dear Mother,

I got here fine. My room was ready, and I am anxiously waiting for my roommate to arrive. She will probably be here soon. Some of her things are already here.

The campus is real nice, and everybody is so nice. I registered today, and I still have all of my money plus some. The check was waiting for me. All I had to do was sign the check, and the cashier gave me the change. I've got to do something with all of this money. I can't carry it around with me everywhere I go.

When I got up at the place where you go to sign up for classes, I saw a Woolworth's peeking through some trees and a tall building next to it. I think it was a bank. I'm going to go there tomorrow and open up an account. Maybe my roommate and I can get our bedspreads from the Woolworth's.

I know what you're wondering. Yes, I've been eating. There is a sandwich shop across from my room, and there's lots of eating places all over the campus and around it too. I bought a baloney meat sandwich from the sandwich shop. It had more meat on it than you buy off of the rolling store. I couldn't even eat it all. So I saved half of it for my lunch. And it didn't cost but fifty cents. Ma, I almost feel rich up her (smile).

And like I said before, I met some real nice people up here. Just today I met a colored woman from Pidcock. Remember we didn't think it would be anybody else up here from down home. I also met another lady who came all the way from the Orient to go to school at Claxville University.

Like I said, people up here are real nice, so tell Daddy I'm fine and he don't need to worry about me so much. You all brought me up right, so I know what to do and how to act.

Kiss all them young'uns for me, and tell them I'll bring them something when I come home. I'll probably bring them a baloney meat sandwich apiece (smile). And, Ma, a pickle as long as the ones come from Aunt Sylvia's garden come with it. And tatter chips, and the drink too. Even a cookie. I just can't believe how cheap things are up here. We'll probably get some curtains to match them bedspreads when we go to the store.

I gotta go now. I was gonna take a nap, but I think I will go to the bookstore first.

Hugs and kisses, Brandi

After rereading the letter, she realized that she had not written about the real purpose for coming to Claxville; she'd told her mother nary a word about school. So her postscript was:

I forgot to tell you what I'm taking. I got three classes: a French phonetics class, English 101, and a PE class. I ought to make all As this time. I couldn't take but three classes. My advisor, a nice white lady, said I shouldn't take but twelve hours—that equals a full load.

Anyway, all of them are in the morning, so I can study in the afternoons.

PPS: My French and English classes meet one hour per day, and we go to PE just two days out the week.

Brandi grabbed her purse, removed some of the money amassed at registration and all that she's bought from home, and secured it in her overnight case before encasing it in a locker above the desk on her side of the room and set off for the bookstore. Dr. McIntyre had told her that once she was signed up for classes, she could go there, ask for the books by the course number and the instructor's name, and secure them without delay. When she got to the bus stop that she had previously used, she noticed that she merely had to cross a bridge about the length of a football field to get to the facility. Suddenly, the campus did not seem as vast, nor was it as threatening as it had appeared on the day of her arrival.

The young woman crossed the street, noting a clump of trees to her right before setting foot on the bridge. Within its boundaries was a small park with wooden tables and benches. Swings made with tires and ropes cascaded from limbs of the imposing oaks found everywhere on the university campus.

Once on the bridge, Brandi looked down and out, through some hedges, seeing for the first time the university's football field and stadium house. She stopped, peering over the bridge; holding fast to its cooling handrail, she sucked in the breathtaking sight. The woman wondered why she had not noticed the beautiful structure in the valley while on the bus earlier that day.

From a distance, its lush, meticulously mowed grass looked as if every neatly cropped blade was the same shade of green—it look like somebody had painted each and every blade with Ritz dye and then taken time to trim it with a pair of hand clippers.

In the center rested the school's mascot, "Ole Rattler." Under the woman's watchful eye, he began a stir. He peered upward at the girl who stood aimlessly by. The mascot seemed to be hissing right at her. She leaned forward, thwarting him, challenging him to rise up from the blanket of green in which he comfortably lazed, that is, until she came along. "I gotcha," she called to the menacing figure. She hissed back at him and laughed aloud, spewing his poison forcefully. His venom couldn't touch her!

CHAPTER SEVEN

Three Billy Goats

A terribly cold wind drew her gaze back to the bridge. A man—or was it a woman?—dressed in a long tan overcoat, black hat, and dark shades had mounted the wrong side of the bridge. The hair on the woman's neck stood at attention; the usually sedate, sandy bristles stood and stiffened with fear and trepidation. Goose bumps ran up and down her spine—she shivered.

Brandi paused, thinking that it would probably be wise to turn around and go back to the dormitory. The young woman mentally started to consider other options, to rehearse what she could do. She could move over to the other side and see what the character would do—but suppose it just crossed over too? Or maybe, she thought, "If I stand here and holler somebody would hear me, come running to my rescue, catch this demon," but there wasn't anybody else around.

"Shucks!" she muttered audibly as she toed the pavement. "I've got to get used to this place, and besides, if he grabs my purse, he won't get much. I'm glad I left most of my money in the room." She pivoted to the right, released her grip on the handrail, and forward she went.

Like the goat on the bridge in one of the stories she had read to Sara when she was a little girl, she sped forward to encounter the adversary and either to pass him or engage in whatever encounter fate had presented her. Seconds seemed like hours—time became surreal. The distance between the strangers shortened—he held fast to his course, so the girl took the "low road." When they were almost directly in front of each other, when only a yard or so separated them, she stepped off the sidewalk and into the roadway. The adversary stepped down as well. For a moment they toyed one with the other, first on the sidewalk, then off and on again. Brandi thought she would try to run by him, so she backed up a bit and began a slow trot. Just as she was about to pass the stranger, the man jerked his coat open, exposing himself as he laughed loud and long. He was naked as a jaybird! And no words could describe his shriek!

The woman did not look back—she kept running until she got to the campus bookstore. A quick jerk on its handle revealed that the store was closed; a sign read "Closed for the Afternoon." Then she noticed that most of this end of the campus was quiet. The bridge separated the world of academe from student and faculty housing—the safety of Davis Hall was temporarily cut off.

She glanced backward, seeing the sparsely clothed stranger enter the park. "Damn, what am I going to do? Maybe there is another route to the dormitory." She looked around—the young woman made a full circle, did a 360. Beads of perspiration popped up on her brow—she swiped at the dew with her arm. It too was wet with sweat. Her whole body felt a mist.

A bus immediately came to a stop in front of the girl—one seemed to always be nearby. For that she was grateful. She mounted its steps. "Nobody will believe this crap!" she uttered.

"Ma'am?" asked the driver.

"Nothing."

She took her seat on the right side of the bus, rendering the park accessible to her roving eye. When the vehicle crossed the bridge, Brandi looked for the stranger, but she saw no signs of him. The park appeared to be as empty as it had been before she had gone to the bookstore—all lay still; no movement was evident.

Telltale signs of Julie's visit to the room while it was unoccupied greeted the tiring student. The note from the father had been removed from its place beside the box of writing paper. Instead, it lay crumpled in the trash can beside the desk.

Although she was exhausted, Brandi still could not sleep. She showered and prepared her clothing for the next day while she longed for her textbooks. It would be a few days before classes started—freshman orientation was not over yet, but the woman thought she would get a head start. Since she was not able to study, she reread all of the information she had received about the university and its environs upon her acceptance in Claxville University's language program.

She thought some music would help, so she turned her music on, twisting the radio's knobs, never able to find the tunes to which she was accustomed, so she elected to just read. The student carefully perused all of the communication that she had received prior to coming to Claxville.

BRENDA SMITH

"Ah! I thought I read that somewhere," she said reading aloud from the student's code of conduct. "Students must room together for two weeks (with two weeks, written in bold, italicized, and underlined) before any changes will be made." She got off the bed, pulled the chair from the desk near the window, shifting it so she could sit up and prop her feet on the bed. Then Brandi reread the opening sentence silently before rereading aloud, "Students must room together for *two weeks* before any changes will be made. A room will be found for the complaining party."

Brandi got up, pushed the chair back under the desk, deciding to plop back on the bed. "How we gonna make it two weeks if we ain't never lived together?" she wondered, an immediate response escaping her.

The woman fell asleep, a fitful, broken, restless, sporadic, erratic sleep. The trolls were trying to cross her bridge, and she wasn't going to let them. Their laughter echoed the thunderous, horrifying cackling emitted by the man on the bridge. The troll-faced goats chorused, "Off my bed . . . get off of my bed, simpleton."

"No. Go away. Please go away." The woman woke with a start and began the new day. She sat on the side of the bed and stared at the clock. It took a few moments for her to realize that it was the next day instead of later in the cumbersome evening and to remember what had happened. Brandi yawned, stretched, finally dressed, left the dormitory, and began the day with breakfast at Stu's Sandwich Shop.

When she had drowned a tuna on toast with Coke from the sandwich shop, she attempted to return to the room to finalize plans for the day. Her effort was thwarted by the resident assistant who called out as soon as she hit the lobby, "Hey you—you girl, Ms. Winthrop needs to talk with you this morning."

"Does she need to see me now?" she implored, wanting to evade the issue brought up the previous day.

Ms. Winthrop pleaded, "I hope that you are satisfied with the choices we gave you for a roommate yesterday. Have you made a decision yet?" the woman asked, never giving the younger lady a chance to respond. "Both girls are willing to share a room with you," she rambled aimlessly on.

Reaching out to touch the woman's arm, Brandi interrupted, "Ms. Winthrop, I sure appreciate your willingness to help me find a place to live, but I already got a place. According to the handbook, me and Julie got to live together for two weeks, then if we aren't happy, the complaining party got to move." With a cursory "I ain't got no complaints," Brandi dismissed herself from the woman's office and headed for the safety of room 306.

When the colored girl was out of audible range,

Ms. Winthrop hissed, "That's a smart ass! She won't last overnight here at Claxville—she got too much mouth." The resident assistant snickered. It always pleased her to see the old lady loose her composure, to see her unnerved by a novice.

CHAPTER EIGHT

La Premiere Classe

The next few days were relatively mundane for the novice; scheduled activities to acclimate freshman students to college life abounded—there were cookouts, sleep-ins, tailgate parties, parties on campus, off campus, in houses, apartments, at clubs, and fraternity and sorority gatherings and preparations for their rushes, dances, and movies. There were intramural sports activities, football games, a basketball game, and the university jazz band put on a free concert for the newcomers. Brandi did not attend any of these activities—she spent most of the time in her room, reading from the texts she had managed to purchase uneventfully on the second try, writing letters, eating, and toileting only when absolutely necessary.

The freshman was so excited that first day of class. She had hardly slept any the night before, so the young woman decided to get an early start before the rush was on—over twenty thousand students had to prepare for class that day. The girl was glad only a couple of hundreds lived in Davis Hall.

Brandi went into the bathroom, brushed her teeth, entered the shower, and began to sing. From somewhere a baritone chimed in, singing her tune, reducing it to a crisp, clear, birdlike whistle as time passed. The woman froze, became a mannequin—she stood still, right hand held high, the shower spray diluting soapy wash cloth's full sudsy strength, letting it run clear as the warm water made a trail down the extended arm, onto her shoulder, downward into the rusty drain.

As she stood still, she held her breath. Water from the other stall ceased. It had been cut off, and the male occupant grabbed a towel, rubbed himself dry, tousled his hair, tied the terry cloth beach towel around his waist, stepped from the cubicle, slipped into shower shoes, and slipped past the only other occupied stall. Brandi got a peek of him! The young woman did not move a muscle, refused to breathe, until she was sure that the man had vacated the community bathroom. Then she rinsed herself completely, barely dried her own buns, slipped into her blue terry cloth robe, and hurried to the room.

The young woman rested, astonished—she was certain that Davis Hall was a girls' dormitory, that it was not coed. Her parents, by their own rights, had noted which housing facilities were girls, boys, coeds, married, student, faculty, etc. "Surely this was a mistake," she decided. Carruthers Brown would have a fit if he knew that boys had a free rein in the girls' dormitories. He'd researched the housing information thoroughly to determine that Davis Hall was not a coed facility—had made a big deal about it!

When she got to her FL-Phonic 111 class, she cautiously approached the classroom door, stood momentarily, and adjusted the skirt that had become larger since she had bought it during the summer before proceeding. No faces like hers were in the room. No signs of acknowledgment were given the Negro girl from Wester. After what seemed like a millennium, the smiling face in the middle of the classroom of a young white man with straw-colored hair and skimpy mustache arrested her roving, searching eyes, so she made her way to an empty seat beside him.

As soon as she was seated, the door widened and Mr. Henri, *le professeur,* came into the classroom. He was a tall, big man with a crop of thick hair peppered with gray. The man placed several books on the teacher's desk beside his filled briefcase and adjusted the podium near the desk to suit his needs. Mr. Henri stood at attention, stared at the class, caught each member's eye, and all mouths closed.

Brandi gawked at the man. He was as ugly as sin; she grew afraid because of his sinister appearance and thought how grateful she was that their meeting took place in the light and in the presence of a class full of students like herself—that it was not night, that they were not alone together on the bridge that separated the university's worlds.

Having gained their attention, he retrieved his class roster from the case and put his eyeglasses on, and he set about placing names with faces. "When I call your name," the bespectacled college professor, the huge man with a voice equally as large, boomed, "repetez the sound given."

Just a few responses to his query had been made before it was time for "Mademoiselle Brown, repetez <u>ou</u>." Brandi's attempts to follow the professor's thunderous instructions were met with "Never mind, Ms. Brown, your lips are too big for that sound. Let's try another."

For a second everyone appeared too stunned to move—the young woman froze, her brain having to work with the obvious put-down, and

BRENDA SMITH

the others; momentarily their giggles shattered the silence. Brandi sat frozen with disbelief, defenseless, unable to fend for herself, taken aback by the surly, narrow-minded man's pugnacious mannerisms.

The only other man in the class sat with mouth agape and eyes wide, obviously as shocked at the teacher's boorish behavior as the girl. His lips began to quiver slightly. Monsieur Dubblerville apparently was trying to speak—he finally made it. "You can't say that to her!" shrieked the young man who sat beside her.

"Monsieur Dubblerville, I can say what I damn well please. Je suis le professeur," the man roared at the student. Turning back to Brandi who sat with lips yet positioned to "repetez ou," the huge man with piercing, cold black eyes and dark hair sprinkled with gray demanded, "Ms. Brown, come by my office apres clase. I need to talk with you about something."

She let her lips relax. Her whole body grew tense. Class continued. Brandi heard little; she sat, anxiously awaiting the professor's self-made appointment, and time crept unmercifully. Each time she looked at her watch, its hands were in the same position—at least they appeared to be. Time always seemed to creep in Claxville. "What does he want? I wonder if Ms. Winthrop talked to him . . . That other colored woman told me to mind my own business. That's all I been doing. What does he want?" Thought after thought threaded its way through her psyche. Her final thought, "I ain't moving. I don't care what nobody say," was abbreviated by students preparing to leave the class. Ten o'clock had finally come!

Brandi waited until the last student had left before approaching Monsieur Henri to ask for directions to his office. "You don't have to come to my office," he barked. "I can tell you everything that I need to right here," the man said, the closure of his half-empty briefcase voicing finality before she could provide any input. "You need to see your advisor today and find yourself another class."

"Why, sir?" Brandi raised her finger, soliciting permission to be heard and to hear the real reasons for the put-down.

"Students from small schools don't have sufficient backgrounds to take my classes. So you need to drop it now while I can still give you a WP. If we wait until after midterm, we'll have to give you an F," the man voiced almost sympathetically, or so it seemed at that moment. Then he gathered his belongings and headed for the door with the young woman on his heels, skipping so that her stride could match his gait.

"But, sir, we haven't done anything yet. Please give me a chance," the girl implored, skipping behind the big burly man, who crossed the room and stepped into the busy hallway. "I could even get a tutor if I need to—I've got money left over from my scholarship check," Brandi begged.

The man stopped at the stairway, adjusting the cumbersome ware he carried. "Listen, girl, you couldn't even say 'ou' when I called on you in class today. Whether you get a tutor or not is immaterial," he snapped at her, brushing past her, briefcase and supplementary textbooks in tow.

Sara's daughter knew she was in for it, that she had waded in deep water, its depths elongated by an unresolved rooming situation. She didn't know where to go, what to do, to whom she could turn . . . if she could turn to anyone.

The young man, Dubblerville, waited at the bottom of the winding staircase that led to classrooms and offices on the second floor. "I'm sorry about what happened in class today," he said, joining Brandi in her descent from the building, looking gawky and awkward, all arms and legs. "Don't pay the ole rat no mind," he continued. "He's just that way. He'll give you a C just to get rid of you if you stay in the class, so just put up with his shit. That's what the rest of us do."

"Thanks," said Brandi as she sped away from the man's soulfully kind eyes. She needed to be alone.

When she was outside, she decided to walk through the orchards along the trails made by students from days past rather that catching the bus. Brandi had a lot she needed to think about. Walks on chilly mornings in Wester seemed like the best times and settings for thinking. Although she was in Claxville, the frosts from first the rooming situation, the encounter with the stranger on the bridge, and now the sting from her first class had sufficiently chilled her to the point where a lot of thinking could take place. Brandi did indeed need to be alone with her thoughts.

As she passed the campus dairy, a girl with a cup of blueberry yogurt in her hand quickened her steps to catch up with her. "Hey," the colored girl called, using her wooden spoon to gesture, to flag her down, "ain't you the one who live in Davis Hall everybody been talking about?"

"I don't know," Brandi responded, never breaking her pace.

"Yes, yes you are." The intruder danced about much like the young'uns back home did whenever overexcited. "I live there too, in another dorm in the same complex, and everybody's been talking about you. If I was you, I would pack up my shit and leave." The speaker's eyes danced with excitement . . . one would have thought Brandi a celebrity, hounded by an autograph seeker, the paparazzi, or a reporter.

The hounded one stopped, and when she did the pursuer almost stepped on her. "What's your name?" she asked pointedly when they both stood still under a tree, away from the sun that was blistering down by now.

"Elnora Jenkins."

"Elnora," Brandi retorted sharply. "I don't know you and you don't know me. And I don't know who you been talking to, but I can tell you this, I won't be run off just like that," she said, snapping her fingers in the inquirer's face. The offender maintained her snug, condescending, knowledgeable air; she scraped the remaining yogurt from the container and cleaned the spoon.

Brandi dismissed her. "See you around," she said, shaking her head as she left the yogurt-eating woman to her own devices.

Dr. McIntyre was not surprised when young Dubblerville showed up at her door immediately after Mr. Henri's class.

"Thanks for sharing," she said to the young man before she dismissed him and placed a call to the dean. The woman really did regret she had had to assign Brandi to the old "geezer's" class the first quarter, but that was the way the cookie had crumbled; there was nothing else the advisor could take right then. More freshman had come that fall than they anticipated, so courses had filled quickly. Nevertheless she felt confident the girl could do the work; she was bright, articulate, and exhibited such good manners, which was more than she could say for many of her advisees. The professor pulled her files from her desk, reviewing her academics, class placement, SAT scores, and recommendations from former teachers. She had everything that it would take to enjoy and successfully matriculate at Claxville University. Brandi just needed a chance.

At the faculty meeting the following Friday, the professor, whose toothy smile and earthy humor usually assuaged the savage beast in people, sidled up to her colleague to ask about the new girl in the department.

"She can't do it, Virginia. That girl just doesn't have enough background to sufficiently respond orally in a second language," the man with a scraggly, battered face—masked by a neatly cropped mustache, sideburns, and a beard, the epitome of conservatism that he was—said forcefully to the woman.

Further attempts to elicit aid for the new student were thwarted by more cutting remarks. "I won't let you teach my class for me," he spewed at the woman whose ambitions he had always thought absurd simply because she was a woman.

The brief encounter stirred quite a furor in the department. When the kindly Professor McIntyre spoke to the dean about the situation, he initially told her to butt out, to mind her own business, but she continued to argue, and the man finally relented, telling the woman, "Virginia, if she stays, we'll give her an A. Mind you, I said *if* she stays," the man stressed the *if* for the woman under his employ. Shortly after Brandi had gotten back to her room, the student laid her books aside and leaned into the large mirror to get a close-up of herself, trying to discover the secret of the ugliness that made Mr. Henri find her so despicable. She smiled, grimaced, puckered, pouted her lips, let her lips relax, hang loose, the bottom drop, and repeated the ritual several times at different angles, face forward, to the right, to the left, to the rear, and with neck craned as eyes besought a view from the rear; then she took the hand mirror from a set she had gotten for graduation to continue her scrutiny before determining that any lip as opposed to no lips on any face as full of color as her own would bring about a similar reaction from the man.

Nothing was wrong with her lips . . . they were beautiful; her teeth were good, and her nose was not big and flat . . . didn't cover her full face, was not bent, crooked, deformed, was shapely, and had never been the object of undue attention.

"Ou, ou, ou," Brandi spoke to her mirrored image confidently as the day's unwarranted, unmerited pain began its ebb. She turned to leave the desk; however, a second thought came. Brandi took a lipstick from her make-up kit—the summer treat, tried until true, under Sara's watchful eye and warnings about the coloring's thickness, heaviness, shade, hue; she covered her full lips with the Revlon's promising pink and took a tissue from the box on her desk, tracing the edges of her beautiful Negroid lips to remove the excess and to stay within the lip line. She looked in her mirror, the one that reassured her once more that with rouge or without rouge, they were not too thick. Brandi picked at the pink with her fingers; her lips were a solid mass, did not flip and flop at the will of her flickering fingers. There were no signs of excess . . . her lips were by all standards a nice set.

A soft tap on the door was almost ignored. Warmth exuded from the visitor who simply introduced herself as Mary Margaret before plopping down heavily, carelessly, on Julie's bed and telling the occupant that she needed to fight back rather than taking "all that shit" from Julie and her friends. "If I was you, I'd beat the living shit out of her," the stranger spoke angrily and harshly of the harassing behavior and its perpetrators.

Brandi, door still in hand, sighed with relief. This girl seemed like her kind of person, and besides, she needed to talk to someone. She shut the door, sat down herself, and the two girls talked; they talked well into the evening about all the insane circumstances that had taken place since her arrival at Claxville University. Mary Margaret finally looked at her watch and then vaulted from the yet unmade bed on which she had sat upon her arrival. "I'm hungry. Let's go to the Burga Barn and get something to eat," she said.

"Where's that?" Brandi inquired, eager to continue their conversation—to establish a congenial relationship with someone, anyone. "Surely," she thought, "this girl must be an angel. She just has to be God-sent. Mama told me he would provide, would make a way out of no way, always be right on time." And Brandi, the girl who always thirsted for sweet conversation, truly needed a friend.

"Oh, it's in walking distance," said the new friend, taking the girl to the window and pointing to a spot through the treetops on a grassy knoll which served as a backdrop for the sandwich shop that had become Brandi's "kitchen away from home." As the days had passed, she had not abandoned the familiarity of the small restaurant, but she had begun to explore its menu as bologna and tuna fish sandwiches for breakfast, lunch, dinner, and snacks had become repugnant—she almost puked at the thought of another.

Sara was so excited when she'd finally had time to get the mail from the mailbox. She had a long letter from her daughter this time. The mother grinned as she read and reread Brandi's letter. Everything was coming along just fine, and the mother was so glad. It had been pretty hard living with Cat ever since the child had decided she wanted to go up to that college, and it was equally hard to reestablish the easy conversations they had always enjoyed before this life-altering event.

Cat still believed that people ought to mingle with their own kind, was not as progressive as his spouse or his daughter or Sylvia for that matter. He didn't care much for white folks and had always told his brood, "Don't trust them no far than you can throw them." While Sara shared his view, but to a lesser degree, she realized that the world was changing—it was bigger than it used to be, and the children would have to mingle with others: black, white, red, locals, and foreigners. They had to go to school with everybody now and work with everybody too. They only real hang-up that Sara had was about interracial marriage. She didn't believe in mixing blood; the woman thought that the consequences were too hard for children born to these couples.

Sara knew that Brandi would be all right. "All you have to do, Cat," she'd insist, "is to watch how she can get along with everybody when we go downtown, and I ain't just talking about Mr. Z and his brother neither. Any of them folks give her the time of day—she can hold a candle to them. She can understand them a heap better that I can—she'll be all right, Cat."

When she'd put the supper on the table and all the children had come and seated themselves on the long wooden benches on either side of the table, she sat in her chair at the end of the table opposite her husband. When every one of the little ones had his or her hands clasped in front of his or her tiny chest, head bowed and eyes squeezed tight, he had blessed the food. Sara helped the little ones put the fried chicken, potatoes and gravy, turnip greens, and buttermilk corn bread that Brandi loved so much on each plate and fixed her own before she spoke of the day's excitement.

"Got a letter from Brandi today . . . It was a long one," she said as she finally readied herself for her own meal.

"What'd she say?" the man spoke with mouth full.

"Said everything was just fine," Sara spoke easy and gently. "Got a nice room, waiting on her roommate to come so they can put them matching bedspreads."

"Shit, ain't no roommate coming," Cat mumbled at his spouse, his mouth as full as it was at the onset of this conversation. "It's going to be hard to get one of them to stay with a colored girl."

"Cat, how come you want to be so negative all the time?" the woman begged.

"Let's talk about something else." Cat stopped the woman short, slicing the air with his right hand in which he held the butter knife.

One thing the Browns didn't do was to argue in front of the children. Cat just didn't think children ought to be brought up in a house where grown folks were always fussing. Yet it just seemed like that was all that had been going on since Brandi had decided that to go to that college—a bunch of fussing—and he'd had his fill of it too; he just didn't want any that day.

Sara grew still, her heart heavy, and the children grew tense too. All picked at their platefuls of food, chewed morsels of its contents softly and quietly. Several bites taken from his meal, the man glanced up from the filled plate to meet the tear-filled eyes of his wife. "Sara," he spoke gently, "mind if I read that letter myself?"

The woman lay her silverware and napkin aside and quickly retrieved the letter from her apron pocket, took it down to the other end of the oversized solid wood table, gave it to her husband, swiped at her watering eyes with her apron hem, bent down and pecked the man on the neck, and hastily returned to her own place at the dinner table.

The man started to read the communications from Brandi. "Sure sounds like everything going to be all right," Carruthers remarked when he was near the double postscript. Almost simultaneously, the tense moment passed, and soon the quiet gave way to the usual dinnertime chatter at the Browns' humble abode.

Back at Claxville University, Brandi asked Mary Margaret if they needed to catch the bus to get to the Burga Barn. She was hungry too; as a matter of fact, she was famished . . . she longed for a real home-cooked meal, one like her mama made.

"No, it's in walking distance. You haven't been there yet? Closest thing you are going to get to real food before Christmas break."

"To tell the truth, I ain't been on that side of the campus," Brandi confessed. "I ain't been nowhere except the dorm, the bookstore, and to class, and back to the dorm," she said to Mary Margaret when they were on the way, but her new friend's mind was elsewhere—on more pressing issues. She spoke of the flasher anew.

"You know you should have called campus security on that dude on the bridge. That isn't the first time that's happened. They just haven't been able to catch the creep. I'm sorry you had to get caught up in that too," she said quite sorrowfully.

"Child, I'm just glad somebody else done seen it too. I didn't tell anybody because I thought they would think I was a plum fool," Brandi responded.

"You didn't even tell your parents?" Mary Margaret probed, thinking how ludicrous this was—she would have called her own folks right away.

"Nope, my daddy would have flown the coop if I had told him about it. He would have been up here and took my tail straight home." The girl added, "Not only that, it would have proved that he was right."

"Right? He was right about what?"

"Never mind," Brandi balked at telling more about her past, heading to the door. "Let's go," she suggested, "We need to hurry anyway. You know, I haven't eaten hardly anything today."

Putting her hand in the waist of her skirt, she added, "Look here, my skirt is about to fall off of me. It was tight when I bought it this summer.

"I can't believe we been talking for six hours," she added when she had glimpsed the time on her watch.

"Who's been talking six hours . . . not me! I been listening for six hours," Mary Margaret said jokingly to her new friend as they walked up the hill to the restaurant.

"Okay, we talked enough about me and my problems. You tell me your dreams, and I'll tell you mine," Brandi stopped and turned to her newly found acquaintance, singing aloud from a song learned in eighth grade choral music, which now seemed so long ago . . . and so far away.

Mary Margaret told Brandi briefly about her home and family as the twosome ascended the hilly knolls of Claxville University, pausing sporadically to point out the various buildings and to tell her friend a little about each.

"A Catholic? What's a Catholic?" Brandi stopped when the other young woman spoke of her religious affiliation. "We ain't got none of them back home. I thought Catholics only lived in places like Rome, Italy, France," she teased.

"No, silly," Mary Margaret shook her head, uncertain about whether Brandi was indeed serious or not. It was hard to tell—the girl wore a mask; she was not the paragon of truth she always pretended to be. In her own way, the new friend recognized and understood that. So she replied, "That's how I got my name. My mama named me after the principal nun at St. John's School." Mary Margaret took the serious route in this verbal exchange.

Soon, the pair was at the Burga Barn. Brandi reached for the handle, tugging gently on the solid glass door with black trim. The whole plate of glass fell from its entrapping and shattered on the cement, releasing the odor of fried chicken, onion rings, and other food scents contained with the restaurant's walls and the acrid smell of simmering food filled Brandi's cheeks with sour, oniony, cold-cutish saliva. She swallowed hard.

Both girls jumped sideways, out of the pane's path, and Brandi released her hold on the door handle now freed of its glass by a mere tug. The shocked duo also gasped audibly.

Thoughts of food clouding her mind, Brandi barely heard the waitress who had seen the glass fall and had rushed to their rescue, asking simultaneously, "Are you hurt, ma'am? Wait right here. Don't move! I'll get the manager. He'll be right here!" the alarmed waitress called back to the two as she scrambled toward the door labeled "Management Only."

The unharmed duo dismissed her warning, entered the restaurant, seated themselves at a small table in the facility's front window which appeared to sit on the sidewalk, secured the menus from their holdings on the clothed tables, and made decisions about their orders before their conversation turned back to the woes of life in Davis Hall.

While a busboy cleaned the shattered pieces, bits and shards of glass, from the sidewalk and the entranceway, the waitress assigned to their table took their order.

Soon, their orders arrived, and the Brown girl sank her teeth into the first hot meal she'd had since she'd left Sara's table on the day she left home for her trip to college. The fried chicken, turnips, and potatoes and gravy selected were quite good. The conversation abated while the girls polished off mounds of food, washing it down with sweetened ice tea with twists of freshly cut lemon wedges.

When the evening meal was nearly complete, a thin young man dressed in a white short-sleeve shirt, black bow tie, and coal black pants came to the table and identified himself as the night manager of the Burga Barn. "I want to apologize for any inconvenience you experienced when you came into our facility tonight," he said, a glimmer of silver showing when he spoke. "Were either of you ladies hurt when the pane fell from its casing?" he went on, professional posture intact. Jotting their responses of denial on a small pad, he told the friends that he had to prepare an incident report.

"No, we're fine," said Mary Margaret.

"Would either of you like dessert?" the man queried, disengaging their bill, which lay face down, on the table from its position.

"Yes, I'll have a peach melba," was Mary Margaret's response.

"How much was the strawberry shortcake with ice cream?" asked Brandi peering upward at the sparkle flashing from the man's upper lips each time he spoke.

He shook his head. "No, it's on me," the manager argued.

The noisome glimpse of silver engaged Brandi's attention while Mary Margaret talked on. It drew Brandi's attention away from the meal. She'd seen Dirk somewhere before. Where was it? He had introduced himself as Dirk when he took information for the incident report. And what kind of name was that anyway? she thought. Who would name a child Dirk? Sounds like something unsanitary, she pondered—her innocent, naïve sense of humor, which had lay dormant since she'd left Wester, being unleashed on the handsome man oblivious to anything except the restaurant's quality service.

The man left to order their desserts and to post "on the house" on the bill before placing it in the cash register's open drawer.

In the meantime Brandi voiced aloud, "Maybe he's in one of my classes."

"Huh?" inquired Mary Margaret.

"Huh?" Brandi echoed.

"You were saying?" Mary Margaret continued.

"Oh, nothing"

Desserts downed, the girls, led by Brandi this time, set foot outside. Clouds of darkness were enacting light switches in the night sky all over the campus and the city that lay at its feet . . . to the girl from Wester it seemed as if they stood alone in a humongous patch of lightning bugs. Not another soul was around.

It was unsettling.

"We better hurry!" Brandi exclaimed suddenly. Sara and Carruthers had warned her about being out after dark in strange places. "It's getting dark," she said, "and chilly too." Her strides lengthened as she spoke, and Mary Margaret thought she was going to break into a run.

"Hey, we can slow down," Mary Margaret said, sensing the urgency in the voice of her new friend, one that matched her stride. "Bus stops are everywhere around here, and this end of the campus is always lighter than the other. And there are fewer trees. The dorms are close to each other, and campus security is everywhere at night." She stopped her and held Brandi still with one hand, pointing in all directions with a digit from the other hand, attempting to reassure her of the safety provided by the university's carefully landscaped environs and capable security police.

A marked car passed within a few yards of where they stood.

Slowing down a smidgen, Brandi said, "Okay, but I'm getting tired. It's been a long day. I have do Monsieur Henri's homework and get my clothes laid out for tomorrow."

Momentarily, the Wester native spoke again. "Let's catch the bus though," her soft plea continued, but none came by. Mary Margaret told her that the buses did not come as frequently at night as they did during the day because there were fewer evening classes than day classes. "Most of the evening classes are for graduates in the master's or doctoral programs. They are generally older, and most of them have their own transportation, small vehicles, mostly sports cars. A few have trucks. They drive to class, take up the few parking areas students could use on the now-cluttered campus . . . don't have to use the transit system."

When Brandi and Mary Margaret got back to Davis Hall, the new friends went separate ways with a commitment to have breakfast together the next morning in a campus cafeteria, then to rent some bikes from the recreation center and explore Claxville University a bit more. The semidark of room 306 was broken by shadows on boxes, clothes, and other stuff on the bed to Brandi's immediate left—and a bicycle, it was there too. A flick of the light switch showed that Julie Blanchard had moved in . . . or so Brandi thought.

CHAPTER NINE

Wash Day Folly

Before Brandi had a chance to draw any further conclusions, the roommate returned from the shower. Dressed in a brightly colored oversized beach towel, draped by waist-length reddish brown curly hair, she came in the room and greeted her, "Hi, Brandi, I'm Kris Maynard. It sure was good to get a room," she went on, disrobing, using the towel to dry her wet locks. Seating herself on the bedside, Kris continued, "I moved down here from Washington State this summer. I've been staying in a trailer park with some of my friends until something came available on campus. Was glad when I got a call that housing on campus was available. It's rough paying rent: light bill, gas bill, buying groceries off campus," the girl continued.

"I'm glad to meet you." Brandi backed up, coming to a rest on her own bed, trying to keep her eyes on Kris's rustic visage and away from the girl's naked, almost boyish, frame. She didn't know what she had expected her roommate to look like, but she did expect someone more feminine in nature, someone as petite as she herself was, someone like Mary Margaret.

Kris put on drawers and a bra, crossed the cold linoleum-covered floor, and reached for the brush she habitually kept on her dresser. Remembering that she had not unpacked all of her toiletries yet, the new roommate walked over to Brandi's desk, got her brush, and began to brush her hair. "Don't mind me using this?" she asked pointing the already-used brush in Brandi's direction.

Brandi, taken aback by this intrusion, stammered, "Uh, no, ugh, ugh."

"Don't have time to dry this. Wish my hair was short as yours," the roommate said, pulling her lengthy, curly locks into a ponytail before retrieving and putting on the tattered faded blue jeans and oversized university T-shirt she'd worn before showering. She grabbed the bicycle, which rested in the middle of the floor, directly in front of the desk, booted the kickstand, and positioned the vehicle for an exit from the room. The departing member said, "See you later . . . we'll talk some more when I get back."

"Okay," Brandi responded as she took to her bed. She lay on her back reliving the day's events. She'd made a friend, enjoyed a hot meal, and gotten a roommate, one who might not be who she had expected; nevertheless, she could tell her parents that she actually had one. "Now I can finally get some spreads and curtains," she thought, "and get this dungeon fixed up!" The young woman grew content—as content as a cow—and she slept soundly for the first time since she had left Wester.

When the night had passed, when she awoke the next morning, Kris was already awake—she stretched and yawned aloud. Brandi rolled over, put her glasses on, and looked at the clock. It was almost six o'clock.

"Good morning," she moaned and said, "what you doing up so early?"

"I have to go to work," said the roommate.

"Where's work?"

"Over at the vet's."

"The vet!" Brandi sprung up from the bed and came to rest on her elbows as she spoke with disgust . . . she detested animals, especially cats. They licked you all over and dropped their mangy skin and hair everywhere and hid their mess. She couldn't imagine why anyone would want to work with them all the time, and she said so.

Kris laughed, cackling at Brandi's expressions of total disgust. "I always loved them—little ones and big ones. Had a house full of cats, dogs, fish, a snake, and whatever else my parents would let me keep while I was growing up."

"We had them too," Brandi remarked. "But they stayed outside"—she placed extra emphasis on the *outside*—"outside where animals belonged. I don't believe anything four-footed belongs inside!" Kris grew serious. "Actually, I want my own clinic one day," she said, now disengaging her fetal positioned corpse from the army green blanket on which she had slept. Reaching for the oversized T-shirt she'd left at the foot of the bed the night before, she slipped it over her head, stepped into the pair of faded blue jeans, shod her feet in the round-toed, metal-tipped work boots required for her responsibilities at Claxville University School of Veterinary Medicine, strung them up, tied them, brushed her hair, knotted it in a bun at the nape of her neck, and bounded for the door, her bicycle in tow. "Talk to you later," she told Brandi, "it'll probably be dark when I get back. I work all day on one Saturday out of each month."

"Glad it was a short week," Brandi mumbled in disbelief. She too got up and got busy—there was laundry to be done, and she needed to study a bit more, especially for Monsieur Henri's class. She already knew she was going to have to hump it; she couldn't afford to get left at the starting gate. "I'm glad this is the only class I got to take from him," she thought.

Brandi gathered her dirty belongings, undressed her bed, and separated the whites from the coloreds just like Sara had taught her to do. Then she secured some washing powder and Clorox and pocketed the roll of quarters she'd attained earlier specifically for laundering. When she left for the laundry room at the far end of the corridor, the hallway was unoccupied except for another student on her way to the bathroom.

Neither Julie nor Brandi acknowledged each other's presence as they briefly traversed to their destinations—Julie, because she had not wanted to speak. She was mad as a wet hen at the colored girl about the room . . . and Brandi, because she had not known Julie, and because of the lesson taught her by the man in the multicolored dashiki. Once burned, twice shy was the latter's case—she now waited to be acknowledged before she spoke.

With the laundry room empty, Brandi placed her already sorted garments into three washers which rested side by side, paying particular attention to the sets of colored lingerie she had ordered from the Sears Roebuck catalog during the summer months. Sara never bought anything except white cotton undergarments for her family. Brandi fawned briefly over the swirl of greens, pinks, blues, and yellows against the polka-dotted porcelain washing machine tub before closing the washers' lids and departing for the bathroom to shower.

The moment Julie saw the girl going to the laundry room, anger's bitter bile overtook her once more. As a matter of fact, she was totally pissed—she'd been fuming every since Ms. Winthrop had enacted the handbook policy to settle her rooming complaint. "The nerve of that old biddy! I can't believe she gave our room to that—that little black bitch. I don't give a shit about what no handbook say. First, the room, then anything else she wants," the distraught coed emitted as she reentered her own newly assigned room, where she woke her roommate with an angry "Ass up!"

"What you talking about? What do you want me to get up for, Jul . . . ?" Laura groggily quizzed the girl who sputtered and spewed profane thoughts still.

"I just don't like what Ms. Winthrop did," she began.

She was stopped short by Laura's plea for peace. "Ah, come on, Jul . . ."—she shortened the friend's name, speaking in terms of endearment—"let's forget about it. We got a room together, and there are other things to do." Laura rolled over, attempting to get comfortable, to go back to sleep. She pulled the covers over her head.

"Forget my ass," the increasingly incensed Julie argued, "we ain't finished with her yet, and Ms. Winthrop either. Next time we catch her ass drunk . . ."

Hands on a head now pounding, Laura winced; she wished they had not started with Brandi. Julie never knew when to stop. She was an only child, extremely spoiled, and accustomed to eventually having her way. "Jul . . . this has to stop sometime. Please. Can't you just forget it?" she pleaded for what seemed like the thousandth time. She was sick of talking about the colored girl—was fed up to her neck with it.

Laura turned over on her belly and placed her pillow over her head, moaning incessantly, trying to drown Julie out.

"Get up!" Julie barked at her. She grabbed the covers and flung them off Laura's bed before dragging her friend and her pillow off of it.

"What the heck for? Why do I need to get up now? It's too early. It's Saturday. We ain't got nothing to do."

Julie pushed Laura and the pillow, which she hugged over, to the door. "Stop!" the girl protested.

"You just stand your puny ass here and watch out for me," Julie said, planting her companion solidly against the open door, using her for a doorjamb.

"Where you going?" asked Laura.

"I'm going down to the laundry room."

"What you fixing to do?" Laura asked.

"Wait till I get back," the college-student-turned-ruffian said as she hurried from the room, leftward toward the laundry room at the end of the hall.

Laura placed her pillow behind her head, shut her eyes, and slid down the door until she was squatting, serving as a mere doorstop. When Julie returned, she had an armload of clothes, some spun almost dry while others still dripped a bit of water.

Laura's eyes opened wide in amazement when she was victimized by the wet garments that struck her about her head, in her face, on her shoulders. "What the heck!" she thought.

"Whew! These clothes weigh a ton!" Julie said, dropping the mound of colored lingerie and towels in the middle of the dusty floor.

Laura straightened up, letting the door shut itself, shocked at what she was witnessing. "What the heck! What you gon' do with them clothes?" she questioned—she didn't have to ask to know whom the clothing belonged. In her heart of hearts, she knew that this was an act of vengeance against the girl in 306.

"I don't know, ain't thought that far yet."

"All's I know is you better do something before that girl finds out and goes running to Ms. Winthrop," Laura admonished her cohort, and then she returned to her own bed to finish her late Saturday morning repose. This was the only day she was going to get a chance to sleep in, and she was determined not to let anything spoil it. She had an eight o'clock class every day, Monday through Friday—she was determined to sleep.

Julie kicked the wet bundle under her bed, pulled off her wet nightshirt and tossed it aside as well, put on a university T-shirt. "I'll do something with it later," she retorted. "Besides, I ain't scared of Ms. Winthrop. I wish she would bring herself up here. I'll call my daddy—let him sink his teeth into her ass." She laughed.

"And you better get that water up too!" Laura exclaimed, shaking her head at Julie's antics—the girl was indeed a fool! She turned over to catnap.

Then Julie grabbed a couple of towels from her clothes hamper, threw them on the growing puddle, swiping at the bleach-scented liquid with her bare feet. She tugged the towels all the way to the door, mopping droplets of moisture as she went, and threw the dirty towels back in the hamper before getting on the telephone to tout her discovery and to brag on herself of the mischievous, revengeful act.

Shortly thereafter, Brandi followed the trail of droplets to the room where she had left her goods. When she lifted the lids of the three washers she had loaded before showering, she found two loads of clothes instead of three. She looked in the tub of each washer on either side of the two left filled, frantically searching the tub of each, first with her eyes, then with her phalanges. The young woman was no longer certain which washer had held her precious goods—she grew confused, looked in the remaining washers, rubbing each tub's bare sides with searching fingers . . . fingers which, when withdrawn, only held moisture, the residue of the last cycle before the final rinse.

Having ascertained that her colorful garments were indeed gone after one wearing and the first laundering, Brandi stayed in the laundry room while the remainder of her clothes dried, folded them, and placed them in her basket before porting her considerably lightened load back to the room. Inwardly she was devastated! She had worked all summer, picking peas and beans, tying tobacco, grading tobacco at the warehouse, all to purchase clothing to bring to college. And now it was all gone!

As she left the laundry room, an unsteady trail of somewhat smudged drops of what appeared to be water sent her eyes to a door with yet unknown occupants, ones with whom she was becoming increasingly more familiar. The girl made a mental note to watch that door, to learn of its occupants, to place faces with names. With dignity in place, jaw firmly set, head high, heartbroken, Sara and Carruthers's daughter, Sylvia's niece, wound her way through a maze of unblinking eyes—some sympathetic, others gleeful—that peered from cracked doors on both sides of the long hallway.

Her phone, like many others, rang to tell about Julie's latest feat. Brandi started not to respond to hers. She was just glad to have the room to herself at the present moment. She didn't want to talk to anybody–she felt like throwing up. Just as she anticipated, it was Mary Margaret; it had to be, no one else had her phone number. They were supposed to have breakfast together.

"Brandi, I'm sorry about—" Mary Margaret greeted her friend, who interrupted her. "Never mind, let's talk about something else. What else do you know about this town? I feel like getting out today."

"Sounds like fun," the caller agreed. "I'll be down there as soon as I get dressed."

Brandi placed some of the clothing in drawers and hung others in the closet. Then she commenced making a list of items she needed to replace, got money from her locker, and waited for her friend to come. Securing the list once more, she added, then scratched from it "poster board and assorted crayons." "Maybe," she thought, "if I put a sign up asking for a return of the garments, they'll give them back."

She looked in the small closet for something to wear, changed her terry cloth robe for the one miniskirt she owned, and flip-flops for sandals. The woman had not worn the outfit, was saving it for some special event. "What the heck! Maybe this will make a dismal day brighter," she thought as she carefully dressed and applied a smidgen of makeup.

Sara always did this—she could be crying on the inside, but she took extra care so that others would not know her burdens. Today the daughter mimicked the mother. The casual observer would not be able to tell how violated she felt.

All too soon Mary Margaret was at the door. "That bitch!" she emitted. Brandi cut her off with a vigorous "uh-uh," a shaking of her head from side to side, and "Don't want to talk about it. Can't we just drop it?"

Then she insisted that the girl sit down for a minute. "I have to finish my hair." Brandi sprayed her hair with moisturizer and picked at her medium-length Afro, giving up, deciding that this was just a bad-hair day and there was no reprieve from that. So she grabbed her purse and said, "Okay, let's go."

They walked outside together—no discourse on bike rental took place. Brandi led the way, and Mary Margaret trotted along, almost precisely following her zigzag lead. Quietness replaced constant chatter that usually takes place when two comrades walk together. The girls just walked, making their way pass the park, the flasher's habitat, through the housing complex-dormitories for males, females, coeds; apartments for faculty and married couples; fraternity, sorority, Greek and non-Greek houses—uphill toward town. Beyond their footsteps, occasional rustling of wind-blown drying leaves from the humongous oaks, and an occasional blare or thump from passing cars' radioed music, there was nothing . . . nothing except serenity, sweet peace. In spite of her circumstances, Brandi had it, was determined to keep it, wasn't going to let the devil steal her joy.

The morning's tranquility was broken by Brandi's discovery that the bus station was just to the left of the imposing archway separating the main campus from the rest of town. She stopped dead in her tracks and looked at her watch, noting the actual amount of time it had taken them to get to this spot from dorm's door. It had taken barely fifteen minutes to get there from Davis Hall. Reflecting sharply on the first day's encounter with the cabdriver, she disrupted the silence with a profane, profound declaration, "Colored folks up here ain't shit either!"

"What?" Mary Margaret asked confusedly.

Brandi had caught a glimpse of the cabby as his vehicle limped into the station. "Wait for me right here," she said to her friend before she trotted over to the bus station, up to the old battered yellow Ford's lone occupant. She pointed her finger straight in his face. "Hey dude, you owe me one!" she said brusquely to the man who had picked her up when she had initially gotten to town.

"Okay, sister, I owe you one," the man said, throwing up his hands, as if he was surrendering, recognizing Brandi immediately. The man gave her a guilty toothy grin before she was off again.

"Nice legs," the amused man declared to himself, turning to a bus arrival.

As quickly as Brandi had left, she returned to her friend's side.

"What was that all about?" Mary Margaret asked her.

"Nothing, nothing you need to know about," she answered. "Where are we going to get some breakfast from? You know I don't know where I'm going."

"Agreed," said the friend. "Woolworth's got a lunch counter. I think they serve breakfast. Is that okay with you? Can we go there?"

"Yeah! That would be fine."

Silence rejoined the girls at the lunch counter. Each ordered pancakes, eggs, bacon, milk, and orange juice and cleaned their plates before shopping. Brandi bought some new undies—white, 100 percent cotton this time because they were cheaper—and bypassed the poster board and crayons, having decided not to beg Julie and her friends to return her clothing. Besides, Sara taught her brood not to fight.

"An eye for an eye ain't a good position for one to take," the mother would tell her offended offspring. "That's the way people did in the Old Testament times," she would add encouragingly. "That's what the Word say. Anyhow, a person would run out of eyes if every time somebody did something to you, you would try to get back at them. Just keep on being nice to them and they'll come around."

When the girls had spent all they had bought with them, they lugged their packages downhill on the lumpy Main Street sidewalk that separated one side of the campus from the other, paced by strains of music, rock and roll, jazz, classical, country and Western, loud, some with lyrics, some free of words but replete with expressions that came from dormitories' partially gaping doors and windows, fraternity and sorority houses, or passersby in their vehicles.

The girls went their separate ways when they were back at Davis Hall. Brandi didn't feel like company, and Mary Margaret, thoughtfully, respectfully, granted her the space and time needed to grieve, mourn, refocus, and become regenerated—to get over being violated so profusely.

Brandi undressed, hung the miniskirt up and put on some shorts, and turned her attention to the remainder of Saturday's chores. She untagged the new items and placed them in the proper places. She cleaned the room. Grit from Kris's bike wheels was everywhere. The coed's toes curled with disgust each time her bare feet hit the floor, so she had to mop too. When the floor was whistle clean, Brandi sat Indian style in the center of her small bed, contemplating what she would do next.

She reached for her books from the desk in front of the window, sorted them, lay them around her, and determined that she couldn't study . . . the thing to do was to study for Mr. Henri's class; that was what she should do, but she couldn't bring herself around to it. It was so hard to get down to business as usual, especially when her personal life was so screwed up.

The offended young woman was revisited by the crazy idea she'd had earlier—it had taken root in her mind and had refused to budge; so she brushed her schoolwork aside and hopped off the bed and secured some sheets of unlined paper, scotch tape, pencils, fountain pens, and ink cartridges from her desk. Then she knelt, as if to pray, and fastidiously fashioned a banner with typing paper and scotch tape, which exceeded the bed's length, on which she scrawled a message to the perpetrators: "WHOEVER STOLE MY DRAWERS, I HAVE CRABS!"

When she had colored each bold block letter in washable blue from dozens of cartridges that came with an ink pen she had received as a graduation gift, Brandi let up the window so her masterpiece could air dry before its mounting on the wall of the laundry room's folding tables. Simultaneously, she released the toxic odor from the ink from its confines of the airtight room into the atmosphere, where it quickly began to dissipate.

With girlhood innocence lost when she committed this first act of vengeance, Brandi decided to use the rest of her afternoon on the environs of the vast campus. She'd fly solo this time! The girl took the steps two at a time and floated from the confines of strife found at Claxville University just a couple of weeks ago. An eternity had seemingly passed since she had taken the Greyhound from Wester.

Laura Mackey, Julie's roommate, was the first person to see the banner; she screamed, dropped her own laundry baskets, spilling its contents all over the floor, before fleeing the contaminated room to get Julie and the others who were engaged in the customary Saturday morning college-girl chatter, this session about Julie's swiping the colored girl's clothes and her stashing them under her bed. "Come here!" Laura stammered breathlessly, her voice pitched a couple of octaves higher than ordinary. She circled the room, ran to and fro, beckoning her friends to hurry to the room at the far end of the hall. All jumped and ran behind her. Their pounding feet flew!

Brandi's billboard widened eyes and created audible gasps. "Julie," one of the girls shrieked, "you better get them drawers out of your room!"—the same thought she herself was having but had not uttered.

All fled the site and scurried back to the room Julie and Laura shared, where they stood back and watched the former fall on her knees to furiously rake the mound of wet garments from under the bed. "Somebody, help me!" she called as she grappled with the slippery, dust-streaked, musty, colorful contents.

Nobody moved. "Help me get these wet clothes out of here!" Julie called out in frustration. "Don't just stand there! Help me!" she said to friends, who were detaching themselves visibly from the situation.

"I ain't helping you with that," said one.

Another exclaimed, "You did this all by yourself! We didn't help with this."

"You just a bunch of damn fraidy cats . . . that's all, you bunch of idiots," she spat at them. Her mouth was dry; she felt like she had swallowed a bagful of cotton balls. "Help!" she shrieked, her voice raspy, and the tears started to fall.

"That sign say she got crabs—cooties—and I don't want them!" someone argued forcibly.

"Move, damn it, move!" the sniveling creature Julie had become yelled at her friends who just stood by as she grappled with the load of wet clothing she was returning to the laundry room, where she plopped the bundle on the table beneath the sign.

Brandi decided to go to the Burga Barn for lunch before resuming her day's adventure. On the newly paned glass was a Help Wanted sign. When she placed her order, she asked for an application. "Can I leave it today?" was her next question.

"If you complete it now, I'll give it to the manager. He will probably see you before you leave. Just let me know when you finish it, okay," said the waitress.

"Thanks," replied Brandi as she pulled pen after pen from her purse, attempting to write, shaking each, attempting to complete the application, finally realizing that it had taken all the ink she had to paint the sign which now hung in the laundry room back at Davis Hall. She smiled mischievously, envisioning the fiasco that was sure to take place when the billboard with the reference to cooties was discovered. Brandi thought that someone else might discover the sign and tell Julie and her girls about it. Then she imagined them tipping down to the room to see it for themselves. It was now that she thought mass confusion would take place; Julie was going to have to get those wet clothes out of her room, and everybody was going to refuse to help her. Nobody wanted crabs—no sane person did anyway! Brandi chuckled mischievously.

"Uh-uh!" she said to herself. "They will probably run and tell Ms. Winthrop, but I don't care." Brandi shrugged her shoulders, ridding herself of further thoughts of her response to the girls' theft of her prized possessions.

She got up and got a pencil from the waitress who was at a table nearby. In the meantime, Dirk had seen her come in. The girl just wouldn't go away. He hoped she wasn't back about the fallen-pane incident. His Uncle Huey had chewed him to bits because of his failure to have the girls sign a release from liability. "Boy," the old man, his mother's brother-in-law, the one who had practically raised him, said, "you got to stop thinking with your balls.

"You must keep the business first and foremost in your mind. Ain't no room for error. A man can lose everything he got if he can't think on his feet. Stay alert, boy, no sleeping on the job," was all the young man ever heard from the man. His own father had divorced his mother when he was a tot, and he'd been at the mercy of Uncle Huey ever since.

The man would continue his tirade with, "You be mindful of that bevy of beauties up there at that fancy college. I ain't never been to no college in my life. All I ever learned is what I taught myself and that was how to work—that's what you got to do, work. See to it you don't get sidetracked."

Dirk worked extremely hard at not getting side-tracked, was basically driven, wanting to do well with the modest business entrusted him by the man, wanting to use the natural business acumen plus the training being received in the university's school of business to catapult himself to first a franchise owner of a restaurant and then to being the CEO of a chain of fast-food establishments. That was the main reason he had come to Claxville—good fortune had lent him an environment where he had the best of both worlds. Claxville's School of Business enjoyed a better reputation than did the state's flagship university; it produced more CEOs than did the larger university. And Burga Barn, the national organization, was opening up opportunities for new talented young managers.

The manager signaled the waitress who attended the colored girl and sighed with blessed relief when he found out what she wanted. "Ever worked in a restaurant before?" he asked the young woman when he joined her at the table where he conducted an informal, brief inquiry about her job skills.

"No, but I learn quickly," she said with confidence.

When the interview was completed, the man scribbled something on the application, told the girl he would call her, and got up from the table for the return to his chores.

"Can I check back later?" she asked. The man assured her that it was appropriate to do so.

He reached for her check that lay beside her almost empty plate. She attempted to keep it, saying, "No." Dirk waved away her weak protest to pay for her own meal, leaving Brandi to finish her meal.

In the meantime, Dubblerville had not wasted any time reporting back to Dr. McIntyre about the way "the old bastard" had treated the girl the first day of class. "Watch your mouth," the professor admonished before hearing of the manner in which the novice was treated in the very first class she attended at the university, telling him, "I appreciate your sharing with me."

The woman summoned the man to her office when the student had left. Upon entry, she accosted the other professor immediately about his unfair treatment of the new girl. "Henri, we told you to lay off," she warned him spitefully. She could barely contain herself; the advisor found his actions so despicable

Robert Henry hated her too. His fiery, red, flaming, menacing, intimidating eye, with no exception the meanest set of eyes Virginia McIntyre had ever peered into . . . they scorched her; they were so full of disgust, anger, putrid hatred for mankind, womankind, any other kind . . . for all that were different than he. Women weren't supposed to be in charge of anything. Despite the woman's obvious capabilities, the man believed that she must have slept her way to the chair of the department. Nevertheless, he didn't care who she was. "I already told you I'm going to teach my class like I damn well please, and you'd be so much the wiser to do the same," he threatened.

"Good day," he said curtly before walking out on his immediate supervisor.

After the FL-phonics 111 instructor had left, the department chair made a few more telephone calls—to other department members, the department's vice-chair, the dean, the vice president of academic affairs, the vice president of student affairs, and to the university president and privately, unbeknownst to the others, to the chancellor of the university system who was a former classmate, one who had been a reference for her when she was initially hired at Claxville University—to gain continued support for an administrative reassessment of the girl's grade at the end of the semester if she stayed in the man's class.

"*If* she stays!" the academic vice president of academic affairs and other committee members said, each knowing that Brandi's skin would have to be made of rawhide to stay in Henri's class long.

From the chancellor, Virginia received encouragement to proceed at all costs and a hopeful and seemingly prophetic "Henri will get caught in his own web of deceit before this thing is over. You just take care of that little girl—the university system can't afford to get caught up in the melee about civil rights. Just do what you can to help her."

"And help she will need," Dr. McIntyre acknowledged, for Henri was a self-professed bigot . . . didn't like coloreds either; all were inadequate and weak, possessed minimal education to say the least, and didn't deserve all the money the government and big corporations were pouring into them. In his opinion, it was all for naught and the man touted it wherever he was . . . he refused to participate in the country's favors, didn't give a shit about all the civil rights stuff, so he abused students like Brandi with a scorn grown mechanical with use; he had no conscience. The professor told them the very first day in his class they couldn't make it, so he felt no remorse when he paid insult to Brandi in class.

Bob Henri knew his stuff, but his tolerance level was zero . . . sub-zero, zero degrees below zero. Silent support came from the masses because of his wealth of knowledge and because many others felt the same way he did; they lacked courage to be openly abrasive, to let their personal prejudices be known.

Kay, the department's secretary, called the resident assistant at Davis Hall to ask her to tell Brandi that she needed to stop by to see Dr. McIntyre real soon. The resident assistant gossiped about the rooming situation, the laundry, the banner, and the response from the coeds involved when they'd seen the sign hanging in the laundry room.

Neither Julie nor any of her friends reported the incident to Ms. Winthrop. No resident of Davis Hall breathed a word about the fracas; the third-floor maid spoke with the resident hall manager about the soiled pile of clothes and the sign in the laundry room, inquiring, "What I do with it?" "Nothing," the woman replied, "leave it be!" Then she and the resident assistant made an infrequent ascent up the staircase to the third-floor laundry. The only time that either bothered to go there was to place a message on a door if a resident had an emergency; to attend to someone reported by another as ill, infirm, drunk, unruly, disorderly, openly engaging in a verbal battle over music too loud; or to respond to a housekeeping inquiry from the maid. When the occasion came for someone to go beyond the office door, it was generally the resident assistant who made the trek; Ms. Winthrop rarely went.

BRENDA SMITH

That Saturday, when both women took the stairs, word went from room to room of their approach. The hallways on first, second, third, fourth, and fifth floors were clear—even the bathrooms were free. Not a single sound could be heard—not even a cough, sneeze, whistle, hum, fart, or the flush of a toilet. Davis Hall was silenced by the laundry incident.

The resident assistant told Kay that Ms. Winthrop had laughed when she had seen the soiled underwear, had picked up the pieces, the bras, drawers, slips, and had laughed drunken belly laughs. "It was obvious she was still loaded from the evening before," the senior in college, who had worked in the dorm for the last couple of years, said. "Ms. Winthrop is usually quiet, sedate."

"What did she say?" Kay asked hurriedly, almost hyperventilating. She needed to know the rest of the story, wanted to tell it to her own boss.

"Nothing really . . . she said that was the funniest shit she had ever seen in her life when she got herself together. Then she started back down the stairs."

"What happened next?" Kay scribbled question and answer in shorthand on the legal pad she kept on her desk. She would transcribe her notes when she was off the phone; she wanted to be able to tell Dr. McIntyre the story just as it was told to her.

"Nothing," the girl repeated before adding, "she told me to just leave it up there. She said she was going to let them little shits from Atlanta take care of their own mess this time." The resident added sympathetically, "I think Julie's old man really got next to Ms. Winthrop when he made such a big fuss over that room. She won't get involved in this."

"I can't wait to tell Virginia about this," Kay spoke of Dr. McIntyre. And when the secretary recanted verbatim the tales to the woman, the professor smiled that crooked, uncanny smile of hers. "A girl after my own heart," she said to Kay, who propitiously panted with excitement garnered from the tales of Brandi's woes in the dormitory.

Soon, realization hit home. Dr. McIntyre and Kay both had neglected to attend to a crucial task; the duo had determined the tutorial assistance should be gotten for Brandi, yet neither had attended to this task. The professor hit her forehead with the base of her hand, rolled her eyes toward the ceiling, sighed, and suggested, "Get Carmen to come by. Now is the time for her to meet Brandi."

CHAPTER TEN

The Affair

Dirk had known the day that she was at the restaurant that he would hire the girl; he telephoned her that very Saturday evening, and she started the following Monday. Brandi's workdays at the newly gained employ varied—Dirk scheduled all employees according to their class schedules and class loads. Except for the custodial help, all of the Burga Barn's workers attended the university. Usually she worked lunch and the three-to-eleven shift on weekends and was on call if someone could not come in; however, one of the part-time helpers had to quit because her grades were slipping and her parents had made her quit.

Dirk asked Brandi if she could come in early in the mornings, around five or six, to do "prep work": chop cabbage for slaw, tear lettuce, slice tomatoes, onions, place vegetables in separate containers, label foodstuffs for use during breakfast, lunch, dinner for each shift, put all containers in their place in the huge walk-in cooler, fill shake machines, wash down counters, polish equipment, perform the work neatly so that customers would be greeted by a warm, caring, clean environment.

"Don't mind at all," she said, giving little thought to the hour of the morning that she would have to walk across campus to get to the restaurant.

"I'll try to get someone else to help out," the man continued, "and I'll be there too.

"Won't interfere with your classes?" he queried the girl, anxious to begin the work.

"Don't mind at all, no," she said. Her classes were going as well as one could expect under the circumstances. However, some days Brandi felt that nobody was in that blasted FL-111 class except her and Monsieur Henri. He quizzed, she responded; she read and he corrected, spitefully and scornfully. The remainder of the class *sauf Monsieur Dubblerville* seemed to enjoy the cat-and-mouse game in which the professor and the student were engaged. Thanks to Carmen and Dr. McIntyre, she always kept her head above water—did actually have a bit of peace.

Brandi went to class every day, didn't miss one. And every day the girls in her class ignored her. Worse than that, they openly disdained her. They would never even exchange a greeting with her; they would never say hello to her when she walked into the classroom and never said good-bye. They never even spoke her name. For the first few days, she did try, would speak, but they rarely responded; and when they did it was out of earshot of another and it was with a cool "hi."

Needless to say, here it was almost half over . . . the days flew by, and it was awful, but Brandi refused to let this treatment shake her; her resolve grew.

The language professor became increasingly incensed as time flew by, especially around the middle of the semester. When the test had been completed and scored, he had returned the papers to the class the very next day. Henri was conscientious; while many professors would keep papers forever, leaving students to wonder about grades, he would work all night if that is what it took to have graded papers ready for his students the next day. "We will review the tests today, and when we have completed the review, please pass your papers to the front of the class," he boomed with instructions as he passed papers to everyone in the class—everyone except Brandi, that is.

"C'est bien," he said to one and to others. "Bien, tres bien" or "tsk, tsk," he emitted as papers were distributed—all verbal clues to passing and failure. In the meantime, Brandi glimpsed the large C+ on the paper in front of her and a bold A and B to her left and right. The others students chatted amiably among themselves, failing to cease their business to pay attention to her concern. A muffled, muted "shit" from Dubblerville claimed her attention for a moment—she knew that someone else knew she wasn't getting a graded paper back.

Soon, the man was back at his desk asking students to read questions and give the correct response. "Marie, question un," then "bien." The students read haltingly the assigned questions—*deux, trois, quatre, cinq . . . quatorze, quinze, vingt . . . trente, trente-et-un*, etc.—until the entire test was reviewed.

Brandi made doodles on scratch paper for each correct response she had made on her now-defunct test and was sure that she had made the perfect score on the test; she knew all the answers, including the bonus questions.

She spoke up when the review was over and papers were being passed to the front as instructed. "Monsieur Henri, I didn't get mine." The professor took the other students' papers from the first seat of each row, lay then on the desk beside his attaché, reached inside the case, and fumbled with several sets of papers in it. "Sorry," he thundered, his unpleasant voice filling the whole classroom, "I don't see it. Come by my office and pick it up."

"When can I come?"

"Don't matter," the professor shrugged his broad shoulders and declared, red faced and almost belligerent.

Brandi knew the statement was weighted. It carried double meanings. Time was not of essence—she could not get the paper at any particular time. It was also clear that even if she showed up, he wouldn't give her the test paper. "I'm damned if I do and damned if I don't," Brandi thought.

Nevertheless, she played the game his way—she had no choice. "This afternoon's good?" The girl prodded until the man gave her a specific time.

"Two-thirty, sharp!" he barked, apparently irritated with Brandi for persisting. "Be there at two-thirty sharp! I don't have time to hang around and wait."

Appointment made, the day's class ensued and ended. "Only 1460 days over four years to be precise, including summer school," Brandi mentally calculated her stay at Claxville. "They can't get any worse!"

Needless to say, the reticent but anxious coed was there ahead of time, more than the customary punctual, but the instructor was not in the office, so Brandi sat on the steps to await his arrival . . . she sat where snatches of conversation could reach her only in spurts, heard doors open and close, felt winds from skirted short dresses and trousers of passersby who sometimes emitted an "excuse me" or said nothing at all. Brandi remained listless, lonesome, staring at tops of heads, vacant eyes, torsos, and toes. She struggled against disappointment; she really hoped the man would come. Deep down in her heart of hearts she knew he wouldn't, couldn't; it would go against his nature.

The girl's repose on the staircase near Henri's doorway did not go unnoticed; the building and the campus buzzed, undergraduates and graduate students, instructors and secretaries, deans, department heads, and administrators—all spoke, whispered, snickered about, or openly expressed chagrin about the professor's obvious negligence. Or was it negligence?

The professor did not show up for this appointment . . . Brandi never successfully connected with the man for future appointments. Thus she never saw a graded paper . . . she was distressed by this, but there was nothing she could do about it—nothing except what her mother always told her to do when things got rough. "Pray about it," and pray about it she did. But stolen glances at yet unsympathetic, uncaring, unconcerned neighbors' papers for correct responses did indicate that she was passing.

Sara's daughter reported the activity back to Dr. McIntyre, as the advisor had requested; however, this girl was not enjoying being a pawn. She played though, for it was expedient that she did.

When she spoke to the tutor about it, Carmen, professional demeanor intact, encouraged her. "Don't get hung up on crap, *mon petit*. Let's proceed to the next *chapitre*. 'Tis a mighty good thing Ole Henri *est systematique*. We can chart our course and stay a couple of *chapitres* ahead of him." The woman intermingled two of the best five of her languages; she was fluent in all the romance languages.

The eldest of the two acquaintances added, "You can only earn his respect by handling things in the fashion that you are. Nothing can be gained by fighting back, and besides, Dr. McIntyre will deliver. You just stay *en classe,* sweets. No matter what he says or does, just stay in the *classe.*"

Brandi smiled. Carmen lay to rest her fears for the moment. She thought the woman could not be much older that herself, yet she seemed so wise. Actually, Carmen was almost twice her age but was youthful. She was petite and energetic, always bubbling with enthusiasm. The woman was herself single and enjoyed scholarly pursuit, finding herself in the States on scholarship because the Americans were giving so much money for minority participation in education. Often she wondered how she was classified as a minority, for she was not a Negro, but that was the American way when it came to distributing scholarships. If you were not a white American, you were by their standards a minority. "Strange," the foreign woman thought when she considered the fate of Brandi.

Brandi was glad that she had Dr. McIntyre, Mary Margaret, Carmen, and now Kris on her side. She especially appreciated the roommate—she didn't pry and gave the young woman the space she needed to sort out things. Kris, upon hearing about Julie's antics with the underwear when she returned to the room to shower, change, and grab a bite from the small refrigerator they now shared before heading back to work, respected her privacy.

Kris had noticed the inky smell—it still lingered somewhat, so she'd had to reopen the windows to let the small room air out some more. Initially she had thought her roommate had wasted some ink but had laughed jovially to herself when she heard some girls in the bathroom talking about the sign that hung in the laundry room. As a matter of fact, Kris had gone to see it for herself. "Go, roomie, go!" she cheered at the girl's quiet courage, yet she never spoke a word about it—never would unless Brandi brought it up.

BRENDA SMITH

CHAPTER ELEVEN

To Work We Must Go!

Dirk showed Brandi how to use the sharp knives to cut tomatoes razor thin before the duo tackled the huge vegetable shredder. Since the young woman had never seen anything like the gadget, he demonstrated, she practiced, they took it apart, cleaned its parts, and put it together again. "Now let me show you how to fill the shake machine," he said when he felt sure that she had mastered this initial task, when her movements were fluid rather than jerky . . . when cabbage fell in fine even layers of variegated green.

"First things first, we gotta get some. Follow me," he said, and then he led the way to and into the bowels of a huge walk-in cooler whose shelves housed all the perishables, including the gallon cartons of shake mix.

"You'll need about nine cartons," the man said.

"Nine," Brandi echoed, making sure that she had heard and that she had the correct number.

"Three of each," Dirk instructed. "Three strawberries, three vanillas, and three chocolates." The man handed several cartons to the new employee, and they returned to the machine where he deposited his ware on a nearby stand. "Don't try to take them all at the same time, they get kind of heavy, and sometimes they are kind of sticky on the outside where some done seeped out. You don't want to get that mess all over your clothes," he said, taking the cartons of strawberry shake mix from her.

She had already felt the cold and sticky on her bare arms. "Yuck!" she exclaimed, wrinkling her brow at the syrupiness.

Dirk secured a towel, wet it in a nearby sink, and wiped some pink from his white shirt; the stain moved. He handed it to Brandi for her arms. She wiped the sticky of the shake mix from herself, looking to see if any had deposited itself on her clothing as well.

Next Dirk showed Brandi how the spigots for each shake compartment of the vast machinery were to be closed off before any of the flavored shake mixes were poured into them.

"If you forget to shut them off before you pour it, you have a sticky mess all over the floor," he added, wiping his hands on the dampened towel he'd tucked in the corner of his pants' pocket to remove the sticky gook.

"Do you have any questions?"

Brandi shook her head assuredly. "No, I don't have any questions," she spoke with confidence, ready to tackle the job, excited about breaking life in Claxville's routine, about having something to do besides sleep, eat, study, and trying to sidestep the many pitfalls of the archaic, segregated society in which she had placed herself . . . her father had been right.

As much as she had wanted Carruthers to be wrong, Brandi's experiences verified what a sage her father truly was.

"If you need me, I'll be in the office," Dirk said, interrupting a moment of nostalgia. "And come by the office and pick up a key. I might be running late sometimes. I don't want you to have to wait outside until somebody gets here," the manager added before he turned once more to leave, then remembered to tell Brandi, "I'm going to pay you a little more than I do the rest of them since you will be helping me to open up too." It was obvious to the man that he had stumbled upon a rare gem. He flashed her a broad grin and left.

Silver's glimmer struck her anew. "Gosh!" she thought, "he's cute," then shook away her admiration of him because he was after all a white man.

Brandi was so excited! That night when she was back in the tiny and congested but private dormitory room, she wrote hastily in brief to Sara:

> Dear Mom,
>
> I ain't believing the luck I been having ever since I been up here. I'm just rolling in dough! That company that gave me the scholarship paid good. I still got some of that left. Plus I got all that money I bought up here with me. And now I got a job.
>
> Today the manager said he was going to pay me more than he pay the others. Oh, Ma, I'm so happy.
>
> Wish y'all were here.
>
> Love,
> Brandi

BRENDA SMITH

When Sara told her spouse about their daughter's letter, the man remarked angrily, "Don't know what she got to do for a few pennies more."

"Now, Cat." Sara shook her head in awe as she admonished her mate for the remarks he'd made about Brandi's letter.

"Don't 'now, Cat' me, woman!" The man banged his hand on the table. "Next time we go to town, you call her from one of them pay phone booths and you talk to her. That gal ain't got a lick of common sense.

"See what she got on her mind!" the man shrieked at his wife. "Help your little fool understand that money ain't everything. Next thing you know, she'll be wanting out of the dorm, wanting her own place, wanting a vehicle to drive. Be thinking she like them little rich white gals she's around now. Won't nobody be able to tell her headstrong self a damn thing!" He continued to voice his concerns at the woman who still thought Brandi a bit wiser than her father did.

Carruthers jumped up from the table and headed out the back door, letting the screen door shut itself.

Immediately Sara got some writing paper off the top of the icebox, took a seat at the kitchen table, and wrote Brandi right back.

Hey Baby!

I told your Daddy about your new job and everything. You be careful up there and don't take more money from that old man what you work for than the job is worth. Don't sell your soul for a nickel. Money ain't everything . . . And you be careful going in early and out of that place so late at night with it just you and that old white man you work for. You know we still living in perilous times.

Here's five more dollars somebody done left here for you. I can't recollect who it was right now. Seems like it was somebody down at the church. But everybody all the time wondering about how you doing.

I'm gonna call you from the phone booth next time I go to town. Maybe you'll be in your room. Your daddy say I need to talk with you a little bit more. He just wants to know what's on your mind. I think it's 'cause you don't talk enough about your classes when you write. Maybe he's thinking you done forgot what you went up there for.

Love,
Your Mamma

P. S. Don't forget to go to church and Sunday school like we taught you.

Sara prepared the letter for mailing, and then she had a second thought, so she ripped the envelope open and added tidbits given by Cat, who was just beginning to use his own personal experiences as references for communication with his daughter. To the body of the letter up to Claxville, Sara added:

And PS again. Can't hardly wait until Christmas comes. All the young'uns keep tugging at me and asking when you coming. I know they let y'all out of school a few days. Cat say when he went out to Texas to play ball for that college the year whilst I was finishing high school, he come home for two weeks for Christmas. You make sure and tell that old man what you work for. You got a family that misses you something awful.

Brandi cackled like one of Sylvia's old setting hens while she reclined on the bed reading the letter from Sara. "Humph!" she grunted in amusement, for there wasn't anything old about Dirk. She rolled over on her back, envisioning how he really did look.

Dirk Abraham Kalin was just a couple of years older than Brandi. She was a freshman, and he a junior. The man was a head taller than the girl, had an olivelike complexion—looked tan at a season when there was little sun—big dark eyes, and dark hair he kept neatly cropped; and every time Brandi had seen him, he was always dressed in the blacks and whites he wore to work. Of course, work was always where she saw him. If she had to size him up for anybody, she would have just said, "Nothing in particular set him apart from other responsible young men his age . . . Nothing except . . . he isn't old, and he is sort of cute." She allowed herself this girlish pleasure. Brandi looked around to see if anyone had heard the words she'd emitted aloud. Nobody was looking; nobody was there. And she resumed her girlish revelry—almost let herself fantasize, free of distractions.

Brandi's commitment to her tasks at the restaurant was only surpassed by that of Dirk. Each found himself or herself anxiously awaiting the wee hours of the morning for the time they shared, alone together, at the Burga Barn.

Each worked, at first alone; then they began to share tasks. He relished the speed and accuracy the girl exhibited as she sliced and pared fruits and vegetables for the day's many homemade goodies; so soon, Dirk washed and passed the groceries to her, making time spent in culinary paring more efficient. Brandi enjoyed these times in this environment, in this relationship with peace and exuberance, and it was during these relished moments that she was free from the folly, pranks, and insolent deeds regularly done by Claxville University's inhabitants.

As Brandi worked harder, faster, and relentlessly, caution evaded her. Nicked fingers required bandages. The red from Mercuricom was splashed everywhere. Brandi's delicate, nimble fingers and hands took on a pale appearance, and they were always so tender.

And as the Burga Barn gained favor, her studies became affected. One day Carmen commented, irritably, about the diminishing quality of her academic work. "You need to give your lessons more attention," the tutor had said when Brandi kept making mistakes in oral and written communications. "You've got to concentrate if you want to be successful."

"I'm just a little tired," Brandi remarked as she pushed her chair away from the table they shared in one of the minuscule study rooms reserved in the library for these sessions, stretching the distance between herself and Carmen, hoping to avoid further confrontation.

As Carmen got up from her seat to stretch her limbs and flex taut muscles, she yawned, then offered, "Maybe you need to quit that job."

"No!" Brandi almost yelled, urgency clearly resounding in her quavering voice.

Carmen flinched, having been caught off guard by the unexpected emotional outburst. She held her hands up. "Hold your horses, mon petite!" she retorted forcefully in a quiet library voice. The argument commenced.

"Brandi, you know you don't have to work. Your scholarship takes care of everything," Carmen persisted, unwilling to let Brandi become entrapped by the obvious security being provided by the place. "Your check was more than enough to take care of all your expenses."

"You don't know what I get!" Brandi fussed.

"I beg to differ with you, missy." Carmen took the offensive. "I know what you get because I get one too. My scholarship like yours is off the Americans. I get enough to rent a place, to take care of my subsistence, and have some left over for folly if I have need of it.

"Why are you spending so much time at that Burga Barn place, working all those long hours when you don't have to, working in the morning, at the noon day, after school, on weekends, Fridays, Saturdays, as well as on Sundays?" Carmen pushed her.

Brandi felt hemmed in. Carmen was in front of the small room's door. She couldn't flee. "I just do it for fun," she yelled, "for fun!"

"For fun!" the Belgian damsel laughed in her face. "For recreation, you work for pleasure. Brandi, that's ludicrous, ridiculous—who works for fun?

Did you ever think about dating?" the woman chided as she retook her seat so she could be eye level with her charge who had returned to her own chair.

"I ain't seen nobody up here I like—or who likes me!" Brandi argued.

"Right!" Carmen pointed out emphatically. "And you won't find anybody behind the counter in that hamburger joint either!"

Brandi, relenting, busied herself, laying her papers, books, notes out on the small table in Hazzard Library they had been using almost daily since Dr. McIntyre had introduced them. "Carmen has worked with other students in our department," she had told Brandi, to which the tutor had nodded affirmatively. "You will have an advantage over the others, even Mr. Henri. English is a fifth language for Carmen—she speaks Spanish, Russian, German, French. She is more capable of helping you if you follow her directions. And she has already secured a place to work if you will accept her help."

Brandi was in no better position the day of their conversation than she was that first meeting day; she still needed help, so she relented, saying, "Let's get back to work. You said yourself that I need to study more. We can't let Mr. Henri get the best of the dynamic duo, and we can't let Dr. McIntyre down either. She's such a nice lady. I still feel kind of bad though because I never have any papers to show her. She's almost like a mama—you know how they are always asking about your homework."

Carmen shrugged her shoulders, her concerns refusing to vanish.

A couple of weeks later, just before the holiday season, Brandi finally overslept. Ever since she'd started opening up for Dirk, she'd wake up in the middle of the night to check the clock. She didn't want to be late, didn't want to let him down, so she'd get up, even dress sometimes, and wait for time to go by; occasionally she'd slip out of the room and go down to the break room on the third floor so she wouldn't wake Kris up. She would watch whatever was on the black-and-white television—many times it was a religious program—but it worked. It kept her entertained until it was time to go to work.

Well, this particular day, she attempted to study to pass the time away, but she'd gone back to sleep at a large table in the break room.

Brandi woke with a start and, books in tow, she flew down the hall to the stairwell and ran down its length taking two steps at a time. The young woman ran all the way from the dormitory to the restaurant. She opened the door with her brand-new key, rushed into the facility, threw her school supplies aside, rushed into the huge wall cooler, grabbed gallon after gallon of shake mix from the shelves, and poured each into the machine. Vanilla first, she poured the three heavy, gigantic cartons into the machine's wells, just as Dirk had shown her several weeks beforehand, and closed each filled compartment before wiping the sticky, milky residue from her hand on the rag atop the shake machine. Then she added the other flavors.

She flipped the "on" switch at the base of the monstrous machine and listened for its motor to rattle to a start, then purr.

Feeling quite pleased with herself for the new accomplishment, she gave the machine a satisfied whack and looked at her watch, deciding it was time to move on to the vegetables, and then she stepped sideways to retrieve the emptied containers. She stopped dead in her tracks . . . she felt sticky gook underfoot. Beads of sweat popped out of her—her forehead, armpits, even the palms of her hands leaked.

"Oh my god!" Brandi exclaimed; she was frozen, rigor mortis had set in . . . had begun at the sole of her feet, crept slowly, unmercifully to her brain. In her haste, she had forgotten to close off each spigot before filling the compartment. Now she freed herself from her solid state; her movements grew fluid as she hastened to close off each spigot from which steady streams of shake mix fell neatly to the floor before making swirls of pink, white, and chocolaty brown ribbons. For an instance, the usually astute worker paused anew; she did not want to track the sticky, murky mess all over the restaurant, to garner the bucket and mop which rested in the utility room just outside the restaurant's rear entrance.

She began to cry. Brandi sobbed aloud as she began the slippery trek through the steadily enlarging yet thinning puddle.

The waitress did not hear the screen door open or plop into place when the manager flew in. Dirk, heart racing, arms outstretched, bolted toward the girl with tears streaming down her face. She saw him when he was directly in front of her, but their pathways were determined by the pool of shake; the man and the woman groped and grappled an awkward dance as each tried to break the other's impending fall.

After what seemed like an eternity, Dirk went down first, making a nice, comforting, and comfortable cushion for the girl who now grieved so painfully for the forewarned error. Realizing what had happened and relieved that his worst fears had not been realized—that the man who had been exposing himself to university students, but who had remained uncaught, was not here and had not attacked the girl, forcing himself upon her—Dirk held her repeating over and over again, "It's okay, it's all right, baby," to Brandi who continued to wail, first for waking up late, then for the crap that took place at Davis Hall, for that bastard Ole Henri . . . Brandi cried her eyes out. At least she thought she would.

Dirk too thought she might never quit sobbing. He raised a sticky hand to brush her hair from her face . . . it hid her eyes—her glasses had been lost in the melee. The man rocked her in consolation, whispering over and over, "It is okay, Brandi, it is all right." No other words would come. Soon, the man's heart's rhythmic pattern realigned to suit the current state of affairs; he found himself staring at her rapt face. The longing in her beautiful, glistening, hazel eyes was more than he could stand. A tightness constricted in his throat, making it impossible for him to swallow.

The tightness spread, gripping the rest of his lean body, knotting Dirk up inside until the man thought he would die from wanting her. His gaze inadvertently shifted to her slightly parted lips. Her warm breath drew him downward.

The man didn't remember moving . . . didn't remember anything until he felt the tentative pressure of her warm lips. Dirk hadn't meant to kiss Brandi, but now he couldn't stop . . . he didn't want to stop.

And Brandi?

She felt his kiss, drank from the well of his mouth, moaned when he moved away, was grateful to feel his lips on her cheeks. He pecked at first one, then the other, raised her face and brushed his burning lips across her forehead, her brow, her cheeks, and tasted the salt of her tears—tears which had abated as she joined him.

The woman leaned into the cradle Dirk made for her body, rocking with him as he made his way for her lips again . . . and back to those eyes . . . those beautiful eyes. He drank the remnants of salt water from each one.

New acquaintances had always asked Sara and Carruthers, "Where does she get them cat eyes from? They almost match her hair."

"I don't know, she was just born with them bright eyes. You can see them in the dark. She couldn't never even pretend to be sleeping neither. Sparkles coming from between them eyelids would part the dark—they just seem to shoot sparks right at you," the mother offered up about her daughter's dark brown eyes flecked with hazel.

"Eyes like them can bore a hole in a person," Uncle Jack would say. "Eyes like them can get a body in trouble."

And boy, was Brandi Leigh Brown in over her head at the moment!

Dirk still lapped at her face—he tongued the corners of her upturned lips. Hungrily, he tasted the ripe curves of her mouth as it melted against his. The sweet from the assorted shake mixes and the salt of her tears reminded him of the remnants from the tub of the old ice cream churn in which Sadie, the cook down at his uncle's Imperial Island summer home, used to make his favorite summer treats.

He would always plead, "Let me lick it, let me lick it!"

"Only if you stand still 'til it's finished," the old colored woman would say to the fidgety little boy.

He'd stand still too until it was finished. Sadie would spoon most of the ice cream in a big dish to transfer to the icebox so that it would keep it chill. And finally, she would spoon the contents left in the container into the little waif's eager mouth, grinning at his obvious delight. Then she would pass the bucket to him for further culinary scrutiny. Soon, the boy would abandon the spoon and swipe at the churn's sides, its bottom, with his fingers.

Dirk would practically wash the container with his tongue until the tin no longer tasted of sweet or bitter. The boy would lick, lick . . . and lick.

Brandi's response was a raspy, throaty moan. She could find no words—they escaped her—couldn't speak because the man had returned to her lips, rested there, and suckled her sweet tongue until he heard the door open. The woman did not hear it.

Dirk turned swiftly but gingerly to allow the woman to free herself from the cradle at a spot where no milk shake lay, and Brandi scrambled to her feet. The man handed her the eyeglasses that rested nearby and prodded her along with, "Better hurry up, we got to open up. I'll clean this up."

She apologized, "Dirk, I'm sorry."

The man shook his head, and finger to his lips, he shushed her. "Get in the restroom and get yourself cleaned up," he ordered.

"What about you? You're a mess!" For the first time, she noticed the mess he really was. He wore much more milk shake mix than she—the man had landed on the bottom, she had come to rest in his lap.

"I keep a change in the office," was his quick and quiet response.

"Here's the mop," chimed in Chuck, the assistant manager who had happened upon the scene but had not made himself known until he thought the twosome should know that he was there. "Bit late today myself," he said to Dirk with whom he shared a trailer, loud enough for Brandi to hear.

Knowingly, Dirk commented, "Thanks, man."

By the time Brandi returned from the ladies' room, Dirk and Chuck had cleaned up the mess and all appeared to be back to normal—at least it appeared to be.

The next two weeks were pure hell for Brandi; they were more hell than any other two weeks in her life had been. Unbeknownst to the young woman, Dirk shared her private inferno. Neither had breathed a word to each other, or anyone else for that matter, about the milk shake machine incident—each wished that the other would. Both wanted to get it over with, yet both let it languish, let it go unattended.

Both brooded.

Where there had been casual conversation, there was none—silence replaced the usual warm chatter between the employees at the Burga Barn. Chuck became the motor that drove the mechanisms for work to be the same. His one attempt to talk to the man who had been his roommate for three years about what he had seen had been met with a cutting, "You'd better keep your face out of this, man!"

"Okay, okay, man! It's nothing to fight about," the huge man had said to Dirk, who was much smaller in stature than he. With raised hands, he backed away.

Chuck had come up to Claxville University the same year that his friend had come. An outstanding linebacker on his high school football team, he had suffered a debilitating injury during his senior year; so unlike many on the team, he was not offered a scholarship. So when he was rehabilitated and felt up to snuff, he had come to play for the Rattlers. But the walk-on did not have a successful preseason; he was reinjured.

The day that Charles Townsend was let go by the coach was a dismal day; since he was a walk-in, he lost his scholarship, lost his room in Russell Hall—the athletic dorm—lost everything. Somehow he found himself in the Burga Barn wolfing down a last meal before heading back home. Dirk's offer of a late-night coffee to the customer who just would not leave led to a lifelong friendship—the man gave him a job, a place to stay, a meal ticket. Chuck wasn't about to let no mess come in between them.

"Going to the game?" he asked Dirk about the second round of the playoffs the next day. The Rattlers faced another undefeated team, the Gamecocks.

"Guess we could," the manager asserted, "won't be many customers with all those tailgate parties going on."

"You want off?" he asked Brandi, who admitted that she didn't enjoy the game, had not attended any all season; as a matter of fact, she had thrown tickets in the trash.

Chuck hit his head with the base of his hand. "Woman, you did what?"

"I threw my tickets away," she reiterated.

"Those tickets were worth a damn mint, woman," he argued. "I could have sold them for fifty dollars apiece. A man in the parking lot when I came in just now was just begging for tickets for tomorrow. You ain't throwed the trash away yet, have you?" he spoke, eyes wide with disbelief, hands thrown upward and outward.

"That's illegal," she spoke innocently and hesitantly, knowing full well that tickets for the big game were back in her room on the desk but she wasn't going to sell them to anybody; that was illegal.

"I am not participating in nothing illegal," Brandi insisted.

"What illegal?" the man shrieked in question.

"That's illegal," she fussed more. "I read an article in the *Commentator* about scalping the other day. It mentioned something about fines being given to anybody upping prices on tickets."

"So?" Chuck asserted humorously, to which Dirk suggested, "So . . . she wouldn't be caught dead doing it. Brandi's as honest as the day is long."

Both men laughed, and the woman did too. Tense moments passed again.

But they had not passed soon enough. Mary Margaret and Brandi had grown closer each day since they had made their way up the dirt-lined path into friendship the first week of school. Their relationship had not been tested; considering circumstances, they seemed unlikely candidates for an enduring relationship. Their backgrounds were dissimilar, they were worlds apart in beliefs, yet their friendship had endured, had grown because of how much they shared, especially in the early days.

But now Brandi seemed distant—so much of the conversation she shared with Mary Margaret was fragmented. Their words seemed to trip over each other all the time, and soon they were quarreling about petty things.

Mary Margaret did not go to the big game either. She made her way through the tailgate parties to the Burga Barn, which Dirk did leave open and in Brandi's charge while he took in part of the game.

Since business was so slow, the girls just sat and shared a banana split boat Brandi had especially prepared for them. They spoke briefly about the number of people in Claxville for the game, the sounds and sights, aromas of the festivities that accompanied the season's impending finale.

"Brandi, I'm sure going to miss you," her friend said when she had almost eaten her half of the shared split, cautiously approaching the line drawn in the bananas, scoops of flavored ice creams, syrups, mounds of whipped cream, and walnuts in syrup by its preparer.

"I'll be back," Brandi spoke listlessly, "I'm just going to be in Wester for the Christmas holidays and then I'll be back.

"I'm talking about when the semester's over," she said. Mary Margaret was becoming increasingly incensed at Brandi's obvious self-centeredness.

"What's happening at the end of the semester?"

"Oh, Brandi, you forgot!" Mary Margaret yelled. "You're always forgetting. As a matter of fact, you haven't been thinking about nobody except for you and your problems ever since you been her." Mary Margaret, upset because her friend had taken over their conversation and was wandering down her own path of thoughts, got up from the table and fled, almost bumping into Dirk as he entered the establishment.

Brandi leapt from her seat and quickened her own steps to reach her friend before she had escaped and was out the door. She grabbed her arm and gently led her back to the table from which the hasty departure had been made.

"Whoa, Mary Margaret," she said, "I must have missed something. I been working my tail off around here," she added apologetically. "Okay, what is it?"

Their eyes locked.

"Please, can't we start over again?" Brandi begged with her eyes, promising to listen attentively, so Mary Margaret returned to her seat.

"You forgot! I told you my old man got a job out of state and the whole family has to tag along."

"That don't make sense," Brandi said defiantly. "You're in college—it doesn't make sense for you to have to change schools too, especially in the middle of the year."

Mary Margaret's frown deepened as she considered asking her father once more to let her stay on the East Coast, but she shook her head. "I know that, but he won't hear it. He just doesn't want me all the way across country—says I need to be near family in case something happens—so he's making me transfer to some school in California."

"Can't your ma help you with that?" Brandi asked thoughtfully, reminiscing about how Sara had always come to her rescue when it seemed that Carruthers was being unreasonable. When she had initially inquired about coming to Claxville, the man's initial response had been, "Let me talk to the spirit about it."

The girl from Wester knew that the probability of a positive response from her father diminished as the nights passed. Every time he woke up, it would always be "The spirit ain't told me nothing yet" or "Let me talk to the spirit a little bit more about it." However, as she grew older it appeared that responses from the spirit were more likely to be affirmative if she consulted with Sara first. She was almost convinced that Sara was the spirit.

Mary Margaret gave an absent shake of disagreement, her expression showing similar displeasure, "No, she isn't a bit of help. My mama doesn't do anything unless he says so." Mary Margaret spoke of the way things were done in her own home. Sighing, she got up from her chair and prepared to leave.

Brandi sprang to her feet with the agility of a cat and quickly stepped in front of her friend to embrace her. "Jeez, Mary Margaret, I'm sorry," Brandi spoke apologetically.

"See you around, Dirk," Mary Margaret called out to the manager.

With a simple "Bye now," he returned her farewell bid.

"Everything all right, Brandi?" the man inquired of the friend who returned to the empty table.

"Yeah, everything's all right, and by the way, I been meaning to talk to you about something else." Dirk sighed with relief; he was more than ready to talk. "Want to come into the office?" he questioned her eagerly.

Brandi shook her head and sighed, choosing to stay put. The man moved closer to her. With her composure regained, she faced him, clasping her hands primly together as if to make a recitation.

"No, we can talk right here . . . I just wanted to let you know that I won't be around in the next couple of weeks. I'm going home for the holidays. I missed Thanksgiving, and my folks are looking for me to show up for Christmas," she said apologetically before querying, "Is that all right?"

Dirk stared at the woman, a hint of relief sprinkled with disappointment showing through. Brandi pressed a hand to her chest to calm her rapidly beating heart . . . being close to the man did that to her. She was so unnerved; his presence, the scent of his spicy aftershave, their closeness in proximity was almost too much to bear. She needed an immediate response.

He shifted his position, stepped backward a bit, fleeing to his own comfort zone. "Oh yeah, sure." He gave his assurances to her as his shoulder shrugged disappointedly. "Just thought something was wrong with your friend. Where is home?"

"Wester." Brandi faltered for an instant. "Wester," she sputtered again.

"That's right," he said, "I remember seeing that on your application when you first came here.

"I know your family will be glad to see you, but you know Chuck and I will be glad when you get back."

"Thanks." She wrapped up their casual discourse, noting the ease with which it had come.

CHAPTER TWELVE

Season's Greetings

From inside the archway's alcove, Brandi peered into a Christmaslike, wintry wonderland that Claxville had become overnight. Downtown actually looked like a picture postcard: deep blue sky dotted with perfect white snowflakes, multicolored lights blinking, decorated storefronts, holly, more bulbs, bells, bows (red ones), streetlight posts wrapped like jumbo candy canes, holly berries everywhere, silvery spray-painted pine cones sprinkled with fake and real snow. She longed for all the young'uns back home, wishing they could behold such wonder. Wester was quite sedate when she compared the festive mood of this city. Nevertheless, she knew they would love the snow as much as she did today—none had stuck on the ground back home since the night she was born.

When she got to the Woolworth's, she carefully deliberated over purchases for each member of the family. She got perfume for Sara, a pair of brown leather gloves for her daddy, and a toy apiece for each of her brothers and sisters, and some candy too. Whitman's chocolates for her mother, boxes of chocolate-covered cherries for her sisters, a gigantic striped red candy cane for Li'l Benji (it was going to take a hammer to break it), orange slices for Cat (that was the father's favorite), and a mountain of double-dipped chocolate-covered peanuts to munch on when she was back in the dormitory; a pair of wool socks and some silk stockings were also purchased for Uncle James and Aunt Sylvia.

Brandi also bought gifts for Carmen, Mary Margaret, and Dr. McIntyre.

Then she got some things for herself: a pair of gloves (her hands were cold right then), a wool hat and scarf set, perfume, and more fancy chocolates. Yet she was not satisfied. Brandi wandered aimlessly throughout the store, up and down each filled aisle trying to find the perfect gift for the man . . . for Dirk.

When it was dark, the young woman left the store burdened down with packages, crossed the street to Macy's, and renewed her search for the perfect gift for Mr. Right. With the remains of money set aside for gifts, she purchased the most expensive gift: a camel-colored knitted shawl and glove set suggested by a saleslady and had it wrapped before leaving the store . . . the rest she had bought wrapping paper for while shopping at Woolworth's . . . they didn't have to be as perfectly decorated as this special gift.

Her return to the archway marked the impending voluntary expulsion from a fantasyland down the now dark, dank, hilly single-lane street with hidden sidewalks, the dirt and wintry brown grasses mingled with gray and pure white snow masking the concrete sidewalks. Brandi didn't know how she was going to make it with all the cumbersome packages. The eerie state of affairs was assuaged by the taxi's familiar toot . . . he beeped and waved at her ever since that day she started to put a cussing on him at the bus station for ripping her off . . . and came the call from his vehicle, "At your service, ma'am?" The driver pulled close to the curb.

She stopped, flashing a smile at the man who got out of his car and took the bags replete with gifts and goodies from her stone-cold hands and cramping phalanges and bruising arms—the packages weighed a ton. Then he let her seat herself before shutting the vehicle's door and getting under the wheel anew to deliver her and all of her goods back to the dormitory.

Brandi teased him when he held the door for her dismount, waiting patiently while she grouped and regrouped her load. "Sure was a quick trip, nothing like the first one I had when I got here!"

The man smiled sheepishly, exposing the whitest, most perfect set of teeth she had ever seen, trying to think of something else to say . . . anything; but words escaped him, so he simply said, "This one's on me! Merry Christmas."

"And merry Christmas to you," Brandi said as she, for some reason unbeknownst to herself, reached into one of the loaded sacks, took out the beautifully wrapped shawl and gloves from Macy's, and handed it to the man, who climbed back into the vehicle and hurried off because he had a run to make.

"Santa Claus comes in all sizes," he remarked aloud to the open air as he sped away. A car in front of the man stopped, enabling him to look over his shoulder to see the girl laden with packages struggling with the dormitory's door. He wished he had taken the time to see her to the door.

Brandi took the Greyhound back home for the holidays; the flats at a distance were no longer scenery to her. There were real places with authentic names, places to help you lick your wounds of which she had plenty: the girls in the dormitory had inflicted some, the black man on the bus had rubbed salt into those, there was the threat from the exhibitionist, intimidation submitted by Monsieur Henri . . . and now there was Dirk and the infatuation that was growing daily.

The young lady looked forward to returning home to civilization and its boundless joys. She passed her time reading signs along the highway. First there was Ochlocknee, Willachoochee, Nahunta, and Sandy Creek. Time seemed to be standing still; the bus ride seemed longer than her first one. Brandi kept looking at her watch. The one layover took forever. Then there was Harlem, Pidcock, and finally, Wester—25 miles, the sign read.

And when she was there, Cat reached her first. He swept her off her feet, and father and daughter hugged, kissed, and cavorted like they had prior to her decision to go to Claxville. "Here's your baby," he said, plunking the girl down at Sara's feet. Mother, daughter, and the circle of young'uns made a spider's web of love at the bus's steps. The driver almost got caught up in the melee while trying to retrieve the baggage from the luggage compartment and place them in the charge of Carruthers before continuing his run.

As the Browns putted slowly back up Dry Lake Road, everybody in every house lined up waving and calling, "Glad you back, child!" "Welcome back! Things ain't been the same without you." It didn't seem like they would ever get home. The bus from Claxville had now seemed to have sped along, but Cat, who customarily drove at a snail's pace, slowed the car to a tortoise crawl at almost every broom-swept yard; and Sara, Cat, or Brandi herself responded to each neighborly salutation.

When Brandi walked in the back door, she was greeted by a homemade banner with humongous block letters Sara had drawn for the young'uns to color while she prepared the homecoming meal. "Welcome Home, Baby," it read. An almost teary-eyed Brandi snickered remembering her own artistic prowess shown at Claxville University when Julie and her girls had stolen and toyed with her laundry.

The undergarments had stayed in a heap on the folding table in the laundry room up on the third floor, and the sign refused to drop off the walls. The custodians, as well as the maids and janitors, shifted them from one end of the table to the other as they cleaned the facility . . . none of the coeds touched them. Neither did Brandi. Ms. Winthrop couldn't even get

BRENDA SMITH

the resident manager to remove the offending reminder of the "tug-of-room" enacted when Julie had tried to wrestle room 306 from Brandi. "I ain't getting no cooties from anybody," the resident manager had argued.

The remaining Browns were ready to eat some of the "birfday cake" Sara had made for Brandi's homecoming. Every iced cake was a birthday cake to the little ones. Sara wanted them to eat some of the smothered chicken feet and rice, turnip greens, candied sweet potatoes, and crackling bread she had fixed first, but Brandi put in, "Let them have a piece of cake now . . . They ain't nothing but young'uns, don't hurt none for them to eat a little bit of it first," before she pulled a knife out of the kitchen drawer replete of utensils and cut a tiny wedge of the coconut cake for each child who seated himself or herself quietly at the table.

Sara gasped; her mouth fell open.

Later that night when the elder Browns were finally in bed, Sara spoke to her husband about their oldest child. "Brandi's done grown up some since she left to go off to school. She's even more patient with the young'uns, wanted me to let them have a bit of that sweet bread before they ate. She just set about giving it to them herself."

"And she was helping you fix their plates," the father added.

"Brandi washed them dishes soon as she finished," the mother went on, "I didn't have to ask her to do them."

"Our baby's growing up, Sara. That's all . . . she going to make you proud one day." The man grinned with pride in the dark.

"Me! Make me proud!" the woman exclaimed, attempting to rise from the mattress, to turn over to face her husband; but Carruthers smiled anew, taking his mate and tucking her into the cozy space made expressly for her by his own body. She nestled against him. No further mention was made of their daughter that night.

Sara enjoyed a restful repose. And Cat slept well that night too, his worse fears not realized; his daughter had not lost her prodigy, integrity, and dignity while away from home. Brandi Leigh Brown was going to be all right.

When everyone in the house was sound asleep, Brandi slipped out the back door and sat on the stoop. The old bird dog across the road howled like he'd treed a coon; the girl didn't pay him any mind. All of her thoughts were of Dirk. What was she going to do about the situation? How did she get herself into the mess? Should she return to work at the Burga Barn when she got back to Claxville? Should she go back at all?

She shivered. The night's chill and her own were too much . . . were overwhelming. And it was so dark, pitch-black, even darker than she remembered her hometown's nights' skies to be. Few stars even winked at her, and there was no moon; she had grown accustomed to the streetlights on Claxville's university campus. Brandi raised herself and made her way back to bed to secure its warmth. Tomorrow was another day.

Every day of the two-week Yuletide break was fun. Brandi had always enjoyed the hog killing, sausage making, chitlin' cooking, cane grinding, syrup making, and cake baking that culminated each year. But it was special this year.

The day before Christmas Eve was there before she could blink her eye; seemed like she'd just stepped off the bus. Well before daybreak, the usually sedate wintry country morning had enlivened in anticipation of the day's activity. Cat and Sara had gotten up and were busy well before the rooster crowed. Sara had fixed Cat's breakfast and had joined him and the others outside for the onset of the annual hog killing.

By the time Brandi joined them, the yard was full of family and friends. Uncle Jack, Aunt Sylvia, Hawk, Russell, Melvin, Tatter, Cooda, Judson, the Stoner boy, all of them were there.

Activities abound. Fuel was being added to the fire under a huge black wrought iron vat of water; carcasses of already hairless pigs, killed with a single shot to the head from a rifle, hung by the legs from a wooden fixture built for this purpose; already sharpened butchers' knives received a final honing.

Uncle Jack, dressed in plaid shirt, overalls, and thigh-high rubber wading boots, stepped forward and slit each hanging pig from "ass to ear" without puncturing chitterlings, livers, hearts, kidneys, and lights. Cat assisted the man in pulling the entrails from each carcass, placing them in tin tubs held by the boys from the neighborhood, who stood in awe, admiring the precision demonstrated by the older men.

"Take 'em over there to the womenfolks," the butcher hurried the young men along. "Be daybreak 'fore you know it, get the least bit warm and gnats, all kinds of bugs and creations be coming from God-knows-where to get at this fresh meat."

"Do like he tell you," Carruthers encouraged them.

"Yassir," all called.

"And you there, bring some of that scalding hot water over here." Uncle Jack singled out one of the helpers. Then the man was back at the first carcass ministering to it once more, making sure there was not a single hair left on it; he scraped the flesh with a razor-sharp butcher knife, stopped and rubbed his hand over the meat, and scraped and rubbed repeatedly until the pork was as clean-shaven as a newborn baby's behind.

"Here, rub your hand 'cross this boy . . . feel any hairs?" he said to an avid watcher who stepped forward, only when summoned, to lean forward and imitate the older man's gestures. The man, proud of his handiwork, laughed long and loud, wiped the pig's blood from his hand on an old wash rag, took his tin of Prince Albert tobacco and rolling paper from his bib pocket, shook some of the tin's contents onto the paper, deftly rolled it into a cigarette, licked the seam . . . making glue with his spittle, and stuck it in his mouth without bothering to light it.

"Not a bit, sir," said the boy who stood rubbing his hand across the dead pig's naked backbone, "don't feel a speck of hair."

"Good, ain't supposed to," the man chided the onlooker. "Bacon gon' be real good. Don't nobody like to pick no hair from betwixt their teeth. Can't think of a single soul who likes to eat hairy bacon." Then Uncle Jack turned back to his duties, noticing that the boy was as intent as ever, so he stepped away from the meat and handed the knife to the boy. "Step 'round the other side," he instructed patiently, "press forward, lean into it, bring the knife straight down, that's right all the way down, far as you can go without releasing pressure off knife, all the hair will come right off. Now, rub your hand 'cross it. If'n you feel the least bit of a stubble, just do it again." The boy tried his hand at hair removal, tested his handiwork, and determined that he must not be doing something just right. The older man took the knife again, assuring the apprentice, "With a little bit of experience, you'll get it right the first time. Won't have to keep raking at it like you was doing just now."

Turning to yet another helper, the man called, "You, boy, bring another tub over here . . . put these heads in it. Sylvia gon' make hogshead cheese out of it." He deftly severed the animal's head from its carcass with little effort, easing it down in the container.

"Ever had any her hogshead cheese?" he spoke anew to his constant attendant.

"No, sir."

"Ain't!" the older man feigned surprise.

"Gon' bring some back over here when it's ready, gonna give you a piece. Be the best chunk of cheese you ever put between your lips. She takes them heads, clean them, puts them in a big pot, and boils them until all the flesh falls off the bone. Then she ground that cooked meat up! And Sylvia, she season it jest right . . . puts plenty fresh, ground, red pepper in it, some vinegar, and sage, salt, black pepper, before she put it in a mold for it to gel. Tell you what, it'll bring snot to your nose, clear your head up if you got the least bit of congestion," the man bragged on his mate's culinary skills. "Where you live anyhow?"

"Right across the field apiece, sir." The boy pointed across the field, "We've only been living in this neighborhood a short time."

"No wonder I can't remember ever seeing you before," the man asserted. "Me and Sylvia come over here every week, sometimes twice a week."

"Well, I tell you what, when you see my truck back over here tomorrow, you come back. I gonna have you a piece. If you ain't here by the time we go home, I'm shore God gonna leave you a piece. You are such a good helper."

"Yes, sir," the boy emitted.

In the meantime, the first fresh liver was sent over to the womenfolk. Sliced while the blood was still warm, Sara handed it to Brandi, who up until this point had done little except observe. "Take this to the kitchen. We are going to have some of this for breakfast."

"Check on the young'uns while you in there," the woman called to her daughter when she was on the top step of the back door, "and turn the stove on so it can preheat . . . gon' make some biscuits to go with that liver and some syrup." She added, "Sister brought fresh butter too. And a pail of this year's sugar cane syrup."

By now Brandi was drooling; she could hardly wait for breakfast. The woman had missed country cooking but had made herself content with the food in the dining halls, Stu's, Burga Barn, Woolworth's, and occasionally, the Varsity.

All of her sisters and brothers were awake, so she helped them to potty, brush their teeth and wash up, and when she returned the other five Browns were in tow.

"Keep them off a distance," Sara said when she noticed them heading her way, Benji with hands outstretched.

"Okay," Brandi acknowledged and invited the youths, "come over here so we won't get in the way." She tried to seat the little ones, who craned their necks to witness the day's excitement.

One said, "I can't see."

"Me neither," another complained.

"Ow!"

Sara stopped working. "What's the matter with the baby, Brandi?" she asked, tenseness increasing with every whine and complaint. The mother's hands were full with chores that came with the hog killing.

"Nothing, Mama," the young woman assured her.

The sniveling youngster fussed, "Somebody stepped on my toe."

The reply was a premature shove and "He pushed me!"

This was almost more than any mother could bear on an average day. But patience was not one of her virtues that morning. "I'm gon' make Brandi take y'all back in the house, put every one of you back in the bed. It's too early for y'all to be up anyhow," the mother verbally warned her brood of sniveling youngsters before returning to the toilsome job she was doing.

Their big sister defended them. "They all right, Mama, I'll entertain them."

"See to it you do," Sara asserted.

Aunt Sylvia remarked, "Shore is come a long way, that one, ain't never knowed her to be so patient with them young'uns before. That school must be good for her. She must be taking up responsibility."

"Me and Cat was talking about that the other night when she got home. It seems like something's come over her since she been gone."

"You got all chitterlings in that tub?" the older woman asked.

"Yeah."

"Let's take them over yonder, start getting some of that mess out of them."

"Okay." The sisters each grabbed the wash tub's handles and ported the heavy load of intestines to another spot in the clearing.

"Whew!" Sylvia exclaimed. "We should have got one of them boys helping Jack come move that thing. It sure is heavy." Sara agreed. After a time, Sara smiled and spoke anew of her daughter's maturity, praising God to herself for the child's exemplary conduct, "Brandi's going be all right. I sure was worried half to death when she decided to go to school up yonder."

"Couldn't nobody tell it," Sylvia reflected back on Sara's reactions to Brandi's choice of schools and the subsequent move away from Wester. "Seem just like you was taking things in stride as they come."

"Pour another dipperful of water in this one," Sara said of the hog gut she gripped firmly in her hand lest it fall in the hole full of fresh swine feces and undigested contents from the boars' and gilts' mauls.

"What's that, Brandi?" the little one who had hollered just a few moments ago asked his sister.

"What?"

"That!" the little one pointed toward his mother and Sylvia. "That long thing Mama holding in her hand."

"Oh, they just cleaning chitlins," the big sister said to Li'l Benji, who acknowledged her response with an "oh" of comprehension. Brandi smiled in amazement at the little chatterbox before turning her attention back to the day's activity. The women had taken a tub over to a hole freshly dug by one of the helpers. Sara cut a piece of the large intestines and held it with her left hand over the pit while she used the other to push its smelly contents downward until they rested in the freshly dug pit. Then she held one end fast while Sylvia poured dippers full of water into the opposite opening. The younger of the two sisters jockeyed the water in the gut from side to side to clean it of the residue from its owner's last meals—meals that had become more nourishing as the men fattened them for slaughter.

Uncle Jack always argued that the flavor of pork differed when the mash given the pigs was more nutritious than the customary fare of slops from the table . . . "Wonders what some good grain do to that meat," he'd say every year.

Sara almost dropped the intestine; she fumblingly held on to it. Arduous demands of the early hours' work were evident. "You tired? You pour, I'll flush 'em," Sylvia suggested.

"That's all right. My hands are trying to cramp a little bit. Each one of them hogs must have had a least five miles of intestines," Sara said, stopping briefly to let her hands relax and to step back from the stench of hog manure and attempt to inhale the wonderful aroma emanating from the other end of the yard where Cat was skinning and cutting skins which were tossed in a wash pot of lard heated expressively for that purpose.

"Lawd, them cracklings sure smell good!" the woman exclaimed.

"Shore do," Sylvia agreed, "but I can't eat a one. Them things give me heartburn like nothing you ain't never seen. You can keep my part of them."

"Naw, sister, you gotta take some of them cracklings away from here. I ain't gonna eat all that grease myself," Sara said, indicating a preference for fruits and vegetables rather than a fare of pork products. "You can have all the chitlins, bacon, cracklings, pork chops, ham steaks you want. I can't eat all that mess. Seems like it runs my pressure up ever since I had that last baby."

"I ain't got no children to eat all that stuff up, and Jack love it, but he don't need it. Old Dr. Watson say he got pressure problems too and that that pork gonna kill him he don't stop eating it every meal. That man of mine could sit down and eat that whole pot of cracklings by his self if you give him a bottle of Tabasco sauce."

BRENDA SMITH

Sara moaned audibly, wrung her hands.

The older woman looked at her.

"Go over yonder, put some warm water on your hands. Make it hot as you can stand it. Maybe that will help," Sylvia suggested. "Funny, but the older I get the more problems I seem to have with my hands. Some mornings I wake up and the feel like they plumb dead. When I put my bath water in the face bowl and stick them in it they wake up."

"I'll be all right," the younger sister spoke shortly, taking a moment to flex her fingers.

"That's better?" Sylvia inquired of her.

"Uh-huh."

When Sara's hands and fingers ceased to cramp and she was back at work in the chitlins, she placed the intestines in a tub of corn shucks and lightly salted water. The most loquacious of the quintet inquired of Brandi, "Why Mama put them corn shucks in there with them?"

A simple "oh" followed her explanation that the roughness from the shucks helped to free the guts of the smallest bits of waste.

Amazingly, by noon that day the butchered meat had been quartered, sectioned, sliced, diced, salted down, seasoned, and either hung in Cat's smokehouse out back or was packaged in butcher's paper, taped and tied, then placed in the deep freezer. Sara and Sylvia had made biscuits for all, buttered some with Sylvia's churned butter, and the sisters had salted, floured, and pan fried some of the thinly sliced meat—bacon, ham, liver—and family, helpers, and friends had rinsed their bloodied hands and eaten the food from tin plates handed out the back door. Jack had gotten some of his syrup from the back of his truck to share with all.

As soon as everyone had had his fill, fires were doused, bloody water was hauled out to the middle of the field and emptied, holes with waste were filled with rich black dirt and packed and booted with feet, holders were dismantled, and tin tubs, pots, and butchers knives were scrubbed, scoured, sterilized, and hanged on hooks in the shed by the side of the tobacco barn to await next winter's hogs killing.

When Hawk, Tatter, Melvin, Russell, Judson, Coota, and the others who had lent a hand were ready to leave, Sara called them into the kitchen where she gave each of them a tin full of goodies, including a bit of bacon, small bottles of syrup, a slice or two of fresh liver, some fruitcake, and nuts and peppermints. "Give this to your mama for me. It isn't much. I just want to share a little of our Christmas with you all." And to each, Cat gave a fifty-cent piece and a hearty thanks and "Merry Christmas!"

"Don't forget to come back over here tomorrow," Uncle Jack said to the boy he'd taken for an apprentice, his voice quivering with excitement, "I'm going bring you a piece of that cheese."

Uncle Jack and Aunt Sylvia had been dutifully the first to come, and they were the last to leave.

Sara asked the woman, who stood by the passenger's side of the truck, "Sister, you feel like making that cheese this evening?"

"Gon' do it soon as I get to the house," Sara spoke decisively.

"Maybe I'll come down there and help you when the young'uns taking a nap this afternoon," Sara offered, thinking she had no other recourse. After all, this was her meat. Brandi was home, so she could babysit.

"No," Jack and Sylvia formed an alliance against the Browns. "Stay on home and enjoy Brandi some, she ain't come home for but a fortnight," they insisted forcefully.

The Browns relented. As soon as they said their good-byes, they turned to go into the house. Uncle Jack put on the brakes of his rolling pickup truck, and Cat, Sara, Brandi, and the rest of the family pivoted on their heels, each to discern what their relatives could have forgotten.

"Gal," the man called out to Brandi when he had stuck his head out of the window, "you ain't get nary one of them white boys while you was up yonder. Be talking with you about that when I get back tomorrow." Then he laughed his customary hearty howl, and she, Brandi, winced, unnerved by a mention of the unspeakable.

Everybody else chuckled and returned the man's farewell wave.

Suddenly, Claxville was no longer as distant as Christmas holidays had made it appear to be. Her uncle's meddlesome manner annoyed Brandi so much that she wanted to flee from her surroundings.

Nobody else seemed bothered. Cat merely picked up his youngest boy and trudged off toward the house, the other children trotting after him. Sara put her arm around Brandi's shoulder, taking her to the house also.

Nevertheless, Christmas day was extra special; she gave much and received much. The youngsters enjoyed the festive reds, greens, silvers, and golds of the colored wrapping paper, ribbons, bows, and ornaments as much as they did the presents their sister had gotten for them. The whole family was excited about the black-and-white RCA television that Santa Claus bought. All twisted knobs, switched channels, elevated the volume, adjusted the contrast, making the hazy picture hazier. "How come it ain't got but one picture?" one asked.

"I got to put the antenna up back of the house. Santa didn't have time to do it," Saint Nick's eldest helper said.

"Take your hands off it now!" The mother encouraged the little ones to play with their new toys. "What'd Brandi get you? Santa bought that one! Santa shore is good," Sara repeated five times.

"Can we put it up now?" another asked the father, whose pant legs she now tugged.

"It's cold outside—let it warm up a bit." The man blew warm breath at his huge hands, emphasizing the current state of affairs outside the house's confines.

"What's in this box?" Brandi inquired about the remaining present tucked at the base of the tree.

"Let's see what else Santa done left," Cat suggested, grinning like a Cheshire cat. "Hand it to your mama." Sara too looked puzzled. She'd not seen this present, was unaware that her husband had a surprise for all of them. The woman tore at the wrapping paper and opened the box to reveal its contents. When she pulled the black toy desktop telephone from the box, Cat started to laugh at her obvious puzzlement. "Real thing be here in about a month, they say." Mother and daughter alike jumped up and down squealing with delight, hugging each other. The eldest three Browns were all laughing, the little ones rested confounded.

"Waited till I left home to get one—didn't want me talking on the telephone all the time," Brandi joked with her father when she and Sara were through with their jubilant dancing. "Your mama needed one so she can keep up with you. Maybe then she will stop worrying about you so much," Carruthers replied.

Sara laughed and threw a ball of the crumpled wrapping paper at her mate. He ducked.

CHAPTER THIRTEEN

After Christmas

Dirk was glad to see Brandi upon her return on the second day of January. The last two weeks had been nightmarish. When he wasn't busy, he'd wondered silently when and if she would return. There was something they needed to talk about; they had to talk.

"Morning, Brandi," he called, "glad you're back."

"Good to be back."

"Business slow—everybody ain't back yet," he said to Brandi who quickened her steps to assume her customary duties.

So the silent presence left by the preholiday occurrence pervaded throughout the remainder of the coed's first full semester and the beginning of the second at Claxville University. When the break came—it was time for Lincoln's and Washington's birthdays—she told Dirk she planned to stay . . . to wait until later to go home and get her spring clothes. The cold had forced her to make her suitcases replete with more warm things when she had been home for the holidays.

"Maybe we can get together sometime," the man suggested nervously when he had claimed her full attention.

"Okay," Brandi relented . . . wanting to take care of, consummate, forget about the infamous mishap that had reshaped their lives forevermore.

By the third day of the break, the campus had emptied, and few customers were coming into the Burga Barn; all machinery had been broken down, serviced, oiled, greased, polished, and put together again. The exterminator had sprayed for bugs; and the floors had been freed of residue left by the exterminator, mopped, stripped, waxed—two coats had been put on.

The odor of the chemicals for killing roaches, ants, chinches, flies, and all sorts of bugs still lingered thickly in the air; so Dirk and Chuck opened all the windows and doors to let Claxville's unusually warm air chase the fumes away. They discussed closure for the remainder of the day as an alternative, but Chuck made an offer Dirk could not refuse. "You need a break, man," he argued. "You spent the whole Christmas here, had to take up the slack while everybody else took a break. Won't be much traffic coming through here for the next couple of days, and you know it. Why don't you go home? Do some of the things you want to do. I can handle it."

Dirk decided to take his friend up on it, and when he was near Brandi he asked, "Do you want to go to my place, talk, watch a little TV? Chuck's going to stay and keep the place open." The man had anticipated her question, but none came. He removed his apron, and she silently undid her own, got her purse from her locker, and stepped quickly through the door he held for her.

When they were around the back of the restaurant, Dirk pointed at his motorcycle. "Ever rode one of these?"

She shook her head.

"There's nothing to it!" He hopped on, told her to seat herself behind him—she was glad she had worn pants to work. When she was on the motorcycle, Dirk urged her to move forward and wrap her arms around his waist. "Hold on to me," he instructed, "and lean when I lean—riding this old Harley is the easiest thing I ever done."

"I don't know about this," Brandi spoke haltingly and quietly with worry when the man was cranking the vehicle. She was scared.

He hollered confidently above the noise of the engine, "It'll be all right, ain't nothing to it. It'll be a breeze."

And a breeze it was not!

By the time Dirk and Brandi got to Hallmark Trailer Park, the man was more than winded . . . he had ridden for two. Brandi had not leaned with him; she'd sat stiffened with fear as they rode through Claxville, to the outskirts, and up the narrow lane to the vast trailer park replete with singles and double-wides: some new, other visibly quite aged, some with shiny veneer, others with green slime snaking its way down the exteriors.

As soon as they were in the tidy two-bedroom trailer, he offered her a beer from the refrigerator and told her to sit. The woman took a seat on the couch.

She shook her head, refusing the alcoholic beverage . . . the girl did not drink.

"How about a Coke?" he asked. Probing further in the refrigerator, he found and offered wine or juice instead of the Coke.

"A Coke's okay, I'll take that," was her reply.

"Ice?"

"No, it okay like it is."

Dirk poured a glass of the soda and handed it to her, put a record on the record player, adjusted the volume, and sat on the couch beside Brandi.

Years later Brandi would not be able to remember much about that late January evening . . . nothing, nothing that is except Taxi's outrage when he had picked her up from the trailer park.

Anyway, after several beers, Dirk had invited her to watch television in the bedroom, where they kissed repeatedly and disrobed themselves, letting the Burga Barn's classic black and whites lay on the trailer's carpeted floor; but their attempt at lovemaking had been thwarted by stolid awkwardness—his and hers, tradition, hers, his, theirs, and Carruthers's forewarning her about being a white man's concubine as well as the jests made by her aging uncle. Momentarily, she was sweating like a hog, and so was he . . . the slippery affair ended with first a cold shower and a few words from the man. "I'm going to ride the bike back. I'll send somebody to pick you up," he said. "Is that all right?" he queried her. "Are you afraid to stay out here by yourself?"

"No, I'm not afraid. I'll be all right."

The man left.

Brandi sighed with relief. She was so glad she didn't have to ride that damn thing back; she'd just as soon walk the five, ten, or however many miles it was back to town in bare feet before she'd ever get on the back of that motorcycle or any other motorcycle again. When the trailer's occupant was gone, she finished dressing, fussing with her hair because it had gotten damp; he had no hair dryer . . . didn't have need of one. Then she got another glass of Coke from the refrigerator, looked around the trailer once more, peeked out the windows of each small room, remade Dirk's rumpled bed, replaced her cosmetics in their proper place in her purse, and sat listening thoughtlessly for the ride, humming.

Back in town, Dirk rode up to the bus station to secure a ride for her. "Got a friend out at my house, need a ride back to town—got time to pick her up for me?" he asked the familiar colored man standing next to the old battered jalopy of a cab, polishing it aimlessly while awaiting such a fare.

"You at the same place?" the man asked Dirk. He had picked up the man's steady and transported her to the Burga Barn on several other occasions.

"Yeah, number 24 Hallmark Trailer Park," he said, impressed that the cabby remembered him. He handed the man a five-dollar bill, and then he rode off.

Taxi stuck the five spot in his jacket and immediately headed west of Claxville across Little River to pick up the girl.

He whistled gaily with the radio as he sped on . . . it was getting dark; dusk was setting in.

The cabdriver whipped his vehicle into the trailer's yard, raising dust and bits of cracked asphalt, and came to a screeching halt before merrily tooting his horn. When Brandi heard the jolly tune, she jumped up from the couch, cut the record player off, locked the door from the inside, stepped backward out of the access, and closed it, turning the door knob to see if the door had locked. It had not shut properly, so she reopened it, turned the lock again, and pulled the door shut one more; this time she slammed it.

She turned, was ready to step, to hit the ground.

Brandi recognized the car, saw the man, was startled by his very presence; she wanted to go back into the trailer. She turned around, grabbed the door knob, and twisted it. It was locked. "Shit!" she emitted at the door refusing to give way to her anxious thrust.

The taxi driver looked up, drawn to attention by the movement on the trailer's steps. Their eyes met.

Hitherto imperturbable, the man suddenly showed signs of alarm. First there was disbelief, then anger replaced disbelief.

He went off. "Damn, damn, goddamn it!" Taxi banged on the steering wheel; he jerked at it, almost wrenching it from its resting place on the vehicle's column when he recognized the woman. He jumped out of his car, running toward the girl already gripped with fear for a third time in a single day, yelling, screaming "*nooo*" at the top of his lungs.

Someone from the trailer directly across the street stuck his head out the door, witnessed nothing alarming, and then went back inside.

"What are you doing here? Bitch!" he screamed at the girl rendered immobile by the unexpected, unanticipated stream of obscenities. "What are you doing here?" the man wailed mournfully. "What in the hell you doing here?" he questioned Brandi who just stood on ground watching the man flailing his arms in the air, waiting for him to take off, soar away. She couldn't move, was frozen; her nervous system had shut down, had failed. The young woman was as stiff as a century-old corpse.

The driver grabbed her by the arm, almost dragged her to the car where he opened the rear door nearest the trailer, and pushed her in the seat before he shut the door and took his own seat behind the wheel. And then the car was loose; the man drove down the street like a bat out of hell, leaping over speed breakers strategically placed to slow speedsters down, careening and swerving to avoid a head-on collision with an oncoming vehicle. The driver of the other vehicle blew at him. Taxi failed to respond . . . kept driving recklessly with no regard for his life or for hers, or for anyone else for that matter.

"You crazy bitch, you crazy," he shrieked tearfully. "I can't believe a fine lady like you gon' let that white boy make a whore out of you!" The irate man choked back sobs of disgust. His words struck the woman like bullets, puncturing her skin, her flesh, searing her flesh, making her double over in pain.

Taxi ran his rickety cab through Claxville's crowded streets like a rodeo steer, zipping through one perilously yellow light after another.

A piteous Brandi sat still in a corner of the backseat, her arms folded, tense, feeling fear at his anger; her eyes closed, she rode the bumps, grunting and groaning periodically—she had so many problems . . . If she had only listened to her daddy, she thought, "I wouldn't be in this mess." She hugged herself tighter still to stop the shivers she could feel spiraling up from her tailbone.

When they were at the dorm, the vehicle lurched toward a vacant spot, the maneuver as frightening as take off from Dirk's trailer; she thought the driver might hit the curb, jump this barrier, and run into the building. Brandi relinquished her seat as it was making a rolling stop. The obviously wounded man, who still saw red, went berserk again; he jumped out of the car, in front of her, accosting her verbally as she attempted to flee up the walkway to the safety of Davis Hall.

"Bitch," he yelled at the top of his lungs, "you need a man, get yourself a real man!" before he got back behind the wheel. He banged on the steering wheel anew as he drove away from the campus. "Gonna kill that bastard. I'm gonna kill his ass, ain't gon' let him make a whore out of her," he whimpered repeatedly. Taxi sobbed—the man was visibly shaken.

Passersby paused but a moment, recognizing no real danger, thinking this a mere lover's spat, a typical occurrence in the life of college students.

The young woman flew up the walkway into the dorm, taking the steps two at a time, her stride lengthened by despair, fright, trepidation, and uncertainty. And shame . . . she was so embarrassed! She couldn't believe how the grown man had behaved.

There was nothing between them . . . they were not lovers, not even friends, had just had a couple of chance meetings. He had driven her from the bus station to the dorm the first day she had arrived in Claxville, she had approached him to give him a piece of her mind the day she met Mary

Margaret, he had picked her up the day she did Christmas shopping, and she had given him the gift that she had bought for Dirk; and of course, he had taken her from the dorm to the bus station when she was ready to go to Wester at Christmastime. While there were other taxis, he had also been the one to pick her up and take her back to the dorm when she returned after the holidays—this last time, he had not taken the scenic route, had taken her directly to her destination.

"Still," she thought as she fled to the sanctuary of room 306, "he had no right to speak to me that way." Her daddy didn't talk to her that way, and her mother didn't either!

Brandi rushed into her room and fell on her bed, sat up, reached down to its foot, got the quilt Aunt Sylvia had made, and wrapped herself in it for security. She couldn't believe what had just transpired. The girl, overwhelmed with guilt, wished she'd not lied to her mother about not having a break at the beginning of the second semester during the presidents' birthday celebrations. She did not even know why she'd lied, but she had. Sara had always said a lie would catch up with you, and she felt that her sin had certainly found her out. If she had taken herself home, she wouldn't have been in this awful fix. Brandi blamed the beguiling influence of a lying tongue for the near loss of her virginity, for the tongue-lashing that she'd taken from the colored man who had been dispatched by the younger white man to pick her up, for the "willies" that she was currently experiencing.

Now her head ached, her stomach churned, her inner thighs and her private parts felt a bit tender from the unsuccessful tryst with Dirk. "What's the matter with me?" she moaned and cried herself to sleep.

Kris knew instantly that her roommate had not had a good evening when she had come in because the young woman lay in a heap on her covers, fully clad, glasses still on, and she whimpered like a wounded animal all through the night—and she muffled cries . . . little by little the cries faded to mere whimpers, and finally a fitful sleep. The veterinary major grew concerned, wondered if she should call the resident assistant or somebody. Something was terribly wrong with Brandi. Kris sat in the center of her bed and kept watch all night long, was vigilant. At one point she went bedside to touch the obviously wounded roommate, determined there was no fever before resuming her watch.

Brandi opened her eyes. Kris was staring at her. She rolled over on her back to escape her roommate's visual scrutiny. Through the pain in her head, in her eyes she saw visions of the day before. Dirk's sweaty body covered hers;

he thrust and pushed at her private parts which refused to allow entry. He left full of disappointment, and then there was Taxi screaming and screeching obscenities at her, calling her names which she had never been called before, challenging her choice for a lover. The young woman shut her eyes to close off the memories, opened them and shut them again.

"Are those girls still bothering you?" Kris asked when Brandi was wide awake the next morning.

"I almost went downstairs to get Ms. Winthrop or the RA," Kris shared her concerns with Brandi.

"Naw, uh-uh," the woman replied to both the question and the ensuing statement.

Wearily she closed her eyes again, wanting to shut out Kris's prodding voice. Talking meant thinking, and thinking meant feeling. Brandi preferred the numbness that had taken hold of her in the backseat of the cab the day before.

"Do you want to talk about it? Want to tell me what happened?" Kris persisted.

"Not now," Brandi insisted, "I got to get dressed."

The woman sat up on the side of the bed for a few moments, slid her feet in the slippers on the floor, dragged her heavy-laden, burdened down body over to the dresser, and stared at her image in the mirror. She took her glasses off, leaned forward, squinted at her reflection and was not pleased at what she saw—the mirror painted a picture of a very disheveled young lady, her eyes bloodshot, her hair a mess, and when she looked down, the young lady noted that her clothing were rumpled. She leaned further into the mirror, stretched her eyes, and looked at her swollen, puffy, red-streaked body parts with displeasure.

"I'm a mess," she muttered to herself. Not only did she look awful, she felt awful. Her head throbbed. She touched the member, moaning quietly.

Kris watched intently, still sitting in the same spot she'd been in most of the night.

Brandi felt her gaze and wished silently that Kris had gone home for the break. They had spoken about it earlier, and Kris had said that Washington State was too far to go home for just a few days, that she would just as soon spend her time making some extra hours at the clinic on campus. She really had a great deal of compassion for the animals, as much as she demonstrated to humankind. Why wouldn't she just go there now?

It was obvious to Brandi that Kris would not give up, but she wasn't ready to talk yet.

She regained her composure in front of the mirror, put her hand on her head, dug into her scalp, felt knots. "Gosh, my hair is a mess," the young woman thought as she ran her fingers through the nappy mass, stretching several strands their full length and sniffing at their ends. "Stinks," she said, turning up her nose at the Afro-ends which were both musty and moldy, smelling of moisturizer, detangler, of buckets of sweat that had poured from Dirk and from herself, of nervous sweat invoked by Taxi's onslaught.

Brandi shook her head vigorously, wanting it to wipe away the near loss of virginity that had taken place the evening before. "I'm going to be late for work, but I can't go out looking like this, and I got to wash my hair too," she told Kris as she prepared for showering.

"Be here when you get back," Kris called after her.

Brandi stuck her head back in the door to say, "No need for that," but her friend insisted that she would not leave until she was sure the woman was fine.

"Go on, go see about your animals," Brandi begged her, feigning a smile of assurance. "I mean it. Go see about your babies. I'm fine. I'll tell you all about it later."

"Do you promise?" Kris queried her playfully with caution.

"Promise!" was the reply.

"How about a scout's honor?" Kris teased.

With "I'm serious now. Go on, Kris," Brandi renewed her efforts at good grooming, personal hygiene, and restored mental suppleness.

When she was in the shower, she scrubbed herself in scalding water until the bronze of her skin was almost beet red, until she was sore . . . almost raw. Then she rinsed with the cool to temper the fever she'd almost evoked. It was only when she felt cleansed from the inside and out that she gave up the stall.

Only guilt remained with her.

Reluctantly she went toward her room, knowing Kris sat awaiting her. But Kris was gone again, and boy, was Brandi glad; she hadn't felt so rotten since she had sneaked out back of the schoolhouse with Russell Thomas at the Halloween carnival when she was in the eighth grade, only to rush from his adolescent arms back into the building after Lurch, the science student teacher, had walked up on them. The girl had rushed back inside the dance, wiping unrouged, youthful, inexperienced lips, pressing wrinkles from navy blue skirt rumpled by her thirteen-year-old boyfriend's exploring boyish fingers before patting with open palms hair disheveled in this, her first pubescent moment of passion.

Brandi found herself a half decade later in front of the mirror mimicking those same movements. She rubbed her hand on the blue terry cloth towel encasing her body as if to free it of wrinkles, she patted her wet hair, pulling the strands to her nose to catch a whiff of the shampoo's refreshing aroma.

Brandi took her hair dryer from the locker over her desk, placed it on the bed, untangled the mess on her head with a wide tooth Afro comb, put some Bergamot hair grease on it, twisted it into some thick braids before putting the dryer's plastic cap on her head. She slipped a pair of underwear under the towel she still wore. Then she lay on the bed to let her hair dry. Soon, the drone from the hair dryer had put her to sleep.

And while she slept again, something was terribly wrong. Taxi was running toward her; he was screaming, yelling for her to stop, wait, and cease, not to do something. Brandi was so confused.

She rolled over, moaned, and rolled over on the coiled clear-plastic tube full of metal spirals that sent warm air to the cap under which lay her now dried hair—it had almost dried to a crisp. She was going to have to put some moisturizer on it fairly quickly. Her roommate came in; Kris had returned for lunch. She immediately went to Brandi's bedside and shook her. Brandi sprung up. "Gosh, you still tired. It is past lunchtime!" the young woman exclaimed, pointing to her wristwatch.

"Sorry, I was gone when you got back," she told Brandi, who rolled over squinting at the timepiece's tiny gold hands, jumped up, turned the dryer off, and reached for the left side of her back to the base of her shoulder blade which stung profusely. She moaned aloud. "Kris, have a look at my back for me," she said, realizing that her right hand could not reach the source of her pain.

Her roommate came back over to her side of the room and pulled her shoulder toward herself. "Shit, girl, you done burnt yourself!" Kris exclaimed, backing her to the mirror for a glance. "Look at it," she said.

The coed leapt from the bed in shock. With back toward the mirror, she peered harder to determine the burn's degree, herself ignorant of first, second, or third degrees. All she knew at the moment was it was stinging something awful.

"Here, use this," Kris said, handing her a long-handled hand mirror from her desk's top. Brandi used both mirrors to determine the extent of the injury and had her roommate put some ointment from the first-aid kit her mother had made when she was getting ready to come to Claxville. "Put some on it," she insisted, jumping when Kris's touch was threatening.

BRENDA SMITH

"Hold still!" Kris argued. "I'm not going to hurt you no more than you have already hurt yourself."

"You might need to go to the infirmary," the roommate added.

"No, I'm going to try this first."

"All right, hard-head, get an infection and you'll be in a mess!"

"Thanks," Brandi said as she searched a drawer for a brassiere.

"Don't know whether you going to be able to wear that," Chris said when Brandi was encircling her chest with the garment.

"Ain't got no choice," she said wincing with pain from her external wound this time.

"Yes, you do," Kris argued. "You can get by without one. I can't . . . I'd be flipping and flopping all over myself," she spoke of her overabundant breasts.

"Wish I had them, I wouldn't complain," Brandi argued. "Think I should put a Band-Aid on it?

"No, burns need air," Kris insisted.

In spite of the discomfort, which was minor in comparison to the inner turmoil she now faced, Brandi got back to her coiffure.

While Brandi straightened and curled her hair with the hot combs warmed on a hot plate on the desk, Kris sat on her friend's bed watching intently. "Wish I could do that to my hair. It's so curly," she said.

"You can."

"Think I can . . . you really think I can?" the woman questioned Brandi once more.

"Don't see any reason why not. Hair is hair. I'll do yours when I've finished mine," she spoke assuredly with youthful confidence.

Wandering over to Brandi's side of the room, where she picked up the jar of blue bergamot, Kris stuck her middle finger in and rubbed its content between her finger and thumb. "Yuck, that's greasy!" she exclaimed, wrinkling her face with utter disgust. "Do I have to use that?" she asked before she wiped the oil on her crusty, soiled jeans.

"Uh-uh." Brandi shook her head in the negative and answered, "Don't think so. Just leave it to me." She took the jar of grease from its new resting place, put it back in its place to accommodate her needs, and continued to press her hair. A new hairdo always made her feel better . . . she was counting on a change from the Afro to a straighter look to help her improve mentally and physically.

Soon, Brandi had straightened and buffed her hair with the hot comb instead of using the curling irons, rolled it with rollers which would be used nightly now that she was changing her hairstyle; then she tied it up with a head rag.

"Am I going to have to roll it?"

"No, don't think so. If so, I got some extra ones," she responded to Kris's inquiry.

Soon, Brandi was finished with her hair. "Sit down here while I get my house coat," she said to Kris as she pulled the chair from the desk and placed it in a strategic location for hairdressing.

Kris sat in the chair while Brandi got a robe from the closet.

"Ouch," she emitted when the cloth touched the burned spot on her back.

"You okay? Don't hurt too much to do this?" Kris asked.

"I'm fine," Brandi assured her as she draped a clean towel over her friend's shoulder, pulled the red waist-length locks from their trappings, penned the towel around the girl's neck, and started to brush at the long hair.

"I didn't need to wash it first, did I?" Kris asked.

"When was the last time you washed it?"

"I think it was yesterday."

"You think?"

"Yeah, it was yesterday. I had to get out of here and get back to the clinic this morning while you were in the shower."

"Girl, you know you love those animals . . . and that job! I don't like anything that keeps me from taking a shower every day," Brandi added, wrinkling her nose with disapproval.

Almost immediately she realized that she was in over her head, was sunk to the ear in a quagmire of tedium . . . Kris's hair was long—it fell over the back of the chair, its tips almost reaching the seat; her tresses were thick and weighty—she had about ten times as much hair as Brandi had on her head, and the mess was curly to boot. It was going to take a week to straighten this mass of hair, but Brandi wasn't a quitter, was always walking around pumping herself up with "A quitter never wins, and a winner never quits."

Second, Kris was too tall. Brandi could barely see the top of her head, and she was on tiptoe. "We have to make a little adjustment," she told Kris. "Get up, I'm going to sit in the chair. You sit on the floor."

"What?" was the woman's query.

"You're too tall. I can't reach the top of your head. Get a towel, sit on it . . . just do what I tell you! I know what I'm doing," she responded to Kris's look of puzzlement.

Third and most importantly, Brandi had never lay hands on any white person's hair, except for Dirk's. She shook her head in protest to chase away thoughts of the day before.

"Anyway, hair was hair was hair," Brandi said to herself.

Kris grabbed a towel from the foot of her bed, spread it out, and seated herself between the young woman's knees.

Brandi parted the mass of hair in quarters and set about straightening Kris's hair. The very first combing with the hot iron partially straightened the first bunch of elongated strands, but the ends remained curly because the comb cooled before it could get all the way from roots to ends. Brandi longed for another straightening comb, maybe two . . . it was going to take forever and a day to straighten all this hair.

"Let me see," Kris whined childlike after some time had passed, so Brandi let her up . . . let her have a peek.

"Satisfied?"

"Neat!" Kris squealed with delight, "this going to take long?"

"I don't know, sit down."

By suppertime the girls were tiring of all except the company and the conversation that had ensued. This was one of the few times that they had actually had a lengthy conversation, talked real girl talk. Brandi talked and her roommate listened.

"So that's what all the fuss was about last night," Kris said to Brandi when she had told her about Dirk and about Taxi's response. "It sounds like this Taxi fellow's a bit jealous."

"He can't be."

"Why?"

"There's nothing for him to be jealous about. He's just somebody I know."

"Would you consider him to be a friend?"

"Not really."

"Well, what would you call him?"

"I don't know," Brandi replied listlessly. She was growing weary, was thirsty—almost to the point of dehydration—and was becoming increasingly famished. She had not had a bite since breakfast the day before the present time.

"That's dumb. He's more than an acquaintance, at least it seems that way to me."

"I really don't know," she repeated.

"Is he your type?"

"He's a bit older than I am."

"How much older is he?"

"I'm not sure."

"Why didn't you ever ask him?"

"We haven't really ever had what you call a real conversation, you know, just talked like we are doing right now."

"Do you want to?"

"I've never really thought about it."

"Well, what will you do next time you see him?"

Brandi sighed. "Kris, I honestly don't know. Maybe best thing I can do is stay away from him."

"What are you going to do about Dirk?" Kris probed further.

Brandi's almost inaudible response was "Don't believe I'm going to have to do anything about that."

"Huh?"

"I think that's done took care of itself," her volume increased with her pulse.

"Well you got to go back to work."

Kris jumped up from the toweled linoleum, flapping her arms up and down as if to take flight. "Holy shit!"

"Shit what! Did I burn you? Couldn't have, I wasn't nowhere near your scalp," Brandi responded, "or your ears."

"Work! Shit, I damn near forgot I gotta go to work! Critters have to be fed and watered!" Kris exclaimed.

Brandi cried out, "But I'm only half done."

Kris cursed anew, berated herself for losing track of time. "What are we going to do?" she wailed.

"I know. I'll pin it up, and we can finish when you get back," Brandi said as she turned to get a rubber band from her desk drawer; but the iron, the one she used to starch press her clothing, caught her eye. "I know what we can do. Sit tight," she said hurriedly plugging the iron up, placing a pillowcase on the desk's top.

"What are you going to do?" Kris asked in puzzlement. "What you plugging that iron up for?"

"Just lean over, I'm gon' iron the other side," Brandi argued.

"What?" Kris laughed at her. "Brandi, you're crazy as hell if you think I'm going let you put that thing on my hair." She pointed at the iron and started to laugh. Tears were rolling down her cheeks—she was obviously getting punchy; there had been so much thoughtful conversation, and she had asked her friend to straighten her hair. Now the girl wanted to apply the electric iron to it!

"It's the same thing! Heat just comes from the iron," Brandi said seriously and encouragingly. "Heat is heat, it don't matter where you get it from. Anyway, there are electric straightening combs too."

Kris thought about this a minute. "You ain't shitting me now, are you?" she asked her roommate.

"No, seriously," Brandi assured her. "My mama bought one, but we don't use it much. She just liked the one you put on the stove better. She's just old-fashioned."

"You better come on now," she prodded Kris, "get on your knees over here by the desk," she said, as she moved the chair to the other side of the small room. "And hold your head over."

"Are you sure?" Kris asked; the other girl did not respond—she was hoping the temperature was right.

Kris kneeled reluctantly and leaned over. And Brandi draped the curly locks on the countertop and pressed the other side of her hair with the iron.

"See," she said after a few minutes when they had finished, "that didn't take but a minute . . . dunno why we didn't think of it earlier."

The roommate briefly looked in the mirror and admired her newly straightened hairdo before putting it up, lest it fly in her face while she labored, and hurried to work at the vet's.

Brandi's failure to show up at work did not go unnoticed, but no word came from anyone. The girl didn't go to class that day either, and soon the telephone rang, nearly scaring her socks off. "What if it's Dirk?" she thought. "I don't want to talk to him," she said aloud before she resigned to answer the instrument's incessant wailing chime.

"Brandi, this is Dr. McIntyre," the woman spoke with her usual syrupy, soothing tone. "I heard you didn't show up for class, and I thought I would give you a ring. Are you all right?"

"Oh yes, ma'am. I just got a little cold, am a bit congested, and my throat hurts—that's all." Brandi sighed with relief and feigned a sniffle and a cough or two. Her throat was parched and her voice raspy; she had not gotten anything to drink yet, so she didn't feel so bad about the deception.

"I'll have Kay drop by and bring you a little something," the woman said.

And she did. The professor's secretary delivered soup du jour, a club sandwich, and a Coke from Stu's, which proved to be quite palatable. She polished it off in no time at all.

Brandi ate, free of guilt, enjoying the attention that she had received before retiring for the evening.

Dirk was already at the restaurant when Brandi got there the next morning. She was a little late; it did not impose any unnecessary stress on her—the business had regained its place in her affections. He worked, she worked, and they worked together . . . things were back to normal . . . the manager-employee relationship having survived a mere fantasy.

"I've been thinking about my hours," she said to Dirk later that same day. "I won't ever finish school if I don't buckle down and study a little bit more. Carmen, my tutor, has been on my case about it real bad lately . . . and I've been thinking she might be right."

"I understand," was his solitary comment. The man spoke these words with relief. He liked her a lot and truly valued the work that she did at the establishment. Dirk did not want to lose her.

And the remainder of the first semester was quite uneventful . . . Brandi had stayed, and Dr. McIntyre did deliver. She passed all her classes.

CHAPTER FOURTEEN

Cross-Cultural Comparisons Class

Brandi did stay in Monsieur Henri's class, and Dr. McIntyre did deliver. The young woman passed all her classes the first semester. Her apparition in CCC100-Cross-Cultural Comparisons, her second major class, received a cordial reception; and because the grades were good, the novice began with renewed, revitalized, and escalated hopes for a successful completion of her degree at the school. Actually, she was excited, felt vindicated, almost jubilant, was restored, so she was ready for her new courses! This one had a special place in her affections—Dr. McIntyre was the instructor. Dubblerville, Elnora, and several other students from previous classes were also taking this class.

And *As* were indeed on the grades mailed to Mr. and Mrs. Carruthers Brown, parents of Brandi Leigh Brown, Rural Route 2, Box 66 in the Wester. Brandi had passed English, Foreign Language, and Physical Fitness with flying colors. Sara, yet ignorant of what it had taken for Brandi to receive the perfect scores, had jumped up and down when the mailman had delivered the letter from the records' office, and Cat had given the mail just as much enthusiasm as did his mate.

The next time the girl's mother went to town, she carried her daughter's grades for Mr. Z to see before posting the exhibit showing "passage" on the refrigerator door for family, friends, church folks, the insurance man, and whoever would take a minute to hear of the girl's successes.

Carmen had also called to congratulate Brandi on her success, offering, "If you need me, call me."

Brandi thanked the woman again for her assistance—she'd been the first person she had called when grades were finally posted beside each office door.

"Did you go by Henri's office?" Carmen asked.

"No way. Dr. McIntyre told me what I got. Final exam day was the last time I ever saw him. I was afraid to go there. You know he always gave me the creeps."

"Me too," Carmen finally admitted to Brandi that the ominous figure that Mr. Henri was intimidated her as well but that she had feigned acceptance just to help assuage the fears of her mentee.

Brandi told her she was glad she faked it for her. "If I had known you were as afraid of the creep as I was, I wouldn't have kept going to that dumb class. All I got to say is if I never see him again, it won't be a moment too soon."

Nevertheless, the young woman did not have much time to rest on her laurels before more insane circumstances transpired.

Shortly after Valentine's Day, Dr. McIntyre started making group assignments—giving research topics and the like—and after considering several alternatives to establishing the groups, she'd simply gone by rows. "Row one will group together for the next several assignments," she said, jotting names in her roll book as she proceeded through the aisles. Ironically Brandi was grouped with four girls, all of whom had been in Mr. Henri's class, neither of whom she had had any contact with beyond being the object of the laughter, snickering, and frivolity while the man had made his own attempts at denigrating her.

"Get in your groups," Dr. McIntyre had told them when she had completed the group assignments. "You may turn your seats around, make a circle. I'll give each a topic, and your responsibility is to plan for how you will make your presentations for the entire class. My expectations for each group is to work cooperatively on the paper and plan your presentations together. Everybody needs to take part, so let's make sure everybody is involved." With, "You'll probably want to plan some library time together," the professor left each group to their own devices.

The girls in the group to which Brandi was assigned determined that they could do all of the work, make individual assignments, determine who was responsible for the written report, and select a method for oral presentation when they met at the library on Saturday morning of that same week. "Do you have any questions?" Deidre had asked as the group leadership became established through no particular order.

"Where will we meet?" Brandi asked, to which the leader quickly replied, "Just show up, we'll be there. It'll be hard to miss us," and the others nodded in agreement. All left the class while other groups continued to work together.

Needless to say, their appointment mirrored those of Mr. Henri—that is, Brandi was at the library at eight o'clock when the doors opened. She did not want to miss the group when they came in. The facility was huge; it had many stories and a collection of tens of thousands in the stacks. "One could get lost in it and not be missed until the buzzards were ready to pick their bones," she'd thought, so Brandi perched herself near the front door so she would not miss her group.

Needless to say, seconds turned in to minutes, minutes into hours, and no one showed. The level of despair was heightened by the fact that she did not know how to get in touch with any of the group members, didn't know their full names, wasn't sure that she could recognize them in the milieu on campus (they all seemed to look alike when they were in a crowd).

Brandi had chuckled when she had thought about everybody looking alike. White people were so indistinct! She was going to speak to Cat about this when they were able to talk about this phenomenon. One of the criticisms that he had of white people was, "They peg us all the same, put everybody in the same category, make like they can't remember a person's name. They claim we all look alike, don't care how dark or light-complexioned you are, you're just the same to them." And here she was having found the same true of them; unless you knew someone personally, they all looked alike. They were just white. She smiled thoughtfully.

After a morning of fruitless waiting, she left Hazzard Library and finally gave up at four and headed back to the dorm feeling dejected, down, depressed, as well as famished.

By Sunday evening she grew increasingly worried, longed again for the assignment, wished that she had written the contents of the assignment down. "At least I could have gotten a start," she thought.

On Monday the professor gave some time for the groups to meet after she had completed her lecture. "I'm sorry I missed you," Brandi said to the other members of the group while dragging her chair, making the effort to complete the circle they had made, to join in, to be a member, to cooperate. No one bothered to shift, to let her fit her chair in. Consequently they made a bulb-shaped group; she stuck out like a pimple and was as good as called out by the group leader who said curtly, "It's pretty hard to find somebody who don't want to be found!" The offender made this statement when Brandi expressed regrets about missing them on Saturday. Others simply snickered at her apology.

Brandi sat stony faced, refusing to acknowledge their folly, attempting to stay focused, merely wanting to secure the assignment sheet. Soon, she detached; she thought, "This lot can go straight to hell!"

The girls played around, giggled, pretended to be on task when Dr. McIntyre approached to check for progress; they chewed gum like it was cud, made bubbles, competed to see who could blow the biggest one and giggled childishly at one who spattered the overextended pinkish gook on her face, and pulled their seats back in order when the instructor announced class's end.

Brandi clearly understood that Dr. McIntyre's grouping system had failed; the other girls had not allowed her to have any input, having put "the ignore" on any comment she attempted, allowing their superior attitudes to be crystal clear. The young woman had no more information that day than she had the first day of the assignment, so she waited until later, went by the professor's office, pretended that she had lost the assignment, and secured a Xeroxed copy of the full assignment from Kay the secretary.

By the first of March the oral presentations began, and Brandi's group showed up, costumed, prepared to present a comedy they had written, choreographed, made props for. Deidre sashayed to the front of the class, presented the cast members, and the act was on, each group member fully participating except Brandi who had not been able to successfully break in to the group—the ceiling, like the floor, was made of glass.

When the girls were completed, Dr. McIntyre asked, "Brandi, do you have a part?"

"Sure do," Brandi said happily, strolling to the front, helping the group to take the set down before returning to her own seat, and passing to the teacher a written report of her own—one accepted by the instructor with no ado.

Once she flipped through the document, her remarks came. "Good job, Brandi," the teacher said, "didn't know you could draw and paint so beautifully. Live and learn," before turning her attention to the full class again. "Let's give this group a hand." Brandi accepted the accolades, the round of applause, with a quick bow.

Deidre and the other girls were flustered, felt upstaged by the Negro woman's obvious creativity and ingenuity. They merely looked from one to another, offering no comments.

Toward the end of the second semester when all groups had reported, the first group assignment having taken much longer than anticipated because the class had really gotten into it—preparing, overpreparing, competing to see whose presentation was the best—Dr. McIntyre's syllabus for the cross-cultural comparisons class changed because some of the girls, especially the upperclassmen in the class, had begun to whine and complain about the course's content and assignments.

"I can't eat another French dish," one had said, feigning a nauseous state, holding her mouth wide open, letting her tongue hang, saliva slide, making choking, gagging, gurgling sounds.

"There goes the escargot," one said, and most of the class erupted in fits of laughter.

"Neither can I's" and "me either's" were elicited from the class.

And without merit, another complained, "We've done Spanish dances in our other foreign language classes. Do we have to do them in here too?"

"Well now, what can we do that could possibly interest everybody?" Dr. McIntyre began her relent from the course syllabus.

"I know," Brandi's group leader spoke up, "we can tell jokes."

More laughter was immediately drawn from the class.

"What kind of jokes?" the instructor probed further, wanting to be fair, to hear all.

"We can find and tell jokes about other cultures. That would be fun," the former beauty queen (she claimed to have been a runner-up to Ms. Alabama) had suggested.

"Uh-uh!" Brandi spoke out, out of order, boldly, unashamedly, and in disgust. "I don't want to make jokes about other people. Don't want any parts of that. If you let them do it, I won't participate." Her tone was offensive; she was yelling, acting like a child who couldn't get her way. At least that was the teacher's interpretation of her thoughts and mannerisms.

All eyes turned in the direction of the young woman, including those of Dr. McIntyre, who did not appreciate her open defiance. After all, she had done more for Brandi than the girl knew.

Momentarily, others in the class were also fussing about a change in the course's content, and they became unruly as well. Dr. McIntyre, who sat near the doorway, reached over, switched the lights on and off, signaling for the bickering to come to a halt, to cease. "So much for academic freedom, gang! Let's put our feelings aside and get to the real issue.

"What the matter with it, Brandi? Can you tell me what concerns you about the assignments?" the professor asked.

"I just don't like it!" Brandi shrugged her shoulders, leaned back in the desk, folded her arms in rebelliousness that matched her voice, failing to support her response, not because she couldn't . . . the young woman grew reticent; she refused to open up, to bare her inner self to the others.

Eyeing her charge once more, trying but failing to establish eye contact or to gain any semblance of cooperation, Dr. McIntyre's voice hardened as she said, "Brandi, unless there is a valid reason for not changing, change is in order."

But Brandi held her stance. She sucked her teeth and made the menacing, childish sound for which Dr. McIntyre had much disdain. The professor had taken a lot of heat for Brandi in the department, from the students, had even received a few pieces of hate mail (from Henri, she thought). Her own usually supportive secretary had made snide remarks about the amount of attention she paid the girl. By now the woman was exhausted, sick of the whole mess, wasn't willing to take one more ounce of shit from nobody. She grew flushed . . . a slow flaring of her nostrils accompanied the reddening of her skin, her neck.

Brandi's ill-mannered gestures antagonized the professor beyond measure. Dr. McIntyre grew increasingly exasperated. She stared at the student, wanting to grab her, rip the obvious narcissism from her breast. Didn't the girl know what she had been through? How old Henri dirtied her name? Called her a whore? Accused her of sleeping her way to the top of the department? Accused others in the department—dissidents from narrow-mindedness—of having ungainly affairs with her? How he had accused her of being a "Nigger" lover?

The professor grew stupefied with disgust. "The little brat, the nerve of her!" she thought. "After all I have done for her . . .

"But you can do it this once! It'd be the same as we have done in the past, the only difference is that we'll search for jokes rather than stories, songs, and recipes." The teacher spoke directly to Brandi, who appeared to be swelling up, puffing up like a hognose, an adder snake.

Having been thrown an emotional wallop by someone she trusted, looked up to, and regarded with the highest esteem, the young woman sat disbelieving Dr. McIntyre would participate, allow the class to participate in "low rent" activities like this. Defeat etching its way deep in her subconscious, Brandi sat motionless, still having trouble digesting this. Why in the world would Dr. McIntyre do this? What was she thinking about?

The Beauty Queen who sat behind her added insult to injury. She reached forward, touched the offended on the shoulder, and stated snidely in a deep Southern drawl which Brandi found as annoying as a swarm of gnats wincing in her ears, "Calm yourself, honey, they got books in the library with jokes. I know they have. I've done seen them before."

"So it wouldn't impose any difficulties on anyone. The assignment is doable then," Dr. McIntyre said, finality resounded, almost assured.

For Brandi, Claxville University lost its academic luster.

Dubblerville, who had set twirling the waxed mustache he'd managed to grow since late August between his forefinger and thumb, renewed the argument. "Dr. McIntyre, I don't know whether we're all mature enough to handle an assignment like that. It could get out of hand, and someone could get hurt," he spoke sympathetically.

Brandi turned to look at the young man and silently studied him, wondering why he always defended her.

Although their relationship never went beyond that of acquaintance, Brandi noted that he was always there; his comforting presence was there when she was faced with Mr. Henri's boorish behaviors—he always spoke out for that which was right.

In the past few months, the two—Dubblerville and Brandi—had shared the same classes. Opportunity was there for them to have become bosom buddies, but they had not. They were wary of and hesitant of each other. It's like they were two people from different worlds shipwrecked on Claxville Island—they cooperated because they knew that if they didn't, neither would survive, both would succumb to hunger, illness, wild beasts, bad weather and ill winds, etc.

Periodically they had talked—never engaged in what you would call a real conversation. It wasn't because of his race—Brandi and Dr. McIntyre conversed, shared, communicated, chatted. Dirk, Mary Margaret, Chuck, Kris, they were lily white too and she had real conversations with them. Philosophically she determined that the masculine and race issue had reared its ugly head again. Just as tradition had thwarted her attempt to have a love affair with Dirk, a white man, it would not allow a friendship with one either.

Certainly if Dubblerville had been a colored boy, they would have hit it off, could have been friends. She probably would've taken him and made a brother out of him. And there was nothing phony about him—everything was real about him except his name, which she had not known . . . the foreign language buff had merely adopted the name given him by his high school French teacher, continuing to use it. She felt a lump in her throat.

The Brown woman was stewing inwardly; her pot was about to boil over; she had had about as much as she could take off of these little "witches." Dubblerville sensed her thoughts and knew she was in misery.

"Dr. McIntyre," the fellow islander called, raising his finger for permission to make an argument.

The other girls booed the class's sole male, told him to keep his face out of their business . . .

Dubblerville, wanting to plunge into the melee to rescue the colored girl, having himself been attacked, rose from his seat and stood in the middle of the aisle and picked up his belongings. Amid their less than ladylike hisses, boos, catcalls, and swats at his flat butt with notebooks, books, tablets, sheets of paper, purses, powder puffs, compacts, and pokes with tubes of lipstick, pencils, ball point pens, fountain pens, whatever they held in their hands, he walked to the door and stepped serenely out of the classroom, having decided to go to the professor's office, wait for her, make the appeal for that which was rational.

He looked point-blank at the teacher before he left.

Brandi felt like following suit but held fast to her seat.

The older woman felt flustered and having second thoughts herself; Dr. McIntyre called the class back to order. "Let's see," she said facing the only other colored person in the class, "Elnora, we've not heard from you. What do you think?" she asked the woman who supported the majority's contentions.

"Dr. McIntyre, I feel that all of us are mature enough to handle any assignment that you give us. I really do," was her reply.

Brandi cast Elnora a reproving look, recalling the day she had first met the heifer near the dairy. She thought she didn't like her then. Now that they had spent almost a semester in the same class, she was sure she didn't—she was always sucking up to the teacher and agreed with everybody about everything, did whatever to ingratiate herself to Claxville's creme de la creme, its high society, its haut couture.

Brandi's classes were full of them; the liberal-arts types seemingly took classes they enjoyed; most had boyfriends in the schools of medicine, law, architecture, and veterinary medicine. All these girls took classes at the university while waiting for their men to graduate, to be catapulted into lucrative careers by their parents, waiting to marry, and to have help—someone else to vacuum all day and make dinner for their providers, take care of their children while they played bridge. Brandi, Dubblerville, even Elnora were misfits; they were treated shamelessly as such by these young women. Periodically they victimized professors such as Dr. McIntyre.

Seemingly Elnora, the older of the two colored women, didn't have a brain in her head—the few attempts at conversation between her and Brandi had been strained and were actually initiated by the upperclassmen, were held when they were out of the white students' sight and earshot; she acted like one of them when she shared space with the class-conscious girls.

Now Brandi shifted nervously in her seat, breathing hard, angered by what the junior said.

She thought, "The no talking so and so, she needed to take Mr. Henri's class. She can't speak English worth a hoot, can't even pronounce her own name right, says 'Nora Jankins' when asked her name—the 'el' silently nasalized—you can see it if you looking, but you can't hear it, slipping right into the second syllable, and says Jenkins like 'Jankins.' One good dose of his class and she'd know the difference between 'en' as in *pen* and 'an' as in *pan*." But she said nothing else, however, realizing that she had lost the battle. Dr. McIntyre was going to allow a bunch of junk in her class!

When class was over, the professor asked Brandi to come by her office. It was obvious to the woman the revised syllabus had bitterly disappointed her charge, and she could feel her pain.

Brandi followed her in silence.

Dr. McIntyre laid her things down before giving the student her attention. "Brandi," the professor said to the woman standing in front of her desk with heart swollen, feeling too big for her chest, beating with odd jerks, hands feeling cold and clammy, "you need to loosen up a bit." Adding, "If you want to be successful, you've got to learn to play along with the others."

"I'm not sure I know what you're talking about," Brandi said, getting more and more pissed the longer she stood there. She was about to explode, so she kept telling herself, "Get a grip, get a grip, get a grip. It ain't worth all this."

Dr. McIntyre sat down and encouraged the girl to do likewise. Brandi reluctantly backed off the desk and lowered herself into the chair facing the desk in the woman's office; all she really wanted was out of there—she didn't want to talk.

The instructor leaned across the desk, drawing closer to the girl, put her hand on the student's cooling, clammy outstretched hand, lovingly, almost protectively, and spoke softly. "Brandi," she said to the girl, who felt her hand trembling slightly, "the other students have really tried to get along with you. They've invited you to study with them, to work on group projects, to . . ."

Brandi moved her hand. She hesitated, fighting the uneasiness she felt at Dr. McIntyre's opening statements.

"I went to the library, sat down to the table closest to the front door, sat there all morning, afternoon, well into the evening, from eight to five. I sat there, didn't even get up to pee, and I had to go real bad. I was afraid if I did go, they'd show up, and I'd miss them," Brandi countered, thinking that the girls had told the woman of the incident that had taken place when she'd given group assignments earlier in the semester.

Brandi started to whimper. Dr. McIntyre reached in her desk drawer for tissue to give the girl.

Brandi blew her nose and resumed. "Then they wouldn't even tell me what the assignment was, wouldn't let me look at the paper. I had to come by your office, get Kay to Xerox a copy of the assignment so I would know what was going on. Don't believe me, you ask Kay, she'll tell you, and that isn't the half of it. You just don't know what kind of shit I have to put up with to get along with them. It's not me—it's them," she wailed, her voice elevating as she spoke.

"I wasn't aware of that," the now floundering professor said, realizing that the last assignment might open a can of worms that might be better left alone. "I'm not talking about that. I'm just making some general observations based on what I have seen," she said.

Dr. McIntyre attempted to smile but changed her mind when she saw the expression on Brandi's face.

"Yeah, I bet! You just talking behind them, that's all you're doing," the distraught student retorted and jumped to her feet, yelling loudly, angrily. "Did they tell you how they walk up behind me, how they step on the back of my shoes and try to make me fall?" Brandi turned around, leaning backside against the desk.

"Now, Brandi?" The woman didn't doubt what she said; her preference was just not to get involved any further . . . She'd seen her through that thing with Henri; she didn't want to be identified as too liberal, didn't enjoy being called "a Nigger lover"—that was what the man had said to the other faculty members, and they'd repeated it to her. Dr. McIntyre rubbed her hand across her aching brow and shut her eyes, blinking back tears.

The girl continued, "Or how they bump into me, prod me with sharpened pencils, apologize, then snicker?" She pulled her shoe off and tore the bandage from her heel, exposing flesh left raw when the Beauty Queen had repeatedly abused it for the past week, stepping on it as each opportunity presented itself—while Brandi sat upright in her desk directly in front of the woman, her feet flat on the floor; when they stood up to exit the classroom paused at the doorway to check the pedestrian traffic before getting into it herself; at the bus stop when she was mounting the bus; and as the bus bounded forward to its next destination.

The professor, leaning over the desk to see, to ascertain the level of physical assault, moaned silently. Disappointment clouded her face.

Along with her pulse, the younger woman's mind was racing. Feeling all the fear, worry, hurt that she'd kept locked inside herself come forth in a gush, she strained to withstand the shivering from inside of her, determined that she wouldn't, couldn't let all come out, not now . . . but words tumbled out, fell freely from her lips, and Brandi made an effort to calm down, to speak more slowly, softly.

Yet the girl's voice betrayed her. It became taut, a quivering string, barely containing bottled-up anger. Brandi heard the crack in her voice and willed herself not to cry. Then she told all once more with passion: bumpins, rammins, kickins, steppins on heels, toes, exposed members . . . uncovered, sandaled . . . covered, covered in cloths, canvas, leather. Brandi was exposed to the most common sorts of harassment on a daily basis, day in and day out of each class day. What made it so invidious is that these acts could be cloaked to look like little more than bad manners. To the offended, though, the difference was obvious—these acts were intentional. A person knew when someone stepped on his toe on purpose!

Yet they had received no mention until this particular day, the day on which Dr. McIntyre suggested that the young lady needed to extend herself to the others, to open up, to be more sociable. Brandi took great umbrage at it! She jumped up from her seat.

Through tear-filled eyes, she watched the teacher's jaw drop.

Dr. McIntyre's ashen face grew whiter. The professor cleared her throat as she retook her own seat. "But you can't be bitter. It'll destroy you," she quietly spoke to Brandi before reaching for the Kleenex atop her desk. Then she came around the desk, facing the coed who turned her head in shame; she didn't want anyone to see her tears—that was a private matter.

"Come on, Brandi, get a grip!" the woman made the statement that Deidre had made, that Brandi had said to herself. Taking her by both shoulders, Dr. McIntyre tried her hand at reassurance. "It's not as serious as all that," the professor spoke soothingly.

Brandi didn't want sympathy, didn't need it, and was fed up to her neck with pretentious attitudes. She bit her bottom lip, drawing blood, broke free of the woman's already loose grip, fled the office totally pissed, so much so that she would have slugged anybody who looked at her funny—she was going to punch their lights out!

"The nerve of the bitch!" she thought, putting Dr. McIntyre into a new category. She couldn't believe the woman; she had suggested that Brandi allow the abuse, that she benefit from it. "How ludicrous! What kind of nut is she!" were her thoughts about the woman's suggestion.

Dr. McIntyre, the woman Brandi had thought to be a benefactor, a real friend, had turned her back on her. Up to this point, the professor had helped her, had been an encourager, provided academic advisement, secured a tutor for her, run interference with Mr. Henri, sent food by Kay when she was ill. And Brandi, she had confided in the woman. Now she felt betrayed.

Brandi paused briefly, closed her eyes, trying to keep herself from spinning out of control.

Almost overcome with emotion, feeling new tears, smelling their salts, tasting saline, Brandi fled from the office, the building, ran across the campus to the dormitory. She blindly took a well-beaten path across the campus, past the dairy, the school of veterinary medicine where Kris worked and practically lived, by the campus laundry, the park—the exposer's hideaway—toward room 306. Head down, snot running from her nose, blending with the tears, the woman ran up Davis Hall's stairwell and to her room.

By the time she got home, Brandi actually felt sick, had a pulsating, blinding headache, was feverish and numb—numb from worrying about the problems that life at Claxville had afforded her since day 1. She hesitated in the doorway—the remainder of her strength ebbed out of her, and she was gripped by a terrible internal shaking. The woman stumbled into the room where she cleaned her snotty nose, wiped her tear-stained face, got something to drink from the small refrigerator she and Kris shared, wondered silently about whether she should go to the infirmary. She felt sick indeed.

The woman laid on the bed, taking comfort from the patchwork quilt Aunt Sylvia had made for her laid at the foot of her bed when she had arrived at Claxville University and moved in room 306 Davis Hall. Brandi felt a sharp ache of longing. She wanted to be home in Wester with her family, away from all the strife, hateful acts, vicious phone calls, and classmates deliberately snubbing her. The woman got up, sat on the side of her bed, took the telephone off its cradle, and began to dial the numbers. "One-four, four, five-two, eight . . . ," she said the numbers aloud as she dialed each digit. "No," she told herself, "that's not a good idea. I'm going to take some Bayer aspirins before I do anything else. I don't want to upset Ma." She hung up and got up from the bedside.

When she stepped on the floor this time, she felt no grit; her full attention was on the drawer where she thought she had placed the first-aid kit her

BRENDA SMITH

mother had made up before she left home in the fall. "I'm putting some ointment in here," Sara told her daughter. "It's an all-purpose cream—good for burns, cuts, scratches, rashes, just about everything—and some alcohol." Sara had held the bottle up. "It's an antiseptic, you can do just about anything with it: clean wounds, cuts, and Sylvia say you can bathe down with it when you have a fever. She told me to put some green and some white in here, but they didn't have nothing but white. If you see some green anywhere while you out shopping some time, you get some."

"Okay," Brandi had assured her mother.

The room's occupant fumbled around in the center drawer, finding first the almost empty mercurochrome bottle—she had used it for the cuts, nicks, scratches she got while working at the Burga Barn and for the marks left by the annoying classmates. "Hadn't been by there in a long time," she thought wondering how everybody was doing and if Dirk had taken her time card out of the slot—she hadn't formally quit, she'd just gradually stopped going. She still held the key that he had given her in case he was ever late coming in. Brandi threw the bottle in the trash and rubbed her hand over her forehead—it was scalding hot. She found the aspirin, popped a couple in her mouth, tasted its bitter contents, and grimaced.

Her throat was dry, so she returned to the metal desk in front of the window and fumbled in the back of the tiny refrigerator, which rested on the desk, took out a carton of orange juice, brought it to her lips, turned it up, and drank straight from the container, draining what was left, suckled at its frazzled edges until it no longer tasted of the citrus fruit, and was still thirsty. She let the empty carton drop to the floor. The neon lights over at Stu's restaurant blinked invitingly at her, beckoning her to "come over, quench your thirst, cool your sweating, aching brow." Its welcoming bid turned down, Brandi scrambled headfirst into the bed, the member pointed toward the door, the pillowed end of the bed reserved for her feet. She couldn't turn around.

"God, I'm sick!" she thought and remembered the only other time she had been sick in her life. She had gone to sleep in class, and Ms. Wilson, her fourth grade teacher, had come to her desk, woke her up, and returned a couple of times before she had determined Brandi should go home. The young woman couldn't remember how the school had gotten in touch with Cat to come pick her up—it didn't have a telephone. As a matter of fact, the Rosenwald Elementary School in Wester didn't have anything—they just had books; and they were old as dirt, ancient, outdated, tattered, torn, worn, written in. The children in the colored schools got them five or six, sometimes seven years to a decade after the white school had finished with them. So the students were always at least five years behind. "Maybe Henri was right." The young woman reflected briefly on the former teacher's arguments that she may not be prepared for his course.

"No, but I was! I was prepared for that class. I was!" the woman resisted anxiety and depression as her thoughts returned to the elementary school experience.

Boys' and girls' lavatories were back-to-back on the side of the schoolyard opposite the playground; each outdoor toilet could accommodate three students at a time. Three holes were cut in long boards that hid the odorous, dark contents in which hoards of maggots lived, survived, thrived, and reproduced. The teacher tried to get her up, to go outside, to get some water from the pump, use the lavatory—thought she had a tummyache, knew Brandi wasn't going in there all by herself. She was scared her tiny butt would fall through one of them holes—nobody else would be in there to help her out.

While there was electricity, there was no running water; the pump was outside near the lavatory. Thirsty children lined up—one pumped the handle up and down until the well gave of its sweet cool riches, and the other children cupped their hands, drank from them, lapped like dogs, to fill themselves, cool their scorching fevers, while the mud from the hole under the pump splattered their feet, shoes, ankles, legs, bare legs and pants' legs. The only time the puddle dried up was during the summer vacation; no mosquitoes nested there because its water never grew stagnant, stale, green, putrid, when the children were at Rosenwald Elementary.

All there was in the classroom was a blackboard, and sometimes the teacher didn't have chalk for that; she kept on teaching, stopping that day long enough to tell Cat that Brandi had a fever, wouldn't use the bathroom, hadn't thrown up. "Thanks for sending Mr. Lane to pick me up." The man expressed gratitude that the principal had not waited until the school bus came, had driven out to their house himself, got him out of the field to let him know his baby was sick.

Brandi whimpered in her sleep, reaching for the daddy now who lifted her from her seat in Ms. Wilson's class to take her home so she could get well.

Sara paced the floor and was glad when Cat brought the girl in the house and deposited her in her arms. Her mother immediately noticed the little red watery bumps popping out all over her—they did it right before their very eyes; chicken pox were all over her torso, in her hair, inside her mouth,

BRENDA SMITH

in her ears, in the crack of her behind, everywhere. "What are we going to do?" the man asked excitedly.

"Let's take her round the house, put her in the chicken coop, let them chickens fly all over her, and they'll go away. That's what the old folks always said to do," suggested Sara.

"No," Brandi moaned from her bed in the dormitory.

The tiny rail-thin eight-year-old moaned and squirmed in her mother's arms. Then she started to cry and reach for her daddy, who took her assuredly in his big arms and walked around the house to the area near the garden where the fowl were fenced in. Sara opened the gate, shooing chickens that tried to escape as the couple brought their child in.

"Put her down, let her stand on her own two feet!" the woman ordered the big man who worked hard at loosening his baby's tight grip on his shirt. He put the girl down.

While their child stood around his knees, clutching his pants' legs, Sara ran clumsily around the chicken yard chasing chickens, trying to make the clucking poultry fly over the squawking, hollering, feverish child's head. Soon, the father, overcome with emotion, grabbed his baby up and the family returned to the house where Cat tried to lay Brandi down. "Daddy's gone go to the store to get you some ginger ale," the woman said as she took over, soothing the sniveling child's steadily bumping temple, worrying that the one she carried in the "oven" wouldn't have the chicken pox so bad when it was born, was the equivalent of Brandi's age . . . or whenever it got the "mess." Cat gladly turned the girl loose and headed to town to get the soda water—tale was that chicken pox would pop out faster if the child was given warm ginger ale to drink.

The medication began to take effect, and soon the coed felt safe again, was very tired and sleepy; her brain, sick of coping with "mess," was shutting down her nervous system.

Meanwhile, Dubblerville was at the professor's office. He had come a few minutes after Brandi's departure. "Dr. McIntyre, I can't believe you are going let them do that," the young man spoke ominously as soon as he was in the office's entranceway.

"She'll survive," the woman spoke quietly, almost as if she was talking to herself, and put both hands on her temple, massaging it where she stood.

"She shouldn't have to," the man said, his face solemn.

"What's it to you anyway, Dubblerville?" The woman let her hands drop, walked past the young man to the door, and widened it for his departure; she'd had enough of his opinions—she didn't need a two-legged conscience.

"Just thought you were different," he said, and with hands buried in his jacket pockets, head bowed, he backed out of the doorway, turned on his heels, and departed.

The professor slammed the door behind him, retook her seat at the desk, and sagged in her chair and wept. Dr. McIntyre cried first for Brandi and then for herself; she couldn't take the scrutiny placed on her by her students and colleagues—she couldn't take being called names like "Nigger lover." All she wanted to do was to help the girl further her education.

Brandi was emotionally bereft, suffering from pure exhaustion; she was dead tired, had a mild case of pneumonia—walking pneumonia. At least that was what the doctor had said when she dragged herself from her quilted nest over to the infirmary where the campus physician told her to "take aspirin, drink plenty of fluids, rest throughout the weekend. You'll be good as new by Monday morning."

Monday came. Brandi felt better, was almost 100 percent physically fit, but was reluctant to go back to Dr. McIntyre's class. Everything within her wanted to flee to the sanctuary of Wester, to Carruthers and Sara Brown's house, but she knew she had to keep going.

Forcing a smile, she put on her mask—the one that grinned and lied, feigned comfort where there was actually distress—opened the classroom door and entered. "Good morning, Dr. McIntyre," she said, and the woman returned her customary cheerful salutation, "Morning, Brandi." Class resumed, and with it came the demise of the cross-cultural comparisons course's content. By week's end, the real catalyst for the change became crystal clear.

For most of the last two weeks in March and well into April, the class chortled, chuckled, hooted, howled as one genteel Southern lady after another trashed the colored race, telling "Nigger" jokes—jokes in which the people fornicated with alligators, monkeys, with themselves, or were brutish, lazy, stupid, and dishonest . . . but with a streak of cunning, when they were in the halls and out of earshot of the teacher, saving that with less zest for classroom activity.

Dr. McIntyre eyed her charge throughout the ordeal, and Brandi eyed her. The student grew obstinate, refused to participate, and would not join in the "fun." Brandi appeared sullen; her arms were always folded across her chest, her feet planted solid on the floor, her posture upright—head high—and she appeared to be in deep thought. The teacher was watchful yet distant.

Dubblerville didn't actively participate either—he leaned back in his chair, hands clasped behind his head; the man joined Brandi's silent protest.

As for Elnora Jenkins, she got carried away. First she snickered lightly, covering her mouth with her hand, wiping it as if to wipe the smile away, but soon she laughed right along with them, seeming to enjoy that which was foolish.

"You're up next, Elnora," Dr. McIntyre called on the fifteenth person on the class' roll, anxious for her to show Brandi how to be cooperative for the teacher had justified, legitimized, supported the assignment with an identified need—that is, that the younger of the two colored girls in the class was going to have to grow thick skin if she was going to make it, if she was going to enjoy a successful life.

The junior vaulted from her desk, engaging herself in a bit of theatrics. She stood, removed her jacket, placed it neatly on the back of the chair, opened her notebook and secured a loose sheet of paper, gingerly and demurely strode to the podium at the front and center of the classroom, laid the paper on the furniture, placed her hands on its sides, and pulled the podium to herself as if to adjust it to suit a particular need. Then she looked first at the professor, then at Brandi, and finally to her other classmates, cleared her throat, and appeared to read, "I'm sorry I don't have any jokes—it seems that people don't make jokes about the majority."

Brandi relinquished her staunch posture, the same one that Dubblerville held, and shook her head with disbelief. Elnora's grandstanding was too much; it was almost more than the freshman could take. The coed sighed, placed her hand on her forehead, letting her eyes drop to her lap to momentarily keep her reaction private. She couldn't believe the silly woman! When she raised her head, Brandi turned a hostile gaze on the other woman.

Nevertheless, Elnora's performance accompanied by the ever-present condescending nature rated "superior" by the instructor and the class. "Let's give Elnora a hand for her participation," the woman said with what Brandi perceived as a toothy smile of deceit. All clapped, gave the older colored girl's performance a thumbs up, and provided congratulatory comments; a few extended lily white palms for a slap from her palm blackened by birth; all celebrated—all except Dubblerville and Brandi, who was really pissed at the only other colored person in the class.

She caught the woman's eyes when she headed back to her desk, was not able to read them, but Brandi felt sure that Elnora had seen and felt her disgust.

Early on Dr. McIntyre had limited the stand-up comedies to one performance per day. Since Elnora's had been brief, Deidre was up next. And that was all right; Brandi renewed her stance—she no longer heard any of the off-colored jokes coming from the white people. She'd detached herself from the situation, allowing her mind to go blank or drift at will, only to return when the day's nightmare had passed.

"Is that right, Brandi?" Deidre solicited, when she had finished her first joke.

"What?" Brandi asked when her name was called.

"How do you think it feels to be dipped in black ink?" Deidre repeated her question as if she expected the woman to verify whatever . . . Brandi didn't even know what the joke was about; she didn't care—just knew she had been singled out.

"Black ink . . ." The words penetrated Brandi's ears, touching a nerve, her last nerve.

This was the third time that she had openly received such treatment since she had been at the university—Julie had done it, Mr. Henri had done it, and now, a student had dared to single her out. Ms. Alabama had overstepped her boundaries. One, two, three strikes, and Brandi came out.

To her own dismay and despite all efforts to stay cool, she felt rigid control snap suddenly. Brandi vaulted from her seat, stood over the offender, poised and erect, her Afro lending height and dignity to an air of newly found freedom, and spoke up like a body possessed; she mimicked the woman's Southern drawl, and with a voice sounding strange even to her, as if her throat was constricted, she pointed toward the row of classroom windows on the building's fifth floor and threatened sharply, "And how do you think you would feel if your ass fell out that window over there?"

All looked at her, mouths flew open, hands covered shocked faces; they couldn't believe Brandi had said such an ugly thing. The room was suddenly quiet as all the jokes, epitaphs, riddles, wisecracks, stories, tales, lies, fables, and myths suddenly became real and concrete—each suddenly took life.

Dr. McIntyre sat immobile; she was visibly in shock.

Deidre failed to respond, felt weak, cowardly, and ashamed. She couldn't get up the nerve to volley, to rally back, and to continue the exchange of insults she had initiated with the personalized joke. The former beauty queen grew flushed, was beet red with embarrassment. She looked to her classmates for support like Julie, Brandi's assigned roommate—the one who stole her laundered belongings—had done, but like Julie, Deidre found no visible support. As the gulf grew, she became first an isthmus, then an island, and a new expression took shape on her countenance: fear.

Then Brandi laughed, alone; her classmates stared at her in surprise, disbelief etched on their brows. Dubblerville glared knowingly at the instructor; just as he had tried to tell her, the demise of the structured class content had led to this. Tempers had flown; and tensions had risen, grown taut, burst from sanity's seams. The woman looking at him through narrowed eyes felt uneasy; her face grew red with annoyance, shifted uncomfortably in her seat, and then she dismissed class prematurely. And each left, alone this time; every student an island, each floating in her own sea of despair.

No one was left in the dimly lit room now except Dubblerville and Brandi.

Dr. McIntyre had led the pack when she dismissed the class. Wearing an expression that wavered between shock and embarrassment, she flicked the lights off and decided to go straight to her apartment in faculty housing rather than the office. She'd had enough of this too!

Dubblerville and Brandi, abandoned by the departed, caught each other's eye. He was the first to smile—the hesitant smile broke across his thin, intense face, and the awkwardness in it that matched the rest of him left. Then her face relaxed, and a warm smile appeared before she sputtered and laughed. In no time they both were in stitches: laughter was rocking them both, each was sliding up and down the wall. When the man had collected himself, he approached the woman and they slapped each other's open palms in agreement. And he sighed with relief, glad that her outburst had not been in derision but was a gleeful expression to the vocalized put-down of the girls who had been a menace since the class' first meeting. "Way to go!" the man exclaimed. "How about a little lunch?"

"Uh-uh," she said as she shook her head in the negative and led their departure from the emptied classroom.

Brandi let out a sigh of relief when she was outside the room's confines . . . God, she felt great!

It had felt good being angry in a world where anger and violence toward her were commonplace . . . it felt damn good being vindictive, shucking off pretense, lifting the mask, letting it fall where it may, reconnecting the raw, honest, instinct that made humankind the brute of the universe. To Brandi, it felt good to be uncivilized . . . natural, powerful . . . good. It felt good to intimidate rather than to be intimidated. It felt good to act white in Claxville! In the state! In America! In the world! On planet Earth! In this galaxy! In the universe!

For the first time since Julie Blanchard had stolen her drawers back in the fall of her freshman year at the university, Brandi Leigh Brown was pleased!

Brandi, cheerful but doubtful about her future at Claxville, took the stairs in Reade Hall in twos. Now that she was beginning to understand the real world (the one that Cat tried to keep her from being exposed to), questions about her schooling flooded her mind. Was she going to be punished for defending herself? What was Dr. McIntyre going to do? Was she going to flunk her? Why was she at Claxville anyway? What was keeping her at a place proving to be quite hostile? What could she do about it? What recourse did she have? Or did she have any rights at all?

Christ, she didn't know. "All I know is I want to make it . . . got to!" she spoke to spring winds' listening ears. "I can't let my family down, and myself neither for that matter."

When Dr. McIntyre was in her apartment, she poured herself a glass of wine and placed Bach's *Toccata and Fugue in D Minor* on the stereo. She went into her bedroom and changed into something more comfortable before checking the refrigerator in the tiny kitchen of her efficiency apartment for cheese. There she found some Gouda cheese and crackers. When she had gotten settled in a lounge chair, she partook of her goodies and let her mind rest.

Brandi couldn't rest; adrenaline flowed profusely, her creative juices were stirred up. Since class was over early, she traipsed with purpose up one of Claxville's many hills and past the bookstore over to Hazzard Library. She knew there had to be some jokes about white people somewhere in the library. "That's where they claim they got theirs from," she remembered.

"Can I help you?" someone asked Brandi, who was leafing through the card catalog in puzzlement.

The student's inquiry at the reference desk was quite generic—it was too embarrassing for her to say what her real needs were. She told the clerk she wanted to look up some jokes and was given the calling card number for a few sources before being dispatched to the stacks. Several hours passed before she abandoned her task for the day—she couldn't find the kind of jokes she searched for, so she left the building as empty-handed as she had come.

"*Ring . . . Ring . . . Ring*" brought the woman from peace evoked by Bach. It was Kay. "Where you been? You didn't come by the office after class. You always come by before you go home. If you don't, you call," rushed from Dr. McIntyre's secretary.

"I'm sorry. I was a bit tired, so I just kept going," the woman spoke lethargically to Kay. She was drained from the day's activity. "Did you need something in particular?"

"Yes and no. I'm not sure!"

"What do you mean you're not sure?" The professor sat up in her armchair.

Kay spoke in a whisper. "Campus security stopped by to see you about something . . . said it could wait 'til Monday."

"Holy shit, I wonder what that little urchin did now!" Dr. McIntyre pulled the lever on the right side of her recliner, allowing her to sit straight up.

"Who? What?" Kay questioned forcefully.

"That damn Brandi. That girl, she's going to drive me crazy."

"What did she do this time?"

Dr. McIntyre recounted the day's event.

"Whew! No wonder you went straight home," commented Kay. "Bet you need a drink?"

"Uh-uh, don't need one, already had one," she responded, adding, "Did they indicate I needed to call or anything?"

"No, it must be personal. They wouldn't talk to me about it. If it had been about a student, they would have talked to me, don't you think?"

"Yes, I guess so. They generally do."

"I asked them if they wanted your home number, and then I remembered it was already in the faculty directory."

"How long ago was that?"

"It's been at least an hour. Surely they would have contacted me at home if it had been about that silly girl. Anyway, I'm not going to worry about it until Monday. I need a break, and I plan to take it this weekend," the professor spoke with conviction.

However, the curious secretary persisted, wanting her to call and find out what campus security wanted and begging the woman to call them and then call her back and let her know what was going on.

"I won't be able to sleep the whole weekend," Kay pleaded with Dr. McIntyre to call right then.

"Okay, what's the number?" the woman said. Kay immediately began to call out the digits, "Four, three . . ."

"Wait a minute, let me get a pencil," her boss insisted.

But before she could retrieve a pencil from her desk, the doorbell rang.

"One minute," she called and returned to the phone to tell Kay she had visitors and would get the number from the directory and call later.

"Don't forget," Kay pleaded.

As Brandi headed downhill to Davis Hall, a streak of mustard caught her eye. Taxi was passing by.

The young woman stopped dead in her tracks. There was somebody who knew everybody and probably a little about everything. "He could probably tell me a few jokes himself," she thought.

But she had not seen the man since he had picked her up from Dirk's trailer that eventful day in January when she had almost lost her virginity. Probably needed to pay him—she did, for she had not done so that day. So with pride tucked between her legs like the tail of one of Uncle Jack's old hounds who'd got himself into trouble, Brandi pivoted, hurried uphill, through the black wrought iron archway, and over to the bus station where Taxi sat in his car as if he awaited her arrival.

Several buses waited on the angle, idling and ready to depart, so she had to walk in front of them to reach her destination. She heard warming engines and the sound of air brakes letting go, inhaled exhaust fumes from the vehicles, and began to cough.

Stifling a cough, she spoke over the noise, "Hi!"

"How you doing?" was the man's lukewarm reply.

With a simple "fine," she laid her books on the car's hood and opened her purse. "I forgot to pay you," Brandi said reaching inside it, fumbling with a zipper caught in tattering fabric.

The man put his hand up and shook his head. "You don't owe me nothing," he barked angrily and emphatically. He was still pissed, and even he could not understand why. She didn't mean anything to him—wasn't his woman. It was just that she was a colored woman, a sister, and white men had been using them from the beginning of time—to suckle themselves when they were babes, to suckle themselves when they were full-grown, and when they were full-grown men to have them suckle their own sons. Taxi was from the old school—the man couldn't get with this interracial-dating shit that was getting to be commonplace, especially over there at that college.

The man looked off; his gaze was afar.

Brandi tried once more. "Let me explain," she began.

But he stopped her with "Done told you, woman, you don't owe me no explanation!" He stirred in his seat; the young woman was getting on his last nerve. He just wished she would leave him the hell alone. "Get off my door," Taxi ordered her, a note of finality punctuating his last sentence to dismiss the pesky young woman.

The woman shrugged her shoulders, gathered up her belongings, and went on her way.

CHAPTER FIFTEEN

At Church's

The young woman's stomach growled, so Brandi decided to get something to eat before she returned to the dormitory. Church's Chicken was nearest the bus station; so she walked there to find, surprisingly, that its manager was a young colored man—his attire was their customary black and white with black necktie. He freed his hands of the residue from the chicken's preparations for frying when she was at the counter.

"Can I help you, ma'am?" he asked before she had time to decide; so she hurriedly selected a "two-piece and a strawberry soda" from the menu, took a seat in the booth nearest the counter, and waited for the chicken to finish frying.

"That'll take about eight minutes," the man called to her from behind the counter. "Want your drink now?" She answered affirmatively, and he handed it across the counter. When she got up to get it, Brandi asked the man how long he had been working there, her interest escalated by his race.

"A while, a couple of years," he indicated.

Soon, the man brought her meal out on a tray, and she took it from his hands.

"Oh, I forgot your pepper!" he said of the green jalapeno. "Want one?"

Brandi nodded; she enjoyed squeezing its juices on piping hot chicken, adding pensively, "That ain't all I need though."

The man smiled with familiarity; he was used to college students coming in dumping on him . . . about money (loans, grants, scholarships, tuition, work-study), about boyfriends, about teachers, about classes, about failure, about their parents—they always had problems; sometimes he thought he ought to have been a bartender or a barber.

"Wait a minute. I'll be right back with your pepper," he said.

When the man had fished the big green jalapeno pepper out of the gallon jar of vinegar on the end of the counter, he placed it on waxed paper and returned to the booth where he seated himself across from the customer.

"Okay," he said, "what do you need?"

Soon, she was talking about school, the most recent assignments; however, she didn't specify the kind of jokes she sought—that was a private matter. The man, who had taken a seat in the small booth with her, suggested a club "or someplace like that" where aid might be found, adding, "Some of the fellows hanging 'round there playing checkers could probably tell you all the jokes you ever want to hear plus more. You know how some of these old guys are."

Well, she really didn't know how some of those old guys really were . . . naiveté was her constant companion; her experiences were minuscule to say the least. Brandi had never been in a club—had never considered going to one. Her upbringing had been narrowly restricted; she'd never ventured beyond the boundaries of Wester's country schools and churches. Her only real friends were family members—folks who shared her values. Besides that, her mama and daddy had taught her early on that ladies didn't frequent "juke joints."

The young woman asked the man if he knew of one nearby, if there was one close to the campus.

"Yeah, sure, the Basement," he said, adding. "I been there a couple of times myself since I moved here, stopped by and got a drink on the way home. Matter of fact, it isn't far from here—it's in walking distance."

"In walking distance," she echoed.

"Yeah, in walking distance," he repeated. "Soon, as you get some of that grease off of your face, I'll show you where it is."

Brandi swiped at her face. The man grinned and said, "I was just kidding, take your time, finish your meal. I'll point it out to you when you ready."

He got up to assist more customers as they came in. "Need more soda?" he asked.

She shook her head.

Brandi shoveled the mashed potatoes down her throat and swallowed the remainder of her chicken. Chewing would take too much time; she had somewhere to go and something to do. She pulled at the straw to get the dregs of the drink from the large paper cup.

"Want a refill?" A waitress passing by offered more from a pitcher as she said, "It's tea."

The manager called, "She got strawberry soda. Just hand her cup here. I'll refill it."

When the server gave her more drink, Brandi relaxed and enjoyed its contents more thoroughly. "Help is on the way," she thought.

Soon, Brandi wiped her lips, face, and fingers, cleared the table, and put her mess in the trash can, and the manager accompanied her to the restaurant's exit.

He held the screen door open and pointed uphill; everything was uphill or downhill in the city. Brandi's attention was drawn to a gray stone wall lining the side of the street, seemingly to keep the hilly embankment and the university itself from sliding or tumbling down smack in the middle of the four-lane street passing through the town.

"Up there," the man stammered as he pointed the way, "up there, past the end of the wall—maybe two or three blocks, no more than that. Cross the street right there at that light, go about two or three blocks, you can't miss it—you'll be right at it."

Confusion showed on her face. Brandi's world had been limited to a few city blocks in either direction of the main campus. She had not traipsed beyond these boundaries since the day Mary Margaret insisted on showing her the campus. Apprehension raised its ugly head.

The man renewed his efforts at giving directions to the Basement. He put his hand on her shoulders, turning her body, giving her eye a recognizable target. "Look over yonder where the bus station is," he said while Brandi glanced to the right. "It's actually kind of diagonal to the bus station, right in back of it really, but sort of at an angle. You might want to just cross over that side of the street, then go uphill, and over." He drew a map in the air with his index finger.

She asked, "Does it have a sign on it?"

"I can't remember, but you won't miss it. A few old fellows will be sitting right outside under some big oak trees, playing checkers, shooting the breeze." She gave him a wary look. The man urged her on. "They're harmless as flies. Don't let them scare you, most of them retired from service or the railroad, got children and grandchildren, go to church most every Sunday, just sit around and play checkers and shoot the breeze most of the rest of the week. When you tell them what you need, they'll be glad to help you."

Brandi sighed, thinking, "It's worth a try," and then she thanked the man and darted across the street, pulling herself up the steep hill, wishing she had not stuffed herself; she was full as a tick. She was about to pop, didn't know how she was going to drag herself up that hill.

Nevertheless she did, and when at the top of the hill, she stood with hands shading her eyes; on one side of the asphalt were storefronts, on the opposite side, fifty yards away, were the backyards of small frame houses circled by rusting wire fences and tall dying weeds; she paused, then looked back, waving at the speck of a man who returned her wave of thanks and farewell. Then the woman disappeared; she went around the corner.

Brandi Leigh Brown had long thought and dreamed about a college education. She was now determined to get it. No words could express the doubt, perplexities, anxiety, and discomfiture beyond those initially expressed by her father. Now they resurfaced. What would people say if she were not successful? Would she be laughed at by the "naysayers," doubters, envious people, people who themselves dare not dream for fear of nightmares' onset, and if she failed, would they mock her?

If she didn't succeed, where would she go? Could she return home defeated? To whom could she turn? Stark reality, cold as it was, stared her in the face. The young lady had made her own choices. Now her inadequacies caused a sense of great despair to come upon her; she stopped dead in her tracks, chilled to the bone, her heart thumping wildly, stomach churning, head aching. Brandi wanted to turn back, to go home to the safety of her mother's arms, wanted to sit beside Sara, lean over, root her head against her mama's side, lean on her sagging breast, feel her warmth, smell her perfume, be hugged, hug back, feel the woman gently push her head into her lap, rub her now aching, throbbing head until the pain dissipated, until she was asleep.

The evening sun winked at her through the treetops—it felt warm and reassuring—and soon faith replaced thoughts of what might befall her. Brandi proceeded—she followed the manager's directions.

Momentarily, the young woman heard voices—she caught phrases and snatches of ongoing conversations, and she heard laughter well before she got to the place to which she had been directed. On the corner of the block was the bricked side of a furniture store—the bricks had been painted white, and the company's name, Schwartz, was hurriedly scrawled in black that had not weathered well . . . it was peeling and fading, was more gray than black. A hot dog stand, a shoe-repair shop, a desolate, unoccupied ancient movie theater, and a small hardware store took up the remainder of the sidewalked block.

The young woman kept walking, taking little note of the ground on which she trod.

Where the sidewalk abruptly ended, the dirt began. Brandi almost lost her footing; she twisted her ankle instead. She had not seen the change coming, now she felt it. Where she stood, at the orifice of the alley between the hardware store and the Basement, she had to stop and examine her ankle, first by simply flexing and stretching its tendons while she held her blue jeans' leg high to get a glimpse of it. Then she bent to touch it, and finally stood on it, testing it with her full body weight.

She winced a bit.

Taxi, on the other side of the building, parked his car, jumped out, greeted the older men—all retirees who now spent their days sunning, playing checkers and poker, people-watching, lying, signifying, tending to world affairs and everybody's business. The driver took a moment to speak to each and to all, for everyone was old enough to be his daddy. "How you, man?"

"Fine, boy, jest fine."

"What's up, pops?"

"Nothing much!"

One after another, the older men returned his greetings, adding, "And your mama, how she doing? I ain't seen Sister Pennington in such a long time."

To which the man chuckled and said, "She's doing fine, just as ornery as ever, keeps on bugging me all the time."

Greetings given, Taxi was on his way again, whistling gaily.

Brandi decided she was not lame, could attend to her business. She started up again.

The two bumped into each other at the Basement's door. "Excuse me," the man said to Brandi as he held her briefly, steadying her, guarding her against an inevitable fall. "Damn, it's you again!" he spoke sharply, bluntly, directly at the young woman when he recognized her.

She saw, heard, felt his obvious disgust; and tears welled up in her eyes. "I'm sorry, I'm sorry," she muttered woefully.

The man felt like crap—never could stand tears. He took her in his arms and rocked her gently. She held on to him for a moment, pressing her head against his chest, sniffing him, inhaling his masculinity—aftershave, sweat, musk.

Taxi pressed his nose into her Afro; the scent of her crept upward, reaching his nose. She smelled good and fresh. Anger released its grip; he relaxed—she was making him dizzy with desire.

Taxi released her for a moment; then the man pulled her to himself again. She went willingly. They hugged warmly; he held her at arm's length. "Am I forgiven?" he asked sheepishly.

Brandi wiped her eyes and pretended to pout. "I don't know," she continued, folding her arms across her chest, stiffening her lower torso, twisting the upper from side to side. She stuck out her bottom lip.

"Damn, you sure are cute when you pouting," he said as he reached for her.

He pulled her to himself a third time, squeezed her tightly; and when they parted this time, Taxi and Brandi laughed until both were in stitches, in tears. When the man had regained his composure, he pulled the young woman to himself for a fourth time, pecked at the cheeks of her now upturned face, let his hands slide from her shoulders downward, rubbed the sides of her arms, sighed, and emitted.

"Damn, you feel good!"

"Does every sentence have to begin with damn?" she inquired teasingly.

"No, just when it feels good," was the response he made as he took her in his arms and repeated his ministrations to her.

She bathed herself in the warmth emanating from a budding relationship.

He was equally as enamored.

Both were oblivious to the evening traffic that was picking up as a work week in Claxville was coming to a close. Both were wrapped up in the moment. Neither wanted it to pass.

Taxi asked Brandi to have dinner with him.

"When?"

"How about Friday week, around six?" He looked at his watch and rhythmically tapped its face.

"No, about five-thirty, that will be better," he said. Six o'clock was a little late. The restaurant would be filling; they might not get a good table—or any seat at all for that matter. Not only that, the man needed to get to the Basement a little bit earlier than usual; the "boys" were going to do a new set, might need to be fine-tuned a little bit, so five-thirty would be better, he thought.

"Sounds great," she said and smiled in agreement.

"Pick you up where I usually drop you off?"

"Okay."

"What's your name anyhow?" the man asked, anxious for a reply as he had some business to attend to—needed to rehearse for tonight.

"What?" the woman, listless with anticipation, spoke.

"Your name? What's your name?" the man repeated, fishing in the air with the fingers of his right hand for a quick response.

"Oh, Brandi," she replied.

"Brandi?"

"Brandi," she repeated before inquiring about his.

"Thaddeus."

"Thaddeus?" she quizzed him.

"Thaddeus Jerome Pennington. My friends call me TJ."

"Can I call you TJ?"

He put his hands on his hips and gave her a smile as he engaged in frivolity. "You my friend, aren't you?"

"Yeah, silly." She smiled, playfully hit his arm, and he laughed. They both laughed. And then he was gone—the man disappeared through the club's front entrance into the lobby, down in the hole.

Brandi turned on her heels to make her way back home. And no sooner than he was gone than she had committed to a date with TJ was she regretting her decision, second-guessing herself. The man was older than she, almost old enough to be her daddy. The Browns would not approve of her going out with somebody that old, and besides that, she didn't know anything about him.

Every time she had seen TJ, he wore the same dark pants and plaid shirt. Sometimes he wore a vest; but other than that, he always dressed the same, always drove his old jalopy of a cab. It was all right to ride in the backseat of a cab, but she just couldn't see going on a date riding in that old wreck.

"God, what am I going to do about this?" The young woman sought divine intervention about the forthcoming engagement, wincing periodically as her ankle twinged, tingled, gently throbbed from the faltered step made just prior to the encounter with the cab driver.

"Jeez, and a cab driver too," she moaned, thinking to herself that a college student deserved more, longing for a medical student, a law student, a future journalist, the kind of men the other women in her classes dated.

When she was near Church's again, she recalled why she had been in the previous location. "Damn," she muttered, "so much for that. I'll get back to that later."

She started to go into the establishment and speak to the manager again, but by now her ankle was getting to her. Going up that hill had been one thing, but practically trotting down with a sore member was quite another.

She went to her room.

Time flew that weekend; it took wings. Brandi couldn't seem to rouse herself from the bed where she lay curled, listening to the soft gurgling of the radiator and the occasional buzz of morning traffic outside her third-floor window.

Monday came; it was right on schedule. As the woman left Davis Hall to go to class, she felt so old, so tired—plum' tuckered out as the folks down home said. Every bone, muscle, joint, ligament, fiber, tissue in her body protested the effort it took to get out of the room and to return to Dr. McIntyre's class, but the ankle felt better. Yet she pondered how she was going to make it down the stairs, to the bus stop, into Reade Hall, up on the fifth floor to room 501B; she couldn't imagine how.

But somehow, by some miracle, by the grace of God, she was to do it—or maybe it was by being cursed with a stubborn will equaled only by that of the likes of her mother Sara and her aunt Sylvia. She was doing it . . . did it!

Galvanizing her will and forcing her feet to move one at a time, she inched her way to class to attend to her academic needs. After all, that was why she was at Claxville University, to earn a degree.

She knew what she was going to do. She'd made a commitment, and she was going to carry it out. That's what she had been taught, that her word was her bond, and indeed it was.

Kay was all over Dr. McIntyre when she came into the office that day. "What happened? What did campus security want? You didn't call me back. I didn't sleep the whole weekend."

"Frankly, I don't know," she told her secretary. "Two officers were at the door when I hung up. They asked some questions about Henri, and then they were gone."

"What kinds of questions?" the other woman begged as the professor stood opening the mail on her desk.

"Nothing real specific—nothing worth repeating. Their inquiry was about his work habits, whether he was punctual, cooperative, how long I had known him, some pretty ordinary questions."

"Dr. M, you didn't ask why they wanted to know," Kay fussed at the woman for not being nosy.

"Actually," the woman finally admitted, "it's quite confidential."

"Aw, come on," Kay begged, "you know I won't tell anybody."

"I have to get ready for my little urchins," the woman spoke with endearment of the students she really enjoyed teaching. She walked Kay to the door and gently nudged her out so she could ponder on the current state of affairs.

Campus security had informed McIntyre of suspicions that Henri may be involved in something devious. There was a secret side, just as Brandi had suggested to her during the previous semester—something sinister was hidden beneath his eyes. "That poor child!" she thought sympathetically.

CHAPTER SIXTEEN

The Dinner

Friday night came soon . . . real soon. Brandi had told Kris about the impending date, admitting that she wished she had not accepted the date but not exposing the reasons for her discomfort, not wanting to share with anyone her private thoughts about the man's dress, his car, his age—about him. She stood waiting on the sidewalk just outside the dorm's door humming a nervous tune, waiting for Taxi to pull up in his old, beat-up, crippled, decrepit vehicle. "Maybe," she thought, "if I dash to it and get in the backseat quickly, no one will know I'm going out with the cab driver . . ."

A tall imposing icon emerged from a sparkling brand-new Cadillac. The man in neo-Edwardian suit adjusted his gangster hat, straightened his tie, tucked his shirt in at his lean waist once more for good measure, shook first one leg . . . then the other, brushed at the pants' legs, and stood up fastening the buttons on his jacket.

He headed for the dormitory. Momentarily, Brandi smiled in recognition. It was Taxi (TJ). Her worst fears had not been realized—he wasn't driving that god-awful mustard-yellow taxi, that old clunker with a broken muffler and fuming exhaust, and he was dressed to kill, looked just like he fell right off the cover of *Ebony* magazine! She hoped she looked as good herself. Brandi tucked the muscles of her already taut, just past adolescent belly in, soothed imaginary wrinkles from her outfit's waist, and hastened down the sidewalk to meet her friend. He hugged her briefly; she smiled.

"You look good in stripes," was all that she could say.

"You look terrific too," TJ said pleasantly to the woman in the skimpy, short black top, which left her firm, taut midriff exposed, and polyester pants split straight up the middle until they were mi-thigh, exposing the nicest set of legs he had ever seen, and she smiled at him. The woman beamed at him, her face red. "Thanks, I'm glad you like it."

And like it he did!

Black sandals and small black earrings finished off the look. She had also taken time to apply a little makeup. That particular evening, a little pressed powder, red rouge, dark brown eyebrow pencil, and a pink lipstick enlivened and enhanced otherwise bland features, except for the hazel eyes—they spoke for themselves. "Done!" she muttered when she had perfected the lip's coloring, rubbed them together, worked top and bottom from side to side, removed the excess with the corner of a wet wash rag, and made the sandy lashes consistently brown with some Maybelline products she had purchased from Woolworth's.

On the way out, she had revisited her mirror, looking to the glass for approval; she modeled, turned, twisted on the narrow three-yard imaginary runway between the foot of the bed and the desk which doubled for a dresser. It was during one of these practice runs that she had changed shoes, and she was glad because their raised platforms heightened her, shortened the distance between their faces, kept her eye out of his chest.

Kris had watched her final stages of dress. "Don't break the mirror now," she chided Brandi who turned around, put her hands on her hips in vexation, made a face, and stuck her tongue out at her roommate.

"You look natural now!" Kris teased the woman.

"Does this look all right?" Brandi asked as she made a 360-degree turn at the end of her imaginary runway.

"Looks all right to me," Kris chuckled.

Brandi, feeling a bit exasperated by now, asserted, "Come on, Kris, be real. Do I look all right?"

"Okay, okay, all jokes aside," Kris reassured her. "You actually look better than that. You look great!" The woman was in stitches before she could complete her statement. Kris was enjoying the discomfort she'd placed on her friend.

"Humph!" Brandi grunted, grabbed her purse, threw it under her arm, and went out.

Now it was obvious to her that the extra effort was paying off—his eyes said so.

He touched the small of her back to guide her to the car. She smiled. Her smile was returned by the man whose worst fears were also not realized . . . she wasn't dressed in the plain old plaid shirts and pants, or skirt and sweaters, or that damn uniform she'd usually worn, and the Afro was gone—her hair fixed, straightened, curled, that bushy 'fro gone. He hated the wet look—different apparel and some makeup—they looked more equally yoked. The man felt now that he would not, could not be accused of cradle robbing; no one would note the differences in their ages.

Taxi was every bit a gentleman. He had pointed the way to the vehicle, let her walk a bit ahead of him, guiding her with hand resting ever so gently on the base of her open, exposed, lean, warm back where he held the door open, awaiting the young woman's suitable, proper seating before returning to the driver's side and getting under the wheel himself. "Thanks," she smiled and said, almost seductively, and the man simply returned her smile before cranking the car.

"Where you want to eat?" he asked when the car was in motion and pulling away from the curb into the busy late, late afternoon traffic.

"Don't matter, wherever you take me, I'll go." Brandi meant what she said. She was overcome with emotion, felt like she had died and gone to heaven, and "Gosh," she thought when she caught a whiff of his aftershave, "he smells so good, good enough to eat a piece of!"

Thaddeus touched her knee, patted the seat next to him, and she slid over, distance between them shortened by his nonverbal overture. Taxi pulled her closer still with his right hand; she rested against his rib cage, nose pressed into his clothing; she allowed herself to be readjusted. "That better?" he asked, shifting in his own seat.

"Uh-huh."

"Feels good to me too," the man offered.

Neither uttered a word as they sped along; a long awkward silence passed between the two. Except for his occasional whistling, singing, humming to accompany the radioed music, nothing could be heard, nothing except the soft purring of the car's quiet engine. When they got to the Fishnet, which was about a thirty-mile journey from the city limits, the man said, "Hope you like seafood, it's good. They got steak and chicken too, if you'd rather have that."

Brandi said, "Don't make me a difference."

Soon, they were seated, and Taxi ordered for both. And both fretted silently about the decision to have dinner. Here they sat, his usually garrulous speech now reduced to monosyllabic responses and wavering queries; Sara and Carruthers Brown's daughter who thirsted for sweet conversation with the cat gripping her tongue; she couldn't talk either.

She looked around the place and was not particularly impressed; the place wasn't anything to look at, was little more than a "greasy spoon" restaurant. It was small, didn't seem like it could accommodate more than sixty people. The young woman felt overdressed, wished she had worn some blue jeans and a shirt, the plastic from the seat cool to her open back, skin pricked by snags in the cracking leathery covering. "Of course, it wouldn't have looked right with his suit," she thought.

The Fishnet, shoddy as its appearance was, enjoyed a good reputation and was rated four-star worldwide in the traveler's guides for its seafood dishes and homemade desserts. The likes of Isaac Hayes, Aretha Franklin, James Brown and his entourage, Gladys Knights, the Temptations, and Sly and the Family Stone had partaken of its delicacies. Taxi told her that, pointing to the lopsided autographed pictures tacked on the restaurant's walls.

"Want some wine?" he offered.

"I ain't never drunk none."

"Ain't?"

"Uh-uh. What does it taste like?"

The man grinned and shook his head in disbelief, "You never had no wine! Where you come from?"

"Wester," she answered him, her response so sincere the man thought it unwise to make light of it, so he told her, "Tell me about Wester."

"There's not much to tell," she said.

"I want to hear it anyway," Taxi said reconsidering his refusal of drinks and summoning a passerby waitress to bring drinks before their fish and shrimp platters arrived. He ordered a gin and tonic for himself and a half carafe of white wine for her.

Soon, Brandi told him all: all about herself, all about Wester, about her family—Cat, Sara, her younger siblings, Aunt Sylvia, Uncle Jack—about the bus ride, the flour-sack money belt, how the tea cakes woke the whole bus up, about the man on the bridge and how afraid she had become, about her rooming situation, the stolen drawers, about Mr. Henri's and Dr. McIntyre's classes, Carmen's help, a few of the jokes she could remember, about Elnora's condescending nature, lunch at Church's, how she had ended up at the Basement's door, twisted her ankle, bumped into him; she told him about everything and everybody—that is, everybody except Dirk. "Thank God for Fridays!" she said, "I almost made a fool out of myself—almost did what my daddy said I shouldn't ever do."

"What's that?" he asked, anxious to hear more. He took the last sip of his drink and held the empty glass toward the waitress who had brought it. The man wanted another.

Taking a cue, she sipped the dregs from her drained half carafe.

"Want some more?" he asked when she picked the vessel up, shaking it.

"No," she replied and responded to his first question.

TJ beckoned the waitress for more wine.

The woman continued, "Stoop down to somebody else's level." Acknowledging that she had the ability to be as ruthless when crossed as the other young women her same age, but never as low or evil as they were, Brandi expressed pride in herself for resisting evil. "I would have been in the same boat they are rocking in!"

The man, watching her face as she told her story, made her confessions, was dazzled with her dancing bright hazel eyes with dark specks that made a wheel's spokes, merry laughter, and was consumed by the desire to touch her, to hold the woman. No one deserved this. "Damn!" he uttered to himself, finding it hard not to curse, not to let loose a mouthful of expletives.

Instead, he told her how sagacious she was.

She appeared quite wise for a woman her age with limited experiences.

The woman stopped talking then for the food had arrived. The seafood platters were humongous—the menu had read "all you can eat," but the feast was more than the woman could eat in a week, and she said as much: "God, I'd weigh a ton if I ate like this all the time, be as big as a house, wider than the side of a barn!"

Taxi laughed at her country ways. "Yeah, you are from Wester," he agreed.

The plateful of flounder was deep fried, flakier than mullet, perch, bream, pikes, catfish, and sucker fish Brandi's family usually had on Friday nights. At least six huge fillets surrounded by a dozen or more fried shrimp and hushpuppies garnished with lemon wedges and green parsley sprigs rested on vast oval silver platters. Dinner fries and mounds of creamy coleslaw topped with a sprinkle of shredded carrots were in separate dishes. Tartar sauce, horseradish, cocktail sauce, pickles, and onions were placed alongside the catsup, mustard, hot sauces—red, yellow, and green—and steak sauces which permanently rested on the crisp red and white plaid tablecloths.

TJ, moved by her confessions, began to nibble his food.

"You didn't say the blessing. Want me to say it?" she asked.

"No," T said, bowing his head, closing his eyes, repeating a familiar blessing, the one he grew up on. "Father, we are thankful for life, health, strength, for your many blessings. We pray your blessings on this meal, that it will be used for the edifying of our bodies and souls. And we ask that you not only bless those who partake of it but the hands that prepared it. In Jesus's name we pray. Amen," his voice resounded reverently.

Brandi was impressed, thought they'd talk about that later. And Thaddeus? His thoughts were of how different the woman was; she was so unlike the women with whom he had been involved in the past. He recounted to himself how she had given him such a nice scarf set when he had picked her up at Christmas. It was several days later when he had taken the gift out of the car and into the house. The value of it surprised him, and he had planned to look her up after the holidays to say thank you. He had considered asking her out for dinner to repay her kindness. The man had not gotten around to it, and then that thing came up out at the trailer park that day.

He shook his head, wanting to let bygones be bygones.

The woman saw his movement. "Everything all right?" she asked.

TJ nodded, chewing bits of the delicious shrimp.

She took a bite or two of the flaky white fish and almost swooned. It was delicious, seasoned to perfection, fried just right. The woman thought it no small wonder that every Tom, Dick, and Harry that had heard about the Fishnet stopped by. Then Brandi sorted through the condiments on the table, secured the hot sauce and mustard, began the ministrations to her food, and she got catsup for her french-fried potatoes. "No grits?" she questioned the menu, not realizing that she had spoken aloud.

"What?" inquired TJ.

She repeated, "No grits?"

The man looked up. "Grits? Why grits? That's a breakfast food."

Brandi shook her head and made a face. "Not where I come from. Everybody back home eats grits for breakfast and with every fish dish. My mama cooks mullet fish and grits almost every Friday if my daddy don't catch some bream, cat, or sucker fish out of the creek down by our house." She tasted of the food on her fork.

The man chortled, shook his head, and said, "You ain't home," before he sprinkled vinegar on the fish that he fastidiously moved around on his plate as he prepared for the tasty feast.

She reached her fork across the table, touched him on the back of his hand to stop him. "Why are you drowning that fish in vinegar?" she exclaimed. "It's already dead."

The man laughed, cut a bite-sized piece of the flaky fish with his fork, reached across the table, and challenged her to "try it." She playfully held her head back, ducking and dodging the probing forkful of food. She held her hand up to arrest the cat-and-mouse game. "Only if you try mine," she relented. "Okay," the man agreed, and they exchanged bites of fish, each with his preferred condiments—his preference reflecting that of Claxville's northerly customs, hers of true down-home Southerners, especially those from down near the Okefenokee Swamp.

While they ate, Brandi resumed the monologue, talked until she had told him all from the trivial to the important. Her date openly scanned her face, wondering periodically how she could go through such harassment yet remain unscathed, could smile, talk about it, laugh, and even empathize with her perpetrators, for at one point she exclaimed mournfully, "I feel sorry for them all. They are a pitiful lot!" The man knew he would have gone off a long time ago, would have shot somebody, taken names and kicked ass.

Several times during the conversation, he tried to stop her. "You don't have to talk about it if you find it too painful," he uttered. But she waved off the man's concerns, shifted in her seat, and kept talking.

And Brandi . . . Brandi felt happy that evening for the first time in what seemed like ages; she let herself go. She was mesmerized first by the confidence that the man exuded; he had known exactly what to order for her—he seemed to know good vintage. She didn't. And second by his humaneness: he listened, without being judgmental; third by his dark eyes, the hair on the back of his hands, his build—it looked like that of an athlete, by . . . (She stopped short. The wine, she thought, must have been taking effect.) No matter what else was happening, at least she felt now that Taxi was there for her. He had become a good friend; her time with him was an island of peace that had at times become a sea of what bordered on stark terror.

She ran her fingers along the edge of the empty wineglass and smiled wistfully. Taxi replenished the goblet, and she talked a bit more.

When the young woman let up for a breath of air, another bite of the delicious food, a swallow from a mason jar of sweet tea, a sip of wine, he asked helplessly, "Is it worth all that?" instantly feeling like a moron for even asking. Brandi was obviously a courageous, albeit young, woman.

She shook her head. "I don't know," she said, shrugging her shoulder before admitting to him how tired she was, how discouraged she often felt. It was hard for her having to take all the crap from the girls in the dorm, and now in class—it was demoralizing to say the least. Taxi could sense that, and his heart went out to her.

He twisted in his seat.

"Maybe it's time to leave," he offered for lack of anything else to say beyond that of his thoughts, which were "to kill the sons of bitches." Enough was enough if this was going on and he was in no position to help her get rid of her problems. All he could offer was a sympathetic ear.

Little did he know that he was exactly what she needed; she just needed to be heard. She shook her head in the negative; a serious look surfaced on her brow. "I don't understand everything I'm going through. I guess everybody gets tested every now and then," she expressed herself with unexpected, unanticipated depth. Brandi matured before his eyes. The man had perceived her to be "one of them little hippies," like the other girls over there at the college. He had almost whipped his own ass a thousand times for asking her out, had been tempted not to even show up, to make like he forgot. "I'm not going to flunk the test," she said. "It may seem like I'm flunking now, but I'm going to hold out until the end."

Brandi smiled.

TJ sighed. "You're quite a woman," he said in admiration. "You'd get an A+ from me. I would have took names, kicked ass, and left long time ago," Taxi countered, no longer able to contain himself; he'd made the statement in such a way as to lighten the burdensome discourse initiated by a callous "Tell me about Wester." Both laughed, he with relief because he knew she was a fighter, that she could take all that "shit" she was going through, that she'd make it; and she because she enjoyed sharing laughter.

He patted her hand, taking it in his own big hand, held fast to it, brought it to his lips, kissed her knuckles lovingly. TJ lifted his head, and when they had locked eyes, he told Brandi, "A year from now, you'll look back at this and wonder how you've survived it."

"A year from now! If I live that long!" she exclaimed, rolling her eyes heavenward, taking another sip of wine, letting her head fall to the table for a moment.

"You will," he assured her. "I'll be right there to give you a shot in the arm when you need one." He released the hand he still held and punched her arm and chuckled.

She looked at him. "I'm counting on you to do that," Brandi said. Waves of gratitude swept over her. She was certain that she had somebody she could lean on. The bond between the duo deepened; their lives seemed to be becoming slowly intertwined. Brandi thought it ironic that he was always there when she needed him: the man was at the bus station when she arrived, was at the gate at Christmastime to help with her descent down to campus where she deposited a load of Yuletide gifts, was at Dirk's when she needed a ride home, was at the Basement's door to arrest her quest for folly, jokes, stories, fables, and here he sat, a listening ear. TJ felt something too.

"How's your wine?" he asked.

"Tastes like mule pee," she spoke and made a face at the man who was taking a sip from his own glass. The man almost choked on the liquid. He placed the glass on the table, withdrew a handkerchief from a pocket inside his jacket, and wiped the corners of his mouth.

TJ laughed heartily—she was quite comical, and when he was no longer in stitches, could speak with a straight face, Taxi asked, "How does that taste?"

"I don't know, ain't never drunk none myself." She giggled a silly giggle, feeling the effects of the warm liquid. The man roared with laughter again, his baritone full, rich, and hearty. Lights flickered. The facility had filled, refilled several times, and was now empty. All dishes had been washed except those on table 2.

TJ looked at his watch, raised himself up, took out his wallet for the tip, and told his date, "Let's get out of here," before taking a moment to swallow the dregs from an after-dinner coffee poured by the waitress on one of her almost unnoticed trips to their table.

"Not before I go to the bathroom. I'm about to pop!" she said. "Where is it?"

"Over there," he pointed out the facility's ladies' restroom, "I think I'll get rid of some of this water too. Meet you at the door."

Afterward TJ guided Brandi over the threshold and into the open air.

The young woman shivered when they were outside, wrapped her arms around herself. The wind rippling through greening oaks sent a cooling breeze across her sweat-dampened skin. It had been relatively warm in the restaurant, which only boasted a couple of antiquated ceiling fans whose rickety blades whipped, churned air from the open windows. Claxville's spring evenings were still cool. Wester was at least 15 degrees Fahrenheit warmer than this town. The man took his jacket off and placed it around her shoulders, offering warmth for her thin torso, arms, and open back. On the way to the car, Taxi asked if she had ever been to the Basement, to which she replied, "Nope, but I heard about it."

"Do you want to go by there?"

"That'll be all right."

Their jovial conversation reduced to fragments once more when they were headed to the club. Brandi had talked out, bared her soul, yet she knew little about the man at the wheel who broke her pensive mood with, "Mind if I stop by my house first?" The young woman wasn't sure about this, didn't like the sound of where it appeared to be leading, so she began a mental and physical withdrawal, subconsciously edging toward the front right car door.

"Hey! Where are you going?" Taxi pulled her close to his side with his right arm, feeling tension where there had been none. Braking for the car in front of him, he took his eyes off the road. He caught her eyes, seeing concern. "What's wrong, baby?" he asked soothingly, his voice full of affection.

"I'm . . . I don't know about going by your house. I haven't had time to think about that," she stammered.

"There is nothing to think about, nothing to worry your pretty little head about. I just need to check on my old lady." He smiled at her innocence in the darkness; it was refreshing. Most of the women Thaddeus Pennington knew were anxious to get into a man's crib, to lay on their backs, get some satisfaction.

He accelerated.

Brandi jumped in astonishment, almost hitting the car's roof with her head. "Your old lady?" she questioned the phrase.

"My mama," the man corrected her, "I live with her."

She sighed with relief, glad he was not referring to a spouse, a lover. She was confused, didn't really know what she thought, was slightly inebriated, didn't trust herself at the moment, was not sure that she had full control of her mental faculties.

TJ gazed at her appraisingly when they were stopped for traffic, thinking how pretty she was and how fresh and desirable in every conceivable way. She was pretty in a colorless sort of way, not flashy, generally modestly dressed, innocent, cultured, respectful to elders, liable to run at the slightest hint of impropriety—straight laced, vulnerable, easy pickings, good-natured, slightly spoiled, as willful as a person could be. The woman had so many praiseworthy attributes—was the kind of woman a man wouldn't mind taking home to his mother.

Her thoughts were of him as well. That old cap he always wore when he drove had hidden gleaming, curly dark brown hair, graying ever so slightly, prematurely, at the temples. He was clean-shaven, wore a neatly trimmed mustache, had a fair complexion, brown eyes, a superb body (exactly five feet nine and one-half inches), tall, well muscled, firm, and taut—didn't have an ounce of fat on him anywhere. And there was no question about his virility, his masculinity—it was like a gloss on him; there wasn't anything "sweet" about him. Thaddeus Jerome Pennington was all man—she was sure of that.

She wondered, "Why couldn't the man have been just a little bit younger . . . ? Under thirty, in his twenties, midtwenties would be all right. Of course, you wouldn't know it," she had thought when he mentioned his age during dinner. He looked so young.

Taxi was almost forty, was just about to reach the big four-oh, more than twice Brandi's age, had enjoyed almost the same number of birthdays as her father. But . . . the man was so knowledgeable, so humane, and for that she was grateful.

And Taxi, the man was glad that he had come tonight, had not chickened out. Brandi had already given him more than he might normally have had in a date—good conversation, witticism, and a sense of being "needed." He was delightfully rewarded by a friendship with a lively young mind and thought it a splendid foundation for something else. Taxi shook his head to chase away any thoughts of love, desire, compassion—all forgotten emotions.

Traffic was rough. The thirty or so miles back to town took a little longer than he had anticipated—almost an hour. He relaxed, as did she, and enjoyed the top pop hits on the radio. At night you could pick up WLAC, Nashville, Tennessee, listen to all the hot numbers on the chart, hear the "Wolf Man" howl, ask you to call in your requests, to dedicate songs to the one you love. Brandi squirmed in her seat—he loosened her; the pressure was off, she was okay. The woman moved over, rolled the window down some more, and hung her arm from the opening to feel the cool breeze, to enjoy the dampness felt in the night's clean air.

The first date went quite well; the man was neither fawning nor flirtatious. Indeed TJ Pennington kept his every emotion tightly cloaked. He pondered this while they rode through Claxville's city streets in the triumphant flow of Sly and the Family Stones' music, never imagining that he was, as he recalled years later, "a bundle of nerves inside a bargain basement suit." The girl did that to him!

CHAPTER SEVENTEEN

The Transformation

B randi enjoyed the college town's bucolic setting, luxuriated in it as TJ headed south then east when they were back in town, down by Little River, an area that she was vaguely familiar with: Dirk lived in a trailer park nearby. A short time later, he turned onto a dirt side street lined with the same oaks found all over Claxville; these were younger though, some little more than saplings. None were draped in moss like those on the university's campus. The man looked at his watch. It was almost seven thirty, closer to eight—the dinner had taken longer than he had anticipated.

The street was deserted except for a few old folks on their porches and some boys playing basketball at one of the neighborhood houses. When he pulled into the yard, it was almost dark—"in the shade of the evening" was what older people labeled this time of day—and the porch light was on. Mrs. Pennington sat in her balding paint-chipped rocking chair enjoying the little puffs of breeze that came up from Little River, slapping with weary hands at the mosquitoes that sang about her ears and legs. Her Bible lay open in her aproned-lap—to her favorite passage, the ninetieth Psalm—and her walking cane rested near her knee.

"Mama, what you doing still out here?" TJ said to the woman after he had let Brandi out of the car and beckoned for her to follow him up the steps onto the porch. "Mama, this is Brandi, she's a friend of mine. Brandi, this is my ole lady, Mrs. Pennington," the man said, and then he hopped off the porch, disappeared around the corner of the house, leaving the two women alone.

Brandi said nothing, couldn't—she was speechless once left with the man's mother. Mrs. Pennington moved first. She laid her Bible on a bench behind her chair, reached for her cane, and pulled herself up from her chair.

"Come on in," the older woman said to the girl when she began her slow descent into the front room of the home, which had been quite grand in her heyday. She pulled the screen door open and let the guest enter.

Brandi stood back a bit, wanting to help the man's elderly mother; she was gaunt with age, ashen. Her bones thinned yet she seemed quite full of life, not at death's door. So the younger woman was reluctant to offer a helping hand, because she was not sure about the old lady's comfort level—she didn't want to be smacked across the head with the thing that the woman was now using as a pointer for all the pictures on the room's moth-ball-smelling walls, rows of framed and unframed photographs that went from the entrance to the far end of the wall, proceeded to that wall's end to be broken near its end by a doorway, took up again on the other side of the doorway, turned the corner and resumed again.

The comfortable living room of the Penningtons' humble abode was like a museum. It was tastefully filled with antiques—a deep-seat sofa and easy chair covered with chocolate brown velvet with a shine on the seats and white lace doilies which had yellowed with age on the arms; plain, sheer, yellowing white curtains moved slightly at a window, stirred by a faint breeze that made a vain attempt to alleviate the room's collected heat; Queen Anne coffee table and matching end tables; a fireplace on one wall, its hearth still holding charred remnants of the winter's last warmth.

And on the long shelf crudely mounted on a wall were trophies, rows of them, trophies of sleek golden and silver athletes posing with bravado on stands embossed with the school's name, TJ's names, and the year that he received the honor.

Off in a corner was a picture of TJ poised in mid-dunk.

Brandi saw, to her amazement, a rosewood piano. When they walked past it, the young woman touched the wood and asked Mrs. Pennington, "Do you play?"

"Uh-uh," the old woman replied, pointing with her cane to a wall on which was a small fireplace with what appeared to be an enamel mantel piece to draw Brandi's attention to the horde of pictures on the walls—walls housing pictures of first Jesus (the baby Jesus; Jesus the man, alone, surrounded by the twelve, Matthew, Mark, Luke, John, James, Peter, Andrew, Simon, and the rest of them; the Lord at the head of the last supper's table) and second of the Penningtons (Thaddeus, the infant and toddler; Junior, the adolescent; TJ the teenager and the military enlistee). Brandi noticed that none were "neo-Taxi"; the man that she now knew—to her puzzlement—the pictures had stopped when the man became a veteran.

"That's Reverend Pennington and me," the old woman told her, pointing to a black, white, and yellowing portrait browning with age right before their very eyes. One was of the wedding day of a handsome, smiling, late-thirtyish couple, another of the couple in front of a church. Brandi gazed at the picture directly in front of her—the tall, stern-eyed, handsome man beside his new bride looked just like TJ. Mrs. Pennington verified her wandering thoughts. "Junior looks just like him, looks just like the reverend spit him out. A body wouldn't think I had no part of the birthing myself."

"God," Brandi thought, "a preacher's son!" Taxi was full of surprises.

She heard the woman say, "And we moved in

This house soon as we got married . . . been here ever since." The Penningtons had always lived on Webster Street, a quiet little unpaved street with no sidewalks; they never could get the city to pour asphalt on their side of town, didn't have representation on the council like some bigger cities "so dirt just stayed dirt," the old woman told Brandi. But everybody had decent housing, all which had indoor plumbing. "And that was a blessing," she added to the monologue. The neighborhood was not as robust as it had been in previous decades. "All the children just grew up and left home, went off to school, got jobs somewhere else because wasn't nothing for them to do right here in Claxville," Mrs. Pennington told her son's new friend.

"Nobody live here now but us old folks and some grandchildren what moved back home because their mamas and daddies too busy to take care of them, make them behave, go to school like they ought to." Forlornly TJ's mother added, "But least they got some—I ain't got a one, least not that I know about. Reverend Pennington and I wasn't blessed with but one, and we was fairly old when we had him—and that boy, he ain't never even married." TJ's mother shook her head.

Brandi smiled pensively, remembering the earlier concern about Taxi having a wife. She sighed with relief, some of the pressure released.

The old woman took a step or two, hesitated a moment, turned and faced the visitor before adding, "This place is dying . . . everything around here is, even the church. Don't nobody stay here. Children get grown, marry, go off, go to the army. Don't never come back except for to visit, for a funeral, family reunion, something like that."

Mrs. Pennington continued.

"Course there ain't nothing for them to do around here . . . ain't no good jobs. And if they are going to college, they are not going 'cross town up on that hill. They tell me they don't treat colored people like nothing over there. That's what the people what work over there say anyhow . . . say they hard on colored people. Lady in church was telling at the mission meeting few Sundays ago how they took one colored girl's clothes over there, stole them out the washing machine, and they say we the ones that steal.

"Humph, humph, humph," the woman muttered as she shook her head in disbelief. Brandi smiled a knowing smile—Mrs. Pennington didn't catch it.

The woman stiffly limped to the next stop. Brandi looked at her watch, wondering where Taxi had gone. Her attention was drawn to the present moment when the man's mother spoke with pride. "And that's Shiloh—Shiloh Missionary Baptist Church," she said about the large white-framed steepled edifice. "Reverend Pennington, my late husband, was the founding pastor—preached right there, stayed in the pulpit up until the day he died." The woman lifted her head proudly as she spoke of the man. "Two things my late husband loved: he loved the Lord's work and loved to take pictures. If he wasn't preaching, he was taking pictures. When he wasn't taking pictures, he was preaching."

Brandi understood now why there were so many photographs on the walls.

"And that's Junior," Mrs. Pennington pointed TJ out in the midst of neighborhood boys, some with those "outrageous nicknames they called themselves while growing up," ones with whom he had forged alliances to last as long as they lived. "They did it right there on the street corner, under the light. These are the same ones he in that band with," Thaddeus Jr.'s mother reminisced. "None come up to the church when they were growing up. He was supposed to let his light shine, drawing them, but that ain't what happened—let them have what little bit he had, ended up joining them," the old woman preached at Brandi her disdain for choices her son had made obvious. "I always told Thaddeus he sleep with dogs, he was going to get fleas—he still don't listen, don't seem to understand what I been trying to tell him. He needs to go to church."

Brandi thought about how much like her own mother the woman was . . . Sara had warned her before she left Wester about her choice of friends and had used the same maxim Mrs. Pennington now spoke.

"You go church?" Mrs. Pennington was asking.

Before Brandi could respond, Taxi was back in the living room; from somewhere in the back, the man had reappeared—he had changed clothes, was more casually attired than during dinner. "I got to get going, Mama," he said. "I'll bring her back another time," he teased the woman whom he had told many times that he would bring a "nice girl" in through the front door. Mother and son grinned, sharing their private moment with no one. He kissed the old woman. She whipped playfully at him with her cane and smiled while her son chuckled anew. Brandi ducked. Taxi took her by the arm and they left, flew hurriedly to the Basement.

TJ initially drove like a bat out of hell but determined it best to slow down because police seemed to be prowling. They were plentiful on Claxville's streets. Blue lights were flashing on every street. On weekends they came out of the woodworks. "That set will be all right," TJ thought of the new numbers the band was going to play tonight. Their plans for a quick session before opening would probably not take place since he was running so late.

The girl stirred in her seat; he played musical chords on the steering wheel when they were stopped for traffic, adjusted the knob on the radio, positioning the band to alleviate the static; he played along with the recorded music.

"By the way, how is it?" TJ asked momentarily.

"What? How's what?"

"Your ankle? How is it?"

"Oh, great," she said, sticking her leg outward, flexing her foot as proof. She hardly felt a twinge, had almost forgotten about the injury—thought he had too.

When Junior had gone into the Basement for a practice session with the band the week before, Brandi had slowed her pace—she had hurt herself when the sidewalk had dropped off suddenly at the club's front doorway. So she gingerly walked back to the campus keeping most of her weight off of the slightly injured ankle, periodically pausing and leaning against the stone wall to rest. She grew lighthearted as she proceeded downhill and as the ankle pain eased too. Nevertheless the young woman knew when she was back in room 306 that she needed to prop it up and get ready for the upcoming Friday-night date.

"Kris?" she called to her roommate as soon as she entered the door. "Have a look at my ankle for me." She lifted her left leg, let its heel rest on the bedside.

"What happened?" Kris asked, and Brandi explained as the veterinary science major handled her ailment with ease, care, and concern.

"Hold still," she commanded when Brandi winced and drew back a little, "I'm going to put a little ice compress on it." She took small cubes of ice from the miniature refrigerator's equally small frozen foods compartment, wrapped the cubes in plastic wrap, and secured it around the puffy, swelling, pulsating, throbbing member. "You better stay off of it!" she warned Brandi as she let her foot drop slowly and easily to the floor, turned herself around, sat herself on the side of the bed.

"Thanks, doc," she joked with her friend. "What do I owe you?"

Kris waved her off.

The wounded woman hobbled around the entire weekend, wallowing in self-pity, whipping herself incessantly for first of all going to search for filth in the form of dirty jokes, then for having run into the man at the club's entrance, and finally for accepting the date. She did this while she did repetitive, boring, mundane tasks to while the time away. Brandi cleaned messy dishes, scrubbed dried food from the jointly owned hot plate's rims, and cleaned grease from the iron.

It needed cleaning real bad.

Since the day that the duo, Brandi and Kris, had used the iron for a hairdressing device, they had found other uses for it, the latest of which was for the making of grilled cheese sandwiches. One or the other would place slices of processed American cheese between slices of white bread, wrap the sandwich in brown paper bag, and iron it on both sides until the cheese melted. When they had ham slices, they made hot ham and cheese sandwiches. If it was not cleaned carefully, their clothes were greasy and they smelled of foodstuffs.

On Sunday she washed clothes and read a novel while she waited for the articles of clothing to dry; Brandi had never left her clothes in the Laundromat unattended since that eventful fall day when Julie Blanchard was on a tear. Once burned, she was twice shy!

CHAPTER EIGHTEEN

Chez le Basement

Junior Pennington was running late. The dinner had take longer than the man had anticipated; then he had had to stop by his house and change before going to work. It wasn't that he had lost track of time—the experiences shared by the young woman had been moving and he couldn't leave right then; nor did he want to.

"Hurry up," he called impatiently when they had parked outside the Basement's back entrance. She got out of the vehicle, hastened to catch up to the man who walked a few feet ahead with hand extended. She caught up with him, and he took her hand and lead her down narrow steps of shaky bricks and mortar into a smoky, dank, drab, huge room lit by a single lightbulb on a chain swinging back and forth each time the door opened and closed.

Reverberations from a jukebox greeted them.

"That you, Junior?" a voice from somewhere in the room's now empty bowels said.

"Yeah, it's me," Taxi yelled back at the voice that spoke from nowhere. Brandi had halted, pulling away from the man.

"It's all right," he said assuredly, leading her anew to the bar where he introduced her to Lou, the Basement's owner and bartender.

"Lou, I'd like to introduce my friend, Brandi . . . ," he stammered and chuckled; he couldn't remember her last name, wasn't sure that he had asked, that she had ever told him.

"Brown, Brandi Leigh Brown," she said, sticking her tiny hand out to the bartender, who put the glass that he had been polishing aside and dried his hand on his apron before reaching across the corner to take her hand into his own.

"Nice to meet you, ma'am! Is this your first time in the Basement? Hope you enjoy it. You can come anytime you want to. Any friend of Junior's is a friend of mine," he said before offering her a drink.

Thaddeus waved off the offer for her, "She don't drink, man."

"Where's the ladies' room?" Brandi asked. The offer of a drink triggered her bladder—she was still full of tea, water, and white wine from the Fishnet, was about to pop, had not felt like this since the day she had come up on the bus from Wester. She was in a tight, wished she'd gone while they were at Mrs. Pennington's, but she had not wanted to appear disinterested while the man's mother was showing her most prized possessions—it was imperative that she indulge the man's nostalgic mother.

The bartender pointed to a curtain-covered aperture. "Use that one behind the curtain," he told her. "It's private."

Beyond the curtain lay dressing rooms, the manager's office, a storage room, and ladies' and men's rooms. At the far end of the well-lit passageway were two rooms, both marked private—one was for ladies and the other for men. Brandi entered the ladies' room. Its only occupant was a woman who sat on a broken backless chair with legs crossed, chain-smoking cigarettes, sucking in tar and nicotine in total abandonment, stomping a butt on the floor, lighting another which she held in her mouth. They barely acknowledged each other.

When Brandi was in the tiny enclosure, she sneezed. The faintest whiff of cigarette smoke always did that to her. She almost wet her pants. Nevertheless, Brandi did her business and hurried back into the hub of the establishment.

Taxi, while waiting for her, was talking with some other fellows. She was almost blinded by the inadequate illumination; she squinted, peered, peeked, barely able to distinguish the floor from the walls lined with red and white Coca-Cola memorabilia and glossy black-and-white photographs of many of Motown's stars—the same ones that had been clientele of the restaurant where they had enjoyed dinner—who had been here too. The man guided her once more with his hand at the base of her back—it felt quite natural; it did every time he touched her there.

The ever enlarging enclosure through which she allowed herself to be led made an L-shape. The man took her hand, and they went a couple of yards before Taxi stopped without warning. Having allowed herself to be blindly guided and led, she almost rear-ended him; the man walked like he drove—full of confidence, oblivious to others. He walked over to the piano, sat on its velvet-covered stool, reached for, and dragged a nearby chair over to a spot beside the instrument. "Sit here," the man spoke authoritatively, and Brandi eased her bottom into a cushioned chair, the only cushioned chair in the room.

Junior raised the piano's wooden cover, exposed the keys, and it became clear to Brandi why the rosewood piano was in Mrs. Pennington's living room. The man paused and struck one of the keys, listening to its clarion ring; then he made a run on the instrument with both hands, and then he glanced over at Brandi, who sat with mouth gaped in astonishment. "Do you play?" he queried her.

"No, wish I could," she said. "Perhaps you could teach me how to play."

"Maybe," he agreed; then he turned to the instrument. Thaddeus began to play . . . chords, Bach's *Inventions*, a little of Schuman's pieces, sprinklings of jazz.

Needless to say, his ministrations to the piano were breathtaking. Brandi had heard nothing like his music before.

"Who taught you that?" Brandi asked when her date paused for a moment, came up for air.

"My mother. She believed in improving one's mind, thought that music was one way," he spoke briefly, anxious to do his business.

Soon, others were coming through the back door and into the club. They called out to Lou at the bar to Junior Pennington to each other. Hammerhead, Goliath, Sweets, Tater . . . others strode by punctuating their called-out greetings full of expletives with handshakes, slapping palms, etc.—chatting incessantly in a verbal and nonverbal way unfamiliar to Brandi, who surmised that these were the friends that Mrs. Pennington had spoken of earlier in the evening.

"Who you got there?" they all asked, to which the pianist simply responded, "A friend."

Greetings extended to T's new friend, all set about the evening's business.

Soon, tinkering from many instruments—the piano, tenor saxophone, alto sax, a couple of guitars, trumpet, string bass, and drums—each tuned sufficiently, ceased. The gig was on! The jukebox music that had ushered Brandi and TJ into the club was replaced by live music which transformed the dank, dark, drab edifice into something ethereal. Soon, there was joy, laughter, awe, wonder, motion, and sound—none like Brandi had felt, seen, heard, experienced. It was Friday night on the south side in Claxville. The woman was glad that she had come.

At a time when Claxville University was losing its academic luster, Sara and Carruther's daughter was becoming increasingly attracted to TJ's world.

When the group had jammed a while, the lighting changed and the man played the prelude to "You're the Best Thing That Ever Happened to Me." Junior Pennington began to sing, and his capacious mouth, toothy grin, grew increasingly sensual—a romantic possibility enhanced by orgasmic rhythms was suggested. Brandi was mesmerized; she didn't know he could play the piano, could sing, not like this anyway. She felt like she had to pee again.

Momentarily, a female vocalist, whom Brandi had not seen, joined the men on the platform and chimed in. Flo's mature, experienced, clear, and crisp, soprano stirred the crowd. They clapped, stood, swayed, chorused several times before the female vocalist loosed the song. "Thank you, thank you, thank you," she throatily expressed her appreciation to the crowd before continuing in song.

The club was packed to capacity—Brandi did not know so many Negroes lived in Claxville. Encounters with other people of her race had been minimal since she had gotten there in late August: there was the doctoral student, the one in 406 Davis Hall who lived only ninety miles from Wester. Brandi counted them on her fingers—Elnora Jenkins, the service workers on campus, maids, janitors, cooks, gardeners, all faces with no names; she clumped them under one finger of the counted hand and, most recently, there was the manager at Church's. Brandi had more phalanges than encounters with her own kind.

There were a few more colored students on campus, but contact with them was casual—they had a way of nodding at each other in the presence of others, thereby acknowledging one another's presence without directly associating. Life at Claxville had offered no positive, joyful community life to balance the mundane campus life offered to students at white colleges like hers. It was just like her daddy, Carruthers Brown, told her it was going to be—exactly like it.

The music drew her attention back to the present.

Taxi played that night, and the yet unnamed vocalist scoffed in lyrics at her lover. Another woman? Who is that woman? Where in the hell did he get on bringing her here? How dare he bring another into the vixen's den!

The crowd enjoyed each one's best and would speak for days about how good Junior Pennington played that night and how Flo expressed herself through song.

And Brandi wondered where she had seen the woman before. Soon, she realized that it was the one from the restroom, the one who sat smoking. She wondered what she was, if anything, to Taxi—nothing showed on the handsome face lit by a small piano lamp, nor did his mannerisms give him away.

However, by evening's end she didn't care; she had enjoyed being with the man. He was so full of surprises . . . too full of them. Between songs, he'd occasionally smile at her in the semidarkness, and her eyes were for him only. Floating glances would take away from her enjoyment of a smile that was big and wide . . . the kind that made her feel good and warm all over.

Nor did TJ . . . Flo wasn't his woman anyhow; she didn't own him.

Throughout the evening he occasionally eyed Brandi, offering apologetic glances; he was sorry that he couldn't talk to her, dance with her, hold her close to himself, caress her, rock her, smother her with kisses.

Brandi refused the verbal apologies rendered as he drove her back to Davis Hall, assuring him that she had a wonderful time.

As the coed left, when he had walked her to the dormitory's doorway and had seen her in and was on the way home, TJ realized he had not asked what happened to the cowardly ruffians who antagonized her—the ones who stole her drawers—so he made a mental note to ask her about them the following Friday night. Were they still on campus? Did she have classes with them? Were they still harassing her?

Julie had not been academically capable of maintaining her grades and had flunked out of school. True to his word, Mr. Blanchard had removed her from the university at the end of the semester. "She left the same day Mary Margaret left," she told TJ at yet another time when he renewed the conversation. "As a matter of fact, their car was parked right beside Mary Margaret's family's car. Her friends bid her farewell, so I know she left Claxville. I witnessed that with my own eyes."

"How was it?" Kris asked about the date as soon as her roommate had awakened the following Saturday morning. "Great," Brandi said, rolling over, hugging her pillow affectionately, tightening the patchwork quilt wound around her body. Although it was spring, she still needed the covers. Kris kept the air conditioner on high.

"Great? What's great?" Kris playfully yanked at the covers as she was anxious to hear about the previous evening's date. "Come on, girl. Get up and spill your guts. I want to hear everything!" she exclaimed.

"Stop!" Brandi shrieked, tugging at the covers Kris now held firmly in her grip. Then she loosed it and got up. "Can you wait till I get back from the john?" she said, and then she threw her housecoat over the pajamas and headed for the potty. "Turn that air down while I am gone. It's cold in here. You won't be able to hear me with my teeth chattering like this." Brandi demonstrated the discomfort.

"Only if you are going to spill you guts!" Kris shrieked playfully.

The other woman got off the bed and headed for the door. "Wait 'til I get back."

When she had given Kris a blow-by-blow rundown of the date—the dinner, the conversation that ensued—the roommate interrupted her and remarked seriously and almost convincingly, "You really unloaded on that guy. He might never come back again," as she shook her head in disbelief.

"That's what you think," Brandi chuckled and continued. "Then he took me to his house—I met his mother."

"Geez, you sure work fast!"

Brandi shook her head. "It was nothing like that. He changed clothes there before we went to the Basement."

"What did you do there?"

When she told Kris about the club, the band, and TJ's musical prowess, she exclaimed, "Gosh, he's full of surprises!" before asking, "Are you going out with him again?"

Brandi gave her a nod of affirmation. "He's picking me up Friday, same time, same place."

"Think you can wait that long?" Kris inquired. "I can see your heart beating across the room."

"Have to," Brandi told Kris as she left for work.

Her consternation about the date, the date itself, future dates with Taxi having overridden her concerns about finding jokes about white folks, she decided to "just leave it be!" which was what she imagined her mother's response would have been anyway. Brandi longed to talk to Sara about these things each time she telephoned, but she thought it not wise to do so.

As the woman's participation level in Dr. McIntyre's class diminished, Brandi grew less bitter about the goings on. TJ, as mysterious and elusive as he was at times, helped with problematic issues in a way that she had never anticipated.

The man continued to take her for casual dinners and to seat her beside him in the Basement. Soon, their weekend dates, which customarily began with supper, ended with breakfast at the International House of Pancakes or the Waffle House before he took her back to Davis Hall. As they spent time together, rode together, explored the city together, Brandi was rapidly falling in love with him.

Several weeks and an equal number of dates passed when the man made a detour on his way to drop her at the dorm. "I have to stop by my house a minute. Don't mind, do you?" he asked. By now the woman was comfortable with the changes he made in their habitual routines; he always had a run to make, somewhere to stop by, some errand to run.

Taxi drove into the yard and pulled around to the back of the house, parking next to his old yellow cab. He opened the passenger door and led Brandi up the steps into the back door—rather, what she believed was the back door of the Pennington house.

"Have a seat," he said when they had entered the large room, one about the size of an efficiency apartment, gesturing toward the room's large sitting area and a gorgeous overstuffed brocade-covered couch facing the foot of a huge wrought iron bed. "Make yourself at home, I got to change," the man told his company.

He took off his dress coat and headed through a door on the left side of a gigantic bed; it was so high until one seated on the couch could almost see the box springs' underside if one raised the beautiful off-white thick chenille spread. A small stepladder with two rungs rested on either side. Left to her own devices, Brandi visually explored the room.

On the coffee table that separated the sofa from the bed rested a hard-pressed rectangular-shaped handcrafted doily. The girl leaned forward, toying with its edges, longing to be able to do the fine needlework herself; she had never seen her mother do it, but she had often seen Aunt Sylvia use balls of yarn and steel crocheting hooks to fashion similar creations. When they were complete, the woman would wash them in thick Argo starch-and-water solution and press them to death with the tiny wrought irons she'd kept for this purpose—said an electric iron couldn't do it. A bottle of forest green pine-scented deodorizer in its center seemingly held it flat on the table, but Brandi knew better: it was weighed down with starch.

A similar doily of the same pattern was on an end table in a corner. A lamp and an eight-by-ten framed photo with its face down were on the table. Right next to the table was an overstuffed armchair, and on the same wall with the end table rested a solid pine dresser and a matching chest of drawers.

On the other side of the bed was a small bookshelf with squatty little pottery figurines set strategically here and there among some novels, a leather-bound set of classics, *National Geographic* magazines, a set of Funk and Wagnall's dictionaries, a thesaurus, several Bibles, and some biblical reference materials.

"Umph," she uttered, thinking about something Sara has said: "You can tell a lot about a person by the books on the shelf." "All of these spoke well of him," she thought, "if they were indeed his." She had no reason to believe they were not his. Like she told Kris, the man was full of surprises.

Everything was so neat, so modern, and so different from the side of the house in which Mrs. Pennington, TJ's mother, lived. This large room had variegated beautiful large-print floral covering on its walls; those of the other were plain old dingy sheetrock. Many old photographs—of family, Taxi by himself, the boy with both parents, the young man standing alongside the father who could have been his twin, friends, church folks, all with the church down the street as a backdrop, seemingly hundreds of pictures—had been tacked to the walls of the Pennington house as the years rolled by, and they were still there. Taxi's abode had yet to accumulate many memories; his walls held no pictures.

Brandi grew restless, curious while she awaited the man's return; so she got up, walked over to the end table, and picked the picture up. It was the girl, the one who sang at the Basement, the one who never spoke. A small movement in the room startled her, and her heart jumped. She almost dropped the picture, realizing that Taxi had reentered the room. "I was just straightening this up. Everything's so pretty," she stammered embarrassedly, attempting to play it off.

The man took the picture from her hands, opened the end table's drawer, placed the picture in, facedown, and closed it. "That's nothing for you to worry your sweet little face about." He held her face in his hand. Taxi stared at her rapt face, saw a longing in those hazel eyes which was more than even he could stand. A tightness constricted his throat, making it impossible for him to swallow, to breathe. The tightness spread, gripping the rest of his body, knotting him up inside until he thought he would die from wanting her. His gaze inadvertently shifted to her lips, soft and innocently inviting. The sight pulled him in, and the man kissed her first on the nose, and ever so sweetly he suckled from her full rich lips—and from her mouth.

Although Taxi had not meant to kiss her, now he couldn't stop himself. Hungrily, he tasted the sweetness of her mouth, drank its sweet, honeyed nectar. The man felt the touch of a tiny hand sliding inside his coat—the contact seared him through his shirt, broke his bronze skin, and touched his heart. An instant later he felt the press of her petite body against his and the childishly small mounds of her breasts.

Abruptly but gently, he pulled away before it was too late.

Brandi, having been pulled to tiptoe by the man's hand under her chin, remained *au pointe,* eyes shut after he released her. The man thumped her on the nose playfully, shook her ever so gently. "We better get going. Let's ride," he said throatily before she could ask what was wrong.

She followed him to the door, noticing that he had changed clothes when he had left the room—TJ was dressed in frumpy jeans, a green long-sleeve shirt, and that God-awful pukey plaid vest; the transformation from TJ to Taxi had been made, and she had been the least unawares; the men had become one and the same, images had blended.

"Wait right here," he touched her arm and said when they had reached the foot of the steps. He hopped in the newest, sleekest of the two parked vehicles and backed it out into the street. Leaving its motor running, he trotted back up the drive around the house where Brandi stood obediently. The driver opened the right front door of the taxi for the girl, who sighed, took a breath of air in, and shook her head in amazement at him.

The man pulled the first car in the drive and got back in the taxi with the woman.

"You're going to work now?" Brandi asked, suppressing a yawn. She was so sleepy, and he, he was still so enervated.

"Man gotta work if he wants to eat."

"Do you ever sleep?'

"Yeah."

"When?"

"When I get time?"

"When's that?"

"When I get time!"

The man laughed. Brandi almost swooned. Here she was overcome with sleep, and Taxi remained just as alert as he had when he had picked her up from Davis Hall at 6:00 p.m. the day before.

She dreamed about him. Taxi was reaching out to her. Brandi saw desire in his eyes, raced to him, impelled more by her own needs than the commanding pressure of his hands on her back when they were in each other's arms. Tilting her head back, she kissed him long and hungrily, thrilling to the caress of his hand on her spine, the small of her back, and to the demanding ardor of his lips which now led their love dance. Straining to get closer, she pressed her body tightly against his hard frame like she had done at his house.

The woman, the singer, the one from down at the Basement, she plucked him out of Brandi's dream.

"Ow . . . ," she whimpered pitifully and painfully into her pillow.

CHAPTER NINETEEN

Flo

Flo had cursed Junior Pennington out that Wednesday night after he brought the "little girl from over to the college" to the club, called him all kinds of sons of bitches, jerking at his clothes, challenging him to fight, threatening to kill him if he ever brought her puny little black ass back in the club. The man had moved himself away from her simply by loosening her fingertips from him and had taken his customary seat at the old upright piano and was fingering chords lightly, one by one, knowing that the difference between an accomplished musician and a mediocre one was knowledge of scales.

The rest of the fellows tuned their instruments while the singer tuned her vocal chords; she was nagging the hell out of Junior. Lou at the bar washed, dried, and polished glasses until their sheen was perfected. Wasn't nobody paying attention to the woman. Everybody was used to her bitchin'; she was all the time going on about first one thing and then another: songs were too high, too low, it was hard to "pitch" her. One thing was sure, when she got it she had it and wasn't likely to turn it loose. That was why Junior Pennington and the Boys, as the group had dubbed themselves, had put up with her.

It wasn't because Flo was Junior's woman—at least, that was what he always said; she wasn't his old lady. But here she was acting like it, and nobody knew what to make of it. Everybody had been watching the man bring the girl into the club, "setting" her right beside him while he played, but nobody had accosted him; it wasn't their business.

"Poor Flo," a few of the women had whispered sympathetically when the woman was out of earshot. "She done put all her time in him, helped him build on to his mama's house, put all her money in it, decorated it herself, would sit right there in that same chair making crocheted things for it, ordering stuff out of the Sears and Roebuck Catalog . . . now he done gone over there to the college and got himself one of them little rich girls. Bet her people's got lots of money and he trying to get his sleazy hands on that."

"You know you right," another joined in, "but that's the way niggers' do you, that's why come I don't trust them."

Brandi was anything but rich. Cat had inherited the small farm from his aged parents, both of whom had passed when he was back home from his brief hiatus at college, after he and Sara had married and had their first baby. So the Browns had stayed right there in Wester planting seasonal crops, rotating them as the agriculture department deemed appropriate; hiring neighbor hands to pick cotton, break corn, pick butter beans, crowder peas, squash; to harvest okra, tomatoes, collards, turnips, mustard greens, sugar cane, tobacco, watermelons, whatever he could grow on the hundred or so acres where the Claxville University student's daddy had been born, reared, where he intended to die.

Near the house was the livestock used for food and a small garden that Sara and her brood of children tended. They had some cows—cows for breeding, beef, and two, "Bell" and "Gal," who supplied the family with milk, thick cream for Sara's frozen fruity homemade hand-churned treats, butter as well as ice cream. And pigs, sows, boars aplenty, and besides that the couple of billy goats left over from one of Brandi's 4-H club projects. Round back of the house near the storehouse was a pen with a chicken coop full of squawking pullets, chickens, guineas, a rooster, and a section cordoned off for the sole tom turkey and several turkey hens.

Bordering the small garden from which Sara got peppers (bell, yellow, hot, red for homemade Tabasco, and green for vinegary pepper sauce) to pour over the greens (collards, mustards, turnips, and onions, radishes, rutabagas, strawberries) were fruit trees (plum, peach, pear, kumquat, one orange, fig, mulberry). And back off from the garden toward the woods was a small grove of young nut trees—pecans, black walnuts—which now yielded enough to sell a few, do some baking, candy-making, for roasting in butter and salted, to eat warm or cold, and to help pay property taxes imposed by the local government.

The Browns didn't have a lot of money in the bank, but one could safely say that, barring a natural disaster, the family could survive. And that if Brandi had not secured that scholarship up to the university, Cat and Sara would have made sure that she did receive an education, some sort of training. They saw education as a "way out" for colored people . . . they wanted more for their children than they had had, so they would have made provisions for her.

BRENDA SMITH

And here was their eldest, Brandi, in the middle of a domestic mess, a "colored people's dilemma." Flo was wanting to scrap with her, had told her bosom buddies that she was going to "kick her butt" next time she came in the club "'cause all them bitches over there at that college think they white, think they can just come into town, think they are more than we is."

Thirty-five years after they had met, the boy-next-door had, with the flick of a hand, severed his ties with the girl-next-door—the first love, first piece, first date, stand-by, whatever he had needed her to be whenever . . . TJ had outgrown Flo, come to despise her beauty; in it was no vanity . . . every penny she got her hands on was spent for makeup, clothes, jewelry, shoes, hairdos, cigarettes. The man hated smoke; she lived for the next cigarette, joint, anything wrapped in cigarette paper, burned, inhaled, exhaled, polluting the air. She stunk, always reeked of it! Her once clean flesh-colored fingertips were yellowed. Her overly expensive clothes all had small dotted windows in the bodice—windows made by roasted marijuana seeds that flickered, popped, and exploded, leaving their marks wherever they lay . . . And most despicable of all was her foul mouth. Flo could no longer make a decent sentence, couldn't communicate, without the F word, could only refrain from obscenities when singing, and that was because someone else penned the lyrics.

Not only that, the man was also sick of helpless, soft women who feigned ignorance, couldn't do a thing for themselves, not even think. They became a bore, a nuisance after a while. They didn't even know how to dream—sisters would steal yours if you had one, would rob you blind. He knew all too well. Flo was a leech—she had almost done it to him, had almost sucked the life out of him.

Soon, Flo's loud talking grew overwhelming; it's volume and content grated on T's last nerve. "All I know is this," she said jabbing at his face with a pointed finger, "you keep bringing her puny ass back in here, I'm gone put my foot up it to the knee." The man shot her a warning glance. "You heard what I said," the woman argued incessantly, not even pausing for a drag. Ash from the cigarette's tip fell to the floor.

The man vaulted from the piano stool, grabbed the squawking woman by an arm, and led her through the bar, up the steps, out the back door. When they were beside his car, well out of the earshot of the checker-playing men he respected so much and of Lou and the fellows, he made his intentions known. "Listen, woman," he said to the one who had raised his dandruff, "you don't own me, and I don't own you. You've known all along what it was all about, what I'm about. You know better than anyone else," he accused pointedly, reminding her of an understanding that they had always had. "I love her," he emitted quietly.

Flo was thunderstruck. The grieving woman shook her head vigorously and tried to push her way into his arms, wanting the security that he had always provided.

He stepped aside; she fell forward, almost falling, but regained her footing. "T, please!" the woman, obviously stung by the revelation, cried out.

"What's love got to do with it!"

"Everything," he countered before going back indoors to practice.

When Brandi had seen Flo in the bathroom that first night at the Basement, she had paid the woman little attention but gave her more notice as time passed.

The young coed said nary a word to her, nor did she elicit any conversation. She longed to find out more about the perceived adversary, but there was no one to ask except Taxi, and that was out.

A couple of Friday nights after T officially broke up with Flo, Brandi was back at the club by his side. Soon, nature called, so Brandi got up to go to the john. Flo was quick to notice her movements; she knocked back the rest of the Seagram's Seven she was drinking and swiped at her mouth with the back of her hand like a drunken cowboy. After setting the glass on the table, she slid her chair back, stood up, picked a napkin off the table, and mopped sweat off her forehead. "Boy, it's hot in here!" she exclaimed to no one in particular. Her nose ran too, so she swiped that too with a crumpled, soiled, damp napkin from the table. She let the snotty paper fall to the floor; and staring toward where Brandi descended, she blinked away the smoky fog surrounding her before she began to walk toward the curtained exit where she'd last seen Junior's new woman's back.

"God, how I hate this part. If there was a way around it," she thought. Her bedeviled, wicked conscience, which was full of drink and smoke, exhorted, "Quit stalling! Get on with it . . . git that bitch!"

Flo let go of the back of the chair; the piece of furniture fell, making a clap like thunder on the Basement's cement dance floor.

A muffled cough, a tug at her dress' bodice, and she was ready.

Flo strutted across the room and into the bathroom in the back when she saw that Brandi had gone there rather than the bar. The younger woman was in the stall, so she waited for her. When Brandi came out, Flo was sitting on a backless chair smoking a Kool Filter King.

Brandi sneezed.

The older, experienced woman drew on the cigarette, took a deep breath, let the nicotine flow from lips to chest, to breast, be filtered by her lungs, travel upward to her brain, make its deadly deposit of tar in her gray matter, reroute itself before she exhaled. And when she was done, Flo threw the butt on the floor, squashed it with her foot, elevated herself, and sauntered over to share the mirror with Brandi who was washing her hands.

"I ought to kill you," the aggressor thought, yet she said nothing; she didn't have to. Her eyes spoke it to Brandi's mirrored image; thus, the taunted grew wary. The singer raised her right hand and stuck it in her bosom. Brandi eyed her closer, catching a glint of silver.

She grew afraid. "What if she's got a knife?" she thought. "Lord, what am I going to do?" She'd never fought anyone in her life, hadn't fought anything except gnats out of her face during dog days in Wester.

Fear became her companion—she tried to move, to return to the safety of the ballroom, but she was frozen.

She caught more of the glimmer from the object nestled in Flo's bosom—Brandi squeezed her eyes shut, peering through narrowed lids.

Her movement or lack of movement did not go unnoticed. Flo felt her fear and enjoyed the emotion her mere presence evoked.

Flo reached further into the bosom of her low-cut royal purple frock, taking as much time as she desired, withdrew a ruby red lipstick, applied a generous amount to her full lips, and returned it to her bosom. Next she spat on the middle finger of her right hand and laid her neatly cropped, freshly plucked eyebrows down with the body fluids. Then she soaped and washed her hands and looked at cigarette-stained fingertips, nibbled nails. The woman made a mental note to shape them, file them—she had torn her hose trying to put them on before the show, put some polish on them, before she shook her phalanges until they were air dry.

Brandi sighed with relief. Her exhaled breath released slow, her rigid posture intact, refusing to allow any motion to detract the singer from the ministrations to herself.

Finally, Flo straightened her dress, smoothing it with her hands, shimmied, shook her shoulders, adjusted the dress's shoulder straps, pulling and separating the already-low-cut bodice open to expose more of her full cleavage, shimmied once more wiggling her buttocks, departed with her four-inch heels clacking.

Brandi almost collapsed; a wave of relief swept over her!

Flo strutted across the room, proud as a peacock, and went back over to the table and told her friends how she had told the little tart off, how she wasn't going to fool with Junior Pennington no more, calling him a "used-up mother fucker," saying, "He ain't worth a fart, can't even get it up anymore, gonna find myself a real man."

All nodded in agreement, and one said, "You should have been got rid of him."

"Yeah," another argued, "he wasn't doing nothing but using you."

And yet another insisted, "He ain't gone never marry nobody anyway. He's a mama's boy. You'll be better off without him, and her too for that matter. That old lady ain't nice as people make her out to be."

In reality these friends had remained at the table while the two women were closeted together in the restroom, had spent their time drinking, shooting the breeze, delighting in Flo's misfortune. They had snickered, getting their kicks out of seeing "high yellow Ms. Snug Butt with her uppity ass" get hers. All delighted, jealously, as neither had gotten a crack at the good-looking man. It was known around the south side and over on the West Side that Junior Pennington and Flo were a number, were tight, that he was Flo's man, and everybody had been scared to mess with him. Now this pretty young thing come over from the college and took him. Flo was a laughingstock.

The pianist had noticed the movement at the table across the way when Brandi had gone to the bathroom. Flo, in her drunken stupor, had pushed her chair back so hard it fell on the floor—it was obvious to the man that her adrenaline was pumping at maximum level. She had reached down and picked the chair up before heading in the same direction as his friend. TJ kept a watchful eye as long as he could, started to go to the john himself but stayed put, praying that nothing unseemly would transpire while the two women were back there behind the curtain; he'd kill Flo if it did, "would choke the life out of her with his bare hands," he thought, looking down at his phalanges tinkering the ivories on the keyboard quietly and softly. His ear was attuned to the area beyond the curtain.

As soon as Brandi was back in her seat, Taxi leaned over and asked, "Everything all right?"

"Uh-huh, yeah," she assured him, touching his arm lightly.

The man relaxed, resumed playing with fluidity almost abated when the two women were not sharing the same space with him.

Brandi tried to sleep the next morning, was tired to the bone but was awakened by the telephone. "Hey, what you doing?" said the caller.

"Hey, Ma," Brandi called back excitedly, "got your phone put in!" It was now March—three months had passed since the Christmas gift had been given.

"Yeah, it took a while for the man to come put it in. Cat had to go back down to the telephone company a couple of times. He almost gave up on it. One time I thought he would, but he talked the Browns, Washingtons, Shermans, Fullers into getting one, and it caught on like fire from there." Thoughtfully, Sara added, "Made sense though, they all just like us, got children moving away from home too. Some of them in college just like you, some in the service." Sara nostalgically spoke of change and how important communication devices had become as change occurred. "Then they told your daddy that more lines had to be run out here before they could put it in." The woman rambled on. "We had to go around and get some more people to say they'll put one in before they got started. Sylvia put their name on the list, but your uncle say he doesn't want one. Anyway, I've been trying to get you since yesterday. But we are on a party line, and everybody was trying to use their phone too—seems like everybody's all of a sudden got something to talk about.

"And Minnie, child when she get on, she just stay on—oh gosh, I better shut my mouth, talking about people, we're on a party line. I'll have to talk about that when you're at home."

Sara paused for breath.

"When you coming back to get your spring clothes? It must be getting hot up there—it is down here. Weatherman says dog days gone come early this year. It's bone dry. We ain't hardly had any rain, and he says we ain't gonna have much rain," the mother kept talking, not giving her daughter a chance to reply.

"Here, speak to your sister, your brother," Sara handed the phone to each of the little ones.

"Did you hear what they said?" she asked Brandi after each gave his or her simple salutation.

"Well, gal, I better get off this line," Sara said when all had had a chance to say a few words. "Don't know how much this is going to cost. Cat says hey. You write me, tell me when you coming get them clothes," the woman spoke hurriedly. Brandi could hear her father in the background prodding the woman to end the long-distance call. "Ain't going to be able to keep it if y'all talk too long," he argued.

And then she was gone. Brandi couldn't go back to sleep—her thoughts returned to the man; she could still feel TJ's mouth on her own. His kisses were so sweet. She wanted that man, and she wanted him bad, but she just wasn't pretty like Flo. Her mirror told her that: Flo was high yellow, almost as tall as

TJ. Brandi was at least a foot and a half shorter than the two—was squat by her own definitions.

She got up to look in the mirror. Brandi rubbed her face: it was plain—faded acne scars gazed back at her. The other woman looked like one of them models from *Ebony Magazine*; Flo's skin was as smooth as a baby's butt. She was quite stunning!

Brandi was just like Sara who was twice her age, looked just like her, was cute, average, had no features that set her apart from the rest beyond the brown hair and funny-colored eyes, and Sara in turn was a replica of Sylvia who was almost eighty-one. The women from Wester were not as richly endowed as the singer; nevertheless they were built "like small brick houses" and had nice legs.

The girl looked in the mirror, even more displeased with what she saw. She lifted her pajama top, stuck her chest out, cupped her small breasts with her hands, pushing them upward, jutting toward the looking glass. Brandi turned sideways to study her profile, to clearly discern the difference in the before and after looks. Where Flo was full and rich, the girl was almost boyish—her bra size was AAA. Although she was beautiful, possessed natural beauty, and had a graceful walk, she longed to dress like a woman, a real woman . . . like Flo. Then she would be ravishing. So she got dressed and went to Woolworth's to do some shopping.

After work, Taxi ran by to pick Brandi up before dressing for the customary dinner and evening at the club. She bounded from dorm's doorway with her arms folded over and on her chest a bit. When she got in the car, Taxi looked at her, shook his head knowingly and said emphatically, with purpose as he'd seen the difference from afar and had had a moment to think about her obvious insecurity, "One day, no titties, the next day too many. Go back and take that thing off. Don't you know I like you just like you are." He kissed her on the forehead, loosed her face, and she slid butt first out of the car. The young woman, arms making a vise on her chest, head down, went back to her room.

Brandi was so ashamed—she started to stay in the room, but she knew the man would come after her. She raised her burnt orange sweater, took her arms out of its sleeves, and replaced the new black lacy B-cup padded brassiere with her usual 100 percent cotton triple-A bra. She was almost out of the door again before she decided to remove the skimpy black lace drawers too and put on her plain white cotton briefs.

Momentarily, shame was replaced with relief. "Whew," she emitted as she inspected herself in the mirror before leaving the room, "looks better and feels better too." Brandi was glad the man had sent her back to change. Sara would have liked that, and so would Carruthers. The Browns had given many lectures on being oneself, not keeping up with the Joneses, as well as on not trying to impress other to the degree that one would compromise one's self, one's integrity, on not letting the world define who a person was or could be.

Back in the car, TJ's conscience whipped him unmercifully. He wished he had been more tactful. He groaned. The man had been afraid that Brandi would want to emulate the other woman. He thought if he had talked to her about Flo, the current fiasco could have been avoided. But Flo wasn't his woman. The gentle giant also wished he had not spoken so forcefully, with little regard for tact, to the object of his affections. What if she didn't come back? He looked at his watch and tapped a nervous tune on the car's red dashboard, quit long enough to adjust the band on the radio, looked up and sighed with relief when he saw burnt orange and her. Brandi was jogging merrily back to the car.

The man sighed with relief.

Taxi jumped out, went around the car to the curbside, held the door open until his date was seated, and off they went, weaving and bobbing through the university's busy Friday evening traffic until they were on the open stretch that led to their habitual evening's dining place. The man, smiling thoughtfully at his woman, considered how lucky he was and promised to keep his electric temper in check, to handle future situations more tactfully.

He had acted like such a fool out at the trailer park that day the white boy had sent him out to pick up the woman. Then he had almost lost her when she stopped by the station to make up, his unforgiving spirit prevailing, and had just now gone ballistic because she tried to make herself look good for him.

The man patted her left thigh affectionately, apologetically, promisingly. Brandi wiggled in her seat, sliding as close to him as she could get, looked upward and gave him a knowing smile. "That's my girl," Taxi said, and he leaned over and pecked her on the forehead before turning his eyes back to the road.

Brandi knew that the incident would never be spoken about again . . . she also knew better than to ever try to be anybody but herself again.

They sped along in silence a few more miles.

Soon, the young woman renewed previously asked questions about the man who remained elusive, mysterious . . . the man who refused to be pinned down to anybody or anything, for that matter. She wanted to know who he really was, where he came from, how he managed to stay in this hell hole, not only to survive, but also to thrive.

TJ told her that he had been at Fort Hood for eight years, had escaped "Nam" because he was an only son to aging parents, and was contemplating whether he was going to re-up when the message had come that he was needed at home—that Reverend Pennington had expired. "My old man's dead?" He returned to Claxville right away; the only son of an elderly couple, Thaddeus Sr. and Sister Pennington, drove all night and most of the next day to be with his mother.

He went by the church first, half expecting his father to be there—he always was; he always had been there before. Thaddeus Pennington had come home few times since his departure several years earlier: first to make the big times—he was a musician—and then to go into the service when that didn't work out.

"How are you, boy?" Rev. Flewellyn, Shiloh's associate pastor, had greeted him. The two men hugged; the older held the younger at arm's length, then hugged him some more, giving him a bear hug. "Just like your daddy boy, look like he spit you out . . . He was always talking 'bout how he was hoping you take over the church one day."

"I ain't no preacher!" the man shrieked at the minister. TJ wasn't up to any reminiscing, especially about church, so he spoke more forcefully than he had intended to. He hadn't set foot in one since the day he had finished high school.

"How's Ma?" he asked, worry in his voice.

"You ain't been to the house yet?"

"Nope, just got in town . . . was half expecting Daddy to be here . . . he always was."

"She about the same as usual," Rev. Flewellyn assured him. "She is. Your mama's a strong woman. She knows the Lord, and most importantly, he knows her. Sister Pennington will be all right, soon as she sees you . . . see you are fine."

The elder man patted his charge on the back, hugged him anew and encouraged him not to tarry any longer. "She right there on the porch, right now, waiting on you, son."

Mrs. Pennington was right where Junior Knew, or rather, had hoped she would be.

"I'm sorry, Ma," TJ said to the old woman who sat on the porch rocking. It seemed like a day had not passed; she was sitting there when he had left home. A wave of relief had swept over the man; he'd fathomed all sorts of things while he had made his way home. He envisioned an aggrieved woman taken to bed in mourning, surrounded by deaconesses whispering softly with respect while they took over the house. In his mind's eye, church members were raking the yard; little piles of leaves, sticks, dry grass smoldered in preparation for the impending wake, funeral, and its aftermath.

It was not so. A simple black wreath on the door was the only indicator that death had claimed an occupant. It was apparent that the woman was in charge of her own affairs; rested faithful—did not need to be surrounded by mourners, well wishers, do-gooders, the curious.

"You staying?" the old woman said as if questioning her son about his intentions.

"If you don't mind."

"Don't mind at all . . . your room's just like you left it. Stay long as you want to. This is your home . . . has always been your home . . . always will be. We'll talk about the arrangements in the morning." Then she was fast asleep. TJ covered her with the blanket, which rested half on her, half on the porch. He brushed his hand across her silver crop of hair; TJ had not seen his already aged parents grow increasingly older.

The yellowed and yellowing pictures on the wall of his parents as newlyweds, of TJ (TJ the baby, the toddler, a youth, a teen, a high school graduate, a military enlistee), of family and friends, and of more than a few which included Flo—the preponderance which had Shiloh Missionary Baptist Church, which his father had founded and pastored until his untimely demise, as their backdrop; each claimed his attention.

Thaddeus Pennington Jr. had always been a hustler, so work came easy for him. He showed up at the Basement, the local joint/nightspot after the funeral, and Lou took him in right away. "Man, I've been looking for a good piano player," he said. "Make yourself right at home." And TJ had sat down on the stool and had done just that.

Fortunately his period of enlistment in the army was almost over. The man had taken terminal leave and only had to return to Fort Hood to complete some paperwork and take care of a few other affairs.

Some of his partners had also hooked up with him, and they had formed a group which played weekends at the club—they played for tips only and did other social events: proms, weddings, house parties, birthday parties, family reunions, any kind of party, etc. Soon, his nights were taken up, but days proved to be a drag. "Ma," he had asked when he wasn't home over a week or two, "how about I add on a room to the back of the house, and another bathroom too? You don't mind?"

Mrs. Pennington didn't mind, so TJ had gotten some of his old jackleg buddies to come around to the house, got some boards, studs, nails, sheetrock, a couple of handsaws and sawhorses, a gallon of moonshine, and they had made the newest-looking shotgun house on the narrow dirt street take on a T-shape. A full bathroom with a shower separated TJ's room from the kitchen of the Pennington household.

Thus the man was able to keep his past separated from his present. He visited his mother daily; she never set foot in his less-than-humble abode—his every invitation was met with, "I ain't going in no whore house. I know you bringing women in there."

Then he would tease her. "When I find a nice one, I'm gone bring her in through the front door," he'd say.

And she'd reply, "I won't hold my breath none," before playfully poking her walking stick at "the only offspring the good Lord ever blessed her with."

After adding to the house, Taxi had purposed to seek gainful daytime employment; however, he couldn't find anything that suited his fancy. Claxville had no real industry. It was just a college town—it wasn't a real big one at that as it was not the state's flagship university, and it boasted only half the population of such; so everybody he knew worked for the college in housekeeping, maintenance, grounds, transportation, laundry—all menial tasks. "Just didn't see how I could jump for anybody anymore. I'd done enough of that when I was in service," he had told Brandi, who had asked him how he got started in the taxi-driving business. "I was passing by the bus station one day, saw some colored folks get off. They had to wait till the white man took all the white folks where they needed to go, so I stopped and picked them up. They were talking about how they hadn't never been no place where there wasn't a taxi for colored people."

He went on, "I didn't say a word to nobody. I got me some paint, splashed it on that old heap I had when I left Texas, and old TJ was in business. People was needing a ride everywhere, over to the college to work, up town, to church." The man laughed. "You can't beat it! I set my own hours, work when I want to," he had told her one weekend.

Brandi marveled at the wisdom shown by the man. "If I'd run my mouth all the time like some folks I know, somebody would have come along, took my idea, and run with it before the paint on my rig got dry," he asserted, enjoying the attention given by the young woman.

"Ever thought about expanding your one-man show?"

"You mean get a fleet!" Taxi exclaimed, not because they idea was new or preposterous but because she was leading the discussion about expanding his business. "I've thought about it," he said seriously, "but I ain't done nothing about it. I've been saving a little money—I figured that plus the money that my daddy left me, a little insurance money, I'll be able to get it going in another couple of years."

Brandi shook a warning finger at him. "Don't put off for tomorrow what you can do today. At least that's what my mama always says."

The mention of her mother embarrassed him slightly; he suddenly recalled how the mother's wisdom was more congruent, more in line with that of his own parent's sageness. Sara and he were equals, were the same age; her daughter with whom he now spoke, spent all his time with, was half her age—and "half mine," he thought mournfully.

"What do you think about that?" she asked the listless man. She tugged at his sleeve when her question received no reply.

"What?"

"Oh, you weren't listening." She dreamed aloud. "I was saying you ought to buy another car, get someone else to drive the old one—stretch out, flex your muscles. That way you can slow down, relax some, won't have to make so many runs. And you need to get your own place. You can have telephones—your own phones—and a secretary, a dispatcher." By now she was bouncing up and down in the car seat, was unable to contain herself, and the ideas continued to pour forth. "Taxi," she said seriously to the man, using the nickname she'd given him, one that he had accepted early on in their relationship, "you could really buy a couple of new cars, hire some drivers, manage the business, expand it . . . make it a limousine service—for proms, for when singers and folks come to town—they won't have to be borrowing one from the funeral home." Her words tripped over each other as she spoke excitedly.

"Whoa! I ain't no pencil pusher," he argued. "You ain't going to sit me behind no desk!" The man loosed the steering wheel, threw his hands upward, arresting the daydreams, the revelations—it was overwhelming.

Thaddeus pulled into his yard.

Now that the two were officially seeing each other, Brandi increasingly spent Saturdays' and Sundays' early hours at his abode lolling on his bed, waiting for him to change clothes, daydreaming and fantasizing about what could be—recreating *True Stories*, creating her own. The man made no attempts at seduction . . . it was almost overwhelming. Brandi could hardly stand the anticipation—she had wet dreams.

Their relationship was equally perplexing to the man accustomed to "getting laid" whenever he took somebody out. He had longed for a little "nookie" several times; he'd been tempted to take Flo over to his house just to "get off," but there wasn't any sense in that right now . . . he wasn't her man, and she wasn't his woman. Besides, she had called him all kinds of "sons of bitches" after he had taken the girl from the college to the club that first night. She had gone on like a crazy woman.

"And you let her sit her puny ass in *my chair*," Flo said to him, placing extra emphasis on the seat as she had continued to berate him, almost making him punch her, so there wasn't no sense in fooling with her anymore. The man smiled, remembering another scrap over a seat . . . a visiting sister had sat in his mama's seat down at Shiloh—wasn't much church that Sunday. There wasn't any peace in the valley again until it was clear that the ushers were to direct others away from Sister Pennington's pew seat on the front row. "Something about women and seats," he mused thoughtfully.

"I sure would like to visit Shiloh sometime," Brandi told the man before the holidays, renewing her efforts to get him to take her to the upcoming Easter service. "My mama's really been on my case," she said. "I ain't been to church since I been up here, used to go every Sunday . . . and Sunday school too."

"You really miss it?" he asked, readily wishing that he had not, for her response was, "Sure do. I really miss going."

"I'll take you," he relented halfheartedly, acknowledging to himself that he was getting to be a Santa Claus; he was pretty damn near a sugar daddy. All this woman had to do was say "I want" and he broke his neck to get it. That just wasn't like old TJ. It was a good thing that she wasn't a "taker," wasn't one to be kept, was independent, self-reliant, stood on her own two feet. The man admitted to himself that all she had to do was ask and he would turn his pockets inside out for her.

The man was in an extra pensive mood one day when he picked her up—had heard something on the news that disturbed him a bit. "How's class?" he asked as soon as greetings had been exchanged.

"It's fine," she responded to his obvious consternation, "I just tune them people out—they don't bother me no more." She attempted to shrug off more questions for she didn't want to talk about it anymore. He paused, wearing that brooding, serious, almost gloomy look he'd been wearing a lot lately.

"Are they still into the joke thing?"

Brandi didn't want to dwell on this any longer, was disinterested. She shifted in her seat nervously, was uncertain about where this conversation was leading.

Thaddeus was persistent.

"What's some of the jokes they been telling?" he asked tentatively, sensing her own discomfort. But he probed on because he never would have known anything about it in the first place if she had not dumped on him that first night they went to dinner. Now he was concerned that Brandi, in her naiveté, was so vulnerable that she could get hurt physically and emotionally in the girlish games.

"I never could tell a joke, can't remember the punch line, so you'd be better off if I don't ever try," she said earnestly. "What made you think about that stuff anyway?" she asked quite embarrassed.

"College students must be pretty dumb everywhere," the man uttered.

"What you mean?" she asked.

He shrugged his shoulders. "I just heard something while I was driving over to get you about some college students somewhere taking over the administration building. The National Guard had been called in . . . Anyway, seem like a few of them got killed because they started throwing rocks, sticks, bottles, books, anything they could get their hands on at the guards, and somebody let loose a few rounds in the crowd."

"Humph," she muttered, "sound like them white kids. They'll do stupid stuff like that and won't have any remorse either."

"That's what I was thinking too. You be careful messing around with them crazy white girls," he forewarned her. "Their mamas and daddies probably belong to the Klan, and you know they don't know how to do nothing but lowdown stuff." Like Carruthers, TJ was blunt, but she admired that in him even when it made her squirm as it did at the moment.

Silence overtook them as they sped into the night. It was broken when he said, "By the way, give me your telephone number. I been thinking I need to check on you more regular, like during the week."

She sighed with relief, glad that he was changing the subject.

The woman turned in the passenger seat to face him and drew her knees up under her buttocks. "Only if you give me yours," she teased spryly, desperate to lighten his pensive mood.

"I'm serious," Taxi refused to play along, to relent, wouldn't give up—he challenged the mask she wore. The man placed his hand on her arm, applying pressure. "I'm dead serious, Brandi Leigh Brown," he insisted. "Promise me you will be careful."

She rubbed her arm when he released it, promising weakly, "I will!" The woman wanted to argue that she could manage things because she was different.

It was Mr. Z who had labeled her "different," had told her in an oddly wry but supportive way when she had stopped by the store to say good-bye the day before she had left Wester. "You're different," the Jewish man had said. "You have the mark on you. You'll go far partly because you're not afraid to be different."

Different? Was that why most all her young life she had felt as if she was swimming against the tide? Why she always saw the cup half-full rather than half-empty? Saw things upside down rather than right side up? she wondered.

It was that same kind of upside-down thinking that could make her want to argue at that very minute of this present conversation that the girls with whom she was in conflict were but spoiled, so she spoke up. "Ah, they're kind of devious . . . not like that," she told him to keep her voice even. "They're just spoiled," Brandi spoke unconvincingly to the man who retorted forcefully. "Spoiled my ass, you talking about the Klan's breeders. They tote dragons in their ovens. You better be careful."

She grew quiet, and rationality questioned her: What if Taxi was right? Was she in any kind of danger?

TJ's warnings, unlike those given by Cat before she left home about the other students' raucous behavior, did not fall on deaf ears. Now that she had been the object of some of their hateful acts, the warning had a different effect—it unnerved her, and she grew frightened. Brandi Leigh felt like she was drowning, had gone down for the third time; she drank from life's chlorinated waters . . . her nostrils stung; her warm breath smelled like bleach, like Clorox.

That night when she lay in her bed, Brandi tried to forget about the conversation, to think positive, good thoughts, but the good thoughts wouldn't stay; she couldn't make them stay. She tried to go to sleep and sleep refused to come so she went on a letter-writing blitz—wrote to Sara a catch-up letter, a necessary evil now that the Browns had a telephone. It was so much easier just to pick it up and call. Brandi also wrote to Aunt Sylvia, a few distant cousins, some folks from down at the church, a couple of neighbors, and teachers.

After the letter-writing blitz, she got comfortable and curled up in the bed with some notes taken in class. She kept an eye on the clock on the desk, and when it was almost noon that Saturday, she had become pleasantly relaxed and went to sleep.

Julie and Laura were on either side of her dragging her facedown, by her arms, toward the cross; her bare toes made a reluctant trail in the dirt over by the campus' athletic field. The other girls jeered, booed, hissed, cat-called, encouraged the perpetrators on. Old Rattler, the university's mascot, raised up from his bed of green, made a coil, let his reddish orange tongue hang loose, drew back his scaled head as if to strike—instead he belched a long loud laugh. Ms. Winthrop stood at the base of the twenty-foot-high wooden oak cross where she called for the resident assistant to bring another can of kerosene. The resident assistant dragged the heavy five-gallon keg of fuel over to the cross and placed it at the woman's feet.

Davis Hall's third-floor occupants—all female—were too short, too weak to hang her on the cross, so they tied her arms and legs around the bottom of the pole. Brandi wailed, moaned, begged for mercy. "No, please, don't stop, uh-uh, *no* . . ."

"Can't get the cap off this can!" the resident assistant yelled, and Mr. Henri, dressed in contemporary Klan's white, edged his way through the crowd, wrested the cap from the container, grabbed the can, and encircled the wooden fixture, sprinkling the fuel evenly as he went by the young woman.

"Jesus, keep me near the cross . . . ," Brandi whimpered in her sleep; she was hot, burning up. She toed the bed linen and the patchwork quilt that was always at the foot of her bed.

"In the cross, in the cross . . ." The chorus drew her back to nightmare's fiery scene. She looked beyond the blazing inferno.

In a distance she could see Sara, arms outstretched, wailing inaudibly in horror at the ugly sight while Carruthers tore at the invisible veil that separated reality from dream, sublime from surreal. Her father's warm breath against the coolness of the imaginary wall made a thick fog, which soon cut her parents from her view and she from theirs.

Brandi tried to sit up, to raise her body from the bed. She couldn't move. Nightmare's evil arms held her in place.

The flames of hatred licked at her . . . her head rolled vigorously from side to side. She could smell burning flesh.

Sir Dubblerville, the knight in shining armor, ran through the covey of white-hooded Claxville University students. The girls from the class snatched at him, but he broke loose and sprinkled iodized salt on the fire, putting it out. That was what Sara had always done when grease on the rims of the electric range had caught fire.

Dr. McIntyre stood by, a water hose held limply in her hand leaking a few drops of water, and Elnora Jenkins stood by the faucet. "Turn it on, please turn it on . . . ," Brandi screamed, the humiliation more than her sleeping psyche could bear.

Actually, Brandi lay shivering on her bed in her third-floor room alone, her knees pulled toward her stomach, arms wrapped tightly against her chest. She rolled over on her back, sat straight up in the bed. The young woman could not stop the shivers, grew nauseous, and her stomach felt queasy. And she kept having to swallow away the saliva that was accumulating in her mouth.

"God," she thought, "it ain't time for Granny to come again," before she was out of the room making a run for the bathroom. The woman vomited, the slime getting all over her clothes, her feet, the toilet seat, the floor; and when she was finished she went to the sink where she leaned on it, broke down and cried. When no more tears would come, Brandi rinsed her mouth, splashed cool water on her face, checked her eyes in the mirror. "Ooh, I look a mess," she muttered. The woman grew despondent.

It only lasted a moment though—her normal cheerful optimism overruled her fears. A new day was there . . . new days always brought new beginnings with them.

CHAPTER TWENTY

Easter Sunday

"Remember, this is just to satisfy your mama," were the first words TJ spoke when he had let her out of the car as they wound their way through the wave of cars that lined both sides of the dirt street in front of Shiloh Baptist Church. He thought he would set things straight right then, didn't want her to get attached, didn't want to get himself attached to the church again either.

She headed off his superficial effort at putting his foot down. "It'll make your mama happy too. I've been to church since you been." Brandi chided her reluctant companion, punching her elbow in his rib cage hard enough to make him wince. The man playfully grabbed her hand, held it in his as they approached Shiloh's steps.

TJ was not particularly pleased about going to Shiloh this Sunday, but the girl had a way with him. She could get him to do what others couldn't. Here he was dressed up in Sunday-go-to meeting clothes—blue suit, white long-sleeve shirt, and string-up Stacy Adams going to the Easter morning church service. He had not set foot in the door since Rev. Pennington's funeral. The church was full when they got there—everybody in Claxville came to church two days out of every year: Christmas and Easter.

A sea of white, lilacs, yellows, tangerines, pinks, limes of the resurrection-celebration season filled every nook and cranny of the sanctuary. White shoes, white ladies' pumps, white girls' flats, white babies' first walking shoes lined each side of the center aisle narrowed by folding chairs the ushers had placed at each pew's end to accommodate the day's crowd.

One of the ushers greeted Thaddeus Pennington Jr. and his guest and led them toward the front. A gentle tug of her hand set Brandi in motion. Hand in hand they waded through the sea of onlookers, many recognizing and acknowledging the man's presence with a nod, a smile, a wave, a thumbs up, or some suitable greeting. A few "amens" even punctuated the air.

While most women sported hats, others sported their newly straightened hairdos, having given up the stylish, popular Afros for the occasion. Every girl wore a hat, carried a basket of colored eggs in nests of green, shredded cellophane grass in one gloved hand and her new white pocketbook in the other.

Big boys and their dads displayed matching suits, generally navy blue, laid away at J. C. Penney's, Sears and Roebuck, some other retailers by wives and mothers to be worn just this one day. The boys would outgrow them by the next year. Little boys in suits with short pants, from which peeked knotty knees, wore bow ties crooked continually by inquiring fingers, constantly flitted at by attentive mothers. They swung baskets of red, green, yellow, natural stripes in which no more than two eggs swung tentatively from side to side until once solid shells were but bits of cracked, fragmenting shell exposing whites of eggs boiled until almost brown.

Easter's fragrances from lilies, toilette water, perfumes, aftershaves, and eggs—marshmallow, jellied, candied, as well as boiled—had distracted Brandi. The usher seated her on the front left pew right next to TJ's mother who touched her arm with frigid fingers before smiling at her for the first time ever. She jumped and returned the woman's warm greeting.

Mrs. Pennington had seen her son drive by the porch with this little girl several times since that first time—didn't like it a bit, couldn't say nothing 'cause he was grown, but she was glad to see her now, glad she had brought T to church. His mother knew he had not come on his own. Brandi's attempts at waved acknowledgement to the woman who was always on the front porch had been met with a cool stare. Taxi had said reassuringly when she mentioned it to him, "She don't see you. If she did, she'd wave back."

Soon, all were seated in the sanctuary. Brandi looked around for TJ.

The pianist played Easter's prelude, and all grew silent.

Deacon Hezekiah Jr. had just laid the "good book," his Sunday school printed text, and the commentary from the Baptist Convention on his seat on one of the short pews in the amen corner. The head deacon secured his hymnal for devotion's beginning. Instead, he shrieked with joy, "Kill the fatted calf, the prodigal son done come home!" He grabbed TJ, who had made his way to the front to sit with Brandi and his mother, hugged, squeezed, squashed him until he was just about out of wind.

"Who dat?" old Deacon Hezekiah Sr. called out, anxious to get involved, to know what all the commotion was about.

"It's TJ, Papa. Little Thaddeus is back."

"Where he at?" the oldest member of the congregation probed further.

By now everybody in the church stirred in his seat, from pulpit to the last seat on the back row; everybody tried to see what was going on. TJ made his way to the corner and bent down to give the head deacon some brotherly love.

The old man, blinded by age, reached up, tracing the visage of the man who now stood bent over him, the one he hadn't seen in over twenty years. When he had ascertained that this indeed was Rev. Pennington's boy, he made the man take a seat right by him. "Sit right here, boy. I want you right by me." TJ was obedient—he pushed Deacon Hezekiah Jr.'s books over and sat down. The old man sighed—TJ was back.

When the man glanced at Brandi, she grinned like a Cheshire cat. His mother also seemed to enjoy the attention he had received.

Worship service resumed, its order already modified by the prodigal son's return. "Wanna hear little Thaddeus play, sing like he used to?" Old Deacon Hezekiah Sr. had spoken, so the pianist respectfully relinquished his sear, which TJ unenthusiastically assumed.

"A-a-amazing grace," the tenor resounded richly with clarity and purpose after he had played the introductory chords from hymn number 135.

"Praise the Lord," Sister Hezekiah Sr. shouted.

"How sweet . . ." The man at the piano held "sweet" almost a full measure more than the printed music called for, singing and playing with his own bluesy brand of gospel.

The choir echoed, "How sweet . . ."

Flo's soprano from the choir loft added, "How sweet, how sweet, the sound."

Brandi's eyes left the piano where they had rested attentively when the man had taken his seat there. She looked upward: she had not seen the high-yellow woman when she had come in—she didn't know how she had missed her. "Perhaps," she thought, "it was because she was dressed in a choir robe." Nevertheless, the woman's presence there seemed like an intrusion; she was always there. Brandi's second thought was that everyone else in Claxville was there, so it was no small wonder that the woman she admired and resented at the same time was there.

The vocalist had lived next door to the Penningtons most of her life. While growing up she and Thaddeus had done everything together—played, gone to school, sang in the church choir, dated; it was she who had decorated his addition to the Pennington House, she who had warmed his bed on cold wintry nights. Wherever TJ was, Flo was, and wherever Flo was, TJ was. It was clear to all the women in Claxville that they were an item—they were like two peas in a pod. They only thing that they hadn't done was marry.

Mrs. Pennington, having noted a mood shift, followed Brandi's gaze. "Ain't nothing to that," she leaned over, pulled her to herself, and whispered knowingly to the young woman at her side. This time when she had touched her, warmth replaced the frost. Brandi regained her focus.

"Yes, Lord," she heard a sister from somewhere shout. The spirit was high is Shiloh Missionary Baptist Church by now. The full choir was singing TJ's version of "Amazing Grace"; the entire congregation was afoot, many with hands clasped prayerfully in front of them, others with arms raised heavenward. Feet patted first, then stomped on the church's wooden floor.

The sanctified sister on the other side of Brandi lost her brand-new hat and was shouting. Ushers, rushing forward to attend to her, passed out fans from Steve's Funeral Home everywhere. From somewhere in the midst, a little boy shrieked, "My egg! It done fell out of my Easter basket!" before he dropped to his belly crawling under the pew in front of him to grab the rolling foodstuff, which did not rest until it lay squashed to smithereens under the shouting woman's brand-new white pumps. While the ushers groped and grappled with the former, the little boy's mother returned to her seat, as did many other parishioners, to attend to their children.

Soon, Rev. Flewellen, at the pulpit, lifted his robe, took a handkerchief from his pants' pocket, wiped at his sweaty bald pate, and took up where TJ left off. It was two-thirty by the time he had buried Jesus in a borrowed tomb, resurrected him, and seated him on the right hand of the Father. Amen. Amen. Amen.

Thaddeus Jr. invited Mrs. Pennington to dine with them after church; she did. They went to Rosie's Cafeteria, had generous portions of macaroni and cheese, green beans, candied yams, and ham steaks with a pineapple sauce. The old woman overindulged by ordering not one but two slices of egg custard she quickly devoured. "Ma, you are going to be sick," the man admonished her.

They had a pleasant day. For Brandi, it was atypical. Easter Sunday at the Browns was a bit different. "What does you family usually do?" Mrs. Pennington inquired of traditions shared by Brandi and her family.

Customarily all of the Browns gathered around the breakfast table. Each child recited a Bible verse, the little allowed, "Jesus wept"; for others a bit of proverbial prose could be gotten away with if memories failed them. Then Carruthers led the family in prayer.

After breakfast, all brushed teeth, combed hair, dressed up in "Sunday-go-to-meeting garb," check appearances in the mirror and with each other. Then they were off to Sunday school and the Red Hill Missionary Baptist Church.

Usually Aunt Sylvia and Uncle Jack came by to chat, sometimes to share dinner. Their extended family joined for any special occasion as well as on Sundays; good food was love's glue that bound them together. Sara smothered chicken or pork chops and all the fixings. Under Cat's and Jack's watchful eyes, the children took turns churning ice cream for dessert. Soon, the uncle would push them aside under the guise of "helping to keep the fuss down" when actually he enjoyed the task as much as he relished the treats that gushed out when the churn's cap was released.

"Lord, I wish I could have had some of that cream!" Mrs. Pennington interjected.

"Ma, you don't need another thing," her son said.

Brandi continued, "I bet dinner's over now." She looked at her watch. "Uh-huh, everybody's outdoors now. Mama, Daddy, Aunt Sylvia, and Uncle Jack and anybody else come from out of town are sitting on the porch fanning gnats and watching the young'uns play from one thing to the other. They are playing marbles, dodge ball, horseshoes, Red Light, Mama May I, jump rope, hide-and-seek, or hopscotch."

"Wish you were there?" the man asked.

"A little bit," Brandi said with nostalgia. "I've enjoyed my day though. Thanks for taking me to church."

"I kinda enjoyed my day too. How about you, Ma? You have fun today?"

A whisper of a snore was Mrs. Pennington's response.

Taxi looked around briefly. His mother was sound asleep. "Hope her sugar don't go up," the son expressed his concern openly. To which Brandi added, "I don't think so. She's just exhausted. Had too much of a day. That's the same way my Aunt Sylvia does when she's enjoying herself. She just overdoes it."

When they were back at the Pennington household, the man saw his mother to bed. He left Brandi in the museum of a living room to wander around, to be encompassed by the mothball scent, to become contemplative as she got a bird's-eye view of the photographs of her love at different stages in his growth and development. She looked at the same ones and others that Mrs. Pennington had not shown her the first time they had stopped by.

Brandi paused at the pictures of the man in his twenties, the man who was handsome then but had aged gracefully. She thought him a hunk; he was more muscular and sexually appealing to her now than he would have been at twenty . . . And Flo, who seemed to be in every picture in that same decade. "Gosh, what a beauty she was!" Brandi sucked in her breath—the woman was stunning, gorgeous, soft, feminine, sexy, innocent-looking, warmly ravishing, not so heavily endowed as she was today. She studied the hand on the side of the woman's face in one close-up—it was slender, beautiful; its nails were shaped, polished neatly—antithetical of the aging members with drying, cracking skin rent of moisture with broken, stubby, bitten, chewed, yellowed, browning nails the singer now possessed.

As Taxi had grown, matured gracefully, Flo had obviously grown stale, tough, and raucous in appearance. Having finally gotten up close to the woman, the understudy no longer envied the other woman. Jealousy waxed and waned. Brandi pitied her, knowing why she had lost the affections of the man. Flo had let herself go to pot.

When they were on the way back to the campus, Brandi longed again for her clothing. Everyone's Easter apparel had enticed her; she had felt so woefully underdressed in her simple light green polyester short-sleeve pull-over top and skirt set and longed to return home to pick up some of her things. "My mama's done called me again about them spring clothes. I kinda need to go get them. It's getting too hot to wear sweaters and skirts," she said still fanning with the hand fan she had inadvertently taken from the church.

He offered to buy her some new clothes and was not surprised when she shook her head. "I got plenty already. I was just thinking aloud, thinking about catching the bus home to get them."

"How long it take you to get there by bus?" the man asked.

"About eleven or twelve hours."

"One way?"

"Uh-huh."

"Shouldn't be but three or four hours by car," he responded thoughtfully. "How about I take you down there? We can spend the night somewhere on the way back, maybe go down to Miami. You ever been there?" The man now thought aloud. Brandi didn't respond, but he didn't notice the failure to respond. "I haven't taken a vacation since I been back home," TJ continued, getting excited about the prospect of taking the woman beyond Claxville's confounding boundaries.

BRENDA SMITH

He added, "I can get somebody to handle the business for me a couple of days."

"Let me think about it," Brandi replied hesitantly, wishing she had not brought up the subject. She had not told her parents about the man, or any man for that matter, and here was Taxi ready to drive up in their front yard. Concern welled up in her. Her stomach ached.

"I need to turn in a little early tonight. I think I ate too much too."

"We'll get together on our trip a little later in the week," he told her assuredly when he left her at dorm's door on Easter Sunday.

Brandi called home that same spring evening, but the party line was busy; it was always busy—it stayed busy. The young woman longed to wish her family a happy Easter, tell them about church at Shiloh, see if they had had an egg hunt, find out how many each young'un had found, what color Easter dresses and suits they had worn, to hear each chant the two—or three-line speeches they had said at church back in Wester, to find out who came home for the holiday, and to find out whether Cat and Sara went to Easter sunrise service. And who kept the children if they did indeed go—she had done it the last five years. Her thoughts tripped over each other.

The woman would hang up and dial again. She was startled when there was finally a ring rather than the busy signal. Her relentless effort paid off.

"Hello," Carruthers responded to the telephone's annoying chime.

"It's me, Daddy," Brandi sputtered anxiously.

"Hey, Brandy gal," the father used his pet name for his daughter. "How you doing?"

"Fine, what you doing answering the phone?" Brandi teased the man, knowing that he would never touch the instrument unless Sara was gone. "Mama must not be there!" She chuckled knowingly.

"Yeah, she is. She and the young'uns in the backyard eating watermelon. All of them gonna have the bellyache. The things ain't hardly ripe yet, just a deep pink, shallow red, and she's out there stuffing her craw, getting ready for a puking party tonight. Wait a minute, I'll get her for you."

"That's all right," Brandi said, sighing with relief for now she wouldn't have to respond to all the questions Sara was sure to pose. "I was just calling to say happy Easter to everybody and talk with her about a little something else . . . Anyway, just tell her I'm coming home sometimes in the next couple of weeks to get my stuff."

"What bus you gon' be on?"

"Ain't gonna be on the bus—" Before Brandi could complete her statement, Carruthers queried her about whether she had bought a car; he and Sara had already had a conversation about that, so the man was almost certain that his daughter's response would be affirmative.

"Naw, a friend's bringing me," she replied almost irritably. This was more conversation than she had anticipated.

"Oh, you coming with that woman from up close by here," Cat suggested plaintively, "the one that you just about got to room with?" before he felt and heard a discomfited silence. Her father grew suspicious; their conversation wasn't flowing freely, pauses were there where there should have been none, and irritation was in her voice; her breathing appeared shallow and labored.

"Uh-uh." Brandi shook her head, uncertain about where the man was coming from, of whom he spoke—that is, she had been until he'd mentioned the rooming situation. "Uh-uh, not her, somebody else, another friend's bringing me. It isn't nobody you know. Just tell Ma to call me," Brandi voiced pleadingly, wanting to discontinue the conversation, which Cat was enjoying no more than she was. He wished she would stop being so evasive.

Both parties grew quiet, and each thought the line dead. Simultaneously, they took the receiver from their ears, looked at the instrument, and returned it to their hearing organs.

"Is it a boyfriend?" the man inquired when a moment or two had passed.

"Something like that," she spewed at him, begging, almost pleading. "Just tell Mama I'll call her back later," she said for a third time before hanging up, neglecting the customary closing. Cat heard a click in his ear, so he put the phone back on the cradle, headed outside under the shade trees where Sara and the remainder of their offspring stood eating the fresh, obviously delicious, chilled vine-fruit, spitting seeds on the rich earth underfoot. There he shared his and Brandi's conversation and voiced his concern to his wife. "You better call her and find out what she got on her mind," he told Sara.

"Will, soon as I get in the house, get these children cleaned up," Sara said between bites, sensing the urgency in the man's voice.

Back in Claxville, Brandi still sat on the bedside holding the dead phone to her breast, its flat buzzing reaching upward for her ear while she rethought the current affair. The young woman knew that she needed her mother's cooperation, that she needed an advance man, needed for her mother to draw from her responses to questions yet undisclosed, questions certain to include those about TJ's race, age, national origin, religious affiliation, marital status, schooling . . . information that only a mother could provide to a father of a girl about to bring her first date home; she'd had no other, had been disinterested in the boys back home in Wester. Naybird, Tater, Russell, Melvin, etc., were there, and all had desired her affections, yet she had not reciprocated, had resorted to fantasy—been Juliet in Shakespeare's story, Rachel to Andrew, the protagonist in any piece of fictional or factual love lore she could secure.

Actually, TJ was about the same age as her father—she was not sure how Carruthers would take to her dating the man. Sara, on the other hand, would probably be a little more open-minded. At least Brandi thought she might be.

The young woman pondered, her thoughts finally drawn back to the present, when the steady hum from the telephone that she had subconsciously moved from close to her heart to the proximity of her ear came . . . when the hum became apparent, she placed it on the cradle and turned to her studies; she had not done all of her homework. It would be Monday again tomorrow.

CHAPTER TWENTY-ONE

Family Reunion

It was almost semester's end, and Dr. McIntyre's class had become one big bore . . . the jokes. Racial epitaphs, brash comments, snide and curt remarks, foolishness no longer claimed the coed's attention. And the change was noticeable. "Brandi," the professor summoned her charge to the teacher's desk before the final. "I've noticed a difference as time has passed. You have survived insurmountable odds," she said, unwilling to give the "odds" their proper names. "I'm glad you have chosen not to be bitter. You'll be a much better person for it," she said, patting her student's hand, letting it linger sympathetically, lovingly, maternally for a while.

A lukewarm "Thanks" was as much as the student could muster, disappointment with the professor still intact.

"Come by soon," the woman added. "We need to get you preregistered for the summer session." She let go of the girl's hand.

"Yes, ma'am."

Elnora Jenkins awaited her departure that same day. When Brandi hit the building's last step, the intruder joined her. "Are you going to summer school?"

With "uh-huh," the less experienced student kept walking.

Elnora continued to pester her. "I'm going too . . . how about the two of us sharing a room? Saxby's closing until fall semester. Davis Hall generally stays open in the summertime. You can probably keep the same room."

Brandi came to a halt, stopped dead in her tracks. The encounter in itself was overwhelming, but this was more than she could bear. She almost told the woman off, having been tempted to do so ever since their first encounter over by the dairy. Instead, she said, "I'll let you know. I don't know whether my roomie is coming back. We haven't talked about that yet."

Kris had never found another place, and Brandi was glad. The two had become really good friends. They shared each other's joys, sorrows, and did many crazy things like girls in their late teens and early twenties did. Although their schedules conflicted, they generally spent Saturday and Sunday afternoons together. Brandi washed the clothes, Kris put them away; Brandi swept the floor—Kris could never seem to get all the grit off the linoleum—and Kris mopped. They shared everything—toiletries, foodstuffs, personal articles, and stories about their dates. Brandi wished for her return, which was improbable; so after careful deliberations, the girl opted once again to reclaim the privacy of room 306. It would cost a few dollars more to enjoy the privacy, but she would manage.

Sara called Brandi back the very next day to inquire about the impending trip for her summer clothing.

"When are you coming?"

"Soon."

"How soon?"

"I don't know."

"You don't know. What you mean you don't know? Who else will know if you don't know?" her mother badgered her.

Brandi voiced with irritation, "Ma, all the details have not been worked out. I knew I should have waited until they had been before I told y'all I was coming."

Sensing her daughter's impatience, Sara said, "Hold your horses, missy! What's all the fuss?"

"I know Daddy told you somebody was bringing me," Brandi said, still on the defense.

"Yes, he did, and it's all right," Sara told her.

Feeling assurance, Brandi opened up. The girl told the woman bits and pieces about her friend. She ended the conversation by telling her mother how excited TJ was about the trip.

All too soon it was time for the duo to go to Wester for the clothes Brandi had been pining about since Easter Sunday. She had told Sara about the man, the little that she knew: that he had gone into the "war" when he had graduated from high school, was the son of the late Rev. Thaddeus Jerome Pennington Sr., founding pastor of the greater Shiloh Missionary Baptist Church in Claxville, had returned to town when his father had died, shared a home with his mother, had enlarged it himself, done some of the carpentry with his own hands, had his own business, had played the piano at church on Easter, emphasizing that he was a little older than she. Could sing!

She also told her mother that the man had played basketball, was starting center for Booker T. Washington High School, was a longtime powerhouse in the sport.

"My average was twenty-two points a game, and I won all district honors . . . In my senior year, Washington High School fell two wins short of making the state tournament," he told her one afternoon when they were piddling around.

"As a matter of fact, they recruited me to play at the university," he added.

"At Claxville University!" Brandi was surprised upon hearing this.

"Yeah, Claxville University." The man chuckled.

"Why didn't you accept?"

He looked at her. "Can't believe you asked that," he said, causing her to recount strife she currently experienced, that which she had been experiencing since the day she got to the city.

Her face grew glum.

"Sorry," he said when he realized approaching despondency. He reached for her and looked at her fondly with regrets. TJ had not intended to hurt her. The man liked her too much for that. With each passing date, affections grew. Their desire for each other was pristine, beautiful. If it wasn't love, at least their journey seemed to be headed in that direction.

And it was clear to the man that he should be taking her home to her parents.

"How much older?" her mother had asked when Brandi took a breath.

"Not much, just a little bit."

"I hope he ain't old enough to be your daddy," Sara had remarked.

An anguished, "Ah, Ma!" was the daughter's response.

"Is he in one of your classes? Is he on the GI bill? Must be taking up courses in business administration, huh?" Sara probed further . . . questions came one after another. And they kept coming; as the girl attempted to talk to her mother about the man, she could feel her breath coming in shallow bursts, so Brandi grew tongue-tied and sputtered.

"No, ma'am," she responded thrice in a row.

"Where you meet him?" Sara persisted with her motherly interrogation— she could see right through Brandi, even on the telephone. The distance from Wester to Claxville and back did not exceed the length on the mental umbilical cord linking their psyches. That's why Cat had conveyed to her, "You better talk to her, find out what she got on her mind. I don't want any surprises."

Brandi said, "At the bus station, that's where I first met him, at the bus station."

"You all ain't planning to stay none?" Sara added. "I was going to ask Sylvia if he could stay with them if y'all was going to spend a night or two."

"No, ma'am, we coming right back up here," Brandi told a little white lie, a half-truth, delaying discussion about a probable extension of the trip. Taxi had briefly spoken of going to an amusement park of sorts, or a zoo, a museum, do a bit of sightseeing.

The second to the last week in May finally came. Sara cooked all week—cooked up some fresh vegetables, packaged them, froze them so all she had to do was thaw them out, cut some corn off the cob for creamed corn, made turkey and dressing, baked a ham, got fresh fryers ready to dredge in flour and fry the morning of their arrival, made two pound cakes. Brandi was bringing a fellow, her boyfriend, home.

When the woman wasn't cooking, she cleaned—Sara took the linen off all the beds; carried it out back; boiled it in lye soap and a little bit of bleach in heavy wrought iron pots full of boiling water fueled by winter's leftover cord of wood; hung the sheets, pillow cases, and towels on the line strung between the house and the garden for this express purpose; took the mattresses outside, beat them out, let them air out; washed windows for the second time since spring had sprung; raked yards.

Cat stayed out of Sara's way, kept to himself, pondering over his daughter's choice of friends—had been thinking on this ever since his wife told him about some "older" guy his baby was seeing.

Then she cleaned the pantry and examined canned contents for spoilage and leakage. Vegetables, fruits, jellies, jams, and condiments, sauces, relishes were carefully scrutinized for graying pallor around each jar's rim before she sorted and restocked the fruits of her labor—the woman did everything she could to while the time away and to keep from fighting with her edgy husband.

Everybody in the Brown household was on edge. Brandi's forthcoming visit created a stressful climate. All the children sensed the thickness in the air, and all obediently succumbed to their mother's commands to "move this, take that, get out of the way."

Sara worked long laborious hours getting into bed in the wee hours when her husband was about to arise. Their routine having been interrupted, a loving marriage grew increasingly tense with the impending visit almost a reality. Rather than talking to each other, they complained to their relations.

"He's raising more hell now than he did when the girl first went off to college. I'll be glad when she done come, got them clothes, and gone. Are y'all coming over here?" Sara had jumped from one subject to another, barely pausing to take a breath during one telephone conversation with her relative.

"Reckon so," Sylvia told her anxious sister.

Meanwhile Cat said to his brother-in-law, "Woman's driving me crazy. I'll be glad when Brandi comes home, get her clothes, take that rascal back up yonder. Are y'all coming over here?"

"Shore is, wouldn't miss it."

Brandi's aunt and uncle came early the day of their arrival. They bought a box laden down with Sylvia's specialties: fruitcake (aged, left over from Christmas and Easter, wrapped in homemade plum brandy moistened cheese cloth and shut up airtight in lard cans), a lemon-cheese layer cake, some tea cakes, and a couple of jars of pickled peaches, spiced apple rings, and whole candied figs—all for their niece to take back to Claxville. They figured there would be room in the car for all the treats; Sylvia felt she had not done her niece justice when she had left on the bus for that first trip to Claxville—all she had given her was a sack of tea cakes in a light bread sack. That just was not enough.

"That old gal ain't here yet . . . can't wait to see what she done caught whilst she was up yonder," Uncle Jack spoke excitedly, anxiously, when he was at the foot of the steps of the back door. "I knew she was gonna get her one." The man laughed. "Can't never remember her courting nobody when she was home. All them boys 'round her, she ain't never give them the time of day . . . She ain't never done nothing, nothing but read," he remarked proudly.

Brandi slept fitfully the night before the journey home. She waited in the lobby alone with her thoughts until Taxi was at the dorm's entrance the next morning—he had long ago given up his seat behind the wheel as he awaited his date and begun to take the walk to the door to pick her up for a date and deposit her back to the safety of the dorm's lobby when a date was over. Now he helped her to gather the items she planned to take home and exchange for the summer garments.

"Who helped you bring all this down?" he asked.

"I did it by myself," she responded, "and I'm beat too."

"I can tell," he said, taking her face in his hand to look at eyes encircled with sleepy bags.

"You can get some rest while I drive," he told her.

"Uh-uh, I'll be all right," she argued. "I'm not going to sleep. I'm the copilot. I'm going to stay awake to help you drive."

Yet she was sound asleep as soon as they began the trip to Wester and down Dry Lake Road to the Browns' residence, which seemed to stretch to infinity.

No stranger to travel, Taxi had judiciously mapped out the trip. He enjoyed a conversation-free ride—his passenger dozed, waking periodically to toggle the radio's knobs, make a comment or two, question their location—so TJ reflected on the events from the last six weeks or so; he'd finally "met"—officially met—the girl, broken up with Flo, and got "caught up." Now he was taking her home to her mama and daddy. He shook his head with disbelief, fixed his gaze on the dirt road.

She stirred in her seat, her gentle snores like a kitten's purrs. He glanced at her; she looked like she did every time he looked at her—the woman was aglow with youth, so alive. His age stuck out like a pebble under the bottom of a shoe. "When I'm eighty," he thought, "she'll still be young, will have men coming on to her." Worry showed on his brow.

Taxi vigorously shook his head and the car's steering wheel. The car jerked a bit, and the woman stirred in her seat. The man wished fiercely that he could sweep all her fears away . . . and his too—that he could somehow make everything all right.

The man reluctantly awoke the woman when they were in downtown Wester, to be directed to the turn on the unpaved rural route leading to the Browns' house. After some distance and small talk about country miles versus city miles, the man asked to abate fatigue . . . and anxiety: "How much farther?"

"Oh, not far!" she said brightly with excitement. "We are going to make a right turn right down there." Brandi pointed to a break in the field between some large oak trees, for there were no street signs.

The two couples, Sara and Cat and Sylvia and her husband, sat at the kitchen table sipping Sara's hand-squeezed fresh lemonade reminiscing almost mournfully about their own courtships and marriages. Everybody jumped when the awaited girl pulled the screen door open. In spite of the quiet and serene atmosphere, neither adult had heard the car pull into the driveway and almost to the back door. Neither one of her kinfolks had heard the slam of the car when Brandi had gotten out and rushed to the house with TJ in tow.

Brandi had walked up the steps and opened the screen door, was almost inside, and the man was on her heels, holding the door with his left hand before anyone realized they were there. Everyone jumped. Sara spoke up first, "Gal, you like to scare us to death, coming in here like that." She rose to greet her daughter. Everyone else got to his or her feet and reached for her too . . . everybody except her father. He kept his seat at the kitchen's table, peering through under Sara's outstretched arms at the stranger who was entering his house.

The two men caught each other's eye.

TJ stopped. Arrested by Carruthers's stark gaze, he stood still, the door ajar.

"Who that with you?" the uncle called, laughing a hearty laugh as he finished rolling his cigarette in the tobacco rolling paper, licked it to seal the tobacco in, and put it in his mouth.

"TJ," Brandi said as she reached for him, "this is my mama, and my uncle and my aunt," the girl said of each who shook the man's hand in greeting.

Before she could introduce the father, Thaddeus had stepped forward to shake hands with Cat who was yet in his seat. He gripped the man's hand. Cat did not exchange the warm greeting—he let his hand dangle limply, refusing to return the grip.

"Nice to meet you, man," TJ spoke gently with consternation in his voice as he loosed the man's hand. He knew all too well the man's fears and trepidation without Carruthers ever having mumbled a word. Taxi shared his concern about age—he had not wanted to love her either. In spite of all his efforts not to do so, TJ had developed a passion for a woman half his age, a girl, and he was just as pissed as her father was.

The two men held each other's gaze for a moment more, TJ awaiting an acknowledgement of his greeting, but Carruthers didn't crack a smile, said nothing, didn't even give the man a grunt; the girl's father's jaw tightened, and he cut the man a hard look of warning.

Thaddeus Pennington's fair-skinned face reddened, and he wanted to step back, to leave. Fear gripped his feet, and his heart fell. He didn't want to further antagonize Carruthers—he was anxious to forge an amicable relationship with Mr. Brown.

"Brandi's home! Brandi's home." They came running, jumping, squealing, snatching, pulling, pushing, shoving to get to each one's big sister. Young'uns were suddenly running around everywhere, clambering for attention—each jumped into Brandi's arms before leaping to TJ for a brief introduction and a hasty hug before being shooed off by their mother.

"Get back in there!" Sara yelled at her brood. "Back on the bed, stay there, lay down 'til I come get you." They turned obediently on their heels and went back to the room, some wailing, sniveling, crying while others comforted them, reminding them to be good so they all could get some previously promised treats. The woman wanted, needed, these moments alone together with the other grown folks, needed to see this thing "gel," come together before the young'uns got involved.

She looked at Cat. He had raised holy hell when Sara had told him that their daughter was dating a mature, older man. "You would have thought he was a white man the way he went on. It was plum ridiculous," Sara had confided in her sister. "That's just how crazy he done got. The man's about to lose his mind."

"Honey," she spoke to him as gently as TJ had done, "how about going out to the shed, get a leaf for the table?" Originally she had thought the grownups would eat lunch together, spend some time getting to know each other before the young'uns ate. Now she thought it would be better to let everybody eat at the same time.

Her husband got up. "Bring a couple of extra folding chairs too," she called after him, indicating that their other relations and the children would be eating at the same time.

With "okay," he acknowledged her change in plans. "The sooner this was all over with, the better," he thought.

"Brandi, go wash your hands, help me get the table set." The mother gave her daughter several commands.

And with, "Need some help?" TJ had excused himself and followed the girl's father out to the shed, where the man handed first the leaf, then the chairs to the offending stranger. He was nervous, was scared to death of the man who was looking at him. The man from Claxville cleared his throat and spoke weakly, faintly, honestly, "It ain't like what you think, man," he said to the woman's fuming father.

From the back bedroom window, Brandi saw the two men deep in conversation. "Please, God!" she begged, throwing her hands up to her face, shocked by what she saw, felt. "Don't let nothing happen." She ran out the room and headed for the back door . . . her mother stopped her, grabbing her arm, shaking her head when they had locked eyes. The men needed time alone. "Help me set the table," Sara said softly, her voice raspy with fear.

"Everything will be all right," Jack said, and Sylvia added, "Gal, yo' daddy know what he doing, got lot more sense than you give him credit for. He just wants things to be all right for you. Just don't get involved in men's talk. Do like your mama say do, help set that table."

Brandi relaxed, breathing a sigh of partial relief.

"I don't want to talk about it!" Cat snapped, voice trembling as he choked back sobs of disgust. He grabbed his pitchfork from the rack where it hung and poked at TJ in the fleshy folds of his neck. Tines ready to make their mark, he told the man, "You old enough to be her daddy . . . can't you find somebody your own age to fuck with?"

"But I love her," TJ spoke weakly as he tilted his head backward to ease the tension placed on his neck by the fork's razor-sharp tines.

"You tell her that?"

"Not yet!" Beads of perspiration rained on him.

Cat pushed the fork forward once more, pressing the exposed Adam's apple, sticking times in unclogged, clear, gaping pores . . . drawing more perspiration. Taxi thought he smelled blood. He leaned backward at the waist. This was crazy, much more than he had bargained for when he offered to bring the girl home to pick up her clothes. Here he was in a barn with some lunatic with a pitchfork at his throat. The man disbelieved his current state of affairs.

"You mess over her, I'll kill you!" Cat spoke through teeth gritted in anger. Infuriation loosening its grip, the man disengaged the fork from Taxi's neck tentatively and gently, thrust the fork in the ground forcefully, and attempted to resume his task.

Thaddeus spoke up in a whisper. "I won't, man, I promise I won't," before reaching to shake Cat's hand anew. The two shook on it.

TJ sighed with relief, took his handkerchief from his pocket, wiped the sweat from his brow and his neck, looking at the object, verifying for himself that the blood he had smelled was from his blood pressure elevated by the tense moments, that it had not poured from a puncture wound in the neck. "Whew, that was close," he thought.

The tense moment having passed, the two returned to the house for dinner . . . Mother and daughter sighed with relief when both men were back in the kitchen.

Jack swiped his brow too. After that the men moved chairs and enlarged the already-mammoth table and set up a smaller table borrowed from a neighbor to harbor some of the platters of food.

Brandi sat by TJ at the table, across from her uncle and aunt; Sara was on the end closest to the door while Carruthers faced the door as he always did. The other Brown children joined them at the table when their mother called.

Sara scrutinized the table, noticed that no bread was there, got up to add a platter overloaded with big hunks of yellow corn bread filled with cracklings to the table heavy-laden with foods. Carruthers blessed the food.

All ate bountifully.

Over dinner, Sara questioned Thaddeus about his past, present, future, finding comfort in the fact that he came from a stable, good home, was self-sufficient, dependable, intelligent, gifted, thoughtful, generous, loving—not many men would care for his mother like he did for Mrs. Pennington—that the man was ambitious, wanting to enlarge his business, and that he was encouraging to Brandi. And she thanked God that he was not a dope head squandering money on marijuana, cocaine, uppers, downers, bennies, black beauties, liquor, beer, wine, wild women, as her husband had argued. She laid to rest Cat's contentions that he couldn't be little more that a "sugar daddy."

Between bites of the delicious meal, the two, Sara and TJ, conversed pleasantly while the others—Cat, Sylvia, James, and the young'uns—called from the room when the tables were set, when it was time to eat, and Brandi herself listened attentively. Sara, generally quite impatient—who had always flipped to the back of the book, read the end of the story, then went back to the beginning—was forced to exercise discipline today. The woman guided TJ's history, making sure that all was told in chronological order from birth to the present. That way she could repeat it if she had to regurgitate it for Catkiller.

No one chewed loud for fear of missing something important. When TJ had reached the end of the story, had come to a conclusion, was up to the present moment, Sara was satisfied that she had been right.

"Where y'all going when you leave here?" Cat asked when the talking parties briefly broke the steady stream of conversation to take bites of the cooling, cold food. Brandi looked to TJ for a response; after all, it had been his idea—he was the one who wanted to turn the trip home into a vacation of sorts, had been the one to stretch the day-long sojourn in the Browns' company to a fantasia. The man swallowed the mouthful of food, took a sip of the lemonade, swiped at his lips with a paper napkin, and laid it beside his half-filled plate before answering.

A moment of quietness passed. TJ relinquished the napkin from the edge of the dinner plate's brim and rubbed gingerly and thoughtfully at imaginary chicken grease on his fingers.

Brandi's father kept his vigil over the squirming man; he refused to blink and continued to eat, masticating ever so slowly and carefully.

TJ grew more nervous, almost sweat bullets for the second time that day. Cat had made him uncomfortable just by looking at him. He had never felt this strange before. He felt cornered; it was obvious to Sara, Sylvia, and the others that TJ was suffering gravely. Cat, on the other hand, was tranquil; he appeared to enjoy the cat-and-mouse game the query about their departure and imminent destination had brought.

Everybody waited for a response.

While Thaddeus had anticipated the question—he had rehearsed a response while Brandi slept on the drive to Wester—the answer escaped him. He wasn't going to lie though. TJ cleared his throat. "I thought we might go over in Florida a couple of days when we leave here. I told Brandi I ain't been nowhere since I got out of the war," he explained to her father.

"Where?" the father growled.

"Down in Florida," TJ responded sheepishly.

Brandi, awaiting the explosion, scooted her chair back from the table a little, listened for its detonating sound, watched for flares, and sniffed, smelling smoke. Uncle James had taken the hand-rolled cigarette from his shirt pocket, put it in his mouth, reached back into his pocket, pulling from it a kitchen match, tip obviously loaded with phosphorus . . . its flame secured when he struck it against the bottom of his everyday boots.

"Y'all going to be gone long?" she heard her father ask TJ.

Taxi shook his head. "Can't be," he said. "A man can't run a business from the road, unless he's a truck driver. We got to get back."

His response drew no particular attention from the girl's father. Carruthers shoveled another spoonful of sweet potato custard in his mouth.

The moment passed, and TJ sighed. The wonderful meal finished, a gorged TJ spoke. "Ms. Sara," he said, "that sure was good! Can Brandi cook anything like that? I ain't never had any of her cooking."

Sara smiled, completely taken in by his complements.

"She ought to be able to. I showed everything I know," the woman said, pride exuded. "Want some of my homemade cream?" Sara asked him before she got up and went over to the sink to remove a wad of burlap from atop the wooden churn chockful of ice and rock salt that protected the elongated tin's luscious contents.

TJ groaned when Sara set the old wooden hand-cranked ice cream churn on the countertop. She lifted the burlap covering from it, scooped ice full of salt pellets from around the container it encompassed, slowly pulled the three-quart holder from the dregs, sat it in the sink, wiped the container down, exercising care that the goods were not tainted by the salt's savor.

"Why didn't you tell me, Brandi?" the man moaned and complained superficially, an act that the children found funny too. They giggled, making their real presence known for the first time.

Taxi winked at them playfully; the rest of Sara's brood toyed with him as well, winking back. Lil' Benji held his eye open and shut it with tiny fingers. To his amusement, TJ mimicked his wink before turning his attention back to the Browns' oldest daughter.

Brandi smiled, patted his hand, letting hers linger longer than she had intended to.

TJ returned their attention to the scrumptious meal. "I wouldn't have eaten so much if I had known you had that, Ms. Sara," he said. "I haven't had any homemade ice cream since before I went to the war. What flavor is it?"

"Plain vanilla, vanilla custard," the woman said as she scooped and heaped mounds of the flavorful cooked, chilled, churned vanilla custard into dessert dishes, and the meal was completed.

Dinner was over soon, and the already-bundled clothes and some of the leftovers packed in tinfoil and plastic storage containers were packed in the car. All had exchanged good-byes, and TJ and Brandi prepared for their departure for the second leg of their journey. "Oh my god, I almost forgot your other stuff!" Sylvia exclaimed. "Gal, you run back in the house. Get that box off the top of the safe," she said when Brandi was almost in the passenger's seat. "That's for y'all to take back with you."

Brandi leapt out and ran through the back door.

Taxi smiled, recalling the story Brandi had told him on their first dinner date about how the odor from Sylvia's tea cakes had permeated the bus, waking everybody up. He'd anticipated tasting some of the woman's cooking, settled for disappointment, and sat practically drooling as Brandi placed the box in the backseat of the car before reclaiming her seat. The man expressed gratitude to all and smiled a special smile at the aunt, who returned it with her own warm one.

He blew a kiss at the woman; she wistfully returned his impromptu gesture of thanks.

When Brandi had secured the goodies in the back of the car, she jumped out again, kissed the aunt, nuzzled each parent once more, and shook Uncle Jack's thick-skinned, rawhide, skillful, but loving hand. Then she got back in the car amid the young'uns cries. "Gimme one. I want a tea cake."

"Y'all scat," the surrogate took charge. "I got some in the house for you. Come on, get out the way of that moving vehicle. Every last one of you, come on in the house, get some." She and Jack hauled them back into the kitchen while Sara and Cat were busy, alone together, each tending to this and their daughter's first love affair.

Taxi had started the engine and was easing out of the drive.

"Come here," Carruthers said wistfully at the mother of his children, whom he wrapped his arms around, drew to himself as they waved good-bye to the duo through the red dust spun up by the car's rotating tires.

And still in the yard, TJ patted the empty seat to his right before accelerating. Brandi slid over, excitement about the rest of the trip replacing worries about TJ's age, the meeting between her parents and her companion, Uncle Jack's insidious ponderings, and admonitions placed on the man by her father. They waved, exchanging parting good-byes with the Browns.

For the first time in months, for now, for the moment, Brandi Leigh Brown was so happy; she felt as free as a bird. Life swung once more on happiness's hinges.

Brandi dozed in the car.

Several hours passed. When they had crossed another state line and were in Florida, it was dark. Taxi stopped at a Holiday Inn. "Wait here," he said to Brandi and went in the front entrance. He was whistling gaily when he got back in the car. The woman could never remember seeing him as jovial; he almost had two wings.

He drove to the far side of the building, let the woman in the room, and returned for their baggage. She closed the curtains and turned on the lamps and the television before she went to the bathroom to relieve herself. Then she asked Taxi if he needed help with their baggage.

"No, just sit down and relax."

"What about you?"

"I'm all right," he said, waving her away from the door and back into the bowels of the hotel room.

Ignoring the chairs surrounding a small round table, she sat on the bed—rather, she bounced up and down playfully on it before she came to rest. Brandi yawned; the young woman was tired. It had been an extremely

BRENDA SMITH

long day: they had arisen early, driven the four-and-one-half hours rather than the anticipated three and a half to Wester, stayed there longer than they had anticipated, both having enjoyed the family gathering, had left, and were in yet another state.

Taxi shut the door when he had finished unpacking the car and went to the bathroom to relieve himself and to get a glass of water. He took the ice bucket from the sink and went down the walkway to fill it. When he returned he put some in his water, drank from it, and returned the ice bucket to the counter.

In the meantime, the young woman mused about the obviously good first impression Taxi had made. All seemed quite pleased . . . even the young'uns took to him like ducklings out of water.

She lay there smiling to herself.

Before she knew it, TJ had lifted her from the bed near the window, laid her on the one nearest the bathroom, and was kissing her—first as if she was breakable, then more persistently as she'd eagerly accepted his overture. He removed her glasses; she held fast to his arched body. The man planted more kisses on her forehead, eyes, the tip of her nose, her now anxious mouth before swirling his tongue in her ear. The young woman felt as if she was going to explode, suffocate, die.

TJ took his time with her.

Soon, Brandi tried to get up. "We better . . ."

"Uh-uh, can't" the man voiced throatily while shaking his head, held her face in hand, partook of her eyes, arresting apprehension, and bathed her face once more with warm, moist tongue, soft lips.

The man was going to have to conquer her first. "Don't be afraid," he whispered in a deep husky voice. He stroked the side of her face with the backs of his fingers, praying silently that the moisture he felt was not tears. She slowly lifted her face a bit, and smiling anew over the way the woman instinctively tilted her face to the side to gain more access to his caress, he whispered again, "Don't be scared."

"I'm trying, I'm trying not to be afraid," she whispered back.

TJ put his arms around her waist and pulled her up against him. Skin touched skin. Her eyes widened in reaction, but before she could get her wits about her to decide if she liked the feeling or not, his mouth settled on top of hers again.

The man certainly knew how to kiss. She didn't make him force her mouth open—instead she quickly became the aggressor. Her tongue rubbed against his first. Taxi grunted in reaction, her teasing almost too much for an experienced man to handle . . . but he had to.

Their kisses grew wild. Soon, Brandi made little erotic whimpers in the back of her own throat. And Taxi knew that he had accomplished his goal—she was hot for him. She whimpered amid his thoughts. And Lord, the sound made the man ache to be inside her.

He rolled her on her back and was covering her. Brandi's hands gripped his shoulders. The man lifted her up and pulled her tight against his arousal, then drowned out a gasp that intimacy caused with another long hot kiss.

The woman couldn't seem to catch hold of a thought. The sensations his kiss caused were so strange, so wonderful, so consuming. She couldn't even hold on to her shyness. Her body involuntarily responded to the will of his hot flesh.

Suddenly, panic took its grip on her. The haze of passion cleared in an instant. She was afraid; she didn't want to do this anymore. "What if I get pregnant?" she thought. "My daddy will kill me."

But she didn't want him to stop kissing her either. But god was she scared.

He'd be mighty pissed if she started to scream. For that reason, she kept her mouth shut . . . she worked hard at containing the shout locked in her throat.

His knee tried to nudge her legs apart. She wouldn't allow that intimacy and began to struggle against him. She slapped his shoulders with fingers of each hand. He immediately stopped trying for the plunge.

TJ propped himself up on his elbows to ease his weight away from her, then began to nibble on the side of her neck. She did like that. His breath, while somewhat labored, was warm, sweet, teasing against her ear. Brandi shivered in reaction. In a dark whisper he told her how much she pleased him, how much she made him want her, how beautiful he thought she was, how much he loved her. When the man was finished with his words of praise and adoration, he was certain that he had coaxed Brandi into accepting him completely.

He was mistaken. As soon as he tried to nudge her thighs apart again, she went completely rigid on him. TJ gritted his teeth in frustration . . . almost longed for Flo. She had always put out, given up the goods any time he wanted them.

"Shit," he uttered, attempting to chase memories of abandoned, unabashed, free sex away from their love nest.

Brandi stirred under his weight. The feel of her soft skin made him wild with his own need to be inside her. But she wasn't ready for his invasion yet. His forehead beaded with sweat from the effort of holding back. Each time his hands moved to touch her breasts, she tensed up on him. His frustration soon made of his hunger acute pain.

It would be only a matter of minutes before he completely lost control, left his load on the bed. God, he didn't want to hurt her. TJ was feeling desperate to thrust his member inside her, but she was going to be hot for him, ready, when he finally made her.

The most mature of the lovers decided to let the novice have her way for just a minute or two. "Shit," he thought, "maybe that white boy didn't get it when I picked her up out at his place that day." Taxi remembered how mad he had been when he had gone to Dirk's trailer to pick her up. God, he thought, he would have killed for her that day. Now he knew for sure that he would. She was his, and he wanted her now!

A few seconds were no good.

He thought he only needed a couple of minutes to regain his discipline. When his heart quit slamming inside his chest, when it didn't hurt so much to breath, when the god-awful ache in his balls abated a little, he would try again.

Wooing a virgin was harder work than he had ever imagined, he thought, and since he had absolutely no experience with wooing or breaking in virgins, the man felt completely inadequate.

Perhaps one day when the two of them were old, or rather older, he thought, he might be able to look back on this shit and laugh. At the moment he wasn't in the mood to laugh though. He wanted to grab Brandi Leigh Brown and shake some sense into her head while he demanded at the same time that she not be afraid of him.

The contradiction in those conflicting thoughts made him shake his head.

The young woman was trembling from head to foot. As soon as he had moved away from her, the helpless feeling of being trapped vanished. She wanted him to kiss her again.

The look on Taxi's face worried her though. He looked like he wanted to shout at her. She took a deep breath, rolled to her side to face him. "Taxi?"

He didn't answer her. Now his eyes were closed, his jaw tight, his teeth clenched.

"You told me you were a patient man."

"Sometimes," he muttered softly, calmly.

"You're upset with me, aren't you?"

"No."

She didn't believe him. "Don't frown," she whispered. Brandi reached to touch his face.

TJ reacted as though she had just burned him. He visibly flinched. "Don't you want to do this any longer?" she asked almost tearfully. "Have you quit wanting me?"

Not want her? He wanted to grab hold of her hand and force her to feel how much he wanted her. He didn't of course, for he was certain she would become terrified again.

"Brandi, just give me a minute," he said in a clipped voice. "I'm afraid . . ." He didn't finish his explanation, didn't tell her that he had not known that she was a virgin, didn't tell her that he was afraid he would hurt her if he touched her. That admission would only increase her anxiety, so he kept silent.

"You don't have to be afraid," she whispered.

He couldn't believe what he was hearing. The man opened his eyes to look at her. She couldn't really think . . . and yet the tenderness in her eyes indicated she did believe he was afraid.

"For Pete's sakes, Brandi, I'm not afraid."

She put her fingers on his chest, let them slowly trail down his chest. He caught hold of her hand when she reached the flat of his stomach. "Stop that!" he demanded.

"You ain't never had no virgin, have you?" she inquired.

His response was a low grunt.

She smiled. "T, you like kissing me, don't you?"

He'd asked her that question some fifteen minutes earlier when he had been trying to rid her of her fear. TJ thought he would have laughed had he not been in so much pain from wanting her. Now she was treating him like he was a virgin.

He was about to straighten out her thinking when she edged closer to him. He suddenly realized that his love was no longer afraid of him. "Do you?" she persisted.

"Yes, Brandi, I love kissing you." He smiled.

"Then kiss me again," she told him.

The man raised himself up on his elbow and looked her in the eye. "Brandi, kissing isn't the only thing I had in mind," he told her. "I want to touch you everywhere. You understand?"

BRENDA SMITH

He waited for her to freeze up on him again. God, he wished he had the patience for this. His nerves were raw, felt like they would snap at any minute, and all he could think about was spilling his load inside her.

The man closed his eyes and growled inaudibly.

And then he felt her take hold of his hand. He opened his eyes just as she placed her hand on her breast.

TJ did not move for a full minute. Brandi didn't either. He waited to see what she would do next. She waited for him to make the next move.

Brandi soon grew impatient with him. He was gently stroking her breast, rubbing her nipples between his fingers. The feeling made her tingle inside. It made her reckless too. She rubbed her toes up against his leg and slowly leaned up to kiss him.

"TJ, please don't give up on me yet," she implored. "This is a new experience for me. Truly, it is."

He gently caressed the side of her face. "I'm not giving up," he whispered. There was a bit of a laugh in his voice when he reassured her. "Truly," he promised.

She sighed against his mouth and kissed him just the way she wanted to. When her tongue moved inside to mate with his, TJ's control snapped. He became the aggressor again, deepening the kiss even with more wild abandon.

The man kept up his assault until she rolled onto her back and tried to bring him with her. Thaddeus didn't give in to her but leaned down to kiss her neck, to kiss the fragrant valley between her breasts, to suckle her clothed nipples. His mouth teased first one, then the other nipple.

Passion welled up inside of her—the girl had never ever experienced raw passion before.

"Can I take this off?" He lifted her pullover sweater, ungluing first one hand, then the other from his sides so he could get the garment over her head. Instinctively, her hands flew up, cupping the brassiere. TJ reached around her and unloosed the undergarment at her back. The onslaught of kisses was renewed. The same care given her face was ministered to the upper torso—shoulders, fully bared chest, upper arms, nape of slender neck—TJ brushed them all with his hands, lips, tongue.

His mouth teased first one then the other nipple until both were hard nubs. His tongue drove Brandi wild. She winced, gasped, and closed her eyes shut even tighter. He stopped; she waited for him to renew his administrations to her warm flesh. When she couldn't stand the torment any longer, she grabbed hold of his hair and began to tug on him.

He refused to budge. She felt as though she had been hit with hot lightning when he finally took her nipple into his mouth again. She arched up, demanding more. The man began his final suckle.

And passion overtook her. Brandi lay sprawled like an eagle on the plush queen-size bed's covering, and she no longer cared what Taxi did.

Thaddeus pulled her up, holding her body that was limp from passion held to himself with one hand while he stripped the bed of its covers with the other. When he had laid Brandi on the cool sheets, he quickly and quietly disrobed. She looked at his solid, lean, muscular body through slit-open eyes, not looking at him below the waist.

Afterward he lifted the young woman's hips from the bed and removed her remaining garments with little ado.

When TJ had laid himself beside the woman who panted vociferously, he took up where he left off. He paid particular attention to the almost boyish breasts, stroking, caressing, kissing, tonguing, kneading, molding, shaping them to suit his own needs.

By the time he had reached her belly button she was thrashing almost uncontrollably. A warm knot formed in the pit of her stomach. "Please," she moaned. She didn't have any idea what she was begging him for, only knew the incredible heat was driving her beyond control, beyond reason.

"Tell me what you want," was TJ's raspy response to her outcry.

He leaned up on his elbow so he could watch her expression. She tried to hide her face in the crook of his shoulder. He reached, caught her by the hair, and turned her face to his.

He commanded, shaking her gently, wanting the full truth, "Say it! Tell me what you want." The man bent his head for the whispered heart's desire.

TJ already knew the answer. He could sense how ready she was for him.

And this time she did not freeze up but yielded herself to the man who initially moved slowly into her, stopping only briefly to acknowledge the thin resistance of virginity he met at passion's gateway.

He took the lead, conquering the obstacle. With one swift motion, it was done, and what little pain there was existed, abated, diminished.

And then she began to move. Her hips pushed up against his . . . her actions were instinctive, primal, and uncontrollable. He joined her. The mating ritual took over, the bed creaked and groaned from the rocking motions, her sweet moans blended with his raw manly growls, and their brown bodies glistened with beads of translucent perspiration.

Thaddeus and Brandi both went wild to find fulfillment, to put out a towering inferno fueled by several months of waiting and wanting. He couldn't stop his own climax or the near holler he gave when he spilled his hot seed inside the woman.

His head dropped against her shoulder in complete surrender to the blazing orgasm their union had brought on. But he continued to thrust with force until he felt Brandi tense up against him, until he heard her scream, "Taxi!"

The man's ears rang from the noise. He collapsed on top of her, giving her his full weight to stop the shimmers.

Neither of them moved for a long time. TJ was too content, and Brandi was too exhausted.

And when he had taken her—when he was totally satiated, completely depleted—he rolled to his side, pulled her to him, and kissed the eyelids that remained closed. It took his fingers to pry them gently apart.

"Can't believe I got me a cherry," TJ teased the woman. "My mama told me don't never mess with no virgin, won't never be able to get rid of her." He grinned, got up, and pulled Brandi to her feet. The young woman almost teetered over, the effects of their lovemaking, coupled with embarrassment, languished on.

She let him lead her to the bathroom where they showered, and afterward sleep claimed the exhausted duo's attention.

Bright and early the next morning, Thaddeus Jerome Pennington emerged from the hotel's bathroom wearing nothing except a small patch of tissue stuck to a razor's nick on his left cheek. He stood in darkness, waiting to make sure he had not awakened the woman sleeping on the bed. Seeing her immobile, he took a step toward her.

Brandi was lying on her side, her sandy brown hair mingling with shadowed creases on the pillow. Even asleep she looked lovely and smart—the girl from Wester with brains. Taxi smiled. He walked around the foot of the bed, stepped over the heap of covers and clothes that had fallen to the floor sometime during the night, and moved quietly to the table on the side of the double bed. Keeping his eyes on her, he opened the remains of goodies Sara and Sylvia had given them, fished out remnants of staling cake, dropped the frosted crumbs into his mouth, and picked up a glass with water in it to wash it down.

The girl stirred. "What time is it?" she asked. The clock on the table next to the man glowed red with inverted and 4:35.

"Time to get up, Sleeping Beauty," he spoke lovingly to the girl. "Wiley World awaits us . . . and maybe we can take in more sights."

She attempted to get up. The woman was thirsty, dried out, drained, dehydrated by an evening, a night, of total bliss. She lifted the heavy masculine arm from her torso, rolled out of the large comfortable bed, headed to the bathroom to quench her thirst.

Brandi peed first, then went to the sink to fill a glass from a tray on the countertop. She drank the tap water until her thirst was abated before returning to bedside to chase the man from it. "Come on, you have to get up too," she pleaded. "If you don't get out of that bed, I'm going to get back in it too." Her attempt to get back in the bed was thwarted by the man, who jumped up and literally rolled her like a barrel until she was in the shower.

Soon, they were at the theme park. Their stay was short. Neither could endure the crowds and long lines; both desired each other's company, so they decided to return to the hotel that was a short distance away.

"Let's eat before we turn in," TJ told her. They stopped at a restaurant just inside the park's gates. It was a large restaurant, two floors, elegant—octagonal-blocked black-and-white linoleum on the floors, with tables instead of booths, and in the mezzanine, a barrel-vaulted ceiling. Like the Fishnet in Claxville, pictures of stars, some of the same stars were on the walls, however; they shared poses with the theme parks' gaily dressed cartoon characters, and in many cases the theme park founder.

They had to wait to be seated. There was a steady stream of customers. Soon, the hostess showed them to a well-proportioned table with fresh-cut daisies in a crystal vase in the center. She took their drink orders and told them their waiter would be there soon. The woman also inquired about appetizers, which they both refused.

"Having fun?" the man asked while they waited.

She responded, "More than I ever imagined. I hate to go back."

"Me too," the man agreed, "I could spend another day or two just doing what I was doing last night."

The woman blushed with embarrassment. "Don't start now."

"Start what?"

"Nothing."

"Okay, okay," he relented. "What you want to order?"

She looked at the menu and pointed at a picture on its cover. "I think I'll have this burger and some onion rings. It looks good, especially the onions.

Everybody around us seemed to have ordered it," she offered, looking at surrounding tables. "Maybe that's their specialty."

"I need a chunk of beef or something. You took it out of the old man last night."

Her face flushed anew. TJ grinned his toothy grin; the man was beaming. He enjoyed toying with her, and she enjoyed his overtures but was really behaving like one recently deflowered. Her preference was just to daydream about the lust they shared in her private moments.

"Come on, just order," she said more forcefully this time.

The waiter came, rescuing her.

Their meals came almost as quick as the drinks had come. When Taxi cut the filet mignon he had ordered, he found the beef a little overcooked, so he had the waiter take it back to the restaurant's kitchen. He ordered panfish that was served with creamy coleslaw and some french-fried potatoes.

"Don't wait for me," he told her. "Eat up."

"Help me with this mess of onion rings. This is more than I can eat."

"Okay."

"These are great!"

"Bet that's why so many people order them."

"Uh-huh."

"Eat some more," she told him.

"Uh-uh, if I keep eating these, I won't have room for my fish when it gets here."

The waiter stuck around for TJ's comment when he had taken a bite of the fish. The man gave the second meal a "thumbs up." "This is much better, thank you."

Momentarily, it started to rain, softly at first; however, the water came harder, clattering on the building like marbles in a metal bucket. Outside people began to flood the restaurants along the walkway or scurried past them toward the shuttle buses that took them back to the parking lot and their vehicles.

"Maybe the crowd will have cleared by the time we go outside," Taxi commented.

Brandi's most memorable Memorial Day weekend was over all too soon. She slept in the car while they headed home. It was almost dark when she woke up. She'd been napping since they had checked out of the hotel and headed northwestward to Claxville. "It's almost night . . . I thought we'd be home by now."

"No, it's raining up ahead," the man said as he pointed forward to a gray, boiling, rolling sky.

"Raining?" She sat straight up in her seat, stretching and yawning, purring softly like a kitten. "This is odd. I haven't seen any rain since I took the bus to Claxville. Seen snow, but I ain't seen no regular rain."

CHAPTER TWENTY-TWO

Flood of the Century

R egular rain . . .
Brandi's expression amused the man, and TJ smiled, chuckled in spite of the bleakness. The woman had a way with words. Nobody would distinguish between the rains, at least no soul that he knew except Brandi. Suddenly, he was remembering their first date, the dinner at the Fishnet, the night when she had told him the wine, rather than beer, had tasted like mule pee.

He spoke aloud, "It doesn't rain much, but when it does, it's like Morton Salt: it just keeps on pouring . . . Shoot, I remember when I was a boy growing up in Claxville, it used to rain. It rained so hard out by that trailer park I picked you up from that day." (Brandi flinched as she had thought he had forgotten the day he picked her up from Dirk's. She had hoped he had.) "It rained so hard that Little River would swell up, overflow the banks. Water would be all out there where those trailers setting right now."

TJ continued to reminisce about the flood, "Trees were uprooted, floated down by the river, belongings from people's houses, all kinds of debris just floated right away. People living in them two-story houses on the other side of Little River lived downstairs when the river was down moved upstairs when the river rose—moved everything, their families, pets, chickens, hogs, plants, clothes, food, curtains from the windows, everything upstairs . . . then back downstairs again when the river went down.

"People got drowned, some would be found after the rains slacked off, some never was. Coffins even floated up out of that old cemetery down by the river."

"You lying, you got to be lying!" Brandi interrupted TJ's monologue about the river's ravaging tendencies and hearty appetite. She trembled.

"No, I ain't lying . . . don't never seem like it's going to let up once it gets started."

The man turned the radio on, twisted its knob in search of some music. On every station, announcers reported torrential rains and flooding, nothing like they'd seen in some areas of the state for at least a quarter of a century. The man wondered silently why they had not been forewarned about the weather. He made it a point to listen to the news, especially the weather. And his mother did too. This storm must have slipped up on her; she would have mentioned it when he told her that he was leaving town for a few days.

He heard Brandi say something and asked, "What?"

"You would have been a teenager then," offered Brandi.

"Oh yeah, I was," he spoke, worry apparent in his voice. "That was when I was quite young, but you don't forget a thing like that. It was just that bad."

Drops of rain pelted the vehicle's windshield, streaking the clay from Wester, making a paste composed of the red blend, Florida's gnats, lightning bugs, and other creatures that flew senselessly, almost aimlessly into speeding vehicles—seemingly transparent windshields. The rain and wind shoved the insects into the glass. The wipers squashed them and made a murky mess. It was hard to see. TJ decelerated, as did other drivers, to accommodate the current state of affairs.

Soon, windshields were transparent again, the murky mess having given way to sheets of steadily increasing precipitation, and the windshield wipers beat a steady, frantic cadence; and they kept driving. Yet the mile markers seemed to grow farther apart as time passed.

"We repeat, flash flood warnings are in effect for most areas in the northwest part of the state. Torrential rains, some hail, icing bridges and highways. Flooding is already taking place in many towns." The commentator named all the cities and towns affected by the bad weather, including Claxville. "You are advised not to travel," he told the listeners. "Travel should be avoided, the public should stay indoors," the announcer continued with the bad weather advisory. "I repeat, we have a bad-weather advisory . . ." The man started the announcement again.

TJ hit the steering wheel in frustration. "Damn!" he uttered and frowned with worry.

The car slid a little, so the man put both hands on the steering wheel. "Switch that to another station," he told Brandi who was anxious to man the radio so he could be free for driving that grew more tedious as miles passed.

She toggled the knobs, switched from channel to channel, station to station, but all news was similar. "I repeat," reporter after reporter said, "I repeat. We have a travel advisory from the national weather service. You are advised not to travel!"

"Shit!" Taxi's response scared her. He kept banging on the steering wheel in frustration, his impatience showing through.

Traffic moved at a snail's pace. TJ was really tired; he had not slept much in at least five or six days. He generally didn't require that much sleep, but he'd done a lot in preparation for the trip. The man had gotten one of the fellows to man his taxi, practiced with the band, made arrangements with some ladies from down at Shiloh to watch out for Sister Pennington, spent a little extra time with her to make sure she would be all right while he was gone.

He'd done everything except checked the weather. "I wish I had checked the weather out before we left," he told Brandi.

A commentator provided consolation. "Apparently," he said, "the storm caught everybody by surprise. No advance warning was given."

The woman sighed with relief. She hated to see the man experience so much frustration. "Feel better now?" Brandi said.

"A little bit. You know I can't help but think about Ma."

"I know," she responded sympathetically, "but you know the people from down at the church are looking out for her."

Nevertheless the rains were beating him; he was too tired for words. It was also stuffy in the car—both occupants lowered and elevated the windows constantly; the rains swept through even the slightest cracks, even the vents near the floorboard were assaulted by the waters . . . its bubbles small, frothy foam at Brandi's feet. She slid forward in her seat, stretched the tendons in her leg, let her toe become a cork, plugged up the vent to keep the waters out.

Besides that, it was almost dark. They would not make it to Claxville before night. "We probably won't be able to get into the city," he told her, "especially if it's anything like I think it might be."

Momentarily, Taxi pulled the vehicle over, off the highway, and into a hotel's driveway.

Flashing lights reading "Vacancy" drew the weary travelers under the hotel's welcoming awning. The man opened the door. "Be back in flash!" he told her.

She waited, checking her watch after a few minutes because it seemed to be taking a long time for his return.

"Hum, maybe they filled up already," she said to herself.

Then he was back. Thaddeus had a room key, a couple of newspapers, a flashlight, some crackers and Cokes, gum, and a large brown bear dressed in a green and brown plaid vest like the one he wore when he drove the taxi—in what Brandi always called "pukey plaid." He grinned and tossed the ball of fur to his companion.

"This is mine!" She feigned childish delight, hugging the bear to her chest, cooing at the brown, fuzzy, hirsute bundle as if it were a newborn infant.

He grinned at her.

"No wonder you took so long, you were on a shopping spree."

"I got some of what I thought we might need. No telling how long we'll be holed up in that room, and ain't no telling what could happen. Lights could go out. The restaurant might close. Room service probably won't be working. If they don't have their own generator, this flashlight will really come in handy."

"Oh."

He added, "I got a couple of newspapers to read. Hotels don't have anything in the room except Gideon Bibles and telephone directories. They had some books, but I wasn't sure what you liked. I bought couple of different newspapers for myself."

"I like the crossword puzzles. I can do those while we wait."

Taxi cranked the car but had a second thought. "You want to run in and look at them books yourself. You might find something you like. It won't take your smart self any time to do those little puzzles—they aren't that challenging."

"No, I'll be all right. I can look at the rest of the paper too."

The man put the vehicle in motion, pulling the Cadillac from the hotel's awning back into the rains and drove around the building in search of the vacant room. In the downpour it was hard to see the numbers on the doors. When he had passed it a third time, he backed the vehicle up—no other vehicle was on his tail this time—and rolled the window down to get a glimpse of the correct room number.

A sheet of rain washed his face. He grabbed his handkerchief from the car seat, dropped it on the floor board, and hastily rolled the window up. He had to wipe the rain off his face with his bare arm.

TJ parked the car in front of the room, started to open the car door. He jumped back in to avoid the deluge. "Shit!" he groaned in distaste. The man grabbed the ads section from one of the newspapers before leaping from the stalled vehicle to open the room's door. When the dripping man was inside, he beckoned to Brandi to follow him . . . she paid no attention; she sat lovingly caressing her new bear.

BRENDA SMITH

"Damn," he uttered at her unabashed inattentiveness, wishing for a minute he had let the present stay where it was—in the gift shop. TJ threw the soaking wet newspaper down as he couldn't get any wetter, ran to her locked door, whacked the window, which she began to roll down. "Come on!" he yelled against the storm's many angry voices—lightning was flashing, thunder was clapping angrily. TJ snatched the door open while she attempted to gather her purse, the bag of goodies, the newspapers, the bear, herself. "Leave the bear, woman!" the man yelled. "My butt's wet to the bones. Come on!"

Cold rain slid off the roof of the car in sheets and struck him sharply on the spine.

"Leave the bear?" Brandi repeated questioningly. Taxi snatched her and the few belongings she held in her arms and almost dragged her into the hotel room.

"Whew!" he said when they were both in the room, free of the storm's onslaught. TJ went to the bathroom and began to take his wet clothes off, and Brandi voluntarily joined him.

They disrobed, rubbing each other dry, hung their wet clothes in the bathroom to dry, and hopped on to the bed to make love (he was never too tired for that, and she was anxious to continue the relationship consummated the last evening). They munched crackers, drank from their Cokes, and watched the news a little bit—see what they could about the storm. Soon, TJ lay naked on top of the covers dead asleep . . . Brandi, sheet wrapped around her body, walked to and fro in the tiny room. Occasionally she looked out the window longing for the first gift and only present that her lover had bought for her, which now laid on the car's front seat.

Now that the man was asleep, she was bored and wished she had gotten a book. Her attention turned to the newspaper that remained by the door where it had slid when they entered the room. The woman went across the floor, dragging her sheet with her, and picked some of it up. It was wet—the pages were becoming papier-mâché. She went back to her perch at the foot of the bed where the man lay to gently peel the pages apart.

A picture of a man with dark shades in a dark trench coat momentarily claimed her attention—seemingly this was the headliner. The lights flickered . . . she looked around, looked back at the paper again. The man's visage was familiar; it looked like Monsieur Henri. "No," she shook her head. The lights flickered a final time, and the woman let the paper, as well as thoughts of the man, drop.

Just as TJ anticipated, the power did go out, so there was no television, no radio, no sound—that is, except her lover's snores. Brandi joined TJ in restful repose. When they awoke the following morning, the power was still out. The room was cooling. TJ peered briefly out the window. "Seems like it's about to quit," he said of the rain. "Let's get out of here—head for the house."

Immediately they took the still damp, gritty, crusting clothes they had worn from the bathroom and redressed in them in spite of the woman's protestations. "Can't we get some more clothes out of the trunk?"

"Don't make much sense," he argued, "we'll be home shortly, check out the situation, and if it's anything like I think, we'll get even dirtier before it is over."

A reluctant Brandi put the pants and shirt she'd worn the day before on again, and they hastened to the car to renew their journey home to Claxville. When they were in the car and the man turned the ignition on, static from the radio met them, so he turned it off and joined the rest of the northwest-bound traffic, which appeared to be moving along quite well, and there were no detours.

"Maybe things aren't as bad as I thought," he told the woman when they were within the city's limits.

Two days had been added to their journey . . . and TJ was anxious to get by the house and check on Sister Pennington. And it was still raining.

He took Brandi on campus first. "Leave your stuff in the car, and I'll spin back by here later to drop it off," were the last words he said to the girl, who also agreed that she did not want the gift to get wet. TJ gave her a farewell smack on the lips, and she jumped out of the vehicle and ran up the walkway.

A note from Elnora Jenkins was taped to the dorm's door. "Came by to check on the room, you weren't here. Call me, my number is in the student directory if you don't have it," were the note's contents. Brandi called her right away to let her know about her plans to stay alone during the summer. Then she cleaned herself up and straightened up the room which was a mess by now—she'd been gone a lot during the week, and Kris had begun preparations for her move. Like always, Brandi began the cleaning with the annoying grit left by the bicycle's tracks.

Kris had also left a note for her to call Dr. M or her secretary.

"Rats!" she thought. "I forgot to go by and register for summer school." She made a mental note to go by the office the next day.

BRENDA SMITH

Virgina McIntrye could not believe her ears! Henri arrested, jailed for a variety of sex offenses, indecent exposure, propositioning of male students, stalking females. The woman had nearly "shit a brick," at least that is what she told Kay when she had come to the office the morning after campus security returned to her house to let her know that the man had been caught just outside her window.

Needless to say, the headlines of the Claxville Gazette read "CSU Professor Apprehended." As soon as the secretary went to her drive and got the newspaper, she called her boss.

"So that's what all that was about!" she greeted the sleepy woman.

"Oh, hi, Kay," Dr. McIntrye responded.

"Don't hi me, Virginia McIntrye," she argued, "I just got my paper and saw the article about Mr. Henri."

"What did it say?"

"I haven't read it yet. I saw the headline and the picture. Then I called you," Kay said before adding, "you already know about it though."

"Yes," the professor admitted, "campus security was by after he was apprehended last night."

Kay took a seat at her kitchen table. She was ready to talk, to hear straight from the horse's mouth what security had said to her in the previous days. However, Dr. McIntrye heard the movement. "Don't sit, Kay," she told the inquiring woman, "I can't talk now. I've got to get dressed, to get to the office. I've got an eight o'clock meeting with the dean, and I haven't showered yet. It's going to take me a bit. I've got to shampoo my hair too. So I've got to get going. I'll tell you everything when I get to the office."

"Everything," Kay begged, "you promise, you'll tell me everything. I'm very interested in this."

Virginia held her loose hand in the air. "Scouts' honor," she told Kay before hanging up. "I will tell you everything, everything that I know. You know, I am only privy to that in which I was involved, so you will probably find out more from the paper than I know." She put the phone back on its cradle.

Kay quickly scanned the article and went to the office. She wanted to be there when Virginia got there. The secretary made coffee and ordered some Danish from the cafeteria. She wanted all of her boss's attention when she was at the office.

The phone rang; it was Sara. "Been wondering how you all was getting along up there. They said on the news that you all was having some bad weather." Brandi listened as her mother recapped all that she had read and heard. "You all didn't run into any problems trying to get back up there, did you?" the woman asked her daughter, who gave an abbreviated version of the itinerary for the trip made since she and TJ had left Wester.

"Gal, be real careful," her mother admonished before hanging up the phone. "Call me if anything happen up there and you need to come home."

"I will, Ma."

Sara asked her daughter, "Did TJ find his family all right?"

"I don't know. I haven't talked to him since he let me out the car," Brandi said, exasperation apparent.

"I was just concerned," Sara told her. "I ain't trying to get into your business. You are grown now, missy."

Brandi, overcome with guilt, apologized for her impatience. "Sorry, Ma, I'm just a little tired, that's all."

"You're forgiven."

"Ma, thanks for being so hospitable. The food and everything was so good."

Sara chuckled, "I don't know any other way to be but hospitable."

Her daughter tested the waters. "Ma, what you think about TJ?"

"Gal, it's not what me and your daddy think about him that's important. You are the one that's got to do the thinking. Just remember what I told you long time ago."

"What, Ma? You have told me so much."

Her mother responded, "Don't you sleep with no man you can't marry!"

"Aw, Ma! I can't believe you said that. I don't remember you telling me any junk like that."

"Don't 'aw, Ma!' me, child. I been where you trying to get."

Brandi blushed—she wished a thousand times she had not asked her mother's opinion of the man.

"All I know is this," the older woman continued, "you better find you a doctor to give you some of those pills to keep you from getting your belly full while you trying to be grown."

"Ma, ain't nobody fixing to have no baby!"

The older woman continued with her advice. "You probably can go to the infirmary and get them. At least that's what Cat say. He feels like they provide them because they got thousands of fast-ass gals like you up there!"

Brandi really did want to get off the phone. All the talk about precautions was embarrassing, to say the least. She rubbed her hands across her stomach. Neither she nor Taxi had taken any precautions the several times they had made love in the last couple of days. "Ma, I got to go," she said.

"Go where? I'm paying for this call," the mother emphasized, "and I'm going talk just as long as I want to. All you have to do is listen."

"I'm going," Brandi responded, anxious to quit the conversation.

"Your ass better find a doctor tomorrow," Sara warned her. "All I know is it will kill your daddy you go up there and get messed up."

The girl shrieked, "What about me? Don't you trust me by now? Don't you know I ain't going to do nothing to hurt myself!" she argued, anxious to get this "birds and bees" talk over.

"Ma, let me go," she begged again. "TJ might be trying to call me right now."

"All right, okay. Let me know how his mama come out with the storm when you hear from him."

Both women hung up, the mother satisfied that she had carried out her husband's orders to "talk with your little fool"; and Brandi, she was just glad to be off the hook, figuratively and literally, for the moment.

Brandi spent that night and most of the next day in room 306 snacking on junk food, kept at the behest of her mother for emergencies, and food she or Kris had placed in the portable refrigerator they had rented for their perishables. There were soda crackers, cheese, sardines, tuna fish, potted meat, dill pickles, cans of fruit cocktail, sliced peaches, and pickled stuff: pickled eggs, pickled beets, pickled pig feet; although her fare was unlike the sumptuous feasts from Sara's and Sylvia's tables, it did indeed suffice. As a matter of fact, she found the snacks quite delicious.

The reality was that she was staying close to the telephone, waiting to hear from Taxi. Periodically she'd look at the instrument, willing it to ring, jump up and down on the cradle, but it refused to chime. He had not returned as promised with her belongings, nor had she been able to reach him at home or at the Basement. She'd even called the bus station to see if he'd been by there; he hadn't. Brandi had been tempted to call Rev. Flewellen down at Shiloh Baptist Church to see if he had any news about TJ or Mrs. Pennington, but she didn't want to stir up a mess. The preacher had been trying to get TJ to return to church and to play the piano for the junior choir ever since he'd let Brandi talk him into taking her to church on Easter Sunday.

Later in the evening, overcome by worry, Brandi went downstairs, joining many coeds and friends who sat glued in front of the television in the lobby. Students were everywhere . . . seated on the many couches, on chairs' and sofas' arms, in laps, on the floor. Brandi had never realized the number of occupants in one dormitory.

She stood on the fringes of the crowd, having cautiously made her way to a vacant spot beside one of the huge room's support columns. When she was in place, she shifted herself for comfort's sake. Brandi gasped; her mouth flew open—she could not believe what she saw on the TV. She moved closer. There on the screen was Monsieur Henri, and the reporter was recanting a tale of how the "exposer" had been caught. "What in the Sam hill? What's going on?" she emitted.

"It's in all the papers," a bystander told her, "there's one on the counter." Brandi made her way through the crowd in the dorm's lobby, picked up the paper, and saw Henri's picture smack dab under the headline "University Professor Exposed."

She scanned the lengthy article, took a moment to look at the date, noticed it was dated before the flood—actually, it was before their trip to Wester.

"Where was I?" she thought, remembering that she and TJ were preoccupied with their own affairs. The woman looked around for someone to ask if she could have the paper, saw no such person, decided to take it to her room to read. She would return it later.

Brandi tucked the newspaper securely under her arm and left the lobby as quickly and quietly as she had come; the woman wandered back upstairs to the security of room 306.

Back in the room, the woman plopped on her bed to read the article, which began:

> The "jury" is out after a hearing convened Wednesday which will determine the fate of a Claxville University professor's career.
>
> Dr. Robert Henri faces charge of moral turpitude before a panel of five members of CU's Faculty Grievance Committee. The panel has 15 days to recommend whether or not CU President Winston Royals should terminate Henry's employment.
>
> Dr. Henri, a recently promoted associate professor of modern and romance languages, has been a member of CU's faculty for over 20 years.

"Jeepers, he's been teaching ever since before I was born," Brandi commented while continuing to read:

The case against him is as follows:

> Several students had filed affidavits against The man who they say had appeared in various secluded spots on campus, dressed in an overcoat, exposing himself when they were up close, causing them to flee.

The former student found herself jumping up and down. She had seen him, had been a victim herself. He was on the bridge that day back in the fall when she had tried to get from the closed bookstore back to the dorm.

Brandi wondered if he had recognized her when she was in his class, if this event could have contributed to his obvious dislike for her. Her mind was rushing.

"Shit!" she emitted in excitement; the rush of adrenaline was overpowering. Her heart pumped, her head felt tight, her airway was constricting. "I've got to talk to somebody about this. I'm going to burst if I don't," she told herself. "This ain't worth dying over." Brandi grabbed the phone from its cradle, put it back down; she didn't know who she would call. "Damn, Taxi, where in the hell are you? I need you. I need to talk to somebody!"

Instead, she sat and read more from the half-page discourse. Yet another student had alleged that Henri touched his genitals late one evening when he had gone to his office on the second floor of the office building during the winter quarter of the previous year.

"The buzzard, the old buzzard," spoke the girl who had been verbally and mentally abused by the beady eyed professor.

The same male student told the panel that Henri then invited him to his cabin to have a few drinks saying, "Because I know what you like. We like the same things."

Statements from this student and others told Brandi that the man had a darker, more secretive side than even she had imagined. It appeared that all would be vindicated now, including her. She read more:

> "Dr. Henri fondled his genitals at me in the parking lot in a suggestive manner when I saw him in the parking lot at Hazzard Library a week and a half later," another student told the panel.

The woman scanned the article, found more instances of perversion, and saw in the final paragraph that criminal charges against Henri were pending an investigation that campus security had turned over to city authorities and the state's bureau of investigation.

"Damn, I got to talk to somebody." Brandi had let the *Claxville Daily News* drop to the floor. She dialed Dr. McIntyre's number. The woman's line was busy. Actually, the professor was talking to Kay about Henri. They had hardly spoken of anything else since the story broke. The women, like everyone else in the Claxville University community, had talked of little else except the man's perverse nature.

"Dr. M, did you know about all this shit with Henri? Was this what you couldn't tell me about?" Kay had pounced on her as soon as she was in the office's doorway.

No and yes responses were given the couple of questions Kay posed. Dr. McIntyre remained elusive, offering, "He was caught near my apartment. One of my neighbors observed a man dressed in a dark trench coat peeking in my window one afternoon while I lay napping and called campus security. And he was apprehended and arrested."

"What was he doing at your place?"

"I don't have the slightest idea. I'm just glad they caught him." The woman shuddered.

"Me too! It gave me the creeps just reading about him." The secretary offered.

"Me too," the professor agreed.

"Can you imagine now how he made that little colored girl feel?"

"Who?"

"The Brown girl."

"Holy shit! She did have some problems with that old bastard, didn't she?"

"She sure did," the older woman agreed, thinking to herself, "With him, and with some of the rest of us too." Dr. McIntyre grew increasingly guilt ridden. "I wish I knew where she was. I've telephoned several times. And you did too. Didn't you? I did ask you to call her for me. I'll just have to keep trying. Talk to you later."

The professor dialed Brandi's number as soon as she hung up; her line was busy.

Brandi lay the phone back on its cradle, picked up the newspaper again, and put it down, deciding not to read any further. She couldn't handle any

BRENDA SMITH

more, didn't want to have a heart attack. She would wait until Taxi was back and she had someone to talk to about this mess.

And depression began its lift. It had settled around her like a fog during TJ's absence, but here was one bit of encouraging news. There had to be more.

Yet the rains continued . . . day and night it rained. For nine days straight it poured in Claxville and surrounding areas. Classes were discontinued, the campus was shut down, and soon communication problems became evident: the television no longer worked, no mail came in or went out, radios gave off static, phones lay dead.

Most students slept. Their waking hours were spent playing cards, board games, ripping and running up and down the halls, playing infantile games. Brandi slept little and worried a lot . . . Kris was not there; compassion had taken her afield to help tend the animals victimized by nature's wrath. Brandi realized what a godsend Kris had been . . . It was Kris who had been the listening, feminine ear, who often brought a different perspective to things. Maybe it was because she was white, was not colored.

It was Kris who clarified the Ethiopian boy's reaction to her that day on the campus bus. Kris had explained to her that the boy who shared her own hue—basic black—was a victim of white Anglo-Saxon protestant indoctrination; he had been told by the Methodist missionaries that he would lose his financial assistance if he associated with American "coloreds." These so-called Christians told him and others like him that it was sinful to associate with mulatto—people with mixed blood—that all American Negroes were mulatto, were of mixed parentage.

Brandi had eyed her roommate suspiciously when she had said such. "You're lying?" she had retorted questioningly.

"Uh-uh," Kris maintained.

Brandi asked, "How do you know that?"

Kris's sedate, remorseful reply was, "Maybe it's because I'm white, and I'm Methodist."

Brandi grew suddenly somber, did not pursue it any further, wanted no more talk about race, color, gender, doctrine, beliefs, dogmas, ideologies.

She had found Kris easy to be around and easy to talk to, and she wanted to keep it that way.

How she longed for Kris while the storm raged; room 306 presented a stifling atmosphere . . . it was dark, dank, gloomy; and the young woman was lonely. She daydreamed, relived the pleasantries of the last few weeks and days with Taxi, then longed and pined for some contact with the man.

By day 15, contact with the outside world had been reestablished. Television, radio, newspapers, and tabloids showed despair . . . the homeless, school-less, jobless, naked, infirmed, dead, dying; everything not nailed down on the other side of Little River had been engulfed, swallowed up by raging, loose, unconfined water. Dams, bridges, roads, asphalt, graves, vehicles, rooftops, furnishings, boards, nails, and buckets, barrels . . . everything in its path had been eaten by the swollen river. With its thirst quenched, it hungered still . . . Little River had a hearty appetite.

When almost three weeks had passed and there was no word from Taxi, Brandi joined many others in the trek to the river. The bridge remained impassable, so everyone stayed on the side in which he was entrapped. Reporters, journalists, cameramen, policemen, firemen, rescue workers, emergency medical technicians, electricians, line repairmen, doctors, nurses were everywhere. Observers were shooed back and away: there was work to be done. Yet Brandi managed to make her way to the bridge's edge to see firsthand what Taxi had told her about.

A gurney rolled by, its human remains covered in white. Brandi paused, studied the cloth-shrouded cadaver . . . it was too short for Taxi, might have been a woman or a child. She rolled her eyes to half mast, whispered a short prayer, and turned to the river to wait.

Before her eyes, the rolling, raging, tumbling, violently twisting, turning, churning river swallowed everything it could . . . it ate small chunks of Claxville and feasted on its largest as well. People exclaimed and pointed. A tree floated by—in its tops appeared to be a partially clad person. Or what was it! Whatever it was, it was at Little River's mercy. Soon, a boat appeared from somewhere—its occupants yelled to the tree's inhabitant, "Hold on, we are going to get you. Hold on!"

The crowd cheered when the ensnared was rescued.

Brandi returned her gaze to the river to await the next miracle; her wait was not as long as some though.

A mustard yellow fender appeared to be a part of the next wave of debris. "Taxi," the half-crazed, half-sleepy, listless girl moaned pitifully to herself.

She turned to leave.

Brandi looked devastated when she left Little River's banks . . . if there was any solace for her, it could only be that her wait had not been as long as some; hers was over sooner than she anticipated. She would never forget the horror of that moment . . . first, hearing someone yell, "There's a body floating there!" "Where?" someone had asked anxiously, glancing to the spot where all fingers pointed, eyes, cameras . . . then of wading through the crowd, of seeing the patch of familiar plaid, the same pukey green, brown, yellow of the vest Taxi always wore when he drove his cab. Most devastating of all was watching the rescue workers grab at what she believed was her lover's stiff, lifeless body with hooks, with tines like Cat's pitchfork prodding at it . . . poking it, trying to pull it from Little River's rushing flood waters.

Good memories of Taxi and bitter ones of Claxville University assailed her senses.

All she could think of was their last days together, the trip Southeast and back, to Wester and on into Florida. Brandi would never see him laugh again or hear him play the piano, sing secular and sacred songs . . . see him get pissed and whip himself unmercifully for his electric temper . . . or hear her lover whisper sweet nothings in her ears.

Carruthers and Sara Brown's daughter knew she would never forget the horrors of this particular day, and she sobbed openly as she made her way to Davis Hall to prepare for the bus ride back to Wester's red clay hills. There was no way for her to stay here now, she thought.

Sewers had overflowed everywhere too . . . when Brandi reached the third floor, she knew that Davis Hall had been touched by the uncanny storm. Fumes drifted to the top of the stairwell, met her at the door, and the young woman held her breath. "Surely," she thought, "the bathroom had begun to back up . . ." Brandi did not see the feces until she was at her own door. She almost stepped in the odorous contents . . . someone had emptied the slop jar at her door, on her door—it ran down the door, under the doorway. Snickers came from cracked doorways . . . Julie grinned from the bathroom's doorway . . . Dr. McIntyre laughed that peculiar laugh . . . the man on the bridge unzipped his fly, exposing himself once more . . . the guy on the bus turned his nose up at her . . . the girls took turns stepping first on her toes, then heels, skinning first one then the other . . .

And the river, it made a feast of her beloved Taxi. The stench of it all drove the young woman back to room 306, where she lay sprawled in grief on her bed, the patchwork quilt of no particular design wound shroudlike around her lifeless body until the footsteps running up and down the hall ceased in front of her door.

"Brandi, it's me! Open the door, it's me!" TJ yelled above the oblivion that threatened to overtake her. The pounding of his fists and rattling of the knob accompanying his voiced pleas breathed life into her.

She tore the covers from herself, ran to the door, jerked it open, and smiled at him. Taxi had weathered the storm.

The man took her in his arms and hugged her tightly to himself.

"Sorry, but I lost the bear," he said. "I'll buy you a dozen."

Brandi smiled through her tears, glad that the pukey plaid in the river had belonged to the gift rather than the giver.

EPILOGUE

May 4, 2010

Dear Little Sistah,

I saw you on the tube that day, and I didn't catch your name; however, I caught your situation. Girl, I was so upset. I know your situation, your pain—I've had similar experiences. Like the song says, "Been there, done that." Because I was so disturbed over your state of affairs, I left work and came home. I couldn't believe they were still playing games like that, but then I did. I knew they couldn't stop; that's just the way those people are.

You were crying. And that's okay. Cry if you must; hiding hurt is not easy. But when you finish crying, get up, brush yourself off, get back in the saddle; failure is not an option. You have to keep trying. Failure isn't failure; it's a step, and life is nothing but steps. Or failures with occasional widely space successes. I hope you didn't leave that school; that's what they wanted you to do. But if you left, if you just had to leave, I hope you did not abandon your education.

I didn't leave Claxville. I kept going, making one step at a time until I graduated. And I went under the watchful eye of my beloved Taxi—we were married shortly after the flood. He provided the support that I needed during the successes, and when I experienced failure, he provided the balm for my wounds. It was also he who encouraged me to write to you.

There is so much more that I could say. Then again, there's really nothing else to say. While I've never met you, maybe we had a chance encounter over the years, and I didn't know it was you. Yet I feel so close to you—you are my sister. So I thought of something you can do for me. In fact, I insist on it. I'll brook no argument. Tell your story too—do it for yourself, friends, sisters, brothers. Whatever happened to you that day at Claxville University is real. It happened then, and it still happens now. Telling your story is therapeutic, and it's inspirational; it will help someone else to cope with the vicissitudes of life. Do this for me. Please! Because it's not really for me—it's for you and for the rest of the sisters and brothers who will matriculate at their own Claxvilles.

By the way, I cried that day too. I cried for you, and I cried for me. But then, I stopped crying. My intent was to find you, to write to you, to offer up some encouragement. It took me over thirty years, but I finally got it all down on paper. The one- or two-page letter is now almost five hundred typewritten pages long. It will cost me a bundle to mail it, but I intend to send it this time. I'm going to send it by my agent. When you finish reading it, pass it along.

Somebody else may need to hear my story, your story, and our story.

Peace, love, and happiness
Brandi Leigh Brown

BRENDA SMITH

Edwards Brothers Malloy
Thorofare, NJ USA
September 17, 2013